I would like to thank Tracy Brennan, my agent, and the team at HarperImpulse, in particular Charlotte Ledger and Kimberley Young for their belief in both me and Beyond Grace's Rainbow. I feel privileged to have you on my team. I would also like to thank my talented fellow authors at HarperImpulse for the wonderful welcome and for reminding me how much I love to read.

Thank you to my family both O'Gradys and Harringtons for every word of encouragement you have given me since I began this writing journey - my parents Tina and Michael, my siblings and inlaws Fiona & Michael, Michelle & Anthony, John & Fiona, Adrienne & George, Evelyn & Seamus, Leah and my mother-in-law Evelyn Harrington and all the nieces and nephews.

I'd also like to thank my aunt & uncle and wonderful godparents, Ann & Nigel Payne, who might live a long way away from me, but have always been there for me whenever I needed them.

To all my friends both old and new, thank you for the gossipy chats and giggles, cups of coffees, glasses of wine and unrelenting support with a special thank you to Ann Murphy (my person).

To every reader, fan, book reviewer and friend who has ever shared, tweeted, liked or reviewed Beyond Grace's Rainbow, I will always be grateful. You all played a role in helping me go from self published to published author. Tanya Farrell, my writing confidante, you officially rock and to the gang in my writers' group, Imagine, Write, Inspire - keep dreaming.

Lastly thank you to all my H's, my beloved children Amelia and Nate and my stepdaughter Eva, you guys are my everything, my Happy Ever After. Roger, aka Mr H, know this - without your unfaltering love and belief in me, I could not do this, would not want to do this. So this is for you.

Carmel

Beyond Grace's Rainbow

CARMEL HARRINGTON

Harper*Impulse* an imprint of
HarperCollins*Publishers Ltd*
77–85 Fulham Palace Road
Hammersmith, London W6 8JB

www.harpercollins.co.uk

A Paperback Original 2013

First published in Great Britain in ebook format by HarperImpulse 2013

A catalogue record for this book
is available from the British Library

ISBN: 978-0-00-755956-5

Automatically produced by Atomik ePublisher from Easypress

Prologue

Friday 13th February 2012

Grace felt like she was floating up on the ceiling. Down below on the ground, she could see Dr Kennedy sitting in a battered old brown leather chair. He was leaning forward, earnestly, looking at somebody who looked very much like herself.

'That reminds me, I must get my roots done,' Grace thought as she looked down critically at herself. Sitting beside Grace was Sean, her friend. She knew that it was not possible to be in two places at once – she hadn't lost her marbles – yet. But at this very moment here she was up on the ceiling, watching the scene below. Grace knew it had to be her sitting below because she could actually feel Sean's hand gripping hers tightly. So the only logical explanation she could come up with was that she was having one of those 'out of body' experiences. The other possibility was that the shock of the news that had just been delivered stopped her heart and she had actually died.

Oh feck, that couldn't be true. Surely you wouldn't think about the state of your roots just after dying?

'Do you understand what I've just told you Grace?' Dr Kennedy's voice jolted Grace back to reality with a bump and a crash. She felt like she'd fallen from the ceiling and landed unceremoniously into the uncomfortable chair. So she was not dead then, Grace thought wryly. For a second she felt like complaining about the terrible chairs the patients had to sit on, while doctors had lovely comfortable leather ones. The injustice of it seemed unbearable. But maybe this wasn't the time.

'I want to go back up there.' Grace said instead, pointing to the ceiling.

'Grace, honey, you're not making any sense.' Sean said to her, he looked really worried. She knew he was probably thinking she'd gone mad. Maybe she had.

'Grace?' Dr Kennedy said gently. 'Do you understand what I've just told you?'

No more floating on the ceiling. No more analysis on the state of the chairs. She knew she had to answer him. She decided she'd have one more stab at dodging the truth.

'No I don't understand, Dr Kennedy. There's been some kind of stupid mistake and I'll be honest with you, it's not on. I'll be writing a strong letter to complain. I have a cold or maybe even proper flu. That's why I've had this bad pain in my back. You always get aches and pains when you have proper flu.' She turned triumphantly to Sean. As a GP himself he was always complaining about his patients coming in with the common cold saying they were in bits with the flu. As he often said, when you have the flu, you know it, you can't move, your body is aching so much. Unfortunately Sean just looked away from her. He couldn't look her in the eye. That wasn't good.

Grace looked at both of them with growing desperation. She knew that at this stage she was clutching at straws.

Dr Kennedy tried again, this time his tone sharper. 'Grace, you have a form of leukaemia, commonly known as AML – Acute Myelogenous Leukaemia. I know that it's a lot to take in and you must have many questions for me. I'll do my best to answer them as honestly as I can. But there's no doubt I'm afraid.'

2

Grace felt a tear run down her cheek. She felt like a truck had literally smashed into her body and she could hardly breathe. Her son's beautiful face popped into her head. His little voice was saying in his beautiful sing-song voice, 'Mommy, I love you!'

And with that she knew she had to pull herself together. She knew she had to fight this with every core of her being, for Jack's sake. So yes Dr Kennedy, she sure did have questions to ask. Thousands of questions started jumping into her head, so much so she thought it was going to explode.

But the only question she wasn't aware she was even thinking was the one that she whispered to them.

'Dr Kennedy, am I going to die?'

Chapter One

Grace Devlin was standing in the sitting room of her apartment in Swords, a large town in Co. Dublin. It was Valentine's Day and she was awaiting the arrival of her five closest friends. Tom reckoned she fancied herself as a bit of a domestic goddess in the kitchen. Whenever he called for dinner, he always joked 'Watch your back Rachel Allen, Grace Devlin's in town!' But as much as Grace usually loved having her friends over, today she was watching the clock with trepidation. How the hell do you tell the people you love that you have cancer? Grace thought. Walking over to the large black marble fireplace in her sitting room, Grace looked into the gilt mirror hanging above it. She stared critically at the image reflected. Long, wavy, strawberry blonde hair fell down her back, framing a pretty face that as yet was unlined. Large green eyes, her best feature, or at least so she'd been told, were shiny with unshed tears. Grace hadn't cried at all since she'd learnt she had cancer. This surprised her, as in the past she'd never had any trouble having a good cry. When her parents died, she cried for a month solid and now, years later, she still cried for them, the loss at times unbearable to deal with. When Liam and she broke up, she felt like she cried non-stop for a full year. So as a self-confessed crier, she was surprised that since she'd left the doctor's office she'd been quite calm about it all. Maybe it was the shock of hearing she had cancer. Grace had never even considered that she would test positive. That sort of thing happened to friends of friends or elderly relatives.

Will they guess when they see me? Grace wondered. Is it obvious to everyone that I've got cancer? Grace looked down at the array of framed photographs lining her mantelpiece, her photo gallery of family and friends. Centre stage, and quite rightly, was Jack, Grace's three year-old son. The photograph was taken at Christmas, snapped just as he walked into their sitting room to see all the gifts under the tree. Grace had zoomed in with her digital camera, capturing his delight and amazement at Santa's handiwork. He too had strawberry blonde hair and big green eyes, but apart from the colouring similarity, he was the image of his father Liam. Sitting next to Jack's photograph was a smaller picture of Liam. Her friends had asked if it was difficult looking at his face every day, and sometimes it was. But the fact of the matter was that he was Jack's father and for Jack's sake, she wanted him to at least have one photograph to look at, even if Liam wasn't actually in either of their lives. Grace and Liam had split up three years ago. He was the love of her life and they had five wonderful years together. But then Liam started to drink, or rather he started to drink heavily. Grace believed that Liam had always loved her, but over the last couple of years they were together this was totally destroyed by his affair with something she couldn't compete with – alcohol. It was a tough mistress to compete with, and in Grace's case, she wasn't strong enough, and lost not just the battle but the war too. She often thought that if it had been another woman, she might have had a chance at holding them together.

Her pregnancy came as a shock to them both. She had finally finished with Liam and he had moved to London. At first she didn't notice that her period was late. She was so upset that they had split up that she put it down to the break-up. But eventually she realised that the nausea she felt and the extreme tiredness might just be down to something other than a broken heart. So she picked up half a dozen tests in the chemist's and with Tara and Abby patiently waiting on her, sat down and did the pee on a stick dance. To her horror a big fat positive came back. She remembered how terrified she was at the time. But as her bump grew and she felt new life stir within her, so did her excitement to meet her little baby. And nine months later, Grace had a beautiful, perfect, glorious baby boy. The start of the most amazing love affair began.

Until Jack came along, Grace believed she was only treading water. But when Jack came into her life, she felt complete at last. This child was like the missing part of Grace and life looked so much more vibrant and colourful having him by her side.

Looking at the picture of Annie and Mick smiling into the camera was always bittersweet. Grace was adopted as a young baby and had always felt a little bit alone, a little bit different to everyone else. Her adoptive parents, though, were amazing and they couldn't have loved her any more than they did and she knew she had lucked out when Annie and Mick Devlin adopted her. They only let her down once, and to be fair, that wasn't even their fault. They were killed in a car crash, when she was nineteen. Seeing their happy faces in the photo made Grace smile, but then a sharp pain would stab her heart as she realised once again that they were gone. She never stopped missing them and a day didn't go by that she wished they had lived long enough to meet Jack. They would have adored him.

Grace walked over to the drinks cabinet and poured herself a brandy and ginger. She'd never usually drink during the day, but this was not a normal day and she felt she was excused. She knew she was getting maudlin, but couldn't help herself. Smiling, she then picked up the picture of Tara on her wedding day. They'd known each other since they were babies, with only a couple of weeks between them. They were destined to be friends from the moment Grace's parents brought her home following the adoption. Tara's mother, Molly, was Annie's sister, as they'd grown up as cousins. Living on the same road in Drumcondra they had done everything together, from taking their first steps to holding hands on their first day of school. To have gone through *thirty two* years together, including adolescence, and still be best friends was pretty cool. Tara looked so gorgeous – tall, dark and beautiful. Many people thought she was Italian, until she opened her mouth – then there was no mistaking she was a Dubliner through and through.

Standing beside Tara in her beautiful wedding gown, was Sean, her husband. Grace smiled as she remembered the day she introduced them. Grace loved to sing, and in the nineties karaoke-fever-hit Dublin, she used to go to all the competitions and it was at one of these that she met Sean. He was in the final singing against Grace – her choice was Nancy Sinatra's *These Boots Are Made for Walkin'* and Sean had chosen Frank Sinatra's *Fly Me to the Moon*. Grace couldn't believe it when she won, something she never let Sean forget. However, she did share her winnings of €50 with him by buying him drinks for the night. There was never any attraction between them, which always surprised Grace as Sean was quite the handsome doctor. But Sean and Grace did decide to become karaoke buddies and while singing their little hearts out, became firm friends.

Sean was everything a doctor should be, calm and friendly, with a really great way of connecting with his patients. Grace didn't know how he did it, but within five minutes of a consultation, he had an uncanny knack of always allaying any fears or anxieties patients had. Grace always teased him that there were a few broken hearts out there when his female clientele found out he was spoken for! The friends had nicknamed him their very own Dr McDreamy, which Tara said he secretly loved!

For some reason, Sean didn't meet the rest of her friends for a couple of years. They kind of had this private karaoke hobby going on and the gang had long since got bored listening to Grace belt out her tunes. So Sean and Grace would go out themselves. But then, on Grace's 25th birthday, she threw a house party and Sean was invited. She couldn't have been happier when Tara and he hooked up. She'd never thought of them together until that night, but when she introduced them, Grace couldn't believe she hadn't engineered a meeting previously. They were perfect together. Two years later, they were married and Grace was bridesmaid. They were quite a cliché too, as Tara was a nurse. She'd always sworn she'd never date a doctor, never mind marry one, yet despite herself she'd done both!

Standing beside Grace in the photo, in a matching cerise pink bridesmaid dress, was their best friend, Abby. They had met her at college, and soon Tara, Abby and Grace were best friends. They'd got up to some serious clubbing and partying in their college years. Abby looked so tiny and fragile beside everyone else in the photograph. She was only 5' 4 and really petite. Tara said she felt like the jolly green giant whenever she stood beside her. Abby had short blonde hair with really pale porcelain skin. She almost looked like a china doll. A china doll with an astonishing talent though – Abby was a brilliant artist. If you go to the top level in Stephen's Green shopping centre you can feast your eyes on an array of colourful and quite frankly amazing works of modern art sketched by the equally amazing Abby Nolan.

To supplement the sales of her art, Abby also sold really cool charcoal portraits. Grace had an 8x10 charcoal picture of Jack and herself when he was 8 months old and it was her absolute favourite possession. Abby had managed to make Grace look like Mother

Earth – not to mention about a stone lighter than she was post-baby! And more importantly – is there anything more important than a painting that makes you look a stone lighter?!!! – she had captured the very essence of Jack. In that one portrait she portrayed that Jack was all at once fiercely independent, kind, funny, stubborn, yet had the most loving of natures. Some days Grace found herself just staring at that picture and could lose twenty minutes.

Abby was really intense when it came to her art. She was totally focused on it and was happy to miss out on so many luxuries to finance it. Mind you, Grace thought with a smile, Abby was certainly no saint, having been known to party hard with the rest of the gang. Grace always teased her that she was the queen of the one-night stand. She hoped that Abby would meet her Prince Charming soon.

Picking up the last of her photographs, Grace smiled. There was something about this duo that cheered her up no matter what, whenever she thought of them. The last of their gang – Tom and Gerry. When they met, Tom used to joke that he was going to change his name as they couldn't possibly date – the jokes about their names too much to take. But they had survived the Looney tune jibes and had been a couple now for three years and were living together in a beautiful Victorian house in Clontarf. Tom was the joker of the bunch and all of the friends had been on the end of his high jinks at some time or other. He was also the oldest of them all at the ripe young age of 42. He'd been grey since he was 15 and to use Tara's words to describe him – was like a comfortable old slipper. A little bit shabby on the outside but the most perfect fit! But appearances can be deceptive. Tom was a Detective Sergeant in the Gardaí and could be one tough cookie when necessary.

Gerry on the other hand, was the complete opposite of his partner. He was 6'2, wore only designer clothes and never missed his daily workout in the local gym. He was also the baby of the bunch, at a mere 30 years of age. Gerry, an Image Consultant, loved giving people a makeover. The opportunity to insult someone and get paid for it was too good to be true for him. He had recently done a few appearances on breakfast TV doing makeovers, so he was also the mini-celebrity of the group.

Many people at first glance had thought Tom and Gerry were an unlikely couple, complete opposites, but as it often is, that's what made them work so much. Tom was the more grounded of the two, whereas Gerry was a drama queen of the highest order! If he could cause a scene where he was the central character, he'd orchestrate it. He adored movies and was a major movie buff. He had this great knack of equating all big events in life to a suitable movie, and forever quoted lines, sometimes at the most annoying times. He also lived his life like he was in a movie where, of course, he was the leading man. So he loved the fact that he could now tell everyone he was a TV star. Tom told the gang he had found him practising his autographs at home just in case he was recognised. They had all teased him endlessly about that one!

Grace smiled as she remembered the night when she had told Tara, Sean, Abby and Liam about her new friends. Grace just knew that they would all get on well together. And they did. Grace met the boys through her work as it happens. As an interior designer they hired her to redesign their house. It was to be the job of her career. Their house was featured in the *Sunday Independent*, and during the interview, the journalist asked who had done the decor and 'Interiors by Grace Devlin' was launched into the public eye. Before she knew it, she was the hot new talent in town, her phone ringing off the hook with enquiries. Grace remembered calling round Tom and Gerry's with a magnum of champagne to say thanks and Gerry had opened the door to her, saying 'Grace Darling, from the moment we met you, we just knew you were going to be our fag hag!'

Grace glanced at the clock, it was almost one and that meant it was almost time for Tara and Sean to arrive. Tara was never late. Still Grace was pretty organised. She had tuna steaks ready to put on the griddle and the salad and couscous were already on the table. She also had several bottles of wine in the fridge along with some large bottles of Bulmers cider. Tom wouldn't drink anything else, much to Gerry's disgust. As she predicted, Tara and Sean were the first to arrive. Tara was all tumbling dark curls and big rosy cheeks, holding a beautiful bunch of white roses. She knew they were Grace's favourites.

'Be my valentine, Grace?' Tara squealed.

'Too late, she's mine,' Sean retorted, handing Grace a bottle of wine.

'Thank you both, but I'm afraid my heart's already taken – Jack and I exchanged cards at 6.30 this morning, while you too were still snoring your heads off!'

'Oh my god, that's inhuman Grace. How are you still awake? I'd need an afternoon nap if I'd been awoken by a three year old at that ungodly hour!' Tara said with a laugh.

'That's because you're a lazy old tart,' drawled the unmistakable Kerry accent of Tom.

'Move aside Tom, let me kiss this vision in front of me,' Gerry chimed in.

And then all of a sudden Grace was the filling in a Tom and Gerry sandwich. Tom giving her a big slobbery kiss on one cheek and Gerry with his standard air kisses on the other. She closed her eyes for a moment to savour it. Her friends all huddled in her hallway, creating chaos within seconds of arriving, and she started to believe that maybe, just maybe, all was going to work out.

'Jaysus, this is like a bad episode of friends! I demand we stop all this right now and get pissed!' Tom boomed. With that, Abby arrived and the noise level in the apartment jumped by

10 decibels. And it felt great. Grace left the gang to chat while she put the finishing touches to the dinner and also got the drinks ready.

A few minutes later they were all tucking into lunch and Gerry begged Tom to tell everyone about the latest investigation he had handled. Tom loved an audience and everyone was eager to hear the latest instalment from Tom's work.

'Well my last case involved eight victims who was conned by the same guy.' Tom took a gulp of his Bulmers before continuing. 'Each of them was looking for an apartment to rent in Dublin and answered an advert in the *Evening Herald* for a stunning apartment in the IFSC centre. The rent was really reasonable – €1000 per month.'

'That's for nothing,' Sean said amazed. He knew those apartments; they usually cost at least €1500 per month.

'I know. That's why the "landlord" got so many takers. He showed the apartment to the eight prospective renters and then promptly agreed to rent it to each of them!'

'That's crazy!' Tara exclaimed. 'Sure how did he think he'd get away with it?'

'Well the landlord took €500 deposit from each and a further €1000 for one month's rent in advance. They all signed contracts and were given a set of keys, telling them they could move in the following Saturday.'

'That's €12,000!' Abby said, quickly doing the math.

'Not too shabby, hey?' Tom said. 'Well, Saturday comes and eight new tenants all arrive within a couple of hours of each other complete with bag and baggage! You can imagine the chaos when each of them produced an identical contract!'

There was a suitable amount of oohs and aahs from the group, Tom noted with a grin.

'Did they call the landlord? Did he come to the apartment to explain?' Tara demanded.

'Yes and yes to answer your questions. The landlord was traced and called by the property management company for the building. But the problem was, when he arrived it wasn't the same guy who had rented the apartment to them!'

'Oh my god!' Tara and Abby exclaimed in unison.

'Who was the guy who gave them the contracts then?' Sean asked.

'Well after a lot of explaining – the landlord was as confused as these guys – they discovered that the existing tenant was the con artist. He was leaving, but decided to scam a few quid before he left. He lost his deposit but that was only €1000. He's still quids in.'

'How do these guys think of such things?' Tara asked. 'The imagination of them!'

'The cheek of them more like!' Tom answered. 'More than likely he's done this before. He was only in the apartment for six weeks. I'd say he does this on a regular basis. The contracts he gave each of the "new" tenants were very professional.'

'So you're trying to find him?' Abby asked.

'That I am princess. And I'll get him too! I feel sorry for those poor eejits who lost out. They were devastated.'

'Darling, don't worry too much about them,' Gerry interrupted. He turned to the group and told them, 'I was waiting for Tom outside the station and saw the tenants all leaving after giving their statements. Tom, did you see the way that the tall dark guy, Morgan, was looking at the blonde girl, Amy? I'm telling you there were sparks flying between them two!'

'God you're an incurable romantic Gerry!' Tara said with a laugh.

'Can I help it if I notice things? You mark my words; they'll be looking for a double apartment next time!'

'Well there's one way I never considered on how to meet a man,' Abby said with a laugh. 'Maybe I should start flat hunting!'

While everyone was listening to Tom's story, it gave Grace a moment to compose herself. Only Sean looked distracted and kept giving her worried looks. It had been really hard on Sean, she was aware of that. He'd been amazing and she knew it'd been a strain keeping things from Tara in particular. She had been adamant that nobody was to be worried unnecessarily until all the facts were discovered. Looking back, Grace hadn't been feeling well for a couple of weeks now. Grace had lost some weight too and Tara had nagged and nagged her to get antibiotics. Thinking it was a bad cold initially, one that wouldn't go away, she went to see Sean. He did an initial examination and although he agreed with Grace that it was probably the flu, he decided to do some blood tests. Grace had been a bit annoyed at that, thinking Sean was going overboard in his Dr McDreamy routine. But hindsight was a wonderful thing and of course he was right to do those tests. Thank God he did!

Grace was abruptly pulled back from her daydreaming by a demand from Gerry. 'Right Grace, I'm in suspenders here for too long! Why are we all here? Don't tell me you're preggers again!' Gerry laughed.

'Nah couldn't be that Gerry, the spawn of the Devil hasn't been around for years now!' Tara joked about Liam. She never missed an opportunity to have a dig at him, never forgiving him for leaving Grace on her own.

'Very funny Tara. When are you going to stop laying into Liam? He's guilty of a lot of things, but spawn of the Devil is going a bit far I think. Remember he's Jack's dad,' Grace responded a bit sharply.

Seeing Tara's hurt face made Grace feel instantly guilty for snapping at her. She was only joking after all. She smiled lamely to try to take the sting out.

'Gerry is right though. I've put off telling you my news for long enough now. I did get you guys around here for a reason.' Making sure everyone had a full glass, Grace figured it was now or never.

'No getting anything past you lot! Though I'm not sure how to start,' Grace faltered. 'This is harder than I thought.'

'Are we talking *It Could Happen to You* kind of news?' Gerry interrupted with a smile. 'Nicholas Cage, Rosie Perez winning the lotto. Nick giving half his winnings to a waitress played by Bridget Fonda. Rosie goes frigging nuts!' With every word Gerry's voice had raised a pitch with excitement.

'Jaysus Gerry, you don't have to give a synopsis of every movie you quote – we have been to the cinema on occasion too you know!' Tom quipped.

''Fraid not, Gerry. No lotto wins here. No Nick Cage either for that matter! I suppose it's more of a *Terms of Endearment* moment actually,' Grace responded.

Gerry loved it when his friends played along with him. With a big grin he started his narrative.

'Jack Nicholson, Shirley McClaine, Debra Winger. God, Jack was gorgeous in that movie. As for Shirley, divine. Can you guys remember that scene in the hospital? I swear I needed Valium because I was crying so much.'

And with that Gerry stopped. The meaning of what Grace had just said hit him and everyone else. Four pairs of eyes turned away from Gerry and looked at Grace.

'Right, I need you guys to be strong. No tears, okay?' They all nodded silently, so Grace continued, 'It's a bit of a bitch, but I've got cancer.'

It was the first time that Grace's friends had all been silent. Tom found his voice first. 'Grace, this is one sick joke. Not even a good one. See, nobody's laughing.' He gestured around the room.

Grace thought this was the first time she'd ever seen Tom look scared.

'It's not a joke though, is it?' Abby asked Grace.

'No pet. It's no joke. Or at least if it is, the joke's on me.'

Sean then spoke quietly, 'If you guys have any questions, I'll answer them for you.'

Tara jumped up then, angrily pointing at Sean, barely able to get the words out, 'You knew about this Sean? You knew and didn't tell me.'

'Big picture Tara, please, big picture,' Sean answered calmly. 'Grace is my patient and my friend and asked me not to say anything to anyone until she had all the facts. I had to respect that.' He jumped up and pulled Tara in close to him, sitting her down beside him again. Continuing he said, 'Basically Grace's bone marrow is faulty. It's sending out wrong signals in making her blood.'

'Or in layman's terms, my bone marrow is fucked,' Grace clarified helpfully. She felt guilty as soon as the words were out as she saw her friends wince.

'What treatment have they decided on, will they do chemo?' Tara asked.

Grace nodded at Sean to continue. She couldn't even think about the treatment, never mind say it aloud.

'Grace is going to start a course of chemotherapy next Saturday. She's going to have a small procedure in the morning, to install what's called a Hickman. That allows the doctors to give Grace all the meds she needs without damaging her veins.'

'And the chemo, that will kill the cancer?' Tom asked.

'Well, it's not that simple I'm afraid. The chemo will stop the cancer growing anymore. But really what we need to do is to fix the problem with Grace's bone marrow.'

While Sean had been telling everyone her diagnosis, Grace had been watching their faces. Gerry had slipped his hand into Tom's. He looked about ten right now, while Tom looked like he wanted to hit someone. Every word Sean said, Tom looked angrier. Abby was trying so hard to be brave, because Grace had asked her to. So she kept giving Grace a little smile, but the tears were spilling down her face, and Grace realised that Abby wasn't even aware of them. Tara surprisingly enough looked emotionless. She was listening to Sean so attentively; it was as if her life depended on it.

'So are they looking at a marrow transplant?' Tara asked Sean.

'Yes, that's the optimum solution. Assuming that they can find a suitable HLA match that will be the way they'll go. The chemo will also prepare the body for a transplant.'

'Now we're talking,' Tom said, jumping up and breaking into a smile. The frown all at once disappeared from his face. 'Why didn't you just say that? Problem over, I'm the donor! Sign me up McDreamy; I've got plenty of good Kerry marrow ready for the lady!'

Gerry squealed with delight, looking at Tom with unadulterated love on his face. And who could blame him?

Grace walked over to Tom and kissed him firmly on the lips. 'My big gorgeous friend Tom. I'm so sorry pet, it's not that simple. I must have been one bad bitch in a previous life, because the double whammy here is that it will be quite difficult for me to find a suitable match. I've quite a rare blood type, O negative, which makes it difficult for me to get a suitable donor.'

'Sean?' Tom said, 'I'm A positive. Would that be a match?'

'The hospital will arrange a test for you Tom,' Sean said. 'We'll just cross our fingers, okay?'

'What about me Tom?' Gerry asked. 'What blood type do I have?'

'The same Gerry, you are A positive,' Tom replied quietly.

'I don't even know what blood type I have,' Abby stated forlornly. She got up and walked over to Grace, grabbing her hands tightly. 'I don't know what I am, but Grace, I'm going to get tested, and I'm going to pray that I'm a match. There's a chance, isn't there Sean?'

'Course there is Abby, there's always a chance,' he responded. 'And Tom, before you ask, I'm going to set up tests for us all. It's only a slim chance that we'll be a match, as we're not blood relatives. But it's definitely worth a shot. I've already started checking all options. But I'm on this, and I'm not stopping till I find a donor for Grace.'

And with that statement from Sean, Grace was undone. She had kept calm all day, focusing on getting the dinner ready, making sure everyone had a drink, anything but think about the news she had been given yesterday. But seeing the devastation that her news had put on her friends' faces – no, she corrected herself, these were her family now – made the whole thing terribly real. She couldn't hold it together anymore. She had cancer. Collapsing on the couch beside Tara she finally allowed the tears to come.

Chapter Two

Tara and Sean were back at their three-bed semi in Malahide. Her blue eyes were shiny with unshed tears. Everyone had cried at some point over the past couple of hours at Grace's, with the exception of Tara. She had to be strong for her cousin, and she had repeated the words like a mantra over and over in her head as the horror of Grace's illness was revealed. Watching Grace fall to pieces had been unbearable for everyone. They felt at once useless that they couldn't help and guilty that they were not ill and Grace was. They all held her until her sobs eventually stopped. Tom made coffee and Grace had called time on any more questions. It was enough for one day. Then it was time for Grace to go, as she had to pick Jack up from his friend's house, where he was on a play date. And she needed to get back into Mommy mode. No way would she allow her son to see her so upset. But Tara still had some questions to ask her husband.

'What is the prognosis really, Sean? The truth please,' she asked.

'With chemo, 30%. If we can find a suitable donor that increases dramatically.' There was nothing to say to that. Tara walked over to the drinks cabinet and poured herself a large vodka. She noticed Sean raise his eyebrows at her, but one look from her stopped him from saying anything. They were both on a health kick at the moment to help with their trying to conceive. But this was not the time to nag her about drinking.

'Oh my God Sean! What about Jack?' Tara said with a sob.

'Jack will be fine, Tara. He has a mother who loves him and a gaggle of aunts and uncles who would all chop their arms off for him. We'll make sure he's okay. Right now, I'm worried about you. You look really pale, honey.'

Tara stared into the bottom of her glass, deep in thought. Sean let her sit quietly; he knew she would talk when she was ready. After a couple of minutes she looked up at her husband.

'I just feel so guilty, Sean,' Tara said in a small voice. 'This morning, the way I behaved. I thought it was the end of my world. How ridiculous is that?' Sean put his hand up quickly to stop Tara continuing.

'Don't you dare, Tara. Don't you dare apologise or feel guilty about how you feel ever. You were disappointed this morning. We both were. We thought this time we were definitely pregnant. It was understandable that you were upset. I was gutted myself to be honest.' Sean knew how Tara felt. They had been trying for years to get pregnant and it was getting to the stage where they needed to go and get some help as it just wasn't happening for them. The constant cycle of devastation they were on was a nightmare. Like this morning when Tara got a Big Fat Negative. Again. It felt like Groundhog Day. He knew that in a few weeks Tara would be back to religiously peeing on a stick, waiting for the go-ahead that it was the right time. Then would come the fervent days waiting till they could test, both allowing themselves to hope that this month it would be their month. Both would work out in their minds the possible due date of their baby. They knew that was only setting themselves up for a fall, but they couldn't help themselves. And then the crashing realisation that once again this wasn't their turn. But today, Grace's cancer had put their own situation into sharp context. He walked over to Tara and sat beside her, stroking her arm lightly.

She looked up at him and said, 'I can still remember the day Grace got the call to say that Annie and Mick were in a car crash. I'll never forget the look on Grace's face as she took that call. The colour just drained from her. We drove like madwomen to Vincent's, all the time me telling Grace to keep positive, it mightn't be Annie and Mick. Probably just a case of mistaken identity. Grace never said a word. She just sat in the passenger seat, quiet as a mouse. By the time we got to the hospital, they were both gone. Mick had died instantly, and Annie just couldn't hold on anymore. I couldn't believe it.'

Tara stood up and turned to her husband, continuing. 'I really had myself convinced that they'd be okay. That it was all a big mistake. Grace just fell to the floor and the scream that came from her stopped everyone in their tracks. I mean hospitals see some serious tragedy every day, but there was something so heart-breaking about that noise that Grace made. It's stayed with me. I don't think I'll ever forget it.'

'Baby, you're torturing yourself. That's all in the past,' Sean said as he took hold of Tara's hands, his heart breaking as he listened to the raw pain in his wife's words.

'You don't understand, Sean. I'm trying to tell you something. I know I'm not making any sense. What I'm trying to say is that everybody has a sad story. Or if they haven't, it's only a matter of time before they do. Grace has already had her sad story. She's already had one motherfucking tragedy in her life when Mick and Annie died.' Sean winced at the language.

'So, why in all that's sacred, would God ask Grace to deal with this now? It's not fair, Sean. It's just not fair.'

With tears running down Sean's face, there was nothing he could say, so he just pulled his beautiful wife into his arms and held her. Held her so tightly that he wondered who was comforting whom?

Chapter Three

Can this day get any crazier? Tom thought. He had just taken a call from Liam, Jack's father. His timing was bloody marvellous. After the emotional rollercoaster of this afternoon, hearing Grace's news, Tom just wanted to go home, crack open a couple of beers, and chill with Gerry. His brain was literally melting from the news of Grace's cancer. It was a lot to take in, and he was struggling. Tom had already lost his Dad to the 'Big C' and it frightened the life out of him. Always had. Something about the word cancer conjured up the worst fears inside all of us. Mention the 'Big C' and people go quiet. You could make a Stephen King novel about that word alone and it would make all his other horror books look tame.

Gerry was eerily quiet, unlike his normal non-stop chatterbox self. Tom realised that Gerry had said maybe ten words since Grace made her announcement. Abby was quiet too, shit – what did he expect; he wasn't exactly waxing lyrical himself. Each of them needed to be alone with their thoughts.

When they left Grace's, Gerry had insisted that Abby come home with them. This was one of the many reasons Tom loved Gerry. He may hold the title of the biggest drama queen in Ireland, he even gave the word 'queen' a capital Q, however, as Tom had found out, Gerry had hidden depths and was a series of contradictions. For example, on one hand, Gerry was the biggest snob alive. Unless his clothes had a designer label, he wouldn't dare put them on his body. Yet Gerry never, ever, passed a charity collection without making a donation. No matter where they were, if someone was collecting, Gerry would stop and throw in some money. Tom believed it was a complete waste giving money to anyone begging because he had a theory that half of them worked for a large consortium of professional beggars. He preferred to donate to a charity instead. That way he knew his money was going straight to good use. But when he tackled him about this before Gerry had just said, 'Darling, if somebody is willing to risk varicose veins by standing for hours on end collecting for charity that has to be worth a euro!' And that was that.

It was as they were leaving Grace's that Gerry realised that whilst Tara and Sean had each other, and Gerry and Tom likewise, Abby would be going home to her flat on her own. The rest of the group were so wrapped up in their own thoughts, they forgot about little Abby. But not Gerry. He just took matters into his own hands.

'Darling, put your skinny ass into our taxi right this minute. And don't even begin to open that pretty little mouth of yours to tell me all the plans you have for this evening. Tom and I need you to be with us. The spare room is ready and waiting for you. Besides, I have this lovely bottle of Pinot Noir just waiting to be enjoyed. You have just simply got to save me from death by cider. You know what a heathen he is!' Gerry pointed theatrically to Tom.

So Abby had done exactly what Gerry had asked, with no argument, just a little giggle!

Tom walked into the sitting room and stood in the doorway for a couple of seconds just watching them. They were drinking the aforementioned Pinot in beautiful Louise Kennedy glasses. They were an anniversary gift to Gerry from him earlier this year. Gerry reckoned wine tasted better in Louise Kennedy glasses, and who was Tom to disagree?

'Guys, you will not believe who that was on the blower.' Tom realised just how badly Gerry had taken the news about Grace, when he didn't jump up and start guessing. Instead, he just looked up at Tom, semi-interested.

'Liam,' Tom stated dramatically. That got their attention.

'Liam, as in Grace's Liam?' Abby questioned.

'The one and only. He wants to meet up with us to discuss an important matter. He wouldn't expand on that, other than to say that he didn't want to cause any problems, just wanted to chat.'

'Darling, what on earth could he have to say to us, that we need to hear? I'm not in the humour for a drunken scene, Tom. None of us are,' Gerry announced.

'You know what I think about what Liam did to Grace, Gerry. But he sounded sober, and serious. He's back in Ireland, and wants to see us. I'm curious. Anyhow, he's coming here tomorrow. I'd better call Tara. She's going to go mental.'

Liam didn't think it was possible to feel this nervous about anything. And he wasn't even seeing Grace or Jack today. This was just meeting Tom for a chat. He figured he was the best bet to meet with first of all, as he was less emotional than the rest of them, to say the least. He'd be more likely to hear Liam out without blowing a gasket in the first five minutes. He might bluster and shout initially, but he was fair. One of the fairest and most level-headed people he'd ever known. And Liam had always got on well with Tom. They were beer buddies, and had drunk many a pint together over the years. And although there was always a lot of bull spoken with drink, there was a brutal honesty hidden there too. They had discussed their childhoods, Tom's homosexuality, careers, relationships, and Liam would like to think that he was a friend to Tom, at least before the drink took over everything else.

Taking a deep breath, Liam knocked on the door of Tom and

Gerry's house, saying to himself as he did, 'I can't put it off any longer, this is it, don't fucking blow it!'

Tom answered the door, shaking Liam's hand firmly. 'You're looking well Liam. Come on in.'

Liam followed Tom into the living room, to find himself under severe scrutiny from several pairs of eyes.

I should have bloody known, he thought. Of course Tom would have told everyone. His eyes finally rested on Tara. And she looked mad as hell.

'You don't think I'd have missed an opportunity like this do you, Liam?' Tara asked, accurately guessing Liam's thoughts. 'I'm in serious need of a good laugh, so when Tom said you were coming round, I knew I'd have to be here. Never thought I'd ever say I'd miss anything about you Liamo, but in fairness your tall stories were always hilarious!'

'Darling, give the man a chance. Liam, as I live and breathe, you've got more handsome, if that's possible. Have you been working out? Jeez, Abby look at those bloody abs!' Gerry said, jumping up to shake Liam's hand.

'Tara, always a pleasure. Gerry, thank you, you're looking good too. Hi Sean, Abby. And for the record Tara, I'm not here to spin any stories, honestly.'

Tom stepped in, 'Righto, take a seat Liam, and we'll all keep quiet. You're a brave man, I'll give you that, facing us lot!'

'Well, I know you lot don't have a high opinion of me. I know that I've done some goddamn awful things over the years, and I was going to see each of you individually to apologise. I wasn't planning on doing it all on this occasion, but hey, maybe this is better. I never thought it would be easy.'

Silence greeted this statement from Liam. He felt like a rabbit caught in headlights.

Taking another deep breath, he continued. 'I'm an alcoholic.'

'No shit Sherlock, give that man a prize,' Tara shouted.

Gerry giggled. Sean just shrugged at Liam. He wasn't going to tell Tara to shut up. He happened to agree with her. Tom, on the other hand, was determined to let Liam have a fair say.

'All right guys settle down – go on Liam.'

'As I was saying, I'm an alcoholic. You guys have known that for years but I only realised it myself just over a year ago now. And I'm happy to say that I've been clean since that moment. I've finally shaken that monkey off my back, as we say in rehab.' Liam stopped suddenly, feeling stupid and extremely vulnerable for telling them that. They didn't want to know those details. Telling himself to keep it simple, not do too much 'therapy talk', he continued.

'Speaking of rehab, it's amazing the shit you remember. As a rule, we alcoholics have a really selective memory. It's the only way we can keep drinking without the guilt taking over. If we remembered every morning what we did the night before, we probably couldn't live with ourselves. So our minds block out the bad stuff, only remembering the highs of drinking. But when you're in rehab, everything's stripped away. It's raw, and memories come back to you in the middle of the night and you can't switch them off.'

'Get out the bleeding violins,' Tara muttered.

'Most of them,' Liam continued, glancing at Tara, 'most of the bad ones, revolve around Grace. But a lot of them include you guys too. I know I was only Grace's boyfriend, but I'd like to believe that you guys were my friends too. And I did wrong by you lot. I treated you all really badly.'

Liam looked around at the group of people who used to be his friends and he was slightly shamefaced to admit that a small part of him had hoped that someone at this point would jump up and tell him not to worry, he had nothing to apologise about. No such luck. 'I'm really sorry for the stuff I got up to. There's no excuse and I don't expect you to forgive me just like that.'

26

Tom's face was hard to read. Liam felt like heading for the door and running like Forrest Gump. But he needed to face his demons. He would never get another opportunity like this.

'How you treated us isn't an issue,' Tom said finally. 'We're all big boys and girls and we got over it. But what you did to Grace is a different story. You really messed her up, man. She had this painted-on smile that she wore whenever you were drinking. She actually thought we all bought that she was enjoying herself, when in fact we all knew that she was trying so hard to hold it together. Watching you constantly to make sure you didn't say or do anything to upset the group. I don't think she let her guard down at all in the last year before you left, Liam.'

Liam felt like he had been punched in the stomach. He had gone through all of this in rehab but hearing it from Tom, his best friend, was hard.

Tom was aware that his words were upsetting Liam, but he also knew that they had to be said, so he went on. 'It fucking killed me watching our lovely, funny Grace, so stressed, because you basically wanted to get pissed. I hated you at times Liam, because you changed Grace. When you got off your face, she was on edge all night. Wondering what shit you were going to get up to next.'

'I closed my mind to all that, Tom. I had to, because the guilt was too much. I'd have to have a drink to forget. When I was pissed, I felt like I was king of the world!' Liam replied.

The tension was palpable in the room and Gerry picked that moment to throw in: 'Leonardo DiCaprio, *Titanic*, holding Kate Winslet in his arms – what a moment.' Everyone laughed for a second. Then they all remembered that they were giving Liam a hard time.

'Tom, you've been like a brother to me and I know that I've pushed you to the limits. But I miss you man. It would mean a lot to me, if I knew you could forgive me one day.'

'It's all right, Liam. Nuff said, apology accepted,' Tom said with a lump in his throat as he once again shook Liam's hand. 'It's good to see you.'

With that, Tara began to clap. Slowly, but getting louder each second.

'Well done Liam, that's a performance and a half. You almost had me there. But I'm afraid I just don't buy it. Why now have you decided it's time to apologise? You say you've been clean over a year, how do we know that's the truth?'

'Tara, I don't blame you for being suspicious. Why should you believe me? But I'm asking you; please give me the benefit of the doubt. Hear me out at least.'

'All right, Liam. I'll hear you out for one reason only: Grace fell in love with you, so you can't be all bad. So go on. I'm listening.'

'My counsellor said that all alcoholics have a defining moment. Something happens and it shocks us into realising we have a problem, and that we want help. Until that moment, it doesn't matter what anyone says or does, you're in denial. Mine was on January 4th last year.'

'Jack's birthday,' Abby said.

'Yep, that's right, Abby. Jack was two years old and I wanted to see him. I mean Grace has been amazing, sending me photos. I know a lot of women wouldn't in her shoes. But I needed to see him. When Grace was pregnant, she came to see me. I couldn't believe it when she called. I was on a high, thinking that maybe, just maybe, we were going to get back together. I didn't even drink that day. I knew how much my drinking freaked her out, so I thought I'd do without my usual four o'clock cocktail. And before you say it Tara, I know what a fucking moron I was.'

Tara closed her mouth. She had been about to say something smart along those lines.

'I actually thought that by not drinking for a couple of hours, Grace would forget all the shit I'd put her through and we'd be back on track again. But Grace didn't want to get back with me. The opposite in fact. She told me she was pregnant and I was blown away. Not freaked out at all. I'd always wanted kids. Not just any kids, mind you. Kids with Grace. I reckoned they'd be gorgeous.'

'You were right, Jack is divine,' Gerry said.

Liam smiled at this and then continued, 'But Grace asked me to promise her something. If I had ever loved her, I must promise never ever to be involved in the baby's life, that is, as long as alcohol played a part in mine. I didn't want to promise to never to see my baby. But as Grace said, she wasn't stopping me seeing the baby. Just asking me to stay away if I continued drinking. Fair enough, so I promised. No biggy, I thought, I can stop drinking anytime. But as you guys all know, I didn't stop drinking. I kept meaning to, you know. Every morning I'd wake up and think that's it. Today, I'll stay sober and get my act together. But by five o'clock I'd be having a beer. Just to take the edge off.' Liam self-consciously put his face in his hands.

'Anyhow, back to Jack's birthday. I cleaned myself up and got the early-bird flight from Gatwick. Got into Dublin at eight o'clock. But I blew it. I went to an early house and arrived at Grace's that evening drunk.'

'Grace never told us that,' Tara said sharply.

'She never knew. I was outside the apartment waiting for her to get home when a little boy, about four or five, walked by. He was lovely, so I said hello to the little fella. Went to cuff him behind the ear. You know the way you do. Then all of a sudden, this woman came running and picked him up, screaming at me to keep away from her son. I looked at her and started telling her I meant no harm, but the more I spoke the more freaked out she got. I was slurring my words, with bloodshot eyes, reeking of booze. No wonder she was freaking out. It was at that moment, seeing how scared that little boy was and the look of revulsion on her face, that the house of cards all came tumbling down. What the fuck was I doing? I couldn't even stay sober to go visit my son on his second birthday. That's when I knew I needed help.'

'What did you do?' Abby asked, her eyes wide in shock at the story.

'I jumped in a taxi, and did what any self-respecting Irish man does – I went home to Mammy.'

'Jaysus, you must really have hit rock bottom to have done that!' Tom quipped.

The gang all laughed. Liam's mother was a legend in the group. Tom always said she made Mrs Bouquet look tame!

'She saved my life, Tom. I hadn't been home in nearly two years. I hadn't even told her about Jack. I was too ashamed. I think that was the thing she found hardest to forgive. Not knowing that she had a grandson only down the road. Anyhow, she got me into a rehab clinic the following week. I had to be eight days sober at home before they would take me. That was hard. But I'm telling you my mother was a force to be reckoned with. She locked me up in her bedroom. There's an en suite there and a TV, so she said I'd have no excuse to leave. She got my uncle Martin round every day, morning and evening, to bring in some grub, so I couldn't try to escape.'

'It's like *Trainspotting* and *28 Days* all rolled into one,' Gerry squealed. 'And now that I think about it, if Sandra Bullock and Ewan McGregor got together and had a kid, it would look exactly like you Liam!'

'Still the movie buff, I see,' Liam laughed. 'God this soul baring is thirsty work. I need something to drink mate. Any chance of a coffee?'

'Now there's one sentence that I never thought I'd hear you say, Liam,' Tom joked. 'I'll get some coffee going.'

Tara jumped up and joined Tom in the kitchen, leaving Gerry, Abby and Sean to chat to Liam.

'Are you buying all this remorse shit, Tom?' Tara demanded.

'You're making it painfully obvious that you aren't, sweetie, but I'll be honest, I think he's genuine. Give him a chance. I don't believe he's anything to gain by coming around here.'

'Yes he has,' Tara whispered flatly, 'Grace and Jack.'

'Coffee's very good mate,' Liam said, taking a moment to savour the blend. 'At a guess, you guys have got a Nespresso?'

'Yes Darling,' Gerry gleefully shouted, 'it is a Nespresso! Tom would serve instant if I'd let him, the heathen! This is our compromise. When did you get so cultured?'

'New addiction I suppose,' Liam wryly commented. 'I think all alcoholics have addictive personalities. That's why so many of them smoke as well as drink. For me, I chose to get into coffees. It's become a hobby for me now. I enjoy it.'

The phrase 'might as well be hung for a sheep as a lamb,' crossed Liam's mind as he turned to Sean and Tara.

'Tara and Sean, I want to apologise for making a scene at your wedding. I know that I embarrassed you both. That one I don't really remember, but Grace told me about it often enough so I know it happened. I'm sorry for falling on the wedding cake, Tara. And I'm sorry for trying to get Sean's aunt to do the lambada. I didn't know she had a bad hip. I was wasted.'

Gerry and Abby started to giggle at that. And there was definitely the hint of a smile on Tom's face.

Sean finally decided to speak. 'Well they say confession is good for the soul, Liam. So your soul must be in good nick at this stage. For me, I'd forgiven and forgotten about the cake incident ages ago. As for Aunt Molly and the lambada, I've never seen her move like that before; it's a sight I'll never forget! So, I take your apology and accept it. As for Tara, I think you may have to accept that you guys are never going to be buddies. Too much water under the bridge.'

'I can speak for myself, Sean.' Tara's voice was like ice. 'I'll never be buddies with you, Liam. I'll never trust you. Maybe I'm being hard, but I saw what you did to Grace. I've had a bellyful of this soul baring. So spill, Liam. Why are you really back?' Tara asked.

'It's very simple, Tara. I want Grace back. And I want to be a dad to Jack.'

'You've a bloody nerve, Liam. What makes you think Grace would even consider talking to you again?' Tara snapped.

'That's why I came to see Tom. I want to find out what's going on in Grace's life. Is she happy? Is she involved with someone else, someone who's being a father for Jack?' Liam paused, taking a deep breath.

'It would kill me,' he continued quietly. 'But I caused Grace enough pain over the years to last her a lifetime, and I never want to be responsible for hurting her again. If staying away is the right thing for Grace, then I'll do it. When I was in rehab, I had plenty of time to think about my life, where I went wrong. I genuinely thought about all the shit things I did in my time to you guys and to my family. But the things that have haunted me the most are what I did to Grace. I still love her, guys. But aside from Grace, Jack is non-negotiable. I intend to spend the rest of my life making up to him the first three years I've missed.'

'I said it earlier to Gerry, your timing is marvellous,' Tom deadpanned.

'Why? What's so bad about my timing? Does she have someone else? Am I too late? Tom?' Liam asked desperately.

Tara's face and the small shake of her head were blatantly clear to all of the friends. That imperceptible shake was all it took – nobody was to mention Grace's cancer to Liam.

'Why do I get the feeling that there's something going on here that everyone knows about except me? Tom, what's going on buddy?' Liam asked.

The look on his face was so earnest that Tom almost answered him and told him about Grace's cancer. But that wasn't his secret to share. If Grace met Liam, it would be her decision if she decided to tell him.

'Look, Liam. This is how it is. Grace isn't seeing anyone, so don't worry on that score. Tara, there's no point giving me dirty looks. I'm not lying to Liam. He's done some stupid things in the past. But he was our friend once upon a time. And he's still mine,' Tom stated.

'Thanks mate,' Liam replied in a strangled voice.

'For what it's worth Liam, I think you've paid a high price for your sins. You've missed out on having Grace in your life for the past three years. And what's even sadder is that you have no idea how special your son is. You couldn't even begin to imagine it. That, my friend, is a price I wouldn't want to pay.'

'I'm with Tom on this one,' Sean added. 'It's not our decision if Grace sees Liam or not. She's big enough and bold enough to make her own mind up.'

'All I'm asking is that you give Grace this message for me. Tell her I'm sober and to call me at this number. Please,' Liam said.

Chapter Four

'Mommy, is my Daddy coming soon?' Jack asked for the hundredth time that day.

'Not too long now, sweetie-pie,' Grace grimaced as she answered. Her nerves were in shreds. 'Watch your programmes.'

When Tom called to tell her about Liam's visit two days ago, Grace thought her heart would jump out of her chest it started to beat so loudly. She supposed she always knew this day would come, but why now? She had to start chemotherapy in a few days, and boy did she not need this, now of all times.

She had struggled about whether to let Jack see Liam straight-away or not. Should she meet him a few times first and then see how she felt? Or just bite the bullet and tell Jack that his Daddy was in town? Finally, eerily enough it was Jack who made her mind up for her. Picking him up from Montessori school yesterday, he had asked, 'When is my Daddy going to pick me up from school Mommy?'

With those words, Grace had frozen. Why was he asking her this, today of all days? Was he flipping psychic? Before she had a chance to respond, his teacher came out, and asked to have a quick word. Mary was a lovely woman and really easygoing. She'd never asked to speak to Grace before, and somehow or other, Grace figured she wouldn't like what she had to say.

'Hi Grace, don't look so scared, it's nothing major. Jack has started talking about his Daddy in the last week or two and I thought you should know. He's never mentioned him before, so that's why I picked up on it. Is he back in Jack's life?' Mary had asked gently.

'No, in fact he's never even met him. His Daddy writes to him every week but he's been out of the picture physically. Oh my God, Mary. What kind of stuff has Jack been saying? He hasn't mentioned his Daddy to me lately at all. It's always me who brings him up.'

'Well, he's got a great imagination then Grace. He's been telling his friends stories about his dad. Stuff about how his dad took him on holiday this year. How his dad is so strong, he could beat Spider-Man. The usual three year old's "my dad is better than yours" repertoire. Don't go beating yourself up too much. It's probably just a phase. I'll keep an eye on him for you.'

Hearing about Jack's over-fertile imagination really upset Grace. Abby was always telling her that she should relax and not worry so much about Jack. She reckoned Grace had way too much single-mother guilt and that Jack was very lucky to have the life he had with Grace. Grace knew that Abby was right; Jack was loved, not only by her, but also by her extended family. But here she was thinking they were doing okay and that Jack wasn't affected by the lack of a father figure and how wrong could she be? She felt like crying just at the thought of Jack being so upset. If she was honest with herself, she knew that the subject of Liam meeting Jack would come up eventually, but she just wasn't prepared for it so early on. What on earth goes on in the little mind of a three year old? That thought was sobering.

Having processed the news that Jack was talking about his dad so much in Montessori made her decision easier and she told Jack that his Daddy was in Ireland and wanted to visit him, and he was so excited, jumping up and down.

'Yay Mommy, can I wear my Spider-Man outfit?' Jack had said to her. No hard questions, no wobbly lip, just a fashion query. As Gerry had pointed out, Jack took after his Mom in a lot of ways!

So Grace had called Liam and asked him to come round today after Montessori, explaining to him that Jack knew nothing about his drinking, just that he'd been working overseas for the past three years and that Daddy loved him very much. Grace had spent the day tidying her already spotless apartment and then trying on every outfit in her wardrobe. What exactly do you wear to meet an ex-boyfriend and father of your child? Nothing too sexy, but sexy enough he'll realise what he's been missing, Gerry the fashion guru had said to her last night when he called over. One advantage to being ill for the past month, Grace realised, was that she'd dropped a stone. Don't recommend getting cancer as a diet tip, she thought wryly, but so far it was about the only plus Grace could find about this whole cancer trip.

She was ready, buffed to an inch of her life. Gerry had been at her apartment earlier and had done Grace's hair and make-up. He understood more than anyone the need for the perfect appearance for an occasion such as this. By the time he was finished with her, he declared Grace was 'pure Carrie from *Sex in the City* – bohemian New York chic meets Dublin hottie!' And looking at herself in the mirror, she had to agree. She did look like a hottie, or a Yummy Mummy as Gerry called her. Her long strawberry blonde hair was falling in soft waves down her back. Gerry spent over an hour applying Mac make-up to make it look like Grace had none on! She was wearing a bright turquoise t-shirt over skinny Miss Sixty blue jeans, with her favourite navy Converse runners. Jack earned himself a big sloppy kiss when he walked into Grace's bedroom and said 'Mommy, you pretty. Just like Upsy Daisy.' What a guy! At least fifty times a day her little man said something to make her smile. Three was such a great age.

Grace was broken out of her reverie by the sound of the buzzer. Jack jumped up and whispered excitedly 'Is that my Daddy?'

'Let's go find out, sweetie-pie,' she replied, straightening Jack's Spider-Man mask.

'Long time, no see, Grace,' Liam huskily said when she opened the door. Then he cursed himself for saying something so lame.

Grace had thought many times about how she would feel the moment she was faced with Liam. But nothing prepared her for her reaction. She felt like she'd been hit by a truck. She felt winded and also dizzy. Realising Liam was waiting for a response from her, she closed her eyes for a moment to compose herself. Finding it impossible to speak, she decided to simply nod. With her heart beating so hard, Grace was sure he had heard it. He looked good, great in fact. Being sober suited him. He'd dropped a few pounds, and looked healthy like he had done in the early days. She suddenly became aware that she was staring and that her little boy was hiding behind her. Knowing she had to pull herself together for Jack's sake, she mentally shook herself and then invited Liam in. Jack was clinging on to Grace really tightly and suddenly looked like a baby again. Pulling him on to her lap, Grace was overwhelmed by the need to protect him. She really prayed that she was doing the right thing by agreeing to this.

'Jack, say hello to your Daddy,' she said quietly.

Liam dropped to his knees, bringing himself down to Jack's level. 'Cool costume, Jack. I'm a big fan of Spider-Man too.'

Jack rolled his eyes and moved closer into his Mommy. Raising his eyebrows to Grace, Liam looked a bit thrown by Jack's response. Grace felt a burst of protectiveness explode in her. Liam couldn't expect Jack to just throw himself into his arms as if he'd just popped home after buying a pint of milk. He'd been away three years what did he expect. It would take more than five minutes to build the relationship!

Liam tried again, 'Jack, I really am a fan. I've seen the movie loads of times. I have it on DVD in fact. I tried to buy a costume too, but couldn't get one to fit me!' Liam said to his son, laughing.

Jack started to giggle. Maybe this was going to be okay, thought Liam. He moved a little closer to Jack and continued seriously, 'It makes me happy that we both like the same things, Jack. How cool is that?'

Jack just shrugged but he had moved a little further away from Grace. She decided that maybe she should leave them for a few minutes on their own.

'I'm going to make some coffee. Jack, why don't you show your Daddy all your Spider-Man toys?'

Walking away holding her breath, Grace wondered if Jack would follow her or stay with his dad? Ten minutes later, she walked back into the sitting room to find Jack showing Liam every toy he had in his toy box. Her son still had his mask on though, so it was difficult to know what was going on in his mind.

'Jack, honey, why don't you take your mask off? You must be hot under that.' Grace figured, correctly, that Liam must be desperate to see his face too.

'Don't want to, Mommy. Can I watch my programmes now?' Grace knew that this was his way of saying he'd had enough. He couldn't deal with anymore right now.

'Sure pet, no problem. Daddy and I are going to be in the kitchen drinking our coffee. You come get me if you want me, okay?'

'I want a snuggle, Mommy,' Jack said in a small voice.

'I'll follow you in,' Grace said to Liam and sat down on the couch with her little man scooped into her arms. Fireman Sam came on, and as Norman began another adventure that would surely end in disaster, Grace felt Jack begin to relax. She sat with him for a few moments and then, once satisfied he was okay she detangled herself and moved to the kitchen.

Grace poured the coffee, thinking about Jack, how grown up he was sometimes, for a three year old, but also how scary it must have been meeting his Daddy for the first time.

'Grace,' Liam interrupted. 'Thank you.'

'For what?'

'For letting me see Jack. For being an amazing mother to Jack for the past three years. For never saying anything negative about me to Jack. For all of that, I thank you.'

'I don't need your thanks Liam, being a mother to Jack is reward enough. He is amazing, and you'll find that out soon enough. I thank God every night for that gift. As for letting Jack see you, I told you three years ago that I'd never keep you away, as long as you were sober. Jack needs his Daddy.'

Liam nodded silently. They both drank their coffees for a couple of minutes, and there wasn't a need for words.

'Do you think he'll take his mask off before I go? I'm desperate to see his face,' Liam asked worriedly.

'I'm not going to push him, Liam. He has to do this at his own pace. Give him time. This is a big day for him. He'll take it off when he feels comfortable with you.'

'It's a big day for me too, Grace. I've been dreaming of it now for the past year. But don't worry; I don't want to push anything. You're in control, and I'll do things in whatever timeframe you and Jack are comfortable with.'

'Well that's very big of you, Liam,' Grace answered sarcastically. Then she felt instantly sorry for the snap.

'I'm sorry, Liam. That was unnecessary. I thought initially you could see him after Montessori for an hour a couple of times a week. Then maybe you can take him to the park at the weekend or something. Kick a ball about. How long you in Dublin for?'

'I'm back for good, Grace. I've relocated. I'm freelancing for a couple of the tabloids, so my time is pretty much flexible. I'll fall in with both yours and Jack's schedules. I want to be hands-on, Grace. But I don't want you to feel that I'm taking over. I want to help raise our son.' Liam's face was vulnerable as he made his speech and Grace felt a little bit of her heart melt at his words. And that frightened her. She suddenly felt very confused. Liam needed to go. She quickly put her shaking hands on her lap so that Liam wouldn't notice her confusion. She needed to stay in control if this was going to work.

'I appreciate that, Liam. But right now I have to check on Jack. I think that maybe you should go for now. Why don't you come back tomorrow, same time?'

'I'd like that, Grace. I need to talk to you. I have things I need to tell you. They're important.'

'I'm sure you do Liam, but I don't want to hear them right now. Let's concentrate on Jack for the moment. Okay?' Not waiting for an answer, Grace jumped up and walked back into the sitting room.

'Jack, Daddy's going to go home now, but he'd like to visit again tomorrow. Is that okay with you?'

Jack stood up and walked over to his Mommy. He felt a bit scared. Things were changing and it felt weird. But he liked his Daddy. He seemed like a cool guy. A bit like Spider-Man was really. So he simply said 'okay' then turned back to his programmes.

Normally Grace would have chastised him for being rude, but on this occasion she decided he'd earned the right to let his manners slide, just this once.

'Bye, Grace,' Liam said as he walked out of the apartment. He looked her squarely in her eyes with such intensity that Grace had to look away. 'Till tomorrow.'

Chapter Five

Tara and Sean were waiting in Duffy's for the others to arrive. Tom and Gerry wouldn't be long as they were already in Malahide having dinner. Abby was getting the Dart over, so should be here soon too. She lived in Clontarf in a little studio bedsit. It was tiny but in a gorgeous old Victorian house. Abby said that the location and the beauty of the house made up for the size of the studio. Plus it was close enough to all her friends in Malahide and Swords, with the added bonus of living around the corner from Gerry and Tom. One big difference though, they owned a whole Victorian house on Castle Avenue! She could have fitted her little studio into one of their reception rooms alone!

Sure enough, the boys arrived ten minutes later, giggling like kids. Tom went straight to the bar to get drinks and Gerry sashayed over to Tara and Sean, like he was walking the catwalk.

'What the hell are you doing?' Sean asked laughing.

'I'm showing you heathens my new Louis Copeland suit!' Gerry proclaimed.

'And I wouldn't like to tell you how much that little number cost,' Tom said as he joined them. 'I've seen the visa bill Gerry, so don't try to deny it!'

'My skin is very sensitive, you know that darling,' Gerry said fluttering his eyelashes at Tom. 'You wouldn't ask me to put any old man-made fibres on, would you?'

'Yes I would, if I thought you'd listen to me, you daft eejit!' Tom replied, laughing. 'Where's our starving artist?'

Right on cue, Abby arrived and joined her friends, air-kissing Gerry theatrically first of all.

'Darling, you are too thin!' Gerry protested. 'Enough of this starving artist charade, time for an intervention – eat!'

'I'll have you know that I've had two McChicken sandwiches today, a chocolate muffin, one Kit Kat, and I just ate a bag of Tayto crisps on the Dart!' Abby responded. Abby was one of those lucky people that could eat anything and never put on a pound.

Tara threw a beer mat at Abby, shouting, 'Bitch! I only have to look at a bag of Taytos and my thighs grow an inch!' Tara was always on a diet, and was currently trying a low-carb one. Sean thought she was off her head, his wife was gorgeous as she was, but Tara ignored him, telling everyone, 'Carbs aren't my friends, you know!'

Tara turned to Tom asking, 'You heard from Liam?'

'Yeah. We spoke earlier. He was on a high after his visit with Grace and Jack. He's going back today, you know. He did admit he was a little bit disappointed because our Jacky was a bit shy with him.'

'Very discerning judge of character is Jack,' Tara murmured.

'Tara,' Sean scolded quietly. She shrugged, looking like a naughty schoolgirl. When Tara had something to say, nobody was going to shut her up, not even the man she loved!

'We spoke to Grace last night. She was in a right state,' Tara told the group. 'Very worried about Jack. It's all she needs right now, what with chemo starting on Friday.'

'I think it's more than that,' Abby chimed in. 'I called Grace last night too, and she admitted that she found it confusing seeing Liam again. She practically threw him out because she was so freaked out by it all.'

42

'She still loves him, you do realise that, don't you Tara?' Tom decided to say what everyone else was afraid to say out loud.

'Yeah, I know that. Stop looking at me like I'm an imbecile, Tom Whelan. I've known Grace thirty two years now, and seen her do a lot of stupid things. Falling in love with that great big lummox Liam Ryan was just one of them.'

Sean smiled at his wife. She always called people by their full names when she was vexed. When she called him Sean Murphy, he knew it was time to bail!

'It's like *Love Story*, isn't it?' Gerry sighed. 'Or even *Jerry Maguire*. God, I love that bit when Tom goes into the mad woman's support group to get his wife. And he does that big speech. And then Renee just says "You had me at hello." Wasn't he just magnificent?'

'I don't think Jerry Maguire was an alcoholic, but I get your point,' Tom laughed.

'I just hope that Grace gets her happy ending. And Liam and Jack too,' Abby said.

Everyone sobered up with that, bringing them immediately back to Grace's cancer.

'So when is she going to tell Liam?' Tom asked. 'It's going to be hard keeping it from him.'

'She wouldn't discuss it with us,' Sean replied. 'Is everyone set for Friday?' It was decided that Tara and Sean would go with Grace to the hospital for the chemo. She was an outpatient, so she could get home in the evening after her treatment to see Jack. The gang had a rota organised to help with him. Tom and Gerry were taking him to Tayto Park, the kid's amusement park, on Friday after Montessori. They figured he'd be so tired after that he'd go to bed early when Grace got home. Then Abby was going to have him on Saturday, Tara and Sean on Sunday, just in case Grace had reactions to the chemo. He'd be in the crèche during the week and then they'd do the same again each Friday and weekend until

Grace was finished. She was scheduled for three months of weekly chemo sessions which seemed like an eternity.

'I don't think Grace is aware of how sick she's going to get, guys. I want her to move in with Tara and me, but she won't have it.'

'We'll have to go to her,' Tom stated. 'Someone must be there every evening next week, while the chemo treatment is going on. At least until we know how she's coping with it? Agreed?'

'Yes sir!' Gerry mock saluted his boyfriend, with a laugh!

****

Liam and Jack were playing Lego in the sitting room; Jack in his Fireman Sam outfit, complete with mask. He had been wearing it yesterday too when Liam had come to visit for an hour and wouldn't even take the mask off to eat the sweets Liam had brought him. When he went to eat one, he just turned his back on Liam and lifted the mask slightly to stuff a handful in. It was comical.

Grace had been keeping an eye on Jack since Liam's return to make sure that he wasn't unsettled. But she could tell he liked him. He sat in the bay window earlier this evening waiting for Liam to arrive. Then the second Liam rang the bell, he ran back into the sitting room and started playing with his toys, pretending not to care. She had asked Liam to stay for dinner tonight, and he had eagerly accepted. When she opened the door to him, he had a huge bunch of white roses in his hands. The fact that he had remembered how much she loved white roses didn't go unnoticed by Grace. She looked around her apartment living room and thought the house was beginning to look like a florist. Earlier today a huge bunch of gorgeous flowers had arrived from Tom and Gerry. The card just said simply, 'Be strong, we love you.'

44

Having unwrapped and arranged the roses and put them in water whilst the boys played, she now shouted to the guys, 'Dinner's ready. Jack wash your hands please.'

Liam threw his eyes up to heaven theatrically for effect, to which Jack obliged him with a giggle. While Jack cleaned up, Liam came into the dining room.

'Let's not mention the mask,' Grace told Liam. 'If we don't make a big deal about it, he might take it off himself. Alright? Plus, he might have difficulty negotiating spaghetti and meatballs if he leaves it on,' Grace added with a smile.

'God, you're a devious woman,' Liam laughed. 'I love it!'

This was Jack's favourite dinner. He loved sucking the spaghetti up like worms. 'My tummy's really hungry Mommy,' Jack declared.

'Well let's put that right straight away.' Grace spooned a big portion into his bowl.

'Liam, don't be shy. Eat up.'

'This is good Grace. You haven't lost it.' Liam smiled as he noticed the blush on Grace's cheeks. She loved getting compliments about her cooking. Liam was determined to achieve two things today: see his son's face properly and talk to Grace. Properly talk, not chit-chat about the weather. It was killing him being in the same room as her and not being able to put his arms around her and tell her he loved her. A big sigh from Jack interrupted his thoughts. He was bringing his spoon up to his mouth, then back down again just as quickly, because the mask was in the way. Grace was torn between bursting into laughter or just taking matters into her own hands and grabbing the mask off him.

Then Jack announced, 'I don't want to get my Fireman Sam mask dirty, Mommy. Can you mind it for me?' He peeled it off defiantly and looked at Liam as if to say 'so!'

Liam judged the situation correctly and simply said, 'Good thinking buddy,' and then carried on eating.

Grace could see such a range of emotions running across Liam's face, recognising them instantly as she felt a lot of them every day when she played with Jack. She could see wonder, pride, awe, fear and a good deal of amusement juggling around at various times, as Jack battled with his meatball pasta. By the time they were finished Jack had somehow managed to put tomato sauce on every inch of his face!

'All right sweetie-pie, time to get your face cleaned up, and into your jimmy jams.'

Liam jumped up then shouting, 'Hold that thought!' as he ran into the hall, coming back in with a bag.

'I got you a present buddy. Hope you like it.'

'It's not even my birthday Mommy, look a present!' Jack squealed as he ripped the paper off. 'It's Spider-Man, Mommy.'

'They're pyjamas buddy. I thought you might dream Spider-Man dreams if you wear them to bed,' Liam stated.

'Thank you! They're way cool. Look Mommy.'

'I know sweetie. They are way cool. But right now you have to wash up and then put them on. Then you can play for half an hour with your Daddy. Deal?'

Jack's little face was scrunched up and she could tell that he was trying to decide something. She figured correctly it had something to do with Liam.

'Do you want to ask your Daddy something, Jack?' Grace asked him.

He turned to Liam, and with a little voice said, 'Do you want to wash my face, Daddy?'

Liam thought at that moment that life could never ever get any better. Tonight he got to see his perfect little face. Tom had told him that he had a 'mini-me' in Jack, and he was right. It was like looking at a picture of him when he was little. But now this…He had dreamt about Jack calling him Daddy.

'Nothing would make me happier, son,' Liam said. 'Is that okay, Grace?'

'Demoted already! I don't know. I'll wash up!' Grace said protesting playfully, shoving the two of them up the stairs, furiously swallowing the large lump that had appeared in her own throat. She felt so many conflicting emotions as she watched father and son walk out of the kitchen together. On the whole she was really happy to see the relationship between the two flourish. But equally it was hard watching Jack need someone else other than her. And as she felt a stab of jealousy she immediately felt guilty for the thought. Life sure was complicated.

An hour later, Jack was fast asleep, and Liam and Grace were drinking coffee.

'Big day, huh?' she asked Liam, noticing that he looked distracted.

'Something like that. Tom told me last week that I had paid a high price for my drinking. I didn't disagree with him. In fact I had thought the same thing many a time over the last couple of years. But tonight, Grace, when he called me Daddy, I actually felt something give in my heart. It took my breath away. I've missed so much.' Liam could feel himself choking up and he pulled himself together quickly, looking away. He wanted to talk to Grace tonight about the two of them. Every time Liam had tried to talk to her about his drinking over the last couple of days, she had brushed him off. But this time he wasn't going to walk away. 'Grace I've missed you.'

Grace thought she was going to faint. Her head was telling her to get Liam out straightaway; she had too much on her plate right now. But her heart was willing him to continue. Spending time with him over the past week had been unbelievable. It was exactly as it had been in the first couple of years they were together. The pre-drinking years when they were deeply in love. In fact it was even better, because Jack was there now too.

'Grace, I'm still in love with you. I fell in love with you the very first moment I saw you. You took my breath away that night. Do you remember?'

How could she forget? Abby, Tara and Grace were having a Christmas party in their rented house in Drumcondra. They had invited everyone they knew and the place was heaving. Abby had told her about this cute guy called Liam that she had invited to the party. But when Grace opened the door and saw him standing there, she always swore she actually felt electricity fly between them. He didn't leave her side all night, and that was fine by Grace. Abby used to say that they were the perfect couple. And for a long time Grace used to agree with her. They just fit. But that was a long time ago.

'I remember Liam. I haven't forgotten anything,' Grace replied with a hint of sarcasm in her voice. She couldn't help it. He'd hurt her too much. Liam looked away and took a deep breath.

'I know I hurt you Grace. I want to make up for it.' Liam felt that just saying the word sorry was too trite. Somehow he needed to do more to prove himself to Grace. But he hadn't worked out what yet. He knew in his heart of hearts that he and drinking were over. He would never, ever jeopardise his love for Grace and Jack for a drink. But how do you make someone you hurt so much believe that? Maybe he didn't deserve her belief. Maybe his punishments for his behaviour while drinking was to lose Grace, and perhaps he should just be grateful she was allowing him to have Jack in his life.

'Why did you wait so long to come and see us when you said you've been sober for a year now?' Grace accused.

'One year and nearly three months to be exact, Grace. When I was in rehab we were given a list of rules and guidelines to abide by when we left. One of the most important ones was to not get involved in any relationship for at least a year. I made a decision when I left rehab not to contact you or Jack for at least that because I wanted to be sure that I could stay away from the drink. I also wanted to make something of myself. I needed to get working again and get back some self-respect. I picked up the phone to call you hundreds of times, just to hear your voice, and to tell you that I had stopped drinking. But I wanted to wait until the time was right. Can you understand?'

'How do you know that you'll never drink again now, Liam? What makes you so sure?' Grace whispered.

'That's a tough one. I'll never be one hundred per cent certain. But I know that I can live without drink. I've gone through birthdays, Christmas, parties of all shapes and sizes without the urge to grab a six-pack. I go to AA once a week. I've already joined a local support group since I got home. I was there last night in fact. Did the whole "Hi My name is Liam and I'm an alcoholic" lark!'

Grace laughed with Liam at that. It sounded so Hollywood! 'Did everyone clap?'

'Yep, and shouted back like robots, "Welcome Liam."'

'God, I'd be morto!' Grace laughed. 'Did you all start singing *Kumbaya My Lord* then?'

'Nah, these days we alcoholics sing *We've Got the Whole World in Our Hands*!' Liam answered, joining Grace in her laughter. 'But on the plus side, there was a huge plate of cupcakes on the go. Best thing about AA meetings is the free cakes!' He finished with a wink. Grace couldn't help giggling again. 'Grace Devlin, it's good to see you laughing. God, you're beautiful.'

Grace jumped up, picking up the coffee cups and walked into the kitchen.

'That my cue to go, I suppose?' Liam joked.

She felt flustered with Liam now. He was stirring up some feelings that she had thought were gone, or at least buried. He pulled on his coat and walked to the door. Turning around at the last minute, he said very seriously, 'Grace, I love you. I can't be without you anymore. And whether you like it or not, I think you still love me too. I know I will have to spend my life making up for the pain I caused you but I'm not giving up, Grace Devlin, you hear me. I'm not giving up.'

Chapter Six

Grace was scared and, for the first time since this whole thing started, in pain. It was funny, but up until they had installed the Hickman device, Grace hadn't felt like she had cancer. She had conveniently pushed it to the back of her mind, choosing not to think too deeply about it. Who has time to think when they are a single mother of a bubbly three year old? Not to mention the whole situation with Liam that had recently added to the madness that was her life.

But right now, there was no getting away from the fact that she had cancer. She was getting her first bout of induction chemo and it felt lousy. The Hickman device hurt, but she knew she'd be grateful for it as the week progressed. They'd also given her a couple of pints of blood and taken a sample of bone marrow from her hip. That hurt like hell. Today felt like a hurricane – it was a blur of tests, anti-sickness tablets and now the chemo. This was only day one and she was struggling.

'Grace, you need to keep using the mouthwashes while on chemo,' Sean said.

'It'll stop you getting mouth sores,' Tara added.

'One of my patients swears she has shares in Polo mints,' Sean said and held up a bag full of mints. 'Just in case.'

'What other treasures can I expect to get, courtesy of this chemo then?' Grace asked sarcastically.

'Well, the chemo will kill off your white and red blood cells. This will mean that you will be open to infections, so we'll have to be careful. You'll probably feel nauseous too. That'll kick in soon,' Sean told her.

Tara once again chimed in, 'You might not feel like eating while on chemo Grace, but you must try, as you've got to keep your strength up. The anti-sickness tablets should help too.'

'Sean, do me a favour. You doctors are great, but you can make things really complicated sometimes. Explain in words that Jack would understand what chemo is actually going to do. I need to know exactly what is flowing into my blood right now.'

'Righto. Basically, it's an anti-cancer drug. It's carried by the bloodstream to every part of your body, and the drug will kill the cancer cells. It also stops the cancer cells dividing and growing, so that eventually the bad cells will simply disappear.'

'Thank you, Sean. I actually understood all of that. What about the side effects? How bad can I expect them to get?'

Sean and Tara looked at each other helplessly. Tara decided to answer this one. 'It's hard to say Grace how you are going to feel at the end of this chemo. All patients differ dramatically. I've known patients who get up at the end of each session and apart from a couple of hours of nausea they are fine. Others react very badly to the chemo and their bodies can't take it. One patient said to me that it felt like her body was weeping inside.'

'I don't like the sound of that, Tara. But so far so good. I'm healthy and strong. I don't feel sick yet, so maybe I'll be one of the lucky ones,' Grace said defiantly.

'The main thing the doctors will be looking at is your blood count, Grace,' Sean continued. 'You'll hear a lot about your haemoglobin, your red and white blood cell count. Whether they're up or down will determine whether you need bloods or are at risk of an infection.'

Grace closed her eyes then, letting her friends know that she didn't want to talk anymore. She felt like her head was going to explode with so many things in there, fighting each other, demanding an answer from her. What would happen if the chemo didn't work? Would she go into remission? Should she tell Jack? What should she tell Jack? Should she tell Liam? Should she tell Liam that she still loved him and that she never stopped? Would her hair fall out? And the other problem throwing its weight around in her brain – Dr Kennedy had given her some food for thought earlier; the odds weren't in her favour for survival by treating the cancer by chemo alone. She certainly wouldn't put a bet on at Paddy Power's with the odds the doctor had quoted. But if she could find a donor for a bone marrow transplant then they would dramatically rise. No contest then – get a donor.

All her friends, true to their word, went in for blood and tissue tests, but unfortunately none of them were a match. Slim odds really. All of her cousins were in as well. Tara's two brothers and sister, plus her Mam and Dad also tested. Tom's sister in Kerry had even got herself tested. All negative. Getting a match was turning out to be tough. Especially because of the fecking blood type Grace had. They had put all her details on the NMDP – National Marrow Donor Programme – and also checked a worldwide database of donors. But so far no luck. Here was the kicker, there was a thirty per cent chance that Grace would find a perfect match from someone in her family – her biological family that was. That brought her to the crux of her problem. She'd never once felt that being adopted was a problem – until now. Now she needed her biological family, but would they help?

Grace had traced her mother when she was 18, with the total support of her Mam and Dad. She wasn't looking for a mother, as she had a perfectly good one, but was interested in finding out about her heritage. She wanted to know where she got her strawberry blonde hair from. All the Devlins had dark hair. She wanted to know whom she inherited her crooked fingers from. She also had a good singing voice too; did that come from her mother or father? She was interested of course in the circumstances of her birth – and her adoption. But Grace genuinely had no hard feelings about it. She knew she had been very lucky in the parents' stake with Annie and Mick. But still she had lots of questions, which anybody who had been adopted would understand immediately. But Grace never got the answers to her questions.

When she contacted the adoption board and asked for information on her birth mother, she was given her name, Catherine Grace Dunne. Her birth mother was from Meath and was 25 when she had Grace. She was single. Grace's parents explained that they gave Grace her biological mother's second name, so that she would have some connection with her. God, they were amazing people. The adoption board contacted Catherine and let her know that her daughter wanted to make contact. Grace wrote a letter that they forwarded on. It took her ages to write, as she wanted the tone to be right. Grace didn't want Catherine to feel like she was judging her or that she wanted anything from her. Eventually she was satisfied with the letter and passed it to the adoption board. Grace thought she'd never get a reply, but eventually, after six weeks, she received a letter back. Catherine was happy that her daughter had a good life, and that Annie and Mick were such good parents. She had thought about Grace every day since she was born. However, she could not meet her. She wished Grace all the best for the future. And that was it. It was a blow of the highest order. It felt like a double betrayal. First she rejected Grace at birth, then again when she was eighteen. Grace vowed then she'd never try to contact her again. Catherine had made her feelings perfectly clear and Grace wasn't going to beg her to meet her. But Grace hadn't counted on cancer. Cancer changed everything.

Grace opened her eyes and saw two pairs of worried eyes watching her. 'Do you think I should contact Catherine again, Tara?'

Tara looked at her cousin but didn't answer immediately. Grace appreciated that, she was giving the question some thought. After a while she grasped Grace's hand and answered. 'Yes I do Grace. I've spoken about this with Sean and I reckon it's your best bet for a suitable match. It's worth a shot.'

'What if she refuses to meet me, never mind agree to a donor test?' Grace whispered. 'I don't think I could bear the rejection again.'

'Listen to me Grace,' Tara said fiercely. 'You've got to do everything in your power to beat this fucker. And if that means putting yourself on the line again with Catherine, so be it. Don't give her a choice, insist on meeting her Grace. She owes you that much.'

Grace knew Tara was right, so agreed reluctantly. 'Okay bossy boots. I'll do it.'

Chapter Seven

It was Thursday evening, and Liam was dropping Jack home. He had picked him up from Montessori and they had gone to the cinema. He'd seen Jack on Sunday too, but Abby opened the door to Grace's apartment when he called to pick him up. He was surprised and disappointed as he'd been looking forward to speaking to Grace again. But Abby said Grace had gone out with some friends.

Then on Tuesday evening when he'd dropped Jack home, Tara was at the door to meet him. She'd practically sneered at him when he tried to get by her and come into the apartment.

'I'm afraid it's not convenient right now for you to come in. Grace said you can pick up Jack after school on Thursday if you like.' At his nod of agreement, she had shut the door in his face. God, she had a nerve that woman. How on earth Sean put up with that temper he'd never know. Somehow he wasn't really surprised when Tara opened the door to them again tonight. Grace was obviously trying to avoid him. She must really hate him, he realised.

'Hi, Aunt Tara. Where's Mommy?' Jack shouted, as he ran into the hall.

'In her bedroom. She's waiting for you,' Tara replied, pulling Jack in close for lots of kisses.

'What's going on Tara? Why are you here like the bleeding Gestapo every time I call round? Why is Grace avoiding me?' Liam demanded.

'Oh get over yourself, Liam Ryan. Everything doesn't revolve around you, you know. Grace's busy now, that's all. She said she'd give you a call on Saturday to arrange another visit. Okay?'

'God, you've an acid tongue on you Tara. When are you going to give me a break? Second thoughts, don't answer that. Tell Grace I said hello.'

With that he turned on his heel, resisting the urge to stick his tongue out at Tara as he did. He checked his watch and realised he was going to be late. He was going to Tom and Gerry's for dinner. He was looking forward to spending some time with the guys again. He got there only ten minutes late in the end, stopping on the way to pick up a couple of bottles of Pinot Noir. It was Gerry's favourite and he wasn't ashamed to admit that he was trying very hard to get back into his good books. When he got there, Abby was there too.

'I'm here to even up the numbers apparently!' Abby told him.

He was pleased. It was good to see her friendly face. When he handed Tom the wine, the three of them burst into laughter.

'What's so funny?'

'Darling, we have spent the entire night hiding all our alcohol! We thought you wouldn't want it anywhere near you! And after all that, you arrive and hand us booze like it's no big deal!' Gerry explained.

'Oh God lads, don't think like that. You're as bad as my mother. She's put a lock on the drinks cabinet. I tried to explain to her that if I wanted a drink, that little lock wouldn't stop me! Honestly guys. Have a jar. It won't make me want one, I promise.'

They had a great night with great food and great company. Tom as usual had everyone in stitches with his stories about work.

Now, as the evening was winding up, they were drinking coffee and Liam decided he was going to try and get some information from his friends.

'Grace's been avoiding me this past week, you know.'

'Really, darling,' Gerry exclaimed in a high pitch. 'I'm sure you're wrong. She's probably just busy. Don't you think Tom?'

'Yep, reckon that's it,' Tom responded. 'Don't push it Liam. Give Grace her space. She'll let you know when she's ready to talk.'

'It's doing my head in. Jack is amazing. He's so funny, and every minute I spend with him is precious. But I miss Grace. I want to be with her. Life's too short guys,' Liam said with such sincerity.

Abby let out a sob. She tried to cover it up, but Liam caught it. And then he caught the look that passed between Gerry and Tom. He knew that there was something going on that he was missing. But for the life of him he couldn't work it out.

'I thought I was being left out on some big secret the other week when I met you all. It was like I was the only one who didn't get the punchline of a joke. Feeling a bit like that again. Am I missing something?'

Gerry jumped up, pouring another cup of coffee for himself. 'Don't be silly, you're paranoid. Coffee, darling?'

Liam didn't care what they said, something was wrong, he could feel it. Tom broke the uncomfortable silence by asking Abby about her love life.

'What love life? I've forgotten what that is!' Abby declared.

'Darling, that can't be true. You should be one of those girls in *Sex and the City*! The single life you lead, it's fantastic!'

'Gerry, I hate to burst your bubble, I'm living in the city all right, but there's not so much of the sex happening!'

They all laughed at that.

'Well that's a tragedy. A beauty such as you should be worshipped! What is wrong with the men in Dublin?'

'From what I can gather Gerry, only two things. The only men I meet that are over 30 are either gay or married!' Abby waited until the laughs died down, and then continued. 'But seeing as you've asked, I'll tell you guys something – I'm lonely.'

As Tom began to protest, Abby stopped him. 'I didn't say alone, Tom. I know I'm not alone. I've got my family and I've got the best friends any girl could ask for. But that's a lot different to being lonely. You can have a roomful of people around you, you know, and still feel like you're the only person left on this planet.'

Gerry got up and walked over to Abby, putting his arms around her. 'Darling, why didn't you tell us you felt this way? I blame myself. I should have known.'

'Because it's hard to say Gerry, that's why. I feel pathetic even saying it to you now. You guys just don't understand. Remember when we went out for dinner last month for Tara's birthday? Tara and Sean booked the table for six people. Nobody even bothered to check to see if I wanted to bring someone.'

'Ah Jaysus, Abby, why didn't you just tell us if you wanted to bring someone? Sure we'd be delighted,' Tom said.

'That's not the point. I didn't have anyone to bring, but I would have liked to have been asked. I know it's irrational. But it's how I feel. It's as if you've all just given up on me ever having a boyfriend.'

Tom looked helplessly at Gerry. He felt out of depth here. Gerry realised that sometimes there was nothing to say, so he simply put his arms around Abby.

'I know how you feel, Abby,' Liam said after a while. 'I'm lonely too. But I know why I'm on my own. I'm in love with Grace and I don't want anyone else. I'm fucked if I understand why you haven't been snatched up though! God, you're lovely looking. Isn't she Gerry?'

'Darling, she is perfection. Look at that skin, it's flawless. And those lips!' Gerry then broke into his best Clark Gable southern accent, '"You should be kissed and often, by someone who knows how."'

Abby laughed, saying, 'If only I could find my Rhett Butler! Not so many of them wandering around Copper Face Jacks on a Saturday night!'

'What happened with that guy you went out with last week? What was his name again, Kieran or something?' Tom asked.

'His name was Kevin. It didn't work out. End of story.'

'What happened? I thought you liked him,' Gerry questioned.

'I'm not telling you. You'll only laugh,' Abby snapped.

'We won't darling, will we guys?' Gerry responded, gesturing to Tom and Liam, who both shook their heads.

'Okay, we went out a couple of times and everything was going well. Or at least I thought so. But then on Monday, he dumped me – by...'Abby whispered the last bit so quietly that the guys couldn't hear her.

'By what, darling?' Gerry asked, looking slightly horrified.

'By text,' Abby shouted. 'By fucking text, the bastard! A Dear John! "Thanks for a great night, but I think it's time we went our separate ways!"'

'Wanker,' Tom said.

'Gobshite,' Liam added.

'Heathen,' Gerry threw in for good measure.

And with that, all four burst into laughter.

Chapter Eight

Grace felt terrible. The chemo was finished at last, for this time anyhow, but her whole body felt like it had been steamrolled. Everything hurt. She couldn't keep anything down. If it weren't for Tara continually shoving food down her throat, she wouldn't have even bothered to eat. It was a waste of time, because it came straight back again. One of Grace's favourite sayings used to be 'I'm losing the will to live!' and she had used it many times over the years. But never again, as now she really understood what the words meant.

Poor Jack didn't know what was going on. He had so much change in his life at the moment. First of all his Daddy appeared out of nowhere. That must have been traumatic for him, even if it was a good thing. And now this week he'd been shoved from pillar to post every day after Montessori while she was recuperating. Then in the evenings, despite her determined efforts, she couldn't manage more than five minutes with him before having to go to bed. If it weren't for her friends, she wouldn't have managed. The doctors had said yesterday following her last chemo treatment that her blood count was good. She knew she should be happy with that, but right now she was just too tired. Jack was with Liam again for the day. She had practically thrown Jack at Liam when he arrived an hour ago and now she just wanted to sleep.

What felt like five minutes later, Grace awoke to the ringing of her mobile phone and the buzzing of her doorbell. She looked at her watch – shit, it was four o'clock already. She'd been asleep since eleven this morning. That had to be Liam and Jack back. She jumped up, glancing at herself in the mirror. She looked awful. She looked thin, and pale, but God what did she expect? Her plan had been to sleep for a few hours, then have a bath and make herself look presentable for the boys when they got back. She didn't want to scare Jack, and didn't want Liam to guess anything was wrong.

'Sorry, I was asleep and didn't hear the bell,' Grace said to Liam as she answered the door. 'Hi sweetie-pie did you have a good time?' Grace winced as Jack threw himself at her for a big cuddle. It felt like every bone was about to jump outside her skin.

'Grace, you okay, baby?' Liam asked. He was worried. She looked terrible and was far too thin. Before Grace could answer, Jack chimed in.

'Mommy, I'm starving. Daddy said we couldn't have another McDonalds. He said chips once a day was enough for one boy, even a big one like me!'

'He never stops eating,' Liam said. 'We had lunch at one o'clock, and ice cream an hour ago. I don't know where he puts it all!' Liam was worried Grace would think he wasn't feeding Jack properly, but she didn't seem to be listening.

'Mommy, can I watch my programmes?' Grace obliged him by putting Disney Junior on. Mickey Mouse would once again have to take care of Jack right now.

'What's going on Grace? You look terrible,' Liam said.

'Thanks a lot. You certainly know how to charm the ladies.'

'You know what I mean, Grace. Don't try and deflect.'

'I had a crap week at work that's all. Demanding client who doesn't know what she wants. I just needed to catch up on some sleep. A bath and I'll be fine.'

'Something to eat too by the looks of it. You've lost a lot of weight. You're not on that crazy low-carb diet like Tara, are you?' Liam said with irritation.

'No you daft fool,' Grace laughed. 'You know me; my weight has always been up and down.'

'Right, I'm not saying I believe you, but I'll go along with your charade for a while longer. But here's the deal. You go up and have that bath, and I'll see what kind of dinner I can manage to put together. Non-negotiable Grace. Go!'

Grace hadn't the energy to argue and to be honest the thought of a hot bath was lovely. To add insult to injury, she felt like she was getting the flu too.

An hour later, Grace came down feeling like a new woman. The bath was glorious. Gerry had brought over a beautiful beauty hamper from Benefit yesterday and she'd indulged herself totally. Afterwards, she threw on some combats and a baby tee. She'd have to borrow some of Abby's clothes soon. She'd spent most of her adult life being a size 12-14, but she'd lost a stone and a half in the past month. And all her clothes were getting too loose. Grace came downstairs to the beautiful aroma of chicken roasting. She had planned on making a roast dinner for Jack and herself this evening.

Jack was panned out on the sofa, dead to the world, his cartoons playing away in the background. He looked so innocent sleeping there. Looking at her son, she knew she couldn't give in to this evil illness. She had to beat it for his sake. She sat on the sofa beside him and lifted his head onto her lap, stroking his hair. God, she loved him so much it took her breath away. She was in awe that she'd actually created him.

'You look better.' Liam had come into the room and was watching her.

'Thanks. It wouldn't have been hard. I looked like the bride of Frankenstein, didn't I?' Grace asked sheepishly.

'Nah, you were still gorgeous, even if you did look a bit rough!' Liam dodged the cushion Grace threw at him.

'Dinner will be ready in about an hour. I raided your fridge, its roast chicken and veggies. That okay?'

'That's great Liam. I appreciate it. But if you want to get off now, go ahead. I'm sure you have plans made for a Saturday night.'

'Nope, no plans at all. Sure where else would I be on a Saturday night, but with my two favourite people in the world. Besides, I couldn't leave right now, even if I wanted to. I'm at a delicate stage in the cooking. I've got to get the veggies in to roast in about five minutes, not to mention making the gravy. A chef's work is never done!'

Grace smiled at him and their eyes locked. He couldn't look away and neither could she. She looked so vulnerable sitting there with her legs curled up under her. And so young, with her hair tied back and no make-up on. Grace was the first to turn away. 'Can I help?'

Liam walked over to Grace and told her to stay put and relax, leaning down to give her a kiss on her forehead as he left. It was only when he walked out into the kitchen that he realised what he'd done. He'd kissed Grace and she didn't go ballistic. He started to whistle as he chopped the carrots. Maybe he had a shot here after all!

Chapter Nine

It was Sunday morning and Tom and Gerry had been up early. They'd gone for a walk along the estuary in Malahide and had decided to call into Grace's for breakfast. Stopping for rashers of bacon, sausages and eggs at the local Eurospar, they were going to surprise her. But it was them that got the surprise when Liam answered the door, with nothing on but his jeans.

'Tom, Gerry, you guys are up and about early. Come on in. Grace's still in bed. Jack and I are just about to have breakfast.' Liam had to bite his tongue to stop himself laughing at their surprised faces. Tom and Gerry followed Liam inside wordlessly.

'Close your mouths!' he said to them, laughing. The look of shock on their faces was priceless. But before they had chance to delve any further, Grace came downstairs wearing her robe, shouting, 'Who's at the door, Liam?'

'Two very curious friends, who want to know what the hell happened last night. Spill, Darlings!' Gerry exclaimed.

Liam and Grace looked at each other and burst out laughing.

'God, you've a filthy mind Gerry!' Grace answered. 'Liam cooked us dinner last night. Then we watched a DVD. It was late so he crashed here. Sorry to disappoint but it was very innocent!'

'Daddy had a sleepover on my bunk bed, on the top bunk!' Jack helpfully added.

'Very comfortable too, buddy,' Liam replied.

'What has you two here so early on a Sunday?' Grace asked. 'Or need I ask. Here to check up on me I suppose?'

'Don't be stupid, woman,' Tom replied. 'We were out for a walk on the estuary and we decided we wanted a fry-up. You were nearer than our house. Make yourself useful Liam, put the pan on!'

Liam wondered what Grace meant when she asked if the guys were checking up on her. She looked better today than yesterday, but still. With that, the phone rang.

'Any money that's Tara,' Grace said as she walked into the sitting room to answer the phone.

'Darling Liam, you should have answered that,' Gerry said with a laugh. 'Tara would have had a heart attack!'

Breakfast was well under way when Grace came back in, looking a bit distracted. Liam placed a full Irish in front of her, and told her to eat up.

'Bet you didn't tell Tara that the queer fella was here,' Tom said, pointing at Liam.

'Less of the queer fella,' Liam replied. 'Three words mate – pot, kettle, black!'

Jack then asked, 'What's queer mean Daddy? Am I a queer fella?' He didn't know why they were laughing, but he joined in too. He was having a great time. He loved his Mommy and his Daddy, and his uncles were here and he had sausies too. This was great!

Tom and Gerry were cleaning up the breakfast things while the others got ready. Grace had been really quiet during breakfast and hadn't really eaten much. Before going upstairs to get dressed, she'd whispered to Tom that she needed to talk to him.

When Grace reappeared with Jack, the boys were all watching *MTV Cribs*.

'Jack, say goodbye to your Daddy. No buts, Jack. If your Daddy doesn't get home soon, his Mommy will call the guards!'

Grace walked to the door with Liam, closing the sitting room door behind her. She was very much aware that she had an audience.

'Liam, thanks a million for last night. Dinner was lovely and Jack loved having you here.'

'What about you Grace, did you enjoy me being here?'

'Liam, let's not do this. Not right now. Do you want to see Jack as usual on Tuesday after school?'

'Yes, of course I want to see Jack. But I want to see you too. Would you come on a date with me, Grace Devlin?'

'A what?' Grace squeaked in response.

'You heard.'

'A date?' Grace realised her voice had risen further by a couple of octaves.

'God, you'd swear I suggested murder by the look on your face. Yes, a date. You know the kind of thing. A guy collects a girl and they go out together. The girl might even enjoy herself! Don't say no Grace. Think about it.' And with that he kissed Grace on the forehead again and walked away.

What was this kissing on the forehead lark, Grace thought with irritation. He kept doing it then walking away! Did he think she'd hit him if he stuck around? And now he wanted them to go on a date. Oh Lord!

'What put that big smile on your face?' Gerry said.

'I'm not smiling,' Grace protested. But she was. It was like she had a coat hanger in her mouth and she couldn't get it out! What was it about that guy? Five minutes in his company and she felt like she was twenty again. 'He only wants me to go on a date with him!'

'How exciting! What are you going to wear?' Gerry said smiling.

'I haven't agreed to anything yet, Gerry.'

'But you will. I can tell. Won't she, Tom?'

'I don't know, Gerry. Whatever you decide Grace, I'm sure it'll be the right decision. But I've spent some time with Liam in the last couple of weeks. He still loves you, Grace. I didn't want to say anything before. It's between you guys. But from where I'm sitting, I'd say you were still in love with him too.'

Grace didn't answer, she just simply nodded. 'Why didn't this happen a year ago? Why did he have to come back now? How can I start something up with him? I've got cancer. It wouldn't be fair.'

Tom put his hand over Grace's and said, 'Life isn't fair, sweetheart. What's happening to you is far from fair. You say that it's not fair to get involved with Liam now that you have cancer. I can understand why you feel that. But it's not your decision to make. It's Liam's. Is it fair to keep this from him? He loves you Grace. Don't underestimate him.'

'It was lovely having him here last night. Really easy, you know. It's weird. In some ways it feels really new, like having a new boyfriend. But in other ways, it's like we've just picked up where we left off.'

Gerry walked over to Grace and Tom, taking her other hand.

'Give him a chance, darling. If something were to happen to my Tom, I would have to be with him. I wouldn't forgive him if he didn't let me help. Don't do that to Liam.'

'I know you're right. I just need a bit more time to think this out. But if you thought my life was complicated before, hold on to your trousers! That phone call earlier – it wasn't Tara. It was my liaison officer from the adoption centre. My biological mother has agreed to meet me.'

Chapter Ten

Liam couldn't believe it when Grace rang him on Sunday evening and said she would meet him for lunch. So here he was, forty-eight hours later, big stupid grin on his face, with Grace sitting beside him in his car.

'Where we going, Liam?' she had demanded as soon as he arrived to pick her up.

'Well, I had planned on booking somewhere really fancy for dinner, but you put the kibosh on that with your diva-like demands. What was it you said again? "I'll go for lunch with you, but I don't want anything fancy. And we have to stay local. Take it or leave it,"' Liam said mimicking her.

'I don't talk like that! Cheek of you!' Grace replied, laughing. 'So come on, where are we going?'

'Well your criteria didn't leave me with a lot to play around with. I was wracking my brains where we could go. But when I got up this morning, and I saw it was such a gorgeous spring day, inspiration hit me. If I remember rightly, you were always partial to a picnic?'

Grace let out a squeal of delight despite herself. Liam knew her so well. She'd always loved picnics.

They got to their destination, Newbridge Park in Donabate, a few minutes later. This was a favourite haunt of Grace and Jack's.

It had beautiful landscaped gardens for picnics and a brilliant play area for kids. They came up here most weekends when the weather was good, and it was always busy. But today, it was practically empty, except for a couple of people walking their dogs.

Liam laid a blanket on the ground and ordered Grace to take a pew while he sorted things out. It appeared he had thought of everything. Liam pressed play on the small CD player he had brought with him, and Michael Buble singing *Home* was softly playing.

'I thought you hated Michael Buble?' Grace said to Liam suspiciously.

'Ah no, not really. I ended up with some of your CDs when we split up, and this was one of them. Some of his songs aren't bad,' he replied innocently. That much was true. But what he didn't admit to was that he had spent all morning trying to decide which song he should have ready to play when he turned the CD on. He was hoping the words of this song might subliminally work their way into Grace's mind. *Let me go home. I'm just too far from where you are.*

Grace smiled. He was certainly trying hard. They'd always had very different taste in music before. If she'd tried to play this CD a couple of years ago, he'd have had a fit!

'So you've provided me with beautiful scenery, good music, what culinary delights do you have in store for me? Egg and onion sarnies?' Grace teased.

'No, smarty-pants. As it happens, it's kind of an unusual picnic. It's what I like to call – Grace's smorgasbord!' With that, Liam started laying out all the food he'd brought.

There was a tub of home-made pâté from Superquinns, a baguette, a pineapple, cheesy coleslaw, olives, sun-dried tomatoes, Skips, chicken, sushi, rocket salad, garlic and lemon mayonnaise, pork pies, Leonidas chocolates and a bag of Monster Munch.

'That's some array of foods you have here, Liam.' Then Grace realised what he'd done, 'Oh my God. You've brought all of my favourite foods.' She was overwhelmed.

'Well, I've noticed that you've not been eating much lately. Or at least when I've been around. So I thought if I brought all of your favourite things, you might be more likely to eat something! So come on. I've been placing bets with myself all morning as to what you'd go for first! Will it be the pâté; God knows you've demolished tubs of this in five minutes in the past. Or will the spicy lure of Monster Munch be too much for you? Or you might even surprise me by going for the pork pies! No point pretending you don't love them Grace Devlin, I know your sordid secret!' Liam hadn't felt this happy in a long time. Seeing Grace's delighted face made the effort worthwhile. He'd even driven into the city this morning first thing for the chocolates.

'Liam, this is the most romantic thing anyone's ever done for me.' She touched him lightly on his hand. He thought his heart would explode, it was beating so much. Did she have any idea what her touch did to him? He stifled a groan just in time.

'This is tough, what a choice,' Grace started, pointing to each of the foods on display. 'But I reckon it's got to be…' Grace picked up the Monster Munch with a laugh.

'I knew it!' Liam shouted. 'I've never known another woman who loved those crisps like you! You're a lunatic, you do know that?'

They spent an hour munching on the feast, talking about nothing really, just chatting and laughing. Grace surprised herself with how much she ate. She was just beginning to get her appetite back, and it was great to be able to snack on all her favourite foods!

'Come on; let's go for a walk, lazybones.' Liam pulled Grace to her feet. They packed the remnants of the picnic away and started their stroll around the park. 'You know the journalist in me reckons you're hiding something, Grace.' Liam knew he should tread carefully if he wanted her to open up.

Grace froze. She really wasn't ready to talk just now.

'But,' Liam continued, 'I'm going to respect your privacy for a little while longer. I have some suspicions but reckon you'll talk to me when you're ready. But just so you know, I'm here for you, Grace. I'm not going anywhere.'

Grace stopped and turned to Liam. 'Liam, I've had such a great time today. I'm feeling really relaxed for the first time in weeks. There is some stuff going on at the moment, but it seems like a million miles away. If we talk now, I'll lose this great feeling. Do you understand?'

Liam didn't understand, but Grace looked so earnest that he knew he couldn't push her any further. So he simply nodded and pulled her close to him. She didn't resist and they held each other tightly. This wasn't the time for talking; that would come, eventually. For now they just relaxed in each other's arms but the moment was broken as the heavens opened up and it started to pour. A typical Irish picnic it was to be: running for the car to dodge the downpour! Grabbing Grace by her hand they made a mad dash to the car, giggling like a pair of kids.

It had been a perfect day, Grace thought. They were driving home and she couldn't believe that it was almost five o'clock. Time flies when you're having fun! She just didn't want the day to end.

'Sorry about the rain,' Liam said.

'So you should be, Liam,' Grace said mock sternly. 'It was only a shower.'

Grace peered out her car window.

'You still looking for the rainbow's end?' Liam asked her softly.

Grace smiled in response. She'd always felt an affinity with rainbows. She didn't know why. As a child, she'd loved it when it rained. She knew that after the rain, there was a chance there would be a rainbow. Her Dad always told her that rainbows were

God's way of giving everyone a free, spectacular light show. Now, whenever she saw a rainbow, she thought of her parents and she felt close to them. It felt like they were sending her a message.

'No rainbows today,' Grace said quietly, and then closed her eyes.

'How would you feel about some company tonight? I really don't want this day to be over,' Liam said, interrupting her thoughts.

'How do you do that?' Grace asked. 'I was just thinking the same thing. Reading minds a new talent of yours?'

'I wish! I think it's more a case of great minds thinking alike! So, would you mind if I hung around for a while?'

'I'd like that very much,' Grace said softly. She knew that they were heading into un-chartered territory and that soon there would be no turning back, but it didn't seem to matter. She had to trust her instincts.

****

A couple of hours later, a very excited Jack was finally in bed and falling asleep. Grace had read him his favourite bedtime story – *The Gruffalo*. Before he'd closed his eyes he asked her. 'Will my Daddy be here in the morning, Mommy?'

'I don't know sweetie-pie, maybe. Is it okay with you if he stays?'

'I wish my Daddy was here every day,' Jack sighed.

Grace kissed him on the forehead, tucked him in tightly and switched his night light on.

'Sweet dreams my darling.'

Grace smiled as she went to join Liam. It felt really nice to have some adult company.

'You're really good with him, Grace. You've got so much patience. He adores you.'

'You haven't seen me when he's asked the same question 100 times in a row, usually very early in the morning when I'm trying to get him ready for Montessori and we're late. I'm telling you there have been days when I felt like throwing him out the window!'

'He'd probably love that! He'd think he was Spider-Man or something! I made some coffee when you were upstairs. Fancy a cup? Or do you want something stronger?'

Grace felt her heart stop when he asked her that. She knew it was too good to be true. He was going to start drinking again. God, she felt stupid. She was just about to tell Liam to fuck off when he continued.

'Listen Grace, I've noticed that you haven't had a drink when I'm around. Don't feel like you can't have something. It won't make me run for the bottle. It actually makes it harder when people change their habits for me. It makes me feel under a compliment.'

Feeling a little bit sheepish and a whole lot relieved, Grace decided she did need a drink. She shouldn't drink too much with her medication, but the doctors said the odd tipple wouldn't harm her.

Curled up on one end of her leather couch with a brandy in her hand, Liam curled up on the other end with a coffee cup in his, Grace couldn't help smiling.

'What's tickling you?' he asked, matching her smile with one of his own.

'This,' Grace answered, gesturing themselves. 'This is all so surreal. Us two sitting on my couch together again, me drinking a brandy and you with a coffee!'

'I wouldn't want it any other way. Mind you I'm going to have to teach you about proper coffee. This instant stuff you buy is pretty bad!' Liam replied with a laugh.

'Don't you miss it? Drinking?' Grace asked gently through her smile, holding her brandy glass up.

'Yep, of course. I think part of me will always want a drink, but hopefully that part will now always be controlled by the greater part of me that says, "Been there, done that, wore the t-shirt!" It's hard to explain, but do you know that Diageo advert on TV, the one that has the tagline "Stop and think"?'

Grace nodded. She knew the advert. It had kind of a *Sliding Doors* theme to it with a guy seeing a flash of what his night would be like if he drank, and it wasn't pretty, so he decided to stay sober.

'Well, that's kind of how I feel. I've seen what I'm like when I get drunk, and it really isn't pretty. I can't go back to that way of life Grace, I won't go back, and the stakes are too high.' Liam took a deep breath, and then continued. 'I'm sorry for everything I put you through. I was a rotten boyfriend. I blew all our money, all our savings. I let you take all the burden of paying the bills and the mortgage.'

Grace interrupted him, 'You've made up for that over the past couple of years, Liam. You've more than paid back your debt with the allowance you've sent each month for Jack.'

But Liam continued, determined to get some things off his chest. 'Anyone can set up a direct debit, Grace; it doesn't make me a father. Sometimes I break out in a cold sweat when I think about the things I did. Saying sorry doesn't seem enough. But I want to make it up to you and to Jack. I never stopped loving you. Grace, I need you, baby. I want to give it another go. I want to grow old with you.'

Liam stopped abruptly, Grace was crying. He knew he'd stuff it up and say the wrong thing. He should have taken it more slowly, but when he started he couldn't stop. He'd been building up to that speech for weeks now.

'Oh Grace. Please don't cry. I'll stop. We can just be friends if that's what you want. Just tell me what you want.' He grabbed Grace's hand and kissed it.

'I want you, Liam.'

Liam couldn't believe his ears. Grace said it so softly; he thought he'd misheard her at first. But she had said she wanted him, he was sure of it. Before he lost his nerve, he pulled her in close and kissed her face, starting on her eyes, her nose, each cheek, finishing gently on her lips.

Grace began to kiss him back, lost in the moment. It felt so right. She could feel tears running down her cheeks, and she wasn't sure if they were hers or Liam's. What the hell was she thinking of? She had to stop this. It wasn't fair on Liam. He didn't know what he was getting into. The time for secrecy was over. She pulled away and stood up quickly, the look of hurt on Liam's face making her wince. Telling her friends that she had cancer had been the hardest thing she'd ever done, but this was going to be ten times worse.

'What's going on, babe? You've got to let me in, Grace. One minute I feel like we've connected, then bam, you're like a rabbit in lights. This is wrecking my head.'

'I'm sorry. Truly. I'm not trying to play games with you, but this is hard for me,' Grace stuttered in response to Liam's plea.

'I know, baby. I know it will take time for you to trust me again, but you've got to give us a chance. I can prove myself to you.'

'It's not about that Liam. I believe in you, and for what it's worth, I don't think you're going to drink again. You said earlier today that the journalist in you sniffed a story. Well you were right.'

Grace picked up her brandy glass; she was going to need it. 'I've been keeping something from you and I'm sorry. But I didn't know how to tell you. There's no easy way I suppose. There's a reason why I've lost so much weight. I'm not well, Liam. A couple of days before you came back into our lives I was diagnosed with leukaemia.' She took another sip of brandy while Liam absorbed the news. He was shaking. 'I've started chemotherapy already; I've three months of it to take. That's why I was so wiped out last weekend. I'd just finished the treatment.'

Grace wiped a tear away. She had to stay calm for this conversation. If Liam wanted to stay, she didn't want it to be out of pity. 'So you can see, this is really bad timing for us. What with the treatment and everything, it would be madness for us to start up again. So why don't we just stay as friends? I think it's for the best.'

Liam stood up. He had suspected that something like this was wrong, but he had shaken it away, thinking he was being melancholy. He walked over and took Grace's hand. 'Sit down with me babe. I've a couple of things to say, and this time you're going to listen.' He paused. 'There's not a hope in hell that we're going to be just friends. I love you and you love me. Don't you?' He stared at her so intensely that she couldn't lie. She nodded silently to his question. 'So that's an end to this friends malarkey. You've got enough of them already, you don't need another.'

To prove his point he kissed her passionately, then continued, 'I'm here now, and you're stuck with me whether you like it or not. So start from the beginning, I want to know everything.'

Chapter Eleven

Dear Grace,

Thank you for your letter. I'm so sorry to hear your sad news. I will pray for a speedy recovery for you every day. I know you may not believe this, but I cried for days when I received your letter. Although I have not been able to meet you before, I have always thought about you. It was thinking that you were happy and well in Dublin that kept me going. When I received your letter, it felt like the ground opened up beneath my feet, and I've been falling since that moment.

I thought that it was for the best keeping away from you all these years. Maybe I was wrong. I'm coming to Dublin on the 12th March, and I've booked into a Hotel in Swords. I hope that this suits you, as I very much look forward to meeting you again. It's been a long thirty two years.

I've enclosed a picture of myself so you can recognise me. I'm really nervous about this, and I hope and pray that I don't disappoint you in any way.

Yours truly,
Catherine

Grace had the photograph of Catherine in her hands. She couldn't stop looking at it. She looked like her. Her hair was shorter than Grace's and had some grey mixed with the strawberry blonde. She didn't have her eyes though. Catherine had blue eyes and Grace's were green. Grace had never felt so nervous in her life. True to his word, Liam was there for her in every way. When the letter came from Catherine, he started fussing over her even more and it was doing her head in. She knew he was only trying to be supportive, but right now everything was getting on her nerves. She felt so out of control in every aspect of her life. She couldn't control her cancer, and it made her feel sick thinking about the bad cells inside her, that were growing day by day, killing the good cells and taking over her body. She couldn't control whether the chemotherapy would work or not. Now, in a few minutes, she would be meeting Catherine for the first time. And she couldn't control how this meeting was going to go either. She hated this feeling. She'd been scared almost every day since that Friday the 13th when she'd received her diagnosis.

Tara and Sean had called earlier and picked up Jack to take him to the park for a couple of hours. The plan was to call them if the meeting went well, so that they could bring Jack home to meet Catherine. Sean could also give Catherine some medical information too, if she was willing to be tested for the bone marrow transplant.

'I can't ask her, Liam. It's too much to expect,' Grace suddenly declared.

'Yes, you can Grace. This is your life we're talking about. She owes you,' Liam said firmly.

'You're wrong Liam. She owes me nothing. One, she gave birth to me when she had options. She could have got rid of me. Two, she gave me to my parents, and I understand now how hard that must have been. In a million years I could never have parted with Jack. I can only imagine the pain it must have caused her.'

'Okay. I get that. But let me ask you a question. If Jack had been taken from you when he was born, would you have stopped loving him? Is there anything you wouldn't do for him even if you didn't see him for over 30 years?'

'Of course not. I'll love him forever. He's part of me.'

'So, unless Catherine doesn't have a maternal bone in her body, I would assume she will want to do this for you. You have to ask her.'

'And what will I say – Hi Catherine, nice to meet you. Haven't time to chit-chat, fancy giving me your marrow?'

'Grace, nobody is asking you to be that blunt. Just talk to her, tell her your options regarding treatment. Let's just play it by ear, okay?'

There wasn't time to debate the situation any further because the bell was ringing, Catherine was here. Liam opened the door and welcomed her in. She looked terrified, but there was no doubt that she was Grace's mother. They were the image of each other.

'Hi Catherine, I'm Liam, Grace's boyfriend. Come on in, you're very welcome. Grace is through here in the living room.'

Grace watched her mother walk into her sitting room and her life in slow motion. She was beautiful.

'Hello Grace,' Catherine's voice was soft and warm.

'Hello,' Grace answered. She felt sick. Her stomach was doing somersaults. She didn't know what to say.

'I brought you some flowers and I thought we might need a drink. I don't know about you, but my nerves are in shreds.'

Liam felt a jolt hearing Catherine's phrasing, it could have been Grace speaking.

Catherine handed Grace a big bunch of white roses and a bottle of Hennessy. Grace paled and sat down quickly.

'Are you okay, Grace? I'm sorry, have I offended you buying a present? I didn't want to come empty-handed, and I didn't know what to bring. White roses are my favourite; I thought you might like them.'

Grace composed herself. Catherine looked distraught and more than a little bit confused. She must think I'm an imbecile sitting here mute, Grace thought. 'Thank you, Catherine. They're beautiful. The flowers gave me a jolt, that's all. White roses are my favourite too. The coincidence overcame me for a moment.'

Liam felt a little shell-shocked looking at these two women meeting for the first time in thirty two years, God alone knew what was going on in their minds. They were trying so hard to be polite. He grabbed the bottle of brandy from Grace and quickly poured two glasses for them.

'Thank you, Liam. Are you not joining us?' Catherine asked when she noticed there were only two glasses.

'I don't drink, Catherine. You girls look like you needed one though, so fire away!'

Grace was so proud of him. He didn't even miss a beat there. She sipped her brandy slowly, watching Catherine. She found it hard to believe that her mother was actually sitting in her apartment drinking a brandy with her. She'd dreamt of this moment for years and had rehearsed what she would say, but now that Catherine was here, she found she couldn't think of a single thing.

Catherine broke the silence. 'You're beautiful, Grace. The picture you sent me didn't do you justice.'

Grace still hadn't found her voice, so she smiled and hoped Catherine understood. Liam had joined Grace on the couch and held her hand tightly.

Catherine continued, 'You must be feeling very overwhelmed right now. I know I am.'

Grace nodded. It helped knowing that Catherine was feeling as nervous as she was. She felt the lump in her throat growing larger by the second. Liam sensing her distress squeezed her hand.

She took another sip of brandy and a deep breath.

'I didn't think you would come,' she said in a small voice.

Catherine started to twist the ring she was wearing. 'It wasn't an option for me not to come. You're my daughter and when you told me you had cancer and that you needed to meet me, I had to come.'

Grace felt light-headed. It was the first time Catherine had ever referred to her as her daughter. It made this situation seem real somehow. She couldn't hold back the tears anymore.

'I'm glad you're here,' she eventually managed to say.

They both took another sip of brandy and smiled at each other through their tears. They were so unsure as to what to say. The tension and high emotion in the room was palpable.

'How are you feeling, Grace? Tell me about your cancer.'

Grace didn't want to get into too much detail at this time. She was afraid that Catherine might run and leave if she thought Grace only wanted her bone marrow. She couldn't bear that, not now they'd finally met. She had so many things she needed to know.

'I'm doing okay at the moment. I've just finished my first few sessions of chemo. I go in weekly, every Friday. I get bloods done on Thursday morning and as long as there's no problems there, I'm good to go. I'm a little bit tired and have a stupid cold that just won't go away, but apart from that, I'm good.'

'I'm so sorry you have to go through this, Grace. If there's anything I can do, please tell me,' Catherine responded.

Liam nudged Grace, this was the perfect opportunity. But Grace shook her head, telling Catherine she didn't need anything. This was not the time.

Silence again.

'I've noticed you keep looking at my hands, Grace. Why?'

'Oh, I'm sorry. I wanted to see if you had crooked little fingers. I have, and I always wondered if you did too. See.' Grace held up her two pinkies for inspection.

Catherine held up her own fingers, saying, 'Snap!'

They all laughed for a couple of seconds, then silence again. Another sip of brandy. I'll be the alcoholic next, Grace thought.

'You must have been wondering about a lot of things. If you have any questions for me, I'll try to answer them,' Catherine said.

'Tell me about yourself. I'd like to understand a bit more about who you are. If that's okay?' Grace asked.

When Catherine began to tell her about herself, Grace began to feel calm for the first time that day. With every word, the tension began to drain out of her body. Catherine owned a small teashop in Meath. She loved to cook and prepared all the produce for the shop herself. Liam told Catherine that Grace was a fabulous cook too.

'It appears we have a few things in common,' Catherine commented. She was single and had never married. She had no other children. She had moved to Meath thirty two years ago, after she gave Grace up for adoption, but was from Wexford originally. Both her parents were dead but she did have a brother living in Perth in Australia. He was married with three kids.

Before long Grace felt herself opening up and relaxing and she began to tell Catherine about her life: her work as an interior designer, her love for Liam and their recent reunion, Jack and all of her friends. It was a lovely afternoon and only when the phone rang did they realise they had been talking for over two hours. It was Sean wondering whether they should come back to the apartment with Jack.

'Would you like to meet your grandson?' Grace asked. Catherine beamed and told Grace that nothing would make her happier. Ten minutes later, Sean, Tara and Jack arrived.

'Jack, sweetie-pie, I'd like to introduce you to someone special. This is Catherine.'

Jack walked over to Catherine and said, 'Hi. I love Mickey Mouse!'

Catherine started to laugh, 'So do I! Do you love Donald Duck too, he's my favourite.'

'Me too!' Jack squealed. 'And Pluto!'

While everyone chatted, Grace and Tara went into the kitchen to make some coffee and tea.

'Oh my God, Grace, she's the bloody image of you!' Tara exclaimed.

'I know. It's really weird. I suppose I know what I'm going to look like in thirty years' time!' Grace said. She couldn't help it, but as soon as she finished that sentence, she thought to herself, if I'm still here that is.

Tara read her mind. 'No negative thoughts, Grace Devlin. It looks like you guys are getting on well. How's it going?'

'Well, it was awful at first. My heart was in my mouth and I couldn't speak. I was so emotional. She brought me white roses, Tara. They're her favourite. How freaky is that?'

'Way freaky!' Tara agreed.

'But then we started chatting about our lives and I think we both started to relax. I like her, Tara. She's nice.'

'Have you asked her about getting tested yet?'

'No. It doesn't feel right, Tara. I'm going to leave it for today. I'll ask her if we can meet tomorrow, then maybe…I want to ask her about my father too, but so far I haven't found the right time. It seems so,' Grace struggled to find the right word, 'so tacky almost. It's like lowering the tone discussing those kinds of things.'

'You're the boss, Grace. But I'm sure she's expecting some tough questions. It's pretty obvious you'd want to know who your dad is too.'

'I know. But today has been pretty heavy for both of us. I think we both need to absorb our first meeting before we add anything else to the equation.'

Grace and Tara returned to the living room and everyone settled into their hot drinks. They chatted for another half hour or so and then Tara and Sean said they had to leave.

'It's been lovely meeting you both. I've always wanted to meet Grace's friends and family,' Catherine said as they were leaving.

'You too, Catherine. I hope we get to meet again soon,' Tara responded.

'May I walk them to the door?' Catherine asked Grace.

'Sure.' Grace looked at Liam puzzled, him shrugging in return.

Catherine returned a couple of minutes later. 'They are such lovely people Grace. You're very lucky to have such good friends.'

'I know. Tara is like my sister really. We grew up together. I can't imagine life without her there right beside me.'

'I'm sure that will never happen. She loves you too much. I can see that. So does Sean. He seems like a good man.'

'You wouldn't say that if you saw him belting out Frank Sinatra on the karaoke!' Liam joked. 'Speaking of which, can you sing Catherine? Grace has an amazing voice, not that I'm biased or anything. We always wondered if her biological family could sing.'

Catherine started to twist her ring again, looking nervous and agitated. 'She didn't get that from me,' Catherine said in a tight voice.

Both Grace and Liam noticed a change in Catherine. Liam regretted asking her the question; it seemed to upset her. They were back to silence again. So, to break it he asked Grace if she'd taken her vitamins yet. Grace laughed as she replied, 'Yes fusspot. Catherine you would not believe what this man is putting me through. He's not letting me have coffee anymore and has me drinking herbal teas only. Not only that, but we're now an organic family! What with all that and him shoving vitamins down my throat, I don't know if I'm coming or going!'

'The vitamin and mineral content of organic food is much higher than the regular stuff!' Liam replied indignantly.

To show she was only joking, she leaned over and kissed him. The tension lifted in the room and Catherine started to speak.

'Grace, I wanted to let you know something. I've asked Sean to set up a tissue and blood match test for me as soon as possible.'

Grace gave Liam a dirty look.

'I never opened my mouth, I swear!' he stated.

'Liam hasn't said a word to me, Grace. When I received your letter telling me about the AML, I felt useless. So I went to my local library and did some research on the internet.'

Liam smiled at that. He'd done the very same. Hence the new health regime they were all on.

'It's amazing the stuff you can find out about on that thing. Anyhow, bone marrow transplants kept coming up as possible treatments. I know that there is a better chance of a match from blood relatives.'

Catherine took a deep breath, composed herself, and then continued. 'Grace, I haven't been in your life all these years. I couldn't put you to bed when you were small, nurse you through chicken pox or measles, watch you go to school on your first day. But I can do something now. I've been praying that I'm a match and if I am, I'll thank God every day for the rest of my life.'

Grace was overcome. Catherine had offered; she hadn't waited to be asked. She felt the tears rolling down her cheeks again. Where were they all coming from? She got up and walked over to hug her mother for the very first time in her life.

Chapter Twelve

Grace was having a bad day. She woke up feeling terrible. The nagging cold had got worse. Her head was pounding. Liam had called Sean earlier and he had come straightaway. The benefits of having a doctor in the family, she supposed. He examined her, declared she had a cold, to which she joked, 'All that money in med school didn't go to waste so!'

He responded by taking out a needle, saying, 'For that cheek Ms Devlin, I'll have to take some blood from you!'

'Not again, Sean. I'm feeling like a bleeding pincushion here,' Grace moaned.

'I'll be gentle, I promise. But it's a necessity I'm afraid. The chemotherapy will interfere temporarily with bone marrow function, particularly your white cells and platelets. It's normal for the level of these to drop following chemo, which makes it more likely for you to catch an infection.'

That made sense to Grace. She remembered her biology days in school, white cells fight infection, red cells carry oxygen around the body and platelets clot the blood.

'I'll have this blood test analysed tomorrow and if your count is low, we'll sort out some antibiotics for you. I don't want you to worry about this, Grace. This is all normal stuff.'

'Sean, hate to disagree with a doctor, but I'm afraid all this is far from normal. What happens if my blood count doesn't return to normal?' Grace replied.

'If that happens, and that's only if, mind you, we may have to postpone the next dose of your chemo. But let's not jump ahead of ourselves, okay?' Sean said gently.

'Okay, Doctor. Thanks a million for coming over. I appreciate it.' She then caught sight of Liam, furiously scribbling away. 'What in the name of God are you writing, Liam?'

'Just keeping notes of what Sean said, babe. I want to keep it all straight in my head,' Liam replied.

'And I used to think that Tara fussed over me! Come over here and give me a kiss you big eejit!' Grace had been really narky with him earlier, and felt bad now. It was funny really, Liam had only come back into her life in the last couple of weeks, but now that he was back, she really didn't know how she would have coped without him. She got so goddamn tired all the time. Meeting Catherine yesterday had really taken it out of her, even though it couldn't have gone any better. Grace had asked her to come for lunch today but felt she'd have to cancel now. She couldn't get out of bed, never mind negotiate an oven. Sean left with strict instructions for Grace to have complete bed rest. She'd asked Liam to ring Catherine to postpone their lunch and then to take Jack out for a few hours. They were going to visit his Nana – Liam's Mam. She was brilliant with him and already Jack was madly in love with his new Nana.

Despite the peace and quiet in the house, she couldn't settle no matter how much she tried, so decided to have a shower. It felt glorious. The hot water warmed her chilled bones. She washed her hair and used copious amounts of her Benefit shower gel. It was amazing the difference a shower could make. She felt much better now and was sorry she'd sent Liam and Jack out. The house was too quiet all of a sudden.

Wrapping a towel around her wet hair and donning her bathrobe, she went downstairs to make a sneaky coffee for herself. What Liam didn't know wouldn't harm him! Said coffee made, Grace began to brush her hair thinking she should really blow-dry it, as opposed to letting it dry naturally. Now she had to be careful about such little things. It bugged her that everything she did now seemed to revolve around the cancer. She could imagine Liam's voice in her ear saying, 'Dry your hair Grace, you've a cold on you!'

And then something she had been told to expect happened. But what they didn't tell her was how she would feel when she saw the big clumps of golden hair in her brush. Her beautiful hair was falling out.

She ran to the mirror over the fireplace and started examining herself. The more she scrutinised it, the more clumps were falling out. That was it, she couldn't take anymore. She wanted to scream. But before she got the chance to have a much earned breakdown the doorbell went. That was all she needed. She looked through the peephole; it was Catherine. Liam had cancelled lunch, what was she doing here? But funnily enough Grace was glad to see her. She quickly tied her damp hair back into a loose ponytail and opened the door.

Catherine came in and took one look at Grace and gave her a big hug.

'What's wrong pet?'

'Nothing. Just a cold. Come on in. I've a pot of coffee made, just don't tell Liam.'

Catherine knew something was up with Grace. She looked really pale and her eyes were bloodshot. She'd obviously been crying. Did she have the right to push her though? She barely knew her really. 'Liam called me earlier to cancel our lunch today. On impulse I decided to come over anyway. When I was small, if my brother Noel or myself were ill, my mother would make this amazing chicken noodle soup. It always made us feel much better. I thought that maybe I could make it for you today. I've brought all the ingredients with me. But if you don't want any company tell me to go. I won't be offended honestly,' Catherine said to Grace.

'No don't go. That sounds lovely Catherine. It's very thoughtful of you. I'll show you where everything is,' Grace replied.

'Indeed you won't. The deal is that you sit down in front of that TV and don't move. I've worked in kitchens all my life; I'll daresay I'll find my way around yours!' And with that Catherine got up and turned the TV on, flicking through the channels until she found Holly and Phillip on ITV talking about makeovers. 'I always find if I need to forget about life for a while, Holly and Phillip work every time. Now sit back and relax,' Catherine instructed her.

Fluffing the pillows up behind Grace's back on the couch, she picked up her shopping bag and went to the kitchen. Thirty minutes later she was back.

'Soup's simmering. It will take about an hour. I've made enough for a couple of days. As long as you put it in one of your Tupperware containers in the fridge it will stay fresh,' Catherine told her.

'Thanks, Catherine. You're very kind. And you were right; Holly and Phillip did take my mind off things. I love it when they both get the giggles. You can't help but join in.'

Catherine stared at her daughter intently, 'Is there anything you'd like to talk about? Sometimes it's easier to talk to someone who's not so close to you. I'm a good listener.'

'If I started Catherine, I don't think I'd stop. I've had a bad day today,' Grace admitted.

'Who says you have to stop? Get it all out of your system. You feel pretty miserable today?' Catherine said gently.

'You could say that. I'm so tired all the time and I've only had a few chemo sessions so far. I've got loads more to go. I'm scared I won't have the strength to get through this,' Grace confessed.

'That's understandable.' Catherine knew that she needed to just listen. Grace didn't need to hear any platitudes right now.

Grace got up and walked over to the sideboard. She picked up a couple of envelopes and handed them to Catherine. 'And these don't bloody help either.'

Catherine opened them and saw that they had Mass cards in them. 'These are get well Mass cards, Grace. Masses and prayers will be offered up for you to get better. Are you not religious?'

'I know what they are, Catherine. When Mam and Dad died I must have received hundreds of Mass cards for them. To me they are only given when you're dead. So when I opened them up, it was like having a premonition. You know that saying, someone walked over my grave, well I could see mine. I could see myself being lowered into the grave beside Mam and Dad at Glasnevin Cemetery. I could see all my friends and Liam and Jack watching me being buried. And I could see the pile of bloody Mass cards that they would have to go through after the funeral.' She stifled a sob.

'Oh Grace pet, how terrible for you. It must have brought back some really sad memories. I'm so sorry that you lost Annie and Mick. I'm sorry that I wasn't there to help you through it.'

Grace smiled her thanks at Catherine. 'I know the people who sent the Mass cards were only letting me know that they cared, but it was an awful shock.'

Grace put her head in her hands and was quiet for a few minutes. After a while she looked up and continued. 'When I was diagnosed with AML, I made it clear to Liam and my friends that under no circumstances was there to be any tears in front of Jack. It's bad enough that my illness is turning my life and, in turn, my friends' lives upside down, I can't have it affecting Jack too.'

'Do you think he knows something?' Catherine asked.

'He's oblivious so far, but I'm not going to be able to hide it much longer. Look.' Grace took her hair down and showed Catherine the bald patch, where her hair had fallen out earlier.

'Oh pet, that's awful. When did it start falling out?' Catherine said, instantly getting why Grace was so upset.

'Just before you got here. I had a shower and was brushing my hair and then I noticed big clumps in my brush. You're warned that it's going to happen with chemo, you even expect it, but nothing prepares you for the actual feeling you get when you see your hair coming out. I know it's vain, but I love my hair. I'm afraid to finish brushing it, because of how much more might come out. I don't want to be bald,' Grace ended on a sob.

'Oh Grace, my darling. Listen to me. Not brushing your hair won't stop it falling out. It will just look messy! If it's going to go, there's nothing you can do to stop it. Why don't we see what the damage is and then we'll know what we're dealing with? Alright? Can I take a look?'

When Grace gave her consent, Catherine began softly brushing her daughter's beautiful long wavy hair. By the time she was finished there were three bald patches about the size of a two euro coin on her head. She opened her bag and took out one of her hair grips, pulled Grace's hair up in a kind of a French twist holding it in place with the grip, and made sure that the bald areas were covered. 'Now take a look at that. Jack will never notice anything.'

Grace stood up and examined herself in the mirror. In fairness, she couldn't notice anything at the moment. But it wouldn't be long before it would be too difficult to disguise with fancy hairstyles.

'Grace, what are those thingies that all the kids are wearing now? Like a scarf on their heads.'

'Bandannas?' Grace asked.

'Yes, that's the one. They're very trendy now, aren't they? I sometimes watch *Neighbours* and one of the girls a few years ago had cancer and wore them all the time. It looked really good on her and she had hair like yours.'

'Steph. That was her name, the girl on *Neighbours*,' Grace said.

'Yes, that's the one.'

'I suppose Jack would think I was cool too if I wore one. I hadn't thought about them before. I was picturing myself wearing a really bad acrylic wig!' Grace said, horrified at the thought.

'Not at all. Sure you can get wigs made of real hair now,' Catherine informed her. She amazed Grace. She had surprised her several times since they met twenty four hours ago. She was so glad that she had her in her life now. Nothing would ever replace her Mam, but she felt comfortable and secure with Catherine here.

'Thank you so much for listening to me rant and rave. I bet you didn't expect all of this when you called over. I'm sorry for all of the drama,' Grace said.

'Listen Pet, you've nothing to be sorry for. It's no wonder you're so upset with everything going on in your life right now. I know you've been trying to put a brave face on for everyone else, but sometimes you have to let people know you're having a bad day. Now, the soup should be ready. You eat a bowl of this and I promise you things won't seem quite so bad.'

Ten minutes later Grace was sitting at the dining room table with a big bowl of chicken noodle soup in front of her. It was absolutely gorgeous and Catherine was right, she did feel better.

Chapter Thirteen

Abby was sitting in the bar of Café en Seine with Gerry, waiting for Tom to come back with their drinks. Gerry had appointed himself as her own personal social secretary since she admitted to feeling lonely. He had decided that the best way to meet loads of guys was speed dating. She had protested that it wasn't her thing, so Gerry went ahead and ignored her by booking a ticket for tonight.

Tom came back with the drinks – Cosmopolitans for Gerry and Abby and a Bulmers for himself.

'So come on, explain this speed dating to me again,' Tom demanded.

'Well, Abby will get a number when she registers. She'll then take a seat and wait to meet the first of her dates. She'll meet twenty tonight and have four minutes to chat to each of them. Then she marks on her scorecard the ones she'd like to see again! It's terribly exciting,' Gerry enthused.

'It's terribly terrifying you mean!' Abby shrieked. 'What the hell am I supposed to say to twenty strangers?'

'Just tell them about your job and where you're from I suppose,' Tom contributed, only to be shouted down by Gerry.

'Are you mad, darling? No talk about work or home! That's too boring! You must be mysterious and exciting. Come on let's practice! I'll be your first date.' Gerry then put on a deep accent, 'Hi, my name is Gerry. How are you?'

'Nice to meet you, Gerry. I'm Abby and I'm a bit nervous to be honest,' Abby said with a hint of sarcasm.

'No darling – wrong! Don't tell them you're nervous. They'll think you're no fun at all. Remember you're mysterious and always game for trying new things – like speed dating! Now try again, how are you?'

'Terrible because my stupid friend Gerry keeps banging on and on if you must ask,' Abby quipped.

'I'll let you off with that remark because you're obviously highly strung right now. I'm doing this to help you, darling. Come on. When they ask you how you are, what are you going to say?'

Abby gave in and decided to play along with Gerry. It was easier. He wouldn't give up. 'I'm fantastic. Never been better in fact. This is a great idea, isn't it?' She said this in her brightest, most enthusiastic voice.

'The force is with you, young Skywalker, but you are not a Jedi yet,' Gerry responded sadly.

'Haven't heard *The Empire Strikes Back* quote for a while,' Tom drawled.

'It seemed appropriate. You're almost there; just remember to be positive always!'

'God Tom, what am I doing here? Your boyfriend has a lot to answer for!' Abby exclaimed.

Tom then gave her a much needed pep talk. 'Look Abby, ignore Gerry and his words of wisdom. Just be yourself and say whatever comes naturally. You've a great personality; the lads will all be queuing up for you.'

'Thanks for the vote of confidence. Shit, I better go up, I'm late.' Abby downed the last of her cocktail quickly.

'"Seize the day, darling, make your life extraordinary!"' Gerry shouted at the top of his voice. The whole bar stopped and stared.

Abby looked at Tom in horror and said. 'God, I'm scarlet. Tom, is that him waxing lyrical or another movie quote?'

Tom laughed and shrugged. 'I find it hard to separate the two sometimes!'

'As it happens, it's a quote from *Dead Poets Society*,' Gerry laughed. 'And to be honest I've been waiting months to find a time to use it! Now go get them!'

Abby left Tom and Gerry laughing and ran upstairs to the function room. She was given a number and nametag at registration – she was number four, which was a good sign, as it was her lucky number. She was directed over to table number four and took a seat, ordering another Cosmo from the waiter as she sat down. She had a feeling that she would need alcohol to get her through this. She'd just had time to catch her breath when her first date sat down beside her.

'Hi there. I'm Brian, number four. Better get the paperwork sorted first. Right your number four too and your name is Abby?' he questioned. He seemed very serious.

'Yes that's right. Have you done this before?' Abby thought he sounded like he knew what he was doing.

'Yep, I go every month to all of the events. You know there are loads of companies running these now. I've been to them all. You should try the chat fest one too; there is over four hundred people at that!'

Abby was gobsmacked. Meeting twenty dates in one night was bad enough, four hundred seemed crazy!

She needn't have worried about what to say because Brian kept talking about the various speed dating events he'd been to, and the next thing she knew the organiser was shouting 'Time, Gentlemen, move to the next table please! Ladies you stay where you are and your next date will be along.'

God, he was mad that Brian guy. Talk about professional speed dater! He didn't ask her one question mind you, so she wasn't sure how he actually got to know people.

Date no. 2 was Tom who was a farmer from Drogheda – not her type, enough said. Date no. 3 was Mick from Cork – he was older than her old fella! By date no. 10 she was really into the swing of things and having a ball. They called an interval then, so she picked up her bag and ran back to the bar downstairs to catch up with Tom and Gerry.

'Darling, you look happier! Have you met the man of your dreams yet?' Gerry asked excitedly.

'Guys, my head is spinning. It's mad up there!' Abby answered.

'Has anyone ticked your box Abby?' Tom joked.

'He's been waiting hours to say that to you, darling!' Gerry laughed. 'I bet they've all ticked your box! How many have you ticked?'

'Well so far, I've only ticked one box out of ten, with another maybe. Pickings are slim my friends!'

'I hope you're not being too fussy, darling. Tell me all about it,' Gerry said.

'Well so far the tally is this – three were definitely over fifty. I'm not going there yet! One was the opposite who couldn't have been more than twenty. Not sure which would be worse, sugar daddy or toy boy? One guy from Raheny was definitely on something. He was out of his tree! There was also a farmer from Cork who told me he didn't like Dublin girls as a rule, but would possibly make an exception for me! Like he was doing ME the favour. God, lads, he was a minger! Then there were two who were really nice but just not my type – either physically or personality wise.'

'That's eight by my reckoning. What was the crack with the others?' Tom enquired.

'Well one is a guy called Shay. He's lovely looking and an architect. I thought we really got on well, so I've ticked his box! The other guy, who's a maybe, is called Fergus. He works in advertising. He's cute but seemed a bit quiet, I'm not sure if he'd be my type.'

'Oh go on, tick his box! Sure you've nothing to lose,' Tom said.

Then it was time to go back up for the second half. The first of her next set of guys stood her up! He'd obviously had enough in the first half so legged it. After that it was a blur of different guys. It began to get a bit tiring. There were all shapes and sizes there and with the exception of one or two of the guys all were really nice. In the end she even ticked two more boxes. There were two South African guys who were really fit and worked in finance in the IFSC centre. Abby thought why the hell not! So when the event was over she handed in her card with four ticks and made her way downstairs where Tom and Gerry were dutifully waiting. Gerry was half-cut, having downed at least half a dozen Cosmos by this time. He was busy telling Tom how much he loved him when Abby joined them. They had a couple more drinks and Shay the architect guy even came over to say hello. Gerry let out a squeal with excitement when he walked over; Tom had to kick him under the table to shut him up. They finished the night off in Crystals and eventually rolled home singing in the wee hours. The last thing Abby thought of before her head hit the pillow was, God, this looking for a man game is great craic!

Chapter Fourteen

It was Thursday night and the gang were all meeting in the Cock Tavern for drinks. Gerry was beside himself with excitement, as Abby would have the results of the speed-dating event with her. Tom wasn't sure who would be more disappointed if Abby didn't get any matches, Gerry or her!

When everyone had arrived and had their drinks, Gerry demanded a full disclosure from Abby on the results.

'Drum roll please guys,' Abby asked. Liam, Sean and Tom obliged. 'Well out of nineteen guys that I spoke to – one refused at the first fence and didn't even come and say hello – I got, wait for it, fifteen ticks!'

They all exploded with whoops and squeals of delight. Gerry stood up and took a bow, claiming all credit for Abby's success. 'It was my words of wisdom that did it! You seized the day, darling!'

'Well, don't go buying a hat yet, Cilla, I haven't got fifteen dates! I only ticked four guys, so that gave me four matches!' Abby told him.

'Remind me again who they were?' Grace asked.

'Well there's Shay an architect, he's my favourite, Fergus who works in advertising, then two South African guys, Richard and Cameron.'

'Gonna go for a ménage à trois with the two dudes from South Africa?' Sean joked, dodging the beer mat Abby tossed.

'What happens now? Do you call them or do they call you?' Tara asked.

'Well, either, I suppose. I have their contact numbers and they have mine.' Then seeing Gerry's face, Abby continued, 'But I'll wait for them to call me. If they're interested they'll be the ones to get in touch.' Gerry nodded his approval. He had given Abby a present – *The Book of Rules*. This was featured on *Sex and the City* as a dating rule book for the single girl, and as Gerry basically treated the show like his guru, he went out and bought it straightaway for Abby. He already had a copy himself and swore that the reason he ended up with Tom was that he used the rules. The main concept in the book was that you shouldn't waste time waiting for a guy who wasn't interested in you. Let the guy make the first move, and then you'll know he's interested. Then make sure he keeps interested by ensuring he's the one actively chasing you. As she read it, Abby had to admit that there were certainly bits that rang true for her. She recognised mistakes she'd made with guys in the past. So she was going to give it a shot. She reckoned if she could get a guy like Tom she'd be laughing – a straight version that was! When the whole speed-dating night had been dissected and discussed from every angle, Tara asked Grace how she was doing.

'Well, we had some bad news yesterday actually,' Grace responded. 'Catherine's results from the tissue test came back. They weren't a match.' Nobody really knew how to respond to that. They all had their hopes pinned on Catherine being a suitable donor.

'Oh honey, keep positive, I'm sure you'll find a donor soon. Won't she, Sean?' Tara said.

'There's every chance the NBMP will come good for us. People are added to that continually. At least your blood count is on the up again. Are you set for chemo on Friday?' Sean asked.

'As ready as anyone can be I suppose,' Grace replied flatly. Liam clasped her hand. He knew how disappointed Grace had been yesterday when Catherine called round with the news. She was devastated too. They had all believed that when Grace finally met her mother and she was fit and willing to be a donor, she'd definitely be a match.

'I'll be bald soon guys,' Grace said just to break the silence. She had been hiding the bald patches with bandannas and hats, but she knew that the next bout of chemo would probably get rid of the rest of her hair. She looked up and saw the faces of her friends and realised that they didn't know how to respond. So she put a big smile on her face and said. 'So girls, I'm going to need a shopping trip soon to go get myself a new wig! And yes Gerry, don't worry I'm including you too!'

'Fabulous, darling. I can see you with a black bob – very Uma Thurman in *Pulp Fiction*. Or maybe long red curly locks à la Julia Roberts or you could go really blonde like Charlize Theron!' Gerry was in his element. He could see himself transforming Grace into all his favourite leading ladies!

'Hold on there buddy, if you don't mind, I'd like Grace to come home to me as Grace, not as someone else!' Liam added.

'Don't you worry, babe, I'm coming home with a wig as close as I can get to my own! But with maybe one difference, no Frizz!'

Tara and Abby laughed. They understood where Grace was coming from. She had a natural wave in her hair and unless blow-dried really well with a helping hand from the GHDs, it would frizz up.

'Has Catherine gone home now?' Tara asked.

'Yeah, she left yesterday evening. But she's going to come up on Friday to sit with me for the day while I have chemo.'

'I'm looking forward to meeting her, Grace. She sounds like a great woman from what Liam's told me,' Tom commented.

'She is Tom. I really like her. Other than the first half hour of meeting her, I feel really at ease in her company. She's not pushing me in any way, trying to be my mother. She's kind of like a cool aunt or something I suppose.'

'What about your father?' Tara gently asked.

Grace shrugged.

'She hasn't asked Catherine yet. You're going to though aren't you, babe?' Liam said.

'It's been a bit difficult to find the right time. She hasn't mentioned anything, so I don't like to,' Grace said.

'I'd ask her on Friday, darling,' Gerry said.

'Why Friday?' Grace asked.

'Sure how could she refuse to answer you when you're hooked up to a bloody drip! You won't even need to throw in any tears; the hospital alone will be enough to tug the heartstrings!' Gerry declared.

Grace laughed with the others then realised Gerry was actually serious. God, she loved how shallow and manipulative he was sometimes!

Chapter Fifteen

It was Tuesday afternoon and Grace was in the middle of her chemo. She was lucky really, as she hadn't been too badly affected by it. Apart from some nausea each evening and feeling really tired, she was pretty much coping with it. She had still managed to get some mouth ulcers despite trying all the washes and lollies that Liam supplied her with. They were the things that annoyed her the most right now.

Liam had been a godsend too. Knowing that his Daddy was looking after Jack in his own home after Montessori was great. They could do things slightly differently this time. As Liam was at home for Jack, Grace didn't have to worry about finding different people to watch him. They had decided together that they needed to tell Jack that Mommy was sick, but not make it too big a deal. Jack was pretty amazing. They'd been really worried about telling him that Grace had to go to hospital, explaining that she needed to get some medicine. He had just walked over to Grace and given her a big sloppy kiss, 'I kiss it better Mommy.'

Grace felt her eyes mist up. This was so hard. 'Thank you sweetie-pie, I feel so much better already. That kiss really helped. But I better get some medicine too, just to be sure. That okay with you?'

'Mebibine Mommy?' Jack asked, finding it difficult to say the word.

'Yes my sweetie-pie, it's good medicine. You just wait and see. I'll be home before you even miss me!'

Grace opened her eyes when she heard a noise, bringing her back from her thoughts. Catherine had arrived and was sitting beside her hospital bed.

'How long have you been there?' Grace asked her.

'Just a couple of minutes, pet. You looked so peaceful, so I thought I'd leave you resting. How are you feeling?' Catherine said.

'Not too bad actually. You get used to the feeling of the drugs going into your system after the first session. I'm nearly done now. Only another hour or so. Traffic bad?'

'No love, it's grand. I didn't know what to bring you, so I got you some glossies. The girls that work in my shop all say that these are the best.'

Catherine pulled out Tatler, Stellar, Marie Claire, Cosmopolitan, Woman's Way and Image.

'That'll keep me going for a while!' Grace laughed. 'You shouldn't have, Catherine. I keep telling everyone that they have to stop bringing stuff with them when they visit. Having your company is the best present, honestly.'

'How are Liam and Jack?' Catherine asked.

'Great. I think they're secretly enjoying the time on their own. It's good for Liam to be the primary carer for a while. I know he has a lot of guilt for the three years he missed. Spending quality time with Jack on his own helps ease that a little, I think.'

'Do you think he'll ever drink again?' Catherine asked quietly.

Grace thought about it for a few minutes before answering. 'I don't know to be honest. My gut instinct tells me he won't. He's had to deal with some heavy stuff over the last month or so and he hasn't turned to the bottle, so I'm hopeful. We talk about it and I think that helps both of us. We have a deal that we have to be honest with each other and that includes him feeling the need for a drink. Liam says that he'll always want a drink and that he scales it each day from 1 to 10. Anything under five is fine, but if he feels the need is over five, he'll go to an AA meeting.'

'That sounds sensible. How often does he go to meetings then?' Catherine asked.

'Once a week religiously. Last week he went twice,' Grace replied.

'He needed a drink when I wasn't a match?' Catherine said anxiously.

'Don't be silly, Catherine. Don't start blaming yourself for everything. As it happens, I think Jack caused it! Liam had just finished an article for his newspaper and Jack came bounding in and knocked Liam's coffee cup all over the papers. He only writes longhand, so it was a slight disaster!'

'Oh dear. Did he go mad?' Catherine said with a small laugh.

'Nah, just jumped up and told Jack not to worry about it when he started to cry. But I was narky as hell that day too and poor Liam took the brunt of it, so I reckon he needed to get away from both of us!'

Catherine noticed that Grace had her hair covered up completely with a scarf. 'How's the hair situation, pet?'

'Ah, nearly all gone now! I'm going to have to shave the rest of it off. I've been avoiding it, but it's driving me mad. The nurses have all said it'll be easier just to get rid of the scraggly bits in the long run.'

'That makes sense, Grace. It'll be a tough moment for you I daresay.'

'Not looking forward to being bald, but I'm going shopping next week for a wig. You're not going to believe it but I found out yesterday that Liam was going to shave his head in support of me.'

'That's sweet Grace,' Catherine said with a smile.

'Yeah, but that's not the end of it. Tom, Sean and even Gerry decided they'd do the same too. Brotherly solidarity or something. Then to make matters worse, Tara and Abby actually said they'd do it too.'

'Oh my word!' Catherine exclaimed.

'Exactly. I don't know what they were on when they came up with that one. We'd look like a group of Hare Krishnas when we got together for God's sake!' Grace said laughing.

'So you put a stop to it?' Catherine said.

'You bet I did. I told them I'd never forgive them if they did that. Can you imagine the looks we'd get if we all went out together?'

'Ah they were only trying to be supportive. Bit disappointed they didn't go through with it, would have been fun to see!' Catherine finished mischievously.

'I'd say Tara and Abby are relieved anyhow. They only went along with the crazy idea because the guys talked them into it. Poor Abby has a date tonight. Can you imagine the guy's face if she turned up bald!'

Catherine and Grace chatted and laughed for another hour or so. Then the treatment was over and Grace was unhooked.

'Another one down!' Grace declared.

Catherine smiled at her daughter. She was constantly amazed at how brave she was being.

Grace decided it was now or never. 'Catherine, there's something I need to know. Can you tell me about my father please? I'd like to fill in the gaps?'

All at once the atmosphere changed in the small room. Catherine's smile vanished and she started twisting that bloody ring again. 'I don't know, Grace. I don't know who your father is. I'm not proud of it, but I had a one-night stand. I was drunk. I can't remember who the guy was. I'm sorry.'

Grace couldn't believe what she was hearing. She didn't know why, but she knew without a shadow of a doubt that Catherine was lying. She was hiding something. 'You don't remember anything, not even a name? I find that hard to believe,' Grace said gently. She didn't want to frighten her by pushing too hard.

'His first name was Michael. That's all I know. Now if you don't mind, I'd rather not discuss this any further. It's all rather painful.' And with that she got up and picked up her things. She kissed Grace on her forehead and practically ran out the door.

Just as she was leaving, Tom arrived nearly colliding with her. 'Jaysus, what's the rush?'

Muttering an apology, Catherine glanced back at Grace sorrowfully and went out.

'Was that Catherine?' Tom asked.

'Yep,' Grace said.

'Something happen?'

'You could say that. I asked her about my father. She freaked and told me a pack of lies.'

'What did she say?' Tom asked.

'That she got drunk, had a one-night stand with a guy called Michael and got pregnant. She doesn't know any more about the guy.'

'Sounds basically like a hundred stories I've heard before. We sometimes get enquiries from women trying to trace their adopted kids. How'd you know it's a pack of lies?' Tom asked.

'Intuition. Instinct. I don't know how, I just know she was lying. It was written all over her face. I've had a feeling she was hiding something a few times since we met, but thought it was my imagination.'

'She sure doesn't look like the type to have a drunken one-night stand. But you never know, Grace. She could have been embarrassed about it and that's why she seemed nervous when you asked her. Not the easiest thing to tell your newly found daughter I would assume.'

'No, I don't buy that. When she talked about giving me up and why she did it, she looked me in the eye the whole time. She was upset and nervous yes, but I knew she meant every word she said.

She looked everywhere but at me when she told me about this "Michael". She was lying. I'm sure of it.' Grace lay back against her pillow and closed her eyes for a moment. She felt betrayed all over again. Surely she deserved more than that from Catherine?

Tom felt terrible seeing Grace suffer. She was so pale and looked so tiny lying in the hospital bed. Seeing a tear fall down her face was the end of him.

'Ah, Jaysus Grace. Don't cry, you know I'm useless with women in tears. Look, maybe I can help.'

Grace opened her eyes. 'How?'

'Well, I could do a little bit of investigation into Catherine. She had you when she was twenty five?'

'Yeah. What kind of investigation?' she asked.

'Look, I can pretty much find out anything about anyone if I really put my mind to it. There's information about all of us out there just waiting to be found! Have you got her date of birth and all that stuff?'

'Yes I do. She lived in Wexford until she got pregnant with me, you know,' Grace told her friend, beginning to feel more hopeful every minute.

'Well that's a good place to start. Leave it to Uncle Tom. I'll make some enquiries. Find out what kind of girl she was. Whether she enjoyed a jar, that kind of thing? I'll see if I can find out if she had any regular boyfriends. Might give us a lead on who your father could be,' he reassured her.

Tom was relieved to see this put a smile on Grace's face.

'Thanks, Tom. That would be great!'

'Anything for you, Grace. No guarantees, but I promise I'll do everything in my power to find your father.'

Chapter Sixteen

Tom and Gerry were on their way to Wexford. Gerry was singing along to *Staying Alive* by the Bee Gees. God, Tom loved him so much. There was something about Gerry that just made everything they did that bit more exciting. He remembered springing the surprise of the trip on Gerry yesterday and his reaction to it.

'How do you fancy a weekend in the country, Gerry?'

'Twice as much as I fancy Matt Bomer, that's how much!' Gerry responded, laughing. 'Fabulous! Where are you bringing me?' Gerry was beside himself with excitement. He loved it when Tom surprised him.

'Wexford. That do you?' Tom laughed. Gerry was like a small child at Christmas.

'Where are we staying, Tom? The Seafield, please say yes!' he asked. They loved staying there; it was a firm favourite for them both.

'Not this time, pet. But don't worry; I've booked somewhere really nice. It's a beautiful country hotel called the Rose Tree Manor.' Tom passed some brochures of the house to his partner to look at. Tom had been to a small wedding there about ten years ago and he'd always wanted to return. He thought he'd better confess that he had a hidden agenda for this trip too, before Gerry got too carried away. He was already declaring that they'd go horse riding and for long walks in the grounds, not to mention fishing and playing golf!

'Now listen to me Gerry before you start spending money on golfing and fishing outfits,' Tom laughed at Gerry's look of astonishment as he couldn't believe that Tom had guessed he was already planning a shopping spree just for this trip! Gerry forgot sometimes just how well Tom knew him. 'I have some work to do when we're down there. Grace's asked me to do some research on the q.t. on her mother. She wants to find out a bit about her and maybe get some leads on her biological father.'

Gerry didn't mind at all. In fact he was pleased to be doing something to help Grace. He thought it was appalling that Catherine wouldn't tell Grace about her father. 'Can I help in the investigation, Tom?' Gerry pleaded.

'We'll see. You can come with me when I visit Catherine's home village, but try not to say anything!' Gerry was often more of a hindrance than a help when Tom was trying to remain incognito. He couldn't help himself, Gerry was about as discreet as a tribe of Aborigines in O'Connell Street!

****

The traffic wasn't too bad and the journey was going nicely. They had left Dublin at lunchtime to avoid the busy Friday evening rush. It wasn't long before they were getting close to Wexford and the hotel was located just a couple of miles outside it.

'Tell me what you know so far about Catherine?' Gerry asked Tom.

'Well, her full name is Catherine Grace Dunne. She was born in Ballymichael, a small village about five miles from Wexford. She has one brother, Noel, who lives in Australia. She's fifty seven years old and both her parents are now passed on. She does have a couple of cousins living in the area still. Ann Dalton, nee Dunne, is one I'm interested in meeting. She's the same age as Catherine, so it stands to reason that she might know something.'

'Are Ann and Catherine still in touch?' Gerry asked.

'That I don't know. We'll find out soon enough I suppose. Ann and her husband Pat run the local pub in Ballymichael. Reckon we'll have to pay that local a visit!'

'Who's the other cousin?' Gerry asked.

'That would be Mary. She's a bit younger at forty eight, so not sure what she can tell us. She's married to the local Guard, Robert Hegarty.'

'What's your plan? I'm not so sure these women will start spilling their guts the second you question them.'

Tom put on his best German spy voice saying 'Ve have vays of making zem talk!'

'Ha ha very funny, Tom. Seriously, you can't just go up to these women and start asking them questions about Catherine. They'll be suspicious.'

'I know. I thought we'd just have to play it by ear and see how it goes. I may just have one other card up my sleeve too. The pressure's on us for this one, Gerry. It's personal, it's for our girl. We can't mess it up,' Tom said seriously.

They soon arrived at the aptly named Rose Tree Manor. Surrounding the entrance to the hotel were the most amazing rose trees the guys had ever seen. There were luscious reds, vibrant oranges, pure whites and the most beautiful yellow roses. Gerry squealed 'fabulous' over and over and Tom had to agree. It really was beautiful. They grabbed their bags – one small leather holdall for Tom and a beautiful Louis Vuitton case for Gerry – and checked in, before being shown to their room, The Yellow Room. It was lovely, full of gorgeous antiques and period furniture. A big vase of yellow roses cut straight from the garden stood on top of a large mahogany dresser. They had a quick freshen up then went downstairs to have afternoon tea. Gerry had spied it being served in the drawing room on the way in and had declared he simply would die if they didn't go and have some! The tea was served in a beautiful silver tea service with bone china cups and saucers. Home-made scones with strawberry jam and cream accompanied the tea, with a couple of large chunks of fruitcake. A big fire was roaring and playing softly in the background was Adele's sultry voice.

'Jaysus this is a bit of all right! I could get used to this life, Gerry my love!' Tom said then bit into a scone piled high with jam and cream.

'Don't curse in here, darling!' Gerry declared, looking around to make sure nobody had heard.

'Sorry, Gerry. I'll try to mind my P's and Q's! Wouldn't want to offend the genteel country folk!' Tom replied in a faux-posh voice, with a wink at Gerry, who giggled despite himself.

The waitress began to clear away their plates when they had finished the mini feast.

'That was beautiful. Thank you.' Tom said. 'Have you worked here for long? It's an amazing hotel.'

'I'm glad you enjoyed it, Mr Whelan. I've been here for almost ten years now. It's a lovely place to work. My name is Fiona; if you need anything just let me know,' she answered with a smile.

'That's a long time, Fiona. You must really enjoy it,' Tom continued with a smile. 'I suppose you have the longest service here?' Tom further enquired.

Gerry looked quizzically at Tom. Tom was in detective mode, the tone of his voice always changed when he was trying to get some information. It always got quieter, gentler somehow. Why he wanted to know how long Fiona worked here though Gerry couldn't guess.

'Oh no, not at all. Mrs Murtagh has been here for over thirty years now. She's the housekeeper and pretty much runs the place. Her husband is the gardener and general handyman and he's been here even longer. They're lovely. I'm sure you'll see them around during your stay,' Fiona replied, happy to chat to the two nice men.

'I'll look forward to that, Fiona. Thank you again,' Tom said as he handed her a couple of euros for her tip.

'What are you up to, Tom Whelan?' Gerry asked when Fiona had left.

'Nothing. It's always nice to get to know the locals,' Tom said with a grin.

Gerry knew there was no point pushing him any further. He'd reveal all when he was ready.

'How about a walk around the gardens, Gerry? Let's get some of that country air you were talking about.'

'And walk off some of that 2000-calorie snack you just demolished!' Gerry shot right back. He'd delicately nibbled on half a scone while Tom devoured one full one and two slices of fruitcake.

'Do you know how much money I've invested in this baby,' Tom said, rubbing his potbelly with a grin.

'Enough to cancel third-world debt, darling,' Gerry quipped, and then continued seriously, 'You're going on a diet on Monday, Tom. I'm not having you dropping dead on me with a coronary.' Ever since Gerry had seen *Four Weddings and a Funeral* he was convinced that Tom would end up like Simon Callow's character, Gareth, and drop dead unexpectedly with a heart attack.

Tom couldn't resist the urge to tease Gerry, so very melodramatically started reciting the famous Auden poem used in the movie.

Gerry was desperately trying not to laugh but failing miserably. 'Stop it, Tom. I'm serious. I couldn't cope without you.'

Tom knew that Gerry worried about him, and felt bad for teasing him, so quickly promised to cut down on the cakes on

Monday morning. Mollified, Gerry continued his walk with Tom. The gardens were stunning, set on two acres surrounding the house. There were beds of the most colourful flowers Tom and Gerry had ever seen. It was a lovely evening, with only a slight chill in the air. Arm in arm they explored the grounds, eventually finding a pond with swans and ducks swimming on it.

'It's like a postcard, Tom,' Gerry sighed. They sat down on a bench beside the pond, sitting silently and taking in the beautiful surroundings, Tom with his arm around Gerry.

'If you ring down to the kitchen, they'll give you some bread to feed the birds,' a thick country voice interrupted their quiet contemplation.

Looking around, an elderly man was standing beside them smoking a pipe. He was wearing overalls and it didn't take Einstein to work out who he was. Tom and Gerry instinctively pulled apart. Both knew that some people of this guy's generation could have a problem with their relationship.

'Mr Murtagh at a guess?' Tom questioned.

'The very one,' Mr Murtagh responded. 'You must be Mr Whelan and Mr O'Leary.'

Gerry laughed, saying, 'That's right. How'd you know?'

'Ah, we make it a point to know all our guests at Rose Tree Manor. It's a soft day, thank God.'

Tom hadn't heard that phrase since he was a kid in Kerry. 'That it is, Mr Murtagh. The gardens are a credit to you,' Tom responded.

The compliment pleased the gardener. He had put a lifetime into these grounds and it showed. He loved his work, but nothing pleased him more than having the guests appreciating his hard word. It made it all worthwhile.

'Fiona told us that you've worked here over thirty years?' Tom continued.

Gerry glanced at Tom again. Back with the questions about length of service; he was definitely fishing for something.

'It'll be forty years this summer. Started here when I was eighteen as a general handyman. But I always had an interest in horticulture. I couldn't believe it when the O'Connors – thems the family who own the hotel – said I could start work on the gardens. They gave me a free rein and the money to buy the bulbs and trees I needed.'

Tom was nodding encouragingly at everything Mr Murtagh was saying. 'You must have seen some people come and go over the years so.'

'Aye, there have been a lot of people working here in one way or another. They usually move on after a couple of years. We've a lot of temporary workers too for the summer months.'

'I've a good friend who used to work here thirty years ago. Ah, I'm sure you wouldn't remember her. It was a long time ago,' Tom said.

Here we go, Gerry thought. Now we're getting to it.

'The body's getting old, Mr Whelan. But the mind is as fresh as it was when I started here forty years ago. Who was it?' Mr Murtagh replied.

'Her name is Catherine Dunne,' Tom stated.

'Young Kitty Dunne. God, I haven't thought of her in years. She was a grand lass. Worked in the kitchen back then. Lovely looking girl. Yes I remember her well. How's she doing?'

'Kitty! Never knew anyone called her that! She's doing great, Mr Murtagh. Living in Meath now, running her own teashop. She'd give this place a run for its money with the home-made scones!' Tom said with a wink.

Gerry raised his eyebrows at this. Talk about free licence with the facts. Tom had barely met Catherine, never mind knew what she served in her teashop!

'Oh she was a grand cook was Kitty. She did a lot of the food back then. Wait till I tell the missus, she was great friends with her. They started here at the same time.'

This was good, Tom thought.

'Well I'd better keep going. I've a couple of blocked drains to see to before it gets dark. It was nice talking to you both,' Mr Murtagh said. And with a nod he ambled off.

'Damn. I wanted to ask him some more questions,' Tom said to Gerry.

'Catherine worked here! Why didn't you tell me?' Gerry demanded.

'Thought I'd surprise you, my love. Anyway I wasn't sure if it would be a good lead or not. It was a long shot that anyone here would remember Catherine from thirty years ago.'

'Why didn't you stop him going and ask him some more stuff?'

'Don't want to let him think I'm being nosy. Nah, let him go back to Mrs Murtagh with the news and hopefully they'll come to us later on. I've a suspicion that Mr Murtagh enjoys a jar or two, we might just ask them to join us for a drink later on.'

'How'd you know he likes a drink?' Gerry was always amazed at Tom's powers of deduction.

'I reckon it's more than the chill in the air causing that red nose, Gerry. A tenner says he's a whiskey drinker.'

'You're on!' Gerry declared. They got up and started the walk back to the hotel.

Chapter Seventeen

While Tom and Gerry were busy playing Lords of the Manor down in Wexford, Abby was anxiously waiting for her date. She was with Sean and Tara having a quick Dutch-courage drink first. Tonight she was meeting Richard, one of the South Africans, for a drink and she was really nervous. She'd been out with Fergus already and it had been an absolute disaster. He didn't drink and had sat there all night sipping a glass of water. He was the single most boring man Abby had ever dated. He was obsessed with *Who Wants to be a Millionaire?* and spent the whole night discussing every episode he'd ever seen. At the end of the first hour she'd been ready to split, but her inbuilt sense of decency and politeness stopped her from running out the door on him. However, it had been the longest night of her life, and without alcohol to anaesthetise her pain it had been unbearable!

'Why didn't you get yourself a drink? I would have.' Tara declared when Abby told them about her disastrous date.

'I did have two drinks, but as he was sipping his water, I felt like a bleeding alcoholic every time I had a sip of my red wine,' Abby moaned.

'So I take it this Fergus bloke won't be the next Mr Abby Nolan so?' Sean asked.

'Over my dead body! Bloody typical though. He's called three times already since Tuesday night. It's always the same. The guys I don't want keep calling and those I want to go out with dump me by text!'

'Oh come on, that was only one guy!' Tara laughed.

'I know. Still stings though! Right I'd better go across to the bar. Remember ring me in an hour, okay?' They had devised a plan so that Abby didn't have a repeat of the last disaster. If the date was going badly, she could get the guys to come and rescue her. With a last gulp of wine and wishes of good luck from Tara and Sean, Abby ran out of McDaids.

'God, I'm glad I've got you,' Tara said to her husband. 'I don't think I'd have the energy to be on the dating scene anymore!'

'Oh you did well snaring me for sure, Tara,' Sean replied, laughing and dodging the beer mat his wife threw at him.

Abby did a quick scan of the place. No sign of Richard yet. She walked up to the bar and ordered a drink for herself. It wasn't too busy so she got a seat at the bar fairly easily. With the smoking ban in force, nearly everybody was standing outside. She'd just paid for her drink when Richard arrived. He recognised her at least, Abby thought with relief. She was terrified he'd have forgotten what she looked like because it had been a couple of weeks since the speed-dating event. He was quite good looking too in a kind of scruffy way. She felt a bit overdressed in her tea dress from Topshop. Gerry had left strict instructions that she was to wear this outfit, and once again he'd excelled himself, it was gorgeous. Richard, however, was just in faded denims with a t-shirt. He got himself a pint of Guinness and took a seat beside her.

'So Abby, how's things?' he asked casually.

'Great, Richard. How about you?'

'Fanfuckingtastic! You're looking gorgeous,' he said with a wink.

Abby was thrilled. It had been so long since a guy had given her a compliment, she basked in it.

'So tell me all about yourself?' Richard asked.

They chatted away easily for fifteen minutes or so. Abby had finished her drink and there was no sign of him ordering. But to be fair Richard was only halfway through his pint. So Abby caught the barman's attention and ordered a drink for her and another pint for Richard.

She couldn't believe it when her mobile rang; the time had passed so quickly. It was Tara.

She excused herself and took the call.

'Well is he a studly or what?' Tara demanded.

'What kind of a word is studly, you mad thing!' Abby giggled. 'He's all right actually. Seems to be pretty laid-back, easy to talk to.'

'Why don't you bring him over here to join us? Go on Abby I'd love to meet him. We can make sure he's a suitable date for our mate!' Tara broke, in peals of laughter. She'd obviously had a few drinks and was in great form, delighted with herself for rhyming!

'I'll ask him, one sec!' Abby replied. 'Why not!'

Richard thought it was a great idea to join her mates, so they grabbed their stuff, finished their drinks and walked back over to McDaids. Introductions were made, with Tara giving the thumbs up behind Richard's back. Sean jumped up and went to the bar to get the drinks in.

'So tell me Richard. Where do you live?' Tara asked.

'I'm in a flat at the moment with a couple of mates in Rathgar. I'm on the sofa till I get myself sorted.'

'That must play havoc on your back, mate,' Sean said as he passed the drinks around.

'What do you do?' Tara continued her inquisition.

Abby was delighted; she hadn't wanted to ask loads of personal questions earlier. Now Tara was doing it for her!

'This and that,' Richard replied nonchalantly.

Abby was surprised at this answer. She was sure at the speed-dating event he'd told her he was working in finance. Maybe he didn't like talking about work.

'Very mysterious,' Tara murmured.

Sean could see that his wife was beginning to go a bit cold with Richard, so thought he'd better change the subject quickly. He started to tell them about a woman who came into the surgery that day claiming she was pregnant, by an alien! When he finished his story, Tara waved her glass in the air.

'I take it you're ready for another drink?' Sean asked with a laugh. He jumped up to go to the bar, half expecting Richard to stop him. But he was in the middle of what looked like a deep conversation with Abby. Maybe he wasn't paying attention.

Drinks refilled for everyone, they carried on chatting. Tara whispered to Sean after a while.

'He's a tight arse that one.'

'Shush, he'll hear you,' Sean reprimanded with a laugh.

'Don't care. He hasn't bought a round yet. God, I hope Abby doesn't like him!'

Richard got up to go to the toilet so Tara had her chance to ask her. 'He seems nice. Just one thing bothering me though, Abs…'

But before she had a chance to tell Abby what was bothering her, Abby interrupted, 'I might be being too hard on him, but he hasn't bought a drink yet.'

'Not even over in Bruxelles?' Sean asked incredulously.

Abby told them what had happened.

'Look it could just be the way the night has turned out. Let's give him the benefit of the doubt. He's probably buying a round now,' Sean said a bit dubiously.

But Richard returned empty-handed a few minutes later and they all raised their eyebrows knowingly at one another.

After a while the drinks were getting low again, so Abby thought she'd better broach the subject with Richard. 'Looks like we're all ready for another drink!' she said brightly.

To which everyone murmured their assent, including Richard, but there was no move on his behalf.

Sean decided to take matters into his own hands. The softly-softly approach wasn't working.

'Right, Richard. Mine's a pint. The girls are on the vino. Good man.'

Everyone went quiet. Richard looked slightly uncomfortable then turned to Abby. 'I thought we'd go for a walk now and call it a night. Are you ready?' he whispered.

'What?' Abby replied confused. There had been no talk about walks a few minutes ago.

'I've had enough jars. I'd like to go for a walk with a beautiful girl. You!' he said with his most charming smile.

'I bet you wouldn't have had enough if Sean was buying again!' Tara said sarcastically.

Richard shot her a look of annoyance and stood up and put his jacket on. 'Abby are you coming?'

'Actually I'd like another drink. Would you go to the bar and buy me a drink please?' Abby said bravely.

'That's a bit tricky. I'm a bit short at the moment.'

'What do you mean exactly by a bit short?' Abby asked quietly.

'I'm between jobs. You know what it's like,' he answered with a shrug.

'No actually, I don't,' Abby said coldly. 'Do you mean to tell me you asked me out on a date when you didn't have a bean to your name?'

Richard nodded silently.

'Asshole,' Tara helpfully contributed.

'Way out of line, dude,' Sean added.

'Weren't we all having a laugh?' Richard seemed to think this was a satisfactory defence for being a miser!

'Yes we were. I hate to break it to you though, but your company isn't that great that you can get away with freeloading all evening. That's all the laughs you'll be having with my friends and me. Goodbye Richard,' Abby said firmly.

'I'll be off then. Will I give you a call?'

'Yeah, some Sunday there's no mass!' Abby responded before he turned away and left.

'God, he's a neck like a jockey's bollocks!' Sean stated, causing the girls to break into hysterical laughter. He jumped up to get the drinks. Abby looked like she needed one badly.

'Why me?' Abby moaned. Tara gave her a hug and told her it was just bad luck.

'God Almighty. I've had months of bad luck. I must have been some bitch in a previous life! It's doing my head in, Tara. What is it with the guys of Ireland?' She took a huge gulp of her drink.

'They're all blind, my love. They don't know what they're missing. But to be fair, that eejit wasn't Irish,' Tara consoled her.

'That's true. Think I'll stick to the locals in future. At least you know what you're getting with them,' Abby declared.

'Only one thing to do when something like this happens,' Sean stated as he sat down. 'Tequila!'

'Now I know why you love this man, Tara! He always knows what to do in a crisis!' Abby laughed.

Chapter Eighteen

Tom and Gerry were drinking brandy in the drawing room of the Rose Tree Manor, having just finished a gorgeous four-course meal. Tom had devoured home-made pâté with Cumberland sauce, followed by roast rack of lamb with rosemary and garlic, then a mouth-watering cheesecake. Even Gerry had ditched his diet for the evening because the menu was just too tempting. He'd eaten tiger prawns to start with, followed by sea bass, finished with crème brûlée. Both of them could hardly move. They'd also had a beautiful bottle of Sauvignon Blanc and they were feeling nice and mellow. Fiona had insisted they retire to the drawing room for coffee and brandy as they'd be more comfortable, and she was right.

'What do you reckon they think of us?' Gerry asked. 'I've noticed a few funny looks from people.' He was always concerned about how people reacted to them. His family had pretty much disowned him since he 'came out' and he had insecurities as a result. Tom didn't give a damn. He was comfortable in his own skin and never happier than when he was with his boyfriend. Plus he was lucky. His whole family knew about his sexuality and they supported him totally, which had surprised a lot of people, as he was from a very small rural area where you might expect more prejudice. But his parents had been incredible when he told them. To hell with what people thought, they loved him for who he was.

'Listen pet, I'm sure we are a bit of a novelty for a place like this. I'm not sure that Rose Tree Manor has seen many gay couples before, but hasn't Fiona been a sweetheart?' Tom said to his boyfriend.

'Yes. But do you think she knows?' Gerry asked worriedly.

'Of course she does, Gerry. We're in a double room, which she was clearly made aware of when we checked in. They know all right. I daresay they've had a chat about us. Only natural.'

'So I'm worrying about nothing?' Gerry asked anxiously.

'Yes my love, you are. We're just two people in love enjoying a weekend break. We're not all over each other in public so we can't be offending anyone. Don't worry,' he squeezed Gerry's hand reassuringly.

With that a small plump woman, with the rosiest cheeks they'd ever seen walked over to them. 'Hello Mr Whelan and Mr O'Leary. I'm Mrs Murtagh. My husband told me he'd met you earlier.'

Tom and Gerry jumped up and shook her hand, both smiling encouragingly at her.

'Would you join us for a drink, Mrs Murtagh?' Gerry asked. 'We'd love to chat for a while.'

'Oh I wouldn't want to intrude,' she demurred.

'No intrusion, we'd love to chat for a while. Is Mr Murtagh around, we'd love to buy him a drink too,' Tom continued.

'He's in the bar. He wouldn't be comfortable in here,' she indicated the beautiful drawing room.

'Well, why don't we all adjourn to the bar so?' Tom said. 'Lead the way!'

Drinks were ordered in the bar, with a giggle from Gerry when Mr Murtagh ordered a drop of Powers' whiskey. That was ten euro he owed Tom. He'd be unbearable later; he loved it when he got it right!

They grabbed a table in the small lounge and Tom raised his glass to toast the beautiful hotel they were staying in. After a few minutes of chat about the hotel, Mrs Murtagh asked about Catherine.

'I haven't seen her in over thirty years. It's such a pity, we were really good friends,' she lamented.

'It's often the way it goes unfortunately. People lose touch,' Tom concurred sympathetically.

'How is Kitty?' she continued.

'Well, she's great actually. I'm sure Mr Murtagh filled you in about what she does now. Her teashop is a great success down there and the busiest spot for lunch every day,' Tom stated.

'She always had a very light hand when baking,' Mrs Murtagh said.

Tom wasn't sure what that meant, but assumed it was a good thing. 'I can't imagine what Catherine was like back then. I've only known her in later years,' Tom said. Never ask questions directly, just lead people into talking, he found that worked the best.

'She was a lovely girl. A hard worker and I think she was happy here. We started at the same time, me working as a chambermaid, her as skivvy in the kitchen.'

'So this is where she got her interest in catering?' Gerry inquired.

'Yes, I suppose it was. It didn't take long for Mrs O'Reilly, the chef at that time, to realise that Kitty had talent. She soon had her doing all the baking. Kitty was happiest when she was mixing and creating in that kitchen!'

'I hope it wasn't all work and no play,' Tom said jokingly.

'Not a bit of it,' Mr Murtagh took this one. 'We had one day off during the week. We all lived in at that time and if I remember rightly Kitty and Molly – that's Mrs Murtagh – were always off on their bikes into Ballymichael for the day.'

'Are you from there too?' Tom asked Mrs Murtagh.

'No Tom, I'm not. I'm a Waterford girl. But Kitty's family kind of adopted me. It was too far for me to go home, so I went to Kitty's with her. Her parents were lovely people. Really warm and friendly. She had a brother too, what was his name again?'

'Noel,' Tom informed her. 'He's living in Australia now, married with two children.'

'That's nice. Has Catherine ever gone to visit him?' she wondered aloud.

Tom didn't actually know this and hesitated for a second.

Gerry jumped in and answered, 'Oh yes, Catherine goes to visit Noel once every five years. They're very close.'

'They always were,' Mrs Murtagh stated. 'God, all this talk about Kitty takes me back.'

Tom quickly got another Baileys for her and another whiskey for Mr Murtagh. He hoped the drink would loosen their tongues.

'I bet you were a pin-up back then.' Gerry complimented her. 'What cheekbones and those lips!' Mrs Murtagh blushed prettily.

'Oh, she was a bonny lass,' her husband said. 'They were quite a picture back then. My Molly with her lovely dark hair and Kitty with her strawberry blonde curls. I'm telling you there were quite a few fellas chasing them back then. I had my work cut out to get Molly to go out with me!'

'But you got her in the end! How romantic!' Gerry declared.

'Yes it was I suppose. He kept asking me out every week, till I finally gave in!' Mrs Murtagh said with a slight blush.

'So did that put paid to your weekly trips to Ballymichael?' Tom asked.

'To some extent. I started to spend my time off with Tadgh. But I still went to Kitty's every now and then.'

'And Kitty, did she have a boyfriend?' Tom casually asked.

'No not really. There were a couple of dates but nothing serious,' she replied.

126

'What about that guard?' Mr Murtagh asked his wife. 'Didn't she go out with him at one point?'

'Oh that's right. Robert Hegarty was his name. He was madly in love with Kitty, but she really wasn't interested. She broke his heart I reckon.'

Tom's ears pricked up at this information. Robert Hegarty later married Catherine's cousin Mary. This was really interesting. It had to be the same guy. Two guys called Robert Hegarty, both guards in the same village, was too much of a coincidence.

'Did Kitty drink much?' Tom asked.

'That's a strange question to ask,' Mrs Murtagh replied sharply. These guys were very interested in thirty years ago! She began to feel like she was gossiping too much about her old friend.

Tom realised he was pushing too far and needed to back track. 'Oh I'm sorry Mrs Murtagh. Just being nosy I'm afraid. Catherine is always teasing me about my lifestyle. I was just looking for some funny stories to tease her with when I got back home!' Tom said with ease.

Mrs Murtagh relaxed. 'Well I'm afraid there are no such stories to tell. Kitty didn't drink at all back then. I can't remember any time when she drank. She never liked to be out of control and hated seeing people drunk.'

They carried on chatting for a few more minutes then the Murtaghs got up to leave, thanking the guys for their hospitality. Mrs Murtagh gave Tom her phone number and asked him to make sure he gave it to Catherine. She'd love to have a chat with her at some point. Tom was pleased with the information he'd gathered so far. He had another lead to follow up on. Could Robert Hegarty be Grace's father? Gerry was thinking the same thing.

'Darling, Catherine may not want Grace to know because she's afraid it would upset her cousin?' Gerry wondered out loud.

'Certainly possible, Gerry. Plus the story about her being drunk and not remembering who got her pregnant doesn't ring true anymore for me. Unless Mrs Murtagh is covering up for her old pal Kitty, she certainly didn't paint a picture of someone who drank at all, never mind got so drunk she slept with someone she didn't really know.'

'What's our next step, Tom?' Gerry asked.

'I think a little drive to Ballymichael in the morning is required. Let's go visit the village and see if we can get a feel for the area,' Tom said.

Chapter Nineteen

Grace peeked in at Jack who was sitting cross-legged in front of the TV, engrossed in an episode of *Fireman Sam*. Smiling at her son's beaming face, she continued into the kitchen to find Liam dragging the mop and bucket from the utility room.

'Clean up on aisle six,' he quipped.

'Another Jack special?' Grace asked. Their three year old seemed to be the clumsiest child ever and was constantly spilling his juice or milk on the floor. Sometimes it felt like all they did was mop up after him!

'Yep. But it was an abbident,' Liam replied, mimicking their son's voice perfectly. 'All okay?'

'Yeah, fine. I was just leaving a message for Tom. He's down in Wexford remember?' Grace said. 'He probably has nothing to share at this stage, but I'm so curious.'

'If anyone can get to the bottom of who your father is, it's Tom,' Liam said to Grace. 'How are you feeling?'

'Sick of people asking me how I'm feeling, that's how,' Grace snapped and then immediately felt awful for it. 'I'm sorry. I just wish I could have one day where cancer hasn't taken over my life!'

'I get that,' Liam said, taking a seat beside Grace at their dining room table. 'Talk to me.'

'Oh, it's just everything seems to come back to my cancer these days. I don't remember having a conversation for more than five minutes that didn't include the subject. I'm sick of having to watch what I eat, what I drink, whether I'm going to get a cold; it's all a bit overwhelming if I'm honest,' Grace confessed.

'Well we can't have this,' Liam declared. 'Right, go get yourself ready. We're going out for the day. Give me an hour to plan the itinerary and then we're off.'

'Really?' Grace said, excitement creeping into her voice.

'Yes really,' Liam replied, ushering his girlfriend towards the door. 'Go get ready and while you're at it, get Jack organised too!'

An hour later, they were all buckled into Liam's car ready for the off.

'Where we going, Daddy?' Jack asked excitedly.

'Well, first of all, we're going to the cinema!' Liam declared.

'Me too?' Grace asked sceptically. She had been told to avoid public areas as there was more chance of her catching an infection from big crowds.

'Yes, you too,' Liam said, smiling as his wife's expression turned from uncertainty to joy. It was amazing the excitement that the word cinema could bring to his two favourite people.

'Can I have ice cream? Pleaseeeeee,' Jack implored.

'Oh, yes, there'd better be ice cream,' Grace said, wagging her finger at Liam. 'At least two scoops each.'

'Today will be a day of non-stop treats. Stuff your faces at will,' Liam told them, to which he was nearly deafened by their screams.

An hour later, as they sat in front of the big screen, munching on tubs of Ben & Jerry's, watching the dastardly deeds of the latest Disney villain, all thoughts of cancer left both Grace and Liam's minds. When the movie finished, they wondered back to the car, Grace a little reluctantly.

'Why so glum?' Liam asked her, catching her sad face.

'I'm not sure I want to go home,' Grace said, sounding like a three year old herself.

'Who said anything about going home?' Liam replied. 'We're going to the funfair!'

Earlier, he had frantically scoured the internet, using every search engine available and finally hit upon funfair gold. There was a festival on in Dún Laoghaire with a funfair in residence. Grace was an adrenalin junkie and he figured correctly that this might appeal to her.

'Wow Daddy!' Jack declared.

'Yes, wow Daddy!' Grace answered, leaning over the gearstick to give Liam a kiss.

****

The traffic from Dublin to Dún Laoghaire hadn't been too bad and pretty soon Grace was strapped into a seat on a ride called 'Extreme'. Liam insisted that Grace should get to have the first ride. There was plenty of time for Jack to have his rides afterwards. So within a few moments of scanning the funfair, she knew it had to be 'Extreme'. The ride itself looked like a giant, metal spider, with legs going in all different directions. Grace could feel her heart beat begin to speed up as the music pounded into her ears, Jon Bon Jovi belting out *Living on a Prayer*. With a quick wave at her two men, both craning their necks watching her move slowly into the air in her metal seat, she closed her eyes.

Bam! The ride took off and instantly she felt herself propelled up high, then suddenly dropped very low, then back up spinning around and around. Her heart was beating so fast and she hadn't felt so alive in months. As she spun around and around she screamed loudly, safe in the knowledge that all sounds omitted from her were lost in translation amongst the chaos and noise

131

of the ride. She opened her eyes and saw she was up high, at the extreme pinnacle of the ride and she looked up to the sky. It was the most beautiful blue sky with white perfect clouds lazily drifting by.

'I'm still here. I'm still alive. Do you hear me?' she screamed at the heavens. She felt exhilarated, strong and ready to face anything. And as the ride started to spin again, she screamed with joy as she was thrust from side to side.

When the ride came to the end, she realised her face was awash with tears. She quickly wiped them away and ran to Liam, throwing her arms around his neck and holding him tightly. 'Thank you for today,' she whispered. 'I love you.'

'I love you too,' Liam answered her, his voice tight with emotion.

'I want a hug,' Jack declared petulantly, pulling at both of their legs.

Laughing, Liam scooped him up and the three of them snuggled into each other, oblivious and uncaring of who was watching them.

'My turn now!' Jack declared in typical three year old fashion.

'Yes, it's your turn now,' Grace said, smiling. Tomorrow she had another chemo session, but as quickly as the thought popped into her head, she banished it. Today was a cancer-free day.

They spent several hours at the fair, mainly watching Jack go up and down the same bouncy slide over and over again.

'We could have bought the fecking slide ourselves, the amount of tokens we bought for that!' Liam grumbled when they finally managed to get Jack to agree to leave.

'Home?' Grace asked Liam. Jack was already looking sleepy as they buckled him into his car seat.

'Nope, not yet. First of all we are dropping slide boy here off to his Nana's for a sleepover. And then it's just you and me. I've booked a table at Siam's.'

'Can we cancel?' Grace asked him frowning.

'You sick? Oh no, Grace, I made you do too much, didn't I?' Liam said, concern written all over his face.

'Sick? Me? I've never felt better Liam! Nope, I'm just not that hungry. But I could do with an early night,' Grace replied smiling at him.

'As in?' Liam answered, brightening up.

'As in, let's get Jack settled at Nana's because I have plans for us!' Grace replied, giggling.

Chapter Twenty

Tom and Gerry were driving towards Ballymichael. They both had a slight hangover from the night before, having drunk brandy until closing time. Gerry had a pair of Guess sunglasses on to hide what he called the 'luggage bags' under his eyes! Tom had rang Liam that morning to get an update on Grace. She had finished another treatment and was at home now recovering. Liam reckoned the chemo was getting slightly easier, as she wasn't as nauseous this time, just really tired. She came on the phone for a quick chat and an update on their findings. Tom filled her in on his chat with the Murtaghs. She was riveted with it all and clearly excited.

'Do you think that Robert Hegarty could be my father?' she asked.

'Now don't start letting your imagination run away with you Grace, sweetheart. All we know is that they dated for a while. Mrs Murtagh couldn't remember exactly when they finished and I couldn't push her too much. The timings may be completely off regarding Catherine getting pregnant.'

'I know, Tom. I promise not to get too excited by it all, but it's a start isn't it!' Grace said.

The hope and possibility of tracing her father again was giving her renewed energy.

'Liam and Grace seem to be really happy, don't they?' Gerry commented.

'That they do. Liam has really come through, thank God. It's so much easier too knowing that Grace has Liam with her all the time. Imagine how hard it would be with Jack if he hadn't come back into her life?'

'I know, it doesn't bear thinking about,' Gerry answered. 'It's fate, Tom. Que sera sera!'

Tom smiled at Gerry, announcing they had arrived.

Ballymichael was a charming village with stone walls and little cottages. They could be driving into a scene from the fifties. But then, as if to remind them that they were in fact slap bang in 2013, they spied a large Mace sign. The village seemed to consist of a school, post office, church, Mace supermarket, small hairdressers' and the obligatory three pubs – Kinsellas, Whelan's and The Village Inn owned by the Daltons. It never failed to amuse Tom that the smallest of villages in Ireland would still have at least three different pubs to choose from! It was far too early to go for a drink, so they decided to go for a walk instead. Tom wanted to find Catherine's old family home, which was supposed be just after the church at the top of the hill.

After a short stroll they came across a couple of detached bungalows, and sure enough No. 3 was there at the end. This was where Catherine had grown up.

'Imagine that's where Grace's grandparents lived all their lives,' Gerry declared. 'It's strange, isn't it?'

'What's strange?' Tom asked.

'Well, if Catherine hadn't left Ballymichael when she was pregnant, Grace could have been brought up here and we probably would never have met her.'

'That's a sobering thought, Gerry. I couldn't imagine life without our Grace. Or Jack. God, we probably wouldn't know Tara, Sean, Abby or Liam either,' Tom replied, slightly horrified.

'So what do you want to do now?' Gerry asked Tom.

'Not sure. I was hoping that someone might walk past who we could ask some questions to about these houses,' Tom said, looking around him.

'Well your lucks in, looks like someone is leaving No. 1.' With that a woman came out of the first bungalow pushing a pram. She smiled and said hello to the guys.

Gerry walked over and gushed, 'What a beautiful baby. How old?' Tom cooed.

'Six weeks. My little angel. Her name is Mia.'

'Delightful!' Gerry replied. 'You look amazing for someone who's just had a baby!'

The young mother beamed with delight at his compliment. Tom thanked the gods once again for Gerry. He was great in these situations, totally unthreatening. Women always felt quickly at ease with him.

'These are lovely houses. Gerry and I – my name is Tom – have been thinking about moving to the country and one of these would be fantastic.' Tom decided to make himself acquainted.

'Hi Tom and Gerry.' The girl giggled, getting the significance of their names, then swiftly apologised for being rude.

'Don't worry about it. We get it all the time, don't we?' Tom told her. It was true. It was bad enough being gay in Ireland, without having famous names from a cartoon to boot!

'My name is Michelle. These houses are lovely. They have four bedrooms and are quite spacious. Ballymichael is a beautiful village, but then again I'm biased.'

'Oh?' Tom asked.

'Well I've lived here my whole life. My parents live in the village too.'

'Isn't that lovely,' Gerry said with a smile. 'You must know who lives in the other bungalows here. Do you think they'd sell?'

Michelle considered the question for a moment and Tom felt a pang of guilt. 'Well, Mrs Doyle lives in No.2 and she's been there for forty years or so. I don't think she's going anywhere!'

Tom smiled encouragingly. This was great. Mrs Doyle may well be worth a visit later on. She must know the Dunnes.

'No. 3 is rented. There are three lads living there at the moment. Nice enough guys, they have a band and gig a lot in the area.'

'You wouldn't imagine a place like this as a rented home, would you?' Tom said conversationally to Michelle.

'No, suppose not. The owners, Mr and Mrs Dunne have passed on now, and their children just rent the house out.'

'Isn't that a shame that they didn't want to live here. I'd never leave if it was mine,' Tom declared.

Michelle was delighted that these two guys were so taken with the houses. 'Well, the son, Noel I think he's called, lives in Australia and the daughter Kitty lives in the midlands somewhere. She never visits, it's strange really. Her cousin looks after the renting of the house for her.'

'Well that's handy I suppose,' Tom said. He wondered how to further interrogate without causing suspicion. Gerry came to the fore again.

'Michelle, I do declare, there's a little bit of gossip there I'm sure! A daughter never visiting her home village! Come on, spill the beans!' Gerry said dramatically.

Michelle laughed. These guys were hilarious and nothing like she'd ever seen in Ballymichael. They were definitely gay, or at least Gerry was. He was so camp. 'Well, it was before my time. Kitty is the same age as my parents, so I only know bits of gossip I heard as a child. Haven't heard her name mentioned in years,' she said conspiratorially.

'Oh darling, spill. I'm positively gagging for this gossip now!'

'Well, from what I know Kitty got herself pregnant when she was in her twenties. She wouldn't say who the father was and her

137

dad disowned her. She was sent to one of those convent places in Dublin and I think the baby was adopted or something,' Michelle told the men.

'How terrible, darling. The poor girl,' Gerry said. This time he wasn't acting. It was unfortunately a sad and true story.

'Yes it must have been. I couldn't imagine giving up my little Mia.' Michelle looked down at her sleeping baby and lightly touched her on the cheek.

'Did they ever find out who the father of the baby was then?' Tom asked.

'Not that I know of. From what I remember that was the strange thing. Apparently, Kitty wasn't the type to get pregnant. She didn't really have any boyfriends, at least not seriously. That's what killed her father I think. He wanted to know who the dad was so he could make sure he married his daughter. But Kitty wouldn't give a name. He was furious and threw her out.'

'And her mother?' Gerry asked sadly.

'Well Mrs Dunne kept in touch I believe. But it was all in secret. Mr Dunne wouldn't have Kitty's name mentioned ever again in his presence.'

Tom and Gerry were silent listening to this tale. How awful it must have been for Catherine.

'You could write a book about it, couldn't you?' Michelle said to them.

'That you could,' Tom agreed. 'I bet in a village like this, there must have been rumours about who the father was?'

'I'm sure there were, but I'm afraid I don't really know. As I said I was a child. Anyhow, must keep going. I've some shopping to do before Mia wakes for her next feed. Nice meeting you both.'

'Well, well, well. That was interesting. Poor Catherine,' Tom said to Gerry as they watched Michelle walking away. 'Let's go back to the village and see if the pub is open yet for lunch.'

'Do you ever think of anything but your stomach?' Gerry exclaimed. 'I'm still full from breakfast!'

They meandered back into the village square and sure enough there were signs of life in Daltons. That had to be their first stop. Working behind the bar was a glamorous older lady who had more than a passing resemblance to Catherine. She had to be Ann Dalton, Catherine's cousin. Tom and Gerry took a seat at the bar and ordered two coffees. She came back with the drinks and Tom asked her about food for lunch.

'We do one special per day. Today it's Shepherd's Pie. It's good. My husband's the cook. But we also do soup and sandwiches if you prefer something lighter.'

'Sounds fantastic. We've overindulged slightly this weekend. Full Irish for breakfast, so maybe we should just go for the soup and some sandwiches,' Tom said almost forlornly.

Gerry nodded his approval. 'This man could eat for Ireland,' he said pointing his finger at Tom. 'We'll just have the soup please. No sandwiches.'

'You're the boss so,' the barwoman said with a smile.

'That he is. I'm Tom and this is Gerry,' Tom extended his hand.

'Nice to meet you guys. I'm Ann. My husband Pat is in the kitchen finishing the pie. Let me put your order in.'

'She's a bit like Grace, isn't she?' Gerry whispered. 'Are you going to tell her you know Catherine?'

'Not yet. Gonna play it by ear.'

'Are you staying in Rose Tree Manor?' Ann enquired.

'Yes we are. We thought we'd do some exploring this morning. This village is really beautiful.'

'Yes it is, I've lived here my whole life,' Ann told them proudly.

'We were just looking at some of the beautiful houses in the village. There's a house at the top of the hill that's rented out at the moment. Michelle in No. 1 told us about it,' Tom stated.

Ann raised her eyebrows, 'I know the house.'

'Well, Michelle mentioned that somebody in the village looked after the rentals. She didn't give us a name. You don't happen to know who it is by any chance,' Tom enquired.

'You're in luck, Tom. I manage the rent on that place. It belongs to some cousins of mine. What do you want to know?' Ann said.

'What a coincidence. Small village, hey?' Tom said with a grin. 'We are thinking about getting a little house in the country for the summer and I thought that it might be a good idea to rent somewhere for a couple of weeks first of all. Get a feel for the area.'

Genius, Gerry thought.

'Well I'm afraid I can't help you with that property. It's not for rent at the moment. I don't really do short-term lets as a rule. The guys that have it at the moment are on a one-year lease. It's easier,' Ann said.

'What about the owners, do they ever use the house?' Tom enquired.

'No, they don't. That sounds like Pat. One moment I'll go get your lunch,' Ann stated.

'Now what?' Gerry said. 'She's not giving much away.'

'I know. Think I'll be cheeky and see how she reacts. Nothing to lose really,' Tom said.

Ann brought their soup out, carrot and coriander, with thick slices of brown soda bread. It was delicious. They ate their food quietly, cleaning their bowls in full.

'That was great, Ann. Compliments to the chef!' Gerry said.

'Glad you enjoyed it.'

'Do you think the owners of No. 3 would sell?' Tom asked.

'No, they wouldn't. They've no interest in doing that,' Ann replied quickly.

Right, thought Tom. Time to raise the bar. 'I would have thought that the girl would have wanted to sell up. Lots of nasty memories there you would think,' Tom said bluntly.

Ann stopped cleaning glasses and asked Tom what he meant by that.

'Michelle mentioned that one of the owners was in Australia and one lived in the midlands somewhere. She got pregnant years ago and was disowned by her father. That must have been awful for her.'

'Michelle had no business talking about such things with you,' Ann said indignantly.

'Oh please don't be cross with Michelle. She wasn't gossiping, honestly. We were just so interested in the house; we kind of drew her out.' Gerry was dismayed to think that they may have got the lovely mum in trouble. 'I know what it's like to be in that girl's situation,' he finished quietly.

'What, been pregnant and got chucked out of your home?' Ann said with a sneer.

'No, but my parents did disown me. I'm gay. They didn't like it.'

'Oh, I'm sorry Gerry. That's awful,' Ann softened to him immediately. He looked so sad.

'I think that's why I was so interested in this girl's story. Are you still in touch?' Gerry continued.

'Yes, as it happens we are. We don't see each other that often, but we talk on the phone occasionally. She's a lovely woman and everything's worked out for her in the end. She's very happy living in Meath.'

'Oh I am glad,' Gerry said.

'Did they ever find out who the father was?' Tom asked.

'Tom!' Gerry exclaimed. 'Don't be so nosy.'

'What?' Tom said innocently. 'I'm interested. It's like a mystery novel. I need to know the ending.'

Ann laughed at the two guys. They were gas. 'Well I'm afraid your mystery novel will have to remain unfinished. My cousin never revealed who the father of her baby was. Not even to me, and we were good friends.'

'Wow. That's some secret to keep,' Tom said.

'Yes it is. I haven't asked her about it in years to be honest. She doesn't like to talk about it and gets quite cross if it's ever mentioned,' she added.

'There must be some suspects though?' Tom asked.

'Not really. It was the talk of the parish back then. I mean you couldn't keep something like that quiet. She was a tiny little thing, so she started to show quite quickly. Everyone was guessing who it could be. But there were no real leads.'

'Could it have been someone from her job?' Tom probed.

'Not as far as I know anyhow. Kitty never mentioned anyone at Rose Tree Manor. She worked there in the kitchen; there's another coincidence for you, Tom.'

A couple of locals came in for lunch then and Ann walked over to serve them. Tom and Gerry jumped up to go and left some money on the counter.

'Ann we're off. We might see you tomorrow. Thanks for the lovely lunch,' Tom said as they waved goodbye.

Chapter Twenty One

Tom was sitting in their car recapping what they had learnt so far. Gerry was taking notes.

'Right this is what we know. Catherine lived with her parents until she was eighteen in Ballymichael. Her best friend was her cousin Ann, now the landlady of Dalton's pub in the village. At eighteen Catherine got a job at Rose Tree Manor in the kitchen. She lived at the hotel and became good friends with Molly Murtagh. She had one day off per week and always went home for it. And from what we've been told, usually with Molly in tow. She dated Robert Hegarty, the local guard, briefly, supposedly breaking his heart. He then went on to marry her other cousin Mary. She didn't drink. She got pregnant at twenty five. When her parents found out there was blue murder. She refused to name who the father was. Her dad was furious and threw her out, disowning her. Her mother kept in touch with Catherine, but in secret. Have I missed anything, Gerry?'

'No that's everything I think. It still doesn't shed any light on possible suspects though, does it?' Gerry said.

'No it doesn't. And to be honest I don't think that Ann Dalton was hiding anything. By the way, you played a stormer in there earlier, my love. She really took to you. So did Michelle. I'll have to bring you along to more of my interrogations in future.'

Gerry was delighted with the praise. He took a look through the notes he'd made for Tom. He wanted to make sure they were legible and he hadn't missed anything. He knew that a lot of people thought he was just a big old drama queen, but he could be serious too when needed.

Tom looked out the window of his car, taking in the surroundings. Somewhere in this village, someone knew who Grace's father was. He was sure of it. They had two more leads to follow up on today. One was to pay Mrs Doyle in No. 2 a visit and then finally talk to Garda Hegarty.

'Where you going?' Gerry asked.

'To buy some flowers. We're going to pay an old lady a little visit,' Tom said.

Ten minutes later he was knocking on the door of Mrs Doyle's. Tom had a plan half concocted in his mind. He felt that he needed to change his story a bit if he was going to get anyone to open up a bit more and perhaps give some clue as to whom Grace's father might be. He just hoped that Mrs Doyle didn't get out and about too much. If she met up with Ann Dalton, or Michelle for that matter, his cover would be blown. He had told Gerry to stay in the car for this one. There was less chance of her associating him with the 'gay couple' later on when she spoke to the neighbours if he went in alone. He knew that in a small village like Ballymichael, there would be a lot of talk about them. Tom had leaned in the window of their car and putting on his best Jim Carrey accent said, "'If I'm not back in five minutes, just wait longer!'" He was rewarded with a belly laugh from Gerry. Easily pleased!

A little old lady in her late seventies answered the door. She had a kind face and smiled a welcome.

'Mrs Doyle?' Tom enquired.

'Yes.'

'My name is Michael O'Grady.' This was a name he often used as a pseudonym in investigations. It sounded strong and dependable. 'I'm a friend of Noel Dunne's who used to live next door to you,' Tom said, shaking the lady's hand.

'Noel. Oh my, what a surprise. He was a lovely young man. How is he?' Mrs Doyle said with a big smile.

'Well he's doing great as it happens. When he heard I would be in the area he asked me to call in and say hello. I got you these.' He handed her a bunch of lilies. Not exactly a bouquet but the best the local shop could offer. He felt a bit guilty when he saw how pleased Mrs Doyle was. This was the part of his job he hated – telling lies.

'Please come in, Michael. I was just about to have some tea. Will you join me?'

'That would be lovely. I'm parched.' Tom felt like he was walking into his own grandmother's house. The wallpaper was lilac floral with a matching border and there was a Sacred Heart picture with a lighted candle underneath it. Mrs Doyle led the way into her living room, which had a large mahogany dresser against the wall, on which her fine china was proudly displayed. Tom took a seat as directed and waited for her to return with the promised tea. It was proper tea leaves like his Mam always served too. Mrs Doyle used a little silver strainer and the tea was delicious. It really did taste better like this. They chatted for a couple of minutes about Noel and his life in Australia. Or at least a fictionalised version of it! Tom didn't really know what was going on in Noels life, but he tried to make a good guess. He wanted to get the subject onto Kitty, but didn't want to rush things. He decided to lead Mrs Doyle down memory lane.

'This place must have changed a lot over the years, Mrs Doyle,' Tom said. As expected, that got her started on the good old days. And thankfully she finally mentioned living next door to the Dunnes.

'You were obviously very fond of them all, Mrs Doyle,' Tom observed.

'They were lovely neighbours. Mrs Dunne was a great friend to me. I was devastated when she died. Hasn't been the same for me since then. I never married, you see. Haven't got much family to speak of, only a couple of nephews living in Kilkenny.'

'That's tough. It can be lonely I'm sure. What about Kitty? Do you keep in touch with her?'

Mrs Doyle looked sad at this question.

'Kitty sends me a Christmas card every year. She was always a good girl. When Noel and Kitty were children they always came into me after school and I'd have a little treat for them. Then when Kitty grew up and went to work for a hotel locally, she used to call in on her day off and she'd bring me a treat. A bag of soft jellies usually. I loved them.' Mrs Doyle had a lovely smile.

Tom smiled. The more he heard about Catherine the more he liked her.

'It was such a shame what happened to her,' Mrs Doyle's old face looked wistful as she remembered thirty years ago.

Tom had his way in and finally felt that he may be getting somewhere so he gently pursued the subject. 'Noel told me that Kitty left home. That must have been really hard on her mother.'

'Oh it was. It near broke her heart. But Bill – Kitty's father – wouldn't have her name mentioned anymore. He was of the old school and was deeply shamed that his daughter had got caught,' she said sadly.

'Do you think he knew who the father was?' Tom asked.

'No, nobody did. That was the strange thing about it. Usually when someone got pregnant – and Kitty wasn't the first, won't be the last either I'll warrant – you'd have a fair idea who the daddy would be. With Kitty it was different. She didn't go out much. She never drank.'

Tom was getting frustrated. The same story over and over again. She must have gone out, once anyhow. Unless it was another miraculous conception!

'What did she do when she came home on her day off?' Tom asked.

'Well in the early days she'd come home with a friend. Molly her name was, I think.'

Tom smiled. Nothing wrong with this one's memory!

'They used to spend the day at home with Bill and Maura, and then would go out for a drink. They were very popular. All the lads loved them.'

'Did Kitty have any serious boyfriends?' Tom asked.

'She did go out with young Robert Hegarty. He had just moved to the village as the local guard. He was mad after Kitty. But she wasn't that pushed. He wanted her to give up her work at the hotel and move home, get married. But she said she knew he wasn't the one for her, so she finished with him.'

'When was that?' Tom asked.

'Oh when she was about twenty one or twenty two I suppose. Let me think. That's right, it was around the time that Molly stopped coming to Ballymichael with her. She got married.'

'So what about Kitty? What did she do on her days off then?' Tom wondered.

'Well to be honest, Kitty never really wanted to go out. She didn't drink and only went to Dalton's to keep Molly company. Now that Molly wasn't with her, she just stayed at home with her parents. I think she was trying to avoid Robert too. He took their break-up very badly,' Mrs Doyle said.

'Do you think they ever got back together?' he probed further.

'Robert and Kitty? I wouldn't think so. He was never around. Plus he had plenty of new girlfriends when Kitty was off the scene. He was quite a catch to a lot of the local girls. He didn't get married for years though. To a cousin of Kitty's as it happens.'

'That's interesting,' Tom murmured.

'Between you and me I reckon he never got over Kitty and poor Mary was only a substitute for her cousin. I'm not so sure they have a happy marriage. It's a pity because Mary is a lovely woman.'

The more Tom heard about Robert Hegarty the more it seemed likely that somehow or other he had managed to get Kitty back and was Grace's father. His name was the only one that was ever mentioned when anybody talked about Catherine.

'She helped out in the local church too,' Mrs Doyle added.

'Kitty?' Tom said with surprise.

'Yes, she worked there on her day off, doing the flowers. Father O'Hara said she was a godsend. He was very upset when she got pregnant. He was always at the house after Kitty left home, offering his support to Maura and Bill,' Mrs Doyle continued.

'I'm sure they appreciated that,' Tom said. 'Actually there was one other thing I meant to ask you. Noel mentioned a guy called Michael that Kitty and he were friendly with. I didn't get a second name. Any idea who that might be?'

Mrs Doyle closed her eyes and thought about this for a minute. 'I'm afraid I can't help you. I don't remember any friends of theirs called Michael or even Mick.'

Tom looked at his watch and realised he'd been there almost an hour. Gerry would be having a fit. He finished his tea and thanked Mrs Doyle for having him.

'No thank you for the beautiful flowers, Mr O'Grady. It was lovely to have some company. I don't get it very much. You must forgive me for rambling on about the old days. You're very kind to humour an old lady.'

'Not at all, Mrs Doyle. I really enjoyed our conversation.'

Tom leaned in and gave her a quick kiss on her cheek, promising to call again should he be in the area. He also left his phone number with her in case she should remember whom the Michael

148

could be. He walked down the hill to the church car park where Gerry was sitting waiting for him with a face like thunder.

'Some five minutes Ace Ventura,' Gerry said pouting.

'Sorry, pet. That went on longer than I anticipated. But I did get some interesting information.' Tom told Gerry the gist of the conversation he had had with Mrs Doyle.

'So that's two people we need to see now. Robert Hegarty and Fr O'Hara? The Garda station I presume?' Gerry asked.

Chapter Twenty Two

Tom was beginning to get a better picture of Catherine's life in the village. She had no real boyfriends, with the exception of Robert, and he was off the scene at least three years before Grace was born. But by the sounds of it he never got over Kitty, so they could have had a fling later on, resulting in Grace. A moment of madness maybe? But why wouldn't Catherine tell her father it was the local guard who got her pregnant? Or there again maybe Tom was on the complete wrong track. He was going to question the Murtaghs again when he got back to the hotel. Was there a member of staff there that could be responsible? For God's sake it could have been a guest of the hotel. They'd never find out who it was if so. Tom's head was spinning with it all. Well, it was finally time to visit the now infamous Robert Hegarty.

Tom and Gerry walked into the station and rang the bell at the reception. A tall, good-looking man in his fifties walked out. He had salt and pepper hair and was in good shape.

'Richard Gere eat your heart out,' Gerry whispered excitedly.

Tom had to agree, there was a strong resemblance.

'Garda Hegarty?' Tom asked.

'Yes Sir. How can I help?' The guard answered pompously.

'Well, my friend and I are currently thinking about moving from Dublin to the area. We've been looking around today and I thought it would be a good idea to talk to you and find out about the area. What's the crime rate etc.?' Tom said.

Gerry smiled to himself. He had heard variations of this story all day and he almost believed it himself!

Robert Hegarty puffed out his chest and came out from behind the desk. 'Please sit down gentlemen and we'll have a chat.' They all took a seat in the reception area 'Well it's a lovely area. Ballymichael has been a finalist in the tidy town's competition four times in the last ten years,' Guard Hegarty told the couple.

'I can understand why,' Gerry said. 'The area is spotless and obviously well looked after.'

'Well, I'm on the parish committee and every resident in the area has to make sure their gardens are at an acceptable level,' he boasted.

'Proper order,' Gerry stated. 'I'm a keen gardener. If we were to move into the area I'd be very happy to help out anyway I could.'

Garda Hegarty obviously approved of this. 'I'm also pleased to let you know that the crime rate in the village is practically non-existent. I don't tolerate any hooligans.'

'Zero-tolerance?' Tom asked.

'Yes. All the way,' he replied.

Tom and Gerry then listened patiently for ten minutes as he gave them a lecture on the fine art of policing in a small village. Realising that this was Garda Hegarty's favourite subject and they could still be there listening in ten hours, Tom realised he would have to move things along quickly.

'I hope you don't mind me saying so Garda Hegarty, but you're very well liked in this area. We've spent most of the day here and your name has come up loads of times.'

Gerry looked a little scared. He'd never have the guts to come out with stuff like Tom did.

'Nothing bad I hope?' Garda Hegarty said with a self-deprecating laugh. He knew he was a well-respected member of the community and had no worries that anyone would say anything bad about him.

'To the contrary. All good I can assure you. We've been told what a Romeo you were in your younger days.'

The guard laughed at this. He was a good-looking man and he knew it. He'd had his fair share of offers from women over the years. He knew that women loved a man in uniform.

'We also heard a sad story earlier about a young girl who used to live here years ago. Kitty Dunne I think her name was,' Tom said, lowering his tone conspiratorially. The smile instantly wiped off Garda Hegarty's face when he heard this name mentioned.

'Who on earth was talking about Kitty to you two?' Garda Hegarty asked incredulously.

'A couple of people actually. We were interested in buying No.3, but have been told that Kitty and her brother won't sell. In the course of talking to various people about the house we heard the tragic story of her getting pregnant and being disowned by her family.' Tom watched Robert Hegarty's face carefully to gauge a reaction. He was obviously annoyed by the story. Tom decided to stay quiet and let him be the first to talk. It took a few minutes, then he finally spoke.

'Well, that was a sad time for all the Dunnes. But it's all in the past now. Nothing for you two to worry about,' he said finally.

'Oh we're not worried. We were just intrigued, Garda Hegarty. It seems to be the mystery of the century. Remember *Dallas* – Who shot JR? Well Ballymichael should have t-shirts printed with "Who knocked up Kitty?"' Tom said, deliberately goading the guard. Partly because he thought it might evoke a response and partly to annoy him.

Gerry giggled at this, despite being slightly shocked at Tom's disrespect. He knew he was trying to get the guard rattled.

'I think you'll find, Mr Whelan, that most people in Ballymichael wouldn't care for your tone. Kitty was well liked in this area,' he replied sharply.

'Oh I'm sorry. I didn't mean any disrespect, honestly. I just meant it seemed to be a big mystery as to who was the father. Or maybe there's no mystery to you,' Tom continued unabashed.

A flush appeared on the guard's cheek. 'What exactly do you mean by that?'

'You used to go out with the girl, didn't you? Come on, man to man; let me in on a secret. Did you get down and dirty with her? Are you the father?' Tom goaded.

'How dare you,' Robert Hegarty roared. 'Kitty Dunne was a lovely girl and didn't get "down and dirty" with anyone. Of course I'm not the father. I never even slept with Kitty.'

'I apologise, Garda Hegarty. I didn't mean to offend. We've obviously hit a raw nerve. We'll be on our way,' Tom apologised quickly. He knew he had pushed it as far as was wise!

Gerry and Tom hastily walked out of the station and jumped in their car, both giggling like kids as they took off.

'I thought he was going to bloody hit you, Tom! Did you see that vein bulging in his neck?' Gerry said excitedly.

'Pompous old twit. At least we know that Catherine had good taste, dumping that idiot! Come on; let's call into The Village Inn for a quick drink. I need one!' Tom said.

They sat down in a booth this time because they wanted to dissect the information they had gathered so far.

'Do you think he was telling the truth, Tom?' Gerry asked.

'I don't know, Gerry. If you really pushed me, I'd say he was telling the truth. But then again he could be deserving of an Oscar. What about you, what's your gut instinct?'

'Well, like you, I think he appeared to be telling the truth. But

I was looking at his face, to be honest with you, to see if I could see any similarities between him and Grace. I couldn't. They are like night and day,' Gerry said.

'That's true, but I suppose it doesn't really mean anything, she might just have got Catherine's looks rather than his. I wonder if we could get our hands on his medical records. Find out what blood type he is. That could eliminate him or point the finger to him very quickly,' Tom stated.

'If he's given blood before, he'll be on a register,' Gerry said helpfully. 'I'll check it out on Monday.' Gerry often did some of the Internet investigative work for Tom if he needed some done while at home. He was good at it and had managed to establish some strong contacts. They finished their bottles of beer and then jumped up.

'One more call, we'll see if Fr O'Hara can shed any light on all of this and then we'll go back to the hotel. I'm knackered, pet,' Tom declared.

They walked to the parochial house attached to the church and knocked on the door. Tom had told Gerry that they were going to go for the honest approach on this one. 'If we ask him not to contact Catherine, he'll have to agree. Don't they have some kind of Hippocratic oath or something?'

'I think that's only in the confessional, Tom. But by the sounds of it Catherine hasn't really kept in touch with anyone in Ballymichael. We should be safe enough,' Gerry replied.

They knocked on the door and a middle-aged woman wearing an apron opened it. She was obviously in the middle of baking. 'Can I help you?' she asked kindly.

'Yes please. We're here to see Fr O'Hara,' Tom replied.

'Can I say who's calling?' she asked.

'Yes you can.' He gave their names in return.

She brought them into a small room, which obviously acted as a meet-and-greet point for the parishioners. There were leaflets on the table on unwanted pregnancy, alcoholism, drug abuse, marital problems, Trocaire, as well as a bundle of parish newsletters. After a couple of minutes or so, Fr O'Hara walked into the room. He was about sixty or so at a guess. Distinguished looking, with a thatch of silver grey hair. He smiled at the boys as he joined them.

'So sorry to have kept you waiting, gentlemen. How can I be of service?' he asked smiling at them.

'No problem at all, Father. Thank you for seeing us at such short notice. First of all I'd like to ask you for your discretion on the matter we are about to talk to you about. We'd appreciate it if you could agree to keep our conversation between ourselves,' Tom asked. Fr O'Hara nodded his agreement. He'd probably been asked to keep secrets in the past before. God knows what stories he'd been told in the confessional. He may even have heard Catherine's confession all those years ago and know who the father was.

'I believe you knew a lady called Kitty Dunne? She used to do flowers for the church here,' Tom said.

Fr O'Hara looked a bit startled for a moment. 'Kitty Dunne. There's a name I haven't heard for a long time. Yes she helped out in the church on occasion. Why do you ask?'

'We're involved in an investigation on behalf of her daughter, Grace. To be honest Fr O'Hara we are trying to discover who Grace's biological father is,' Tom answered truthfully.

Tom let the priest take in this information.

'I'm not sure I can help you there, Mr Whelan. Kitty was a lovely young lady and was such a help with the flowers. But I'm afraid I wasn't a confidante of hers,' he said gravely.

'I was led to believe that you were a family friend to the Dunnes?' Tom further probed.

'I like to think I'm a friend to all my parishioners. But yes, I was close to the Dunnes. I tried to offer some comfort to them when Kitty left. They were devastated.'

'Kitty was thrown out as opposed to leaving though?' Tom asked.

'Yes, that's right. Her father did ask her to leave. He was a good Catholic man and the thought that his daughter had sinned grieved him,' the priest replied seriously.

'Pretty harsh I would say. Disowning your only daughter, in particular one who was in obvious distress? Hardly the works of a good Christian?' Gerry interjected. He couldn't help himself; it annoyed him when people did downright evil things in the name of God.

'Yes. I can see where you are coming from Mr O'Leary. But you have to remember this was over thirty years ago. Times were different then,' Fr O'Hara answered mildly.

'Do you think Garda Hegarty could be the father?' Tom continued.

'Oh my. What a question. I couldn't say for definite, but they had stopped seeing each other years before Kitty fell pregnant. For what it's worth I'm not sure you'll ever know who the father is. Kitty swore she'd never tell anyone. My guess is that it was one of the guests at the hotel she worked at. Maybe a married man and she didn't really know him. Maybe she doesn't know who it is herself,' Fr O'Hara said, shaking his head sadly.

This wasn't what Tom wanted to hear. He had contemplated this scenario himself and knew it was a possibility. But he still had a gut instinct that the answer to Grace's paternity lay in this village.

Fr O'Hara then continued. 'When did the poor soul die?'

'I'm sorry. Who are you talking about?' Tom replied.

'Kitty. I'm assuming she's dead. That's why your client Grace is looking for her father.'

'Oh Lord. Sorry Father, I should have explained. No, Kitty is alive and well living in Meath. She has her own business there. Grace and her mother have recently met, but I'm afraid Kitty won't divulge who the father is.'

'Is that so? I would have thought she'd tell her daughter the truth?' Fr O'Hara said thoughtfully.

'Yes I know. Grace was very disappointed. She really wanted to know about her background, but Kitty, or Catherine as we know her, refused to say. Or at least said she couldn't say,' Tom continued.

Fr O'Hara raised a questioning eyebrow at this.

'She said she didn't know who the father was,' Tom said in answer.

'There you go. That confirms my earlier suspicion that it was a one-night stand. May God forgive her,' Fr O'Hara replied, his voice raising.

Tom threw his eyes up to heaven – sanctimonious old git, he thought – then blessed himself in his mind for cursing a priest. His grandmother would turn in her grave. 'Well thank you Father for your time. We'll leave you in peace now. Just one last thing before we go. Do you know of any Michaels that Kitty would have known around the time of her pregnancy?'

Was it Tom's imagination or did Fr O'Hara go slightly pale at the mention of Michael?

'No I'm sorry, Mr Whelan. I'm afraid I don't know any Michaels that Kitty may have known. Why do you ask?'

'Nothing for you to worry about, Fr O'Hara. We'll be off for now. Please keep this conversation between ourselves,' Tom said.

'Oh you can be assured of my discretion. God bless you.'

Chapter Twenty Three

It was August 15th and Grace had been banished from her home. She had completed her last course of chemotherapy and in the main was feeling good. Last week she had been told her cancer was in remission and Liam had decided they needed a party. It was also Grace's birthday in a couple of days, so it was a joint celebration. He was at their apartment with Jack finalising everything and she was with Tara and Sean.

'You look good, Grace,' Tara said to her friend. 'Better than I've seen you in months.'

'Thanks pet. I feel great too. It's such a relief to finally have finished the chemotherapy. What do you think of my new wig? Catherine bought it for my birthday.'

Before Tara had a chance to respond, Sean walked in the door whistling at Grace as he did.

'Looking foxy Grace!'

Laughing, Grace turned to Tara and said, 'How do you put up with all his cheesy lines?'

'I don't know; they're getting worse the older he gets!' Tara replied with a laugh.

'Speaking of Catherine, any further word from her on your father?' Sean asked.

'No, it's a no-go area for us. I've realised that if I want to keep seeing Catherine I need to avoid that subject. As soon as I mention it, she gets up and leaves, then goes to ground for a couple of weeks.'

'That's terrible. How do you feel about that?' Tara asked with concern.

'Well to be honest, I can live with the fact that I'll probably never know who my father was. And I don't really need to know either. It would be nice to get some history I suppose, but no one could ever replace Daddy for me.'

Grace smiled at her two friends. She meant what she had said. Finding out who her father was didn't seem to matter anymore. She felt blessed that Catherine had come into her life, and at a time when she really needed the support. She was in remission now and felt great, so a bone marrow transplant wasn't on top of her list, like it had been a few short months ago. Her doctors still felt it was the best long-term option for her, but unless a suitable match came along, she couldn't do anything about that. One thing this cancer had taught her was that she couldn't control everything that happened in her life. Sometimes you had to just roll with the punches.

'Has Tom come up with anything further?' Tara asked.

'No. He reckons that unless Catherine spills, its one secret that will never be unveiled,' Grace answered.

Tom and Gerry had further questioned Mr Murtagh in Rose Tree Manor about Catherine while she worked there. According to him there was never even the hint of scandal that she had may have had any kind of relationship with one of the guests. Apparently it was a sackable offence back then and one that Catherine – or Kitty – as he called her, respected totally. No matter who Tom talked to, he got the same response: Kitty was a lovely woman, who didn't drink and didn't have any romances, except a brief one with Garda Hegarty, she worked six days a week at the hotel then spent one day at home with her parents, even finding the time to do the flowers in the local church.

Grace had gone over and over all of things the guys had told her. She had loads of theories about why Catherine was keeping quiet. The two that Tom thought were most likely were Catherine had got drunk, as she had alleged, and didn't know whom the father was. Because it was so out of character for her, she was too embarrassed about it to discuss. Or the second possibility was that Catherine had to keep the father's identity secret. Maybe he was married. Maybe it was Robert Hegarty and because he had later married her cousin Mary, she couldn't reveal it was him. So in the end, Grace had decided to let it drop. It was using up much needed energy.

'How's love's young dream?' Sean asked with a smile.

'Very happy, I can report, thank you very much,' Grace answered with an even bigger grin. 'I know it's corny, but I seem to be falling more in love with Liam every day. He's just been amazing with me while I've been ill. He spends all his time making sure Jack and I are both secure and happy.'

'He's very good with Jack,' Tara concurred. In fact she really couldn't fault Liam at all over the last few months. He had been there for Grace every step of the way and never once fell out of line.

'I think that's the first positive thing you've said about Liam since we got back together!' Grace said in amazement. 'Don't tell me you actually approve?'

'Don't look so surprised, Grace Devlin,' Tara said indignantly. 'You know I only want what's best for you and Jack. And I can see that's Liam. As it happens, I actually like him. I always did, it was just his drinking that did my head in.'

'Thanks Tara, I really needed to hear that,' Grace said with a smile. 'It's important to me that you two get on.'

'Just don't tell Liam what I've said,' Tara said with a wink. 'I like keeping him on his toes!'

'Right you guys, time to go, Liam was adamant that we shouldn't be late!' Sean said to the girls, shooing them out the door to his car.

****

Arriving at the apartment Grace wondered what was in store for her. Just as she walked up the steps to her front door, Jack opened it, shouting, 'Happy Birthday Mommy!' Grace started to laugh as she took in her son's appearance. He was dressed as Robin Hood and looked just adorable.

'How do I look, Mommy?' he asked earnestly.

'You look so handsome, sweetie-pie,' Grace replied adoringly, planting a big kiss on his head.

'It's a fancy dress party, Mommy! Daddy says go upstairs straightaway. Put your costume on!'

Grace couldn't believe it. Turning around to face Tara and Sean, she started to laugh. Sean held up a bag. 'And these are our costumes. We couldn't put them on, as it would have given the game away. Can we use your room, Jack?'

The three of them went upstairs led by Jack in front.

'Don't come out until I tell you Mommy, okay?' Jack ordered.

Agreeing, Grace walked into her bedroom and let out a squeal of delight. Lying on the bed was a Marilyn Monroe costume, consisting of a blonde wig and the white halter-neck dress made famous by the iconic shot in *The Seven Year Itch*. She loved it. Liam knew that she had always admired Marilyn Monroe and he couldn't have picked a better costume for her. She got changed quickly, taking her own wig off and swapping it for the platinum blonde one. She ran to the bathroom mirror to check out her appearance and was delighted to see that she looked okay. She needed to change her make-up though. She put bright red scarlet lipstick on and pencilled in a beauty spot over her lips. Then the obligatory lashings of black mascara and eyeliner were applied to complete the makeover. She looked great! After a few minutes, Jack came in and announced, 'You

161

look beautiful Mommy. I love your lellow hair!' He had never been able to pronounce his Ys and they always came out as Ls. It was so cute.

Bending down, Grace gave him another big kiss. 'I love you sweetie-pie. Have I ever told you that before?'

'Not since yesterday, Mommy!' Jack said with a smile. 'I love you too, Mommy.' He reached up and threw his two little arms around Grace and gave her a big hug.

'Can we go downstairs now?' Grace asked her son.

'Yep, everyone is waiting.' Jack caught his Mommy's hand and led the way. 'Wait till you see Uncle Tom!'

When they got to the sitting room door, Jack screamed, 'Prise! Mommy's here.'

Opening the door, Grace couldn't believe her eyes. The room looked so beautiful. Liam had placed hundreds of fairy lights around the room, which were now twinkling. Banners of 'Happy Birthday Grace' were aligned on the back wall over the patio doors and their dining room table was laden with trays of hors d'oeuvres of every kind. It was too much to take in. She looked around at her friends' faces one by one, all smiling at her, ending last of all on Liam's face. She felt tears sting her eyes and noticed his were the same. She had never felt so happy in her life.

'You look gorgeous, babe!' Liam said to her. It was only when he spoke that she actually took in the costumes everyone was wearing and she started to laugh.

'Never mind me, look at the cut of all of you!' Grace said with a laugh.

Liam was wearing a fireman's outfit and gave Grace a big wink. He knew that it was always a fantasy of Grace's to see him dressed in this particular uniform. He was looking forward to the after-party they were going to have!

'What do you think, Marilyn?' he drawled suggestively.

'I think you're going to have to put some fires out later on tonight,' Grace said with a laugh, giving her boyfriend a kiss. 'Thank you for this. The room looks amazing!'

'You're welcome babe. You deserve it. This is only the beginning!' he promised with a wink.

Grace then turned to Sean and Tara. They were dressed as Ozzy and Sharon Osbourne.

Sean shuffled over to Grace in Ozzy mode, saying, 'Those dogs have pissed over the floor again, Sharon.'

Tara responded in an over-the-top English accent, 'Well wipe the piss up then Ozzy!'

Grace felt tears coming out of her eyes. Then she saw Abby looking absolutely stunning as Wonder Woman. She had a long wavy brown wig on and the complete red, navy and white costume. Only Abby could get away with red hot pants! She did a twirl for Grace, to which Sean and Liam both murmured their appreciation.

'Down boys,' Grace and Tara said together with a laugh!

'What about us?' Gerry squealed. 'Look at us!'

Grace looked at Tom and Gerry and literally fell to the floor laughing! Sean and Tara were doing the same, as they hadn't time to get used to them either. Gerry was Batman and Tom was his sidekick Robin. Gerry looked resplendent in the Batman costume complete with six-pack and Tom looked like he was going to die of embarrassment in his Robin gear! His potbelly was exaggerated in the red robin top, hanging over his big black belt and green tights!

'I told you I should have been Batman!' he said sulkily to Gerry.

'Darling, I told you, you couldn't pull it off!' Turning to his friends, he said, 'Doesn't he look cute as Robin?'

'I wanted to be the Joker!' Tom continued. 'He wouldn't let me!'

Jack walked over to Tom and said in a really loud whisper, 'I think you look really funny, Uncle Tom. It's my favourite costume!'

Tom looked mollified at Jack's statement and took another sip from his bottle of Bulmers.

Then the door opened and Catherine walked in dressed in a long flowing green robe with a gold tassel belt. She looked gorgeous and much younger than her years.

'Happy birthday, Grace.' She did a twirl for everyone then said, 'When Jack told me he was going to be Robin Hood, I decided I'd be Maid Marian!'

'You look beautiful Catherine.' Grace walked over to her and gave her a hug.

'So do you honey. Stunning!'

Liam ran around getting everyone drinks and turned the music up. Soon the party was in full swing and he even had the theme music to Robin Hood, Batman and Robin, Wonder Woman, The Osbourne Show, Backdraft and lastly Marilyn singing *Diamonds are a Girl's Best Friend*! Whenever he played one of their songs, the relevant people had to get up and do a dance. It was hilarious.

'How did you get all this pulled together?' Grace asked him incredulously.

'Well I hired the costumes, Catherine did all the food, and I downloaded all the music from the Internet onto my iPod! Abby, Tom and Gerry called round this afternoon when you left to help decorate the room! Easy!' Liam said with a shrug.

'I love you.' Grace looked up into his eyes and felt truly and absolutely happy.

'I love you too, babe,' Liam replied. They got embarrassed then as they realised the whole room was looking at them.

Jack piped up, 'I love you Mommy!' as he threw his arms around both their legs. Everyone laughed at that.

Liam had even hired a karaoke machine and soon everyone was up having a go. It was the best party Grace had ever been to and it made up for all of the bad times of the previous six months.

After a couple of hours of eating, drinking and singing, everyone was taking a breather.

'Daddy, is it time yet?' Jack asked his father.

'Yep, buddy, I reckon it is!'

Grace looked questionably at her friends, but they all shrugged.

Liam opened the closet under the stairs and out came a bundle of helium balloons! Each one had a scroll tied to the end of it. Liam explained to the group, 'Jack decided he wanted to give everyone a present tonight. So he's been busy drawing a picture for each of you.' Liam handed the first balloon to Jack who walked over to Tom and Gerry with it. They opened the scroll and laughed with delight. Jack had drawn Tom looking like a sheriff and Gerry with loads of shopping bags around him!

'Fantastic!' Tom roared, grabbing Jack into him for a cuddle.

'Darling, it's a masterpiece!' Gerry said, joining in for the cuddle. 'Imagine a genuine early masterpiece from Jack Ryan! It'll be worth a fortune in years to come! I'm going to frame it and put it in our bedroom!'

Jack was delighted with their reaction. He had worked so hard at these pictures. Next he handed one to Abby, who he had drawn as a fairy. Then Tara and Sean got theirs which was a picture of them working in a hospital as a doctor and nurse. Lastly he handed a picture to Catherine and she started to cry when she opened it. It was Catherine baking a cake and said 'I love you Nana Kitty' on it, which is what he called her. Everyone was laughing and complimenting Jack on their pictures. They couldn't get over how talented he was for a three year old.

'Daddy did the writing,' Jack informed everyone. He thought it was only fair to be honest with them. They seemed to think he was a genius or something.

'Now Mommy's!' Jack said with a big grin. Grace had been itching to see hers and thought her turn would never come. Jack walked over to her very importantly holding the balloon out. Grace looked at Liam and smiled with pride. Their son, what a star! Opening her scroll, Grace couldn't believe her eyes. Written on the scroll was, 'Mommy, will you marry my Daddy?'

'Read it Mommy!' Jack demanded.

Grace did as she was asked in a small shocked voice. There were gasps from the room. Nobody had known that this was planned. Liam walked over to Grace and knelt on one knee in front of her.

'Grace, I love you. Have done for over ten years now. I never want to live another day without you and Jack. I want to grow old with you. Please do me the honour of marrying me?' Liam made his speech as tears flowed from his eyes. He didn't care. He knew that only people who loved him and Grace were watching. Taking a small ring box from his pocket, he opened it to display the most amazing ring Grace had ever seen. It had a single emerald stone in the middle, surrounded by diamonds, and was absolutely perfect. He picked it because he thought the emerald matched the colour of her eyes exactly. The room was silent, waiting for Grace's answer. She too was crying.

'Grace?' Liam asked softly.

'Yes, I'll marry you,' Grace answered, throwing her arms around him.

The room exploded then with everyone shouting their congratulations. The girls were all crying, and Abby said it was the single most romantic moment she'd ever seen. It was a magical night and one that would stay with each of the friends for the rest of their lives.

As Grace looked around her friends, she thought to herself, if this is as good as it gets, then I'm one lucky girl.

Chapter Twenty Four

Grace was out with Tara and Abby for a couple of drinks. It was the first night they'd been out together on their own for months and they were all raring to go. Grace looked great in her blue Guess jeans and pink cami. Tara was wearing a figure-hugging black corset top with her blue jeans that showed her curvaceous figure off perfectly, with Abby wearing low-slung hipsters with a skin tight T-shirt.

'So come on Abby – spill with the latest in your love life!' Grace asked.

'I have nothing to report unfortunately. Nada, zilch! Gerry persuaded me to go to another speed-dating event, which I can't believe I agreed to.' Abby had dated two of the four guys from the first event – Fergus and Richard – which were both disasters. She decided against dating the second of the South Africans, feeling he was probably more of the same, and unfortunately Shay, the architect, didn't contact her.

'No luck then?' Grace asked.

'There were two of the same guys from the first event there!' she said with a laugh. 'That's the end of speed dating for me. I'm going to try the traditional way of meeting guys for a while again!'

'What's that?' Tara asked.

'Flash some flesh,' Abby answered, pointing to her bare midriff, 'and position myself strategically near the bar!'

'Oh to be young and single again!' Tara said with a sigh. Then seeing her friends' faces, she continued, 'Don't worry; I'm not thinking about ditching Sean or anything drastic! I love him to death, but sometimes when I realise that I'll never have that wonder of who might be around the next corner it depresses me!'

'Thanks a lot Tara, for putting that into a newly engaged head!' Grace answered with a laugh.

'I never knew Liam had it in him to be so romantic!' Tara said, taking another look at Grace's engagement ring. 'He took me totally by surprise!'

'Me too. There wasn't even a hint of it to me before the party. He'd robbed one of my rings to make sure he got the right fit and everything; I didn't even notice!' Grace said dreamily.

'Any ideas when the big day's going to be?' Abby asked.

'Well, now that you mention it, we're going to get married this Christmas. Neither of us wants to hang around and we both want a small service.'

'That's fantastic!' Abby said, totally enthralled. She almost sighed, wondering when it would be her turn. But she checked herself quickly. This wasn't about her, it was about Grace.

'Well we just need to find a venue, but we've decided that we're definitely going to Florida for our honeymoon.'

'I take it Jack is going with you too!' Tara said.

'Yep, we both talked about going somewhere on our own, but I don't think I'd enjoy myself without Jack,' Grace said smiling.

'Can you imagine Jack when he gets to meet Mickey Mouse? He'll lose his mind!' Tara laughed.

'I know I can't wait to see it. But, guys, I've one big question to ask you,' Grace said with a smile. 'How do you fancy being my bridesmaids?'

The whoops of delight from the two girls were answer enough!

'Liam is asking Tom to be his best man tonight,' Grace informed the girls. Liam was at home babysitting and the boys were all joining him for a game of poker. 'He's going to ask Sean to be his groomsman too,' she told Tara.

'They'll be made up. I can imagine Tom pretending to be cool about it as he tries to stop himself crying!' Tara laughed.

'What about Gerry?' Abby asked.

'Don't worry, we've thought about him. I've asked him to be my wedding planner!'

'What did he say?' Abby giggled.

'Have you ever seen *Father of the Bride*?' Grace asked her friends. When they both nodded, they all started to laugh and said at the same time 'Franc!'

'Yep, he started quoting bits from that movie in a very bad 'Franc' accent! He's going to do my head in, I know, by the time the wedding arrives, but at least it will keep him happy!' Grace said laughing.

'Speaking of *Father of the Bride*,' Tara said softly, 'have you had any thought as to who should walk you down the aisle.' Tara had thought that maybe Grace would have asked Tom. She knew that Grace thought of him as an older brother.

'Well, I've been thinking of it for ages now, wondering what to do. I did think about asking Catherine.'

'That would be nice,' Abby said with a smile. 'I bet she would be so honoured.'

'I know. It would make her day, but something about it doesn't sit right with me,' Grace answered with a sad smile. 'I'd never say this to her, so please don't repeat it. I love Catherine and I'm so happy she's in my life, but I don't think she's earned the right to walk me down the aisle. Does that make me sound like a right bitch?'

'No pet, not at all,' Tara answered. 'I'd find it weird too, to be honest. If it wasn't Uncle Mick, I'm not sure it would seem right for Catherine to step in.'

'That's how I feel,' Grace said earnestly. 'I feel like I'd be disrespecting Mam and Dad if I asked Catherine. But you know what, I reckon if I really wanted her to do it, they wouldn't mind.'

'You're right,' Tara replied. 'They hadn't a bad bone in their bodies and would support Catherine totally if they were here. I bet Annie and Catherine would be great mates if Annie were still alive.'

'I've thought the same thing myself. But it's not an issue anymore, I've already asked somebody to give me away,' Grace stated.

'Who?' Tara and Abby asked together.

'Jack, of course!' Grace responded with a laugh. 'And who better than my darling son?'

****

Over at Grace and Liam's the boys were having a similar conversation. Jack was tucked up in bed and the guys were sipping cans of beer, with the exception of Gerry who was drinking a Cabernet Sauvignon.

Liam had asked Tom to be his best man and Sean to be groomsman and the two of them were busy pumping his hand up and down, thrilled with themselves! Gerry was running around looking at each of them critically, muttering about shades of grey or navy for morning suits!

'Now hold up buddy!' Liam said with a laugh at Gerry. 'We're having a really small wedding with only immediate family and friends. There will probably only be about fifty there in total. So we don't want anything flash, okay?'

'Are you mad, me do flash?!' Gerry shrieked. 'I've never done anything flash in my life! But just because it's going to be a small wedding doesn't mean it can't be elegant! You just wait Liam; you will be thanking me when you see what I'm going to pull together for you guys! Now first things first, you have to decide venues!

Here's a shortlist of suitable venues I've pulled together. Grace said you want a hotel somewhere with its own chapel in the grounds?'

Liam couldn't believe that Gerry already had a list of venues for them to decide upon. Grace had only asked him to be the wedding planner that afternoon!

Seeing his friend's look of amazement, Tom said, 'When Gerry puts his mind to something; nothing's going to stop him!'

'You know one of the venues on Gerry's list is Rose Tree Manor. It's absolutely stunning and has its own chapel in the grounds, but I'm not sure what Catherine would think about it?'

'See what you mean, Tom,' Liam answered. 'I'll have a chat with Grace about it, but if she wants that venue, Catherine will have to accept it.' Liam was firm on this point. He wanted their wedding day to be perfect and if Rose Tree Manor was the ideal venue, then that's where it would be. Gerry had narrowed the list down to four venues all within two hours' drive of Dublin, all ranked on various criteria from the size of the venue to the food options. This was great!

****

As the boys started their poker game, the girls started getting into the swing of things. They were on their third Baby Guinness shot and were feeling quite tipsy. Abby was on her way back from the bathroom with a shocked expression on her face!

'Oh my God – look over at the bar!' she mouthed to the girls, pointing behind her dramatically. Tara and Grace did as requested, but couldn't see what they were supposed to be looking for.

'Shit, I forgot you don't know what he looks like!' Abby said with a smile. 'Remember that guy I met at the first speed-dating event? Shay the architect?' Both girls nodded in response. 'Well he's only over there propping up the bar. Third guy on the right, drinking Guinness!'

171

'Holy cow, he's gorgeous!' Tara said.

'I know!' Abby responded. 'What should I do?'

'Has he seen you yet?' Grace asked.

'No, I just walked straight by him with my nose in the air!' Abby grinned.

'Well the next round's yours, so I'd say you better go up to the bar and order one right now!' Grace said with a laugh.

'I can't,' Abby wailed. 'What if he sees me?'

'That's the whole idea, you daft eejit!' Grace laughed back in response. 'Go up and order the drinks and if he says hello, say hello right back!'

'Should I let on I recognise him?' Abby asked.

Tara and Grace looked at each other and then both said together, 'No way!'

Grace continued, 'If he says he knows you from somewhere, just say non-committally that his face looks familiar. After all, he never contacted you before, so don't give him a big head!'

'Right. How do I look?' Abby said, flicking her hair.

'Absolutely gorgeous, just one thing,' Tara said, then grabbed Abby's t-shirt and hoisted it up further so more midriff was exposed. 'If you've got it, flaunt it!'

Abby walked to the bar and ordered a round of drinks from the barman, positioning herself just beside Shay. She forced herself to keep looking forward and tried to ignore the giggles from her friends.

Then a voice cut in, 'You all seem to be having a great night.'

Abby turned to her left and sure enough it was Shay who had spoken. 'Yeah, we are thanks. A girls' night out.'

'A dangerous lot when you all get together!' he responded with a laugh.

'That's us – girls behaving badly!' Abby joked. 'What about you? Are you having a good night?'

172

'Yes I am thanks. I'm with a mate. He's in the jacks,' Shay replied.

The barman was looking for his money, so Abby knew she hadn't much more time to chat. Then with that Tara was beside her.

'Thought I'd come help with the drinks!' Turning to give Abby a wink, she said, 'Who's this handsome guy you're talking to?'

Shay laughed and put out his hand to introduce himself. 'Shay Corrigan. Nice to meet you.' Tara responded by introducing herself. 'I didn't get your name,' he said turning to Abby.

'Abby Nolan,' she said softy, taking his hand.

'Why don't you come and join us?' Tara said boldly, ignoring Abby's dirty look.

'Tara, Shay is with his friend, I'm sure he's happy where he is,' Abby replied mortified.

'Actually I'd love to join you girls. I'll bring Paddy my mate over when he gets back. If that's okay with you, Abby?' Shay replied.

She answered him with a smile and, taking her drinks, walked back to the table.

'Smooth, real smooth Tara!'

Grace and Tara were laughing their socks off.

'Anything to help move love along!' Tara answered. 'Now start fluttering your eyelashes, here come the boys!

It was obvious that Shay fancied Abby. He sat down beside her straightaway and they were deep in conversation immediately. As for Paddy, he couldn't believe his luck when Shay had said they were going over to join the three girls. He thought he had his pick of Tara and Grace and couldn't decide if he wanted blonde or brunette. He was quite put out when they told him they were both spoken for!

Chapter Twenty Five

Abby was on the Dart on her way into the city centre to meet Shay. She was beside herself with nerves. At the end of her night out with the girls last Friday, Shay had asked her for her phone number. She gave it to him readily and had sat by the phone waiting for it to ring. She pretended to the girls that she didn't really mind one way or the other, because she'd got used to being let down, but she really liked Shay and this was one guy she hoped would come through. Sure enough on Tuesday evening the phone rang and it was Shay. He had asked her out on Saturday and Abby told him she already had plans – she didn't want to make herself too available. So a date was arranged for Friday night and she was meeting him in The Bailey. Shay had suggested she send him a text as she got near so he could come outside the pub to wait for her. She thought this was really sweet of him and a good sign. Walking up Grafton Street Abby sent him the promised text, crossing her fingers that he would respond. She still had a feeling that he would cancel at the last minute. But a text appeared a couple of seconds later saying he'd be waiting. God, she was nervous. Turning the corner from Grafton Street, Abby saw Shay standing outside the pub looking a bit nervous too. He was anxiously looking up and down the street and when he caught sight of Abby his face broke into a huge grin. She waved at him and found herself smiling too.

'Hi Abby.'

'Hi Shay.' She felt very shy all of a sudden.

'Shall we go inside?' Shay asked her.

'Sure,' Abby replied. Oh my God, she thought. This was horrendous. The conversation was so stilted. Shay led the way to a corner, where he had a couple of seats held. There was a pint of Guinness on the table for himself.

'What can I get you, Abby?' Shay asked.

'A vodka and cranberry juice please,' Abby replied with relief. For one awful moment she thought it was going to be a repeat of her disastrous date with the miser Richard and she'd have to buy her own! While Shay stood at the bar ordering her drink, she had a moment to check him out. He was wearing faded blue jeans, and with a small smile, Abby couldn't help but notice that he had a cute bum! He was wearing a baby blue shirt with the jeans and it showed his tan off perfectly. He looked good and she realised she really did fancy him! Shay walked back and put Abby's drink on the table for her.

'You look stunning Abby,' he said sincerely.

'Thanks,' Abby said with a smile. Maybe this was going to be okay after all! She didn't mention that she had spent the whole day getting herself ready!

'You said last week that you're an artist. Tell me about it,' Shay encouraged.

Abby was delighted that he remembered and was interested enough to ask her about it. She told him about the paintings that she sold in Stephen's Green. 'I sold one yesterday, so tonight is kind of a celebration actually!' Abby said.

'That's fantastic! What did you sell?' Shay asked, looking very impressed.

'Well my work is very modern and colourful. It was a young couple who bought it and they felt it would be perfect for their living room. It was one of my larger pieces and it's been for sale for three months now, so you can imagine how happy I was when they took it!'

'How long does it take you to complete one piece?' Shay asked.

'Well it depends. Some of my smaller pieces I can do in one afternoon. But the larger pieces can take months for me to finalise and be totally happy with. That particular painting took over two months to complete and there was a lot of hard work in it!' Abby admitted.

'I'd love to see some of your paintings, Abby,' Shay declared.

'Well I'm in Stephen's Green every Saturday, Tuesday and Thursday. If you're ever in the area, call up,' Abby said, feeling brave all of a sudden.

'Can you make a decent living from the sales of your art?' Shay asked. Then quickly continued, 'Oh God, sorry Abby that was really rude and nosy.'

'Don't worry about it,' Abby said with a laugh. 'Some weeks are good, like this week because I've sold a large piece, others are pretty tight. But I do charcoal portraits too to subsidise my art, that's where my bread and butter comes from.'

'Wow that's amazing. Do people sit for you?' Shay asked.

'Sometimes, but mostly they give me a favourite picture and then I'll do the charcoal from that. Quite often I get people in who've lost a loved one and they want to honour them in some way. I work really hard at those, because I know it's so important for the people that I capture the essence of their family or friend.' Abby stopped, suddenly feeling a bit shy. There was too much talk about her work and she wasn't used to it. Usually the guys she went out with only talked about themselves and never asked her about her art. Seeing that Shay's glass was nearly empty, she got up to reorder some drinks.

'Abby please sit down. I asked you for a drink so I'm buying, okay,' Shay said firmly as he got up to go to the bar.

Abby smiled with relief. This was going really well. Shay came back with the drinks and Abby wanted to find out some more about him. 'So tell me about yourself. Are you from Dublin?' she asked him, leaning forward.

'No, I'm from Kilkenny originally. I came to Dublin for college and then got a job here, so never went home,' Shay answered.

'Do you have family at home in Kilkenny still?' Abby further probed.

'Yeah, Mam and Dad, plus I have four sisters all living in Kilkenny too. I'm the eldest,' he said smiling.

'Wow that's quite a big family. That must have been fun growing up with four girls! Were you the stereotypical "big brother is watching you" type of brother?' Abby teased.

Shay laughed as he answered, 'I suppose I was a bit of a nightmare. I was very protective of all the girls and still am I guess. I wouldn't let any of my mates go near them, didn't trust them! Still, one of my sisters, Fiona, ended up marrying my best friend Michael anyhow!'

'And are they happy?' Abby asked.

'Yep, two kids later, couldn't be happier!' he answered.

'What about your parents, are you close to them?' Abby continued.

'God yes – I go home once a month to see them and we all talk every week on the phone. We're pretty tight as families go, really. My folks are cool people. They got married really young so are only in their fifties now and I think they have a better social life than I do!' Shay said with a grin.

Abby liked a guy who got on with his family. She knew it wasn't always black and white, but a man who didn't keep in touch with his family always worried her a bit.

'What about you Abby? Tell me about your family?' Shay asked in return.

'A bit like you, Shay. My parents are cool people and we're really close. They both live in Clondalkin and I go home every Sunday for lunch! I have two brothers and they're both married and they both come home every Sunday afternoon with their wives and kids. It's great fun and nobody ever misses it, unless they're out of the country!' Abby said with warmth.

'Sounds like fun,' Shay commented.

'Yeah it is. I'm lucky. I know my parents worry a bit about me – they're convinced I'm not looking after myself properly, not eating enough etc., so I'm looking forward to going home on Sunday to show Daddy my cheque for that painting I just sold! He'll want to frame it!' Abby declared.

'Must have been some cheque!' Shay said with a laugh. 'God, sorry, I'm not prying honestly!'

'Ah you're okay, Shay. It was for €1200,' Abby grinned.

'That's amazing! That really needs celebrating!' With that Shay jumped up and went to the bar and whispered something to the barman. When he got back he refused to tell Abby what he had ordered, but her suspense was over quickly because the barman was soon on his way over with a bottle of champagne.

'Oh Shay that's so lovely of you. Thank you.' Abby leaned in to give Shay a kiss on the cheek, but just as she did, he turned, and she got him on the lips. She pulled back for a second feeling embarrassed locking eyes with Shay. He would think her so forward. But then they both leaned in together for their first real kiss and it was unbelievable. Abby actually felt lightheaded and couldn't remember ever having a kiss like that before. Shay evidently felt the same way because when they broke he just looked at her before saying, 'Wow!'

They spent the next hour staring into each other's eyes and kissing. It was very romantic and Abby felt like they were the only people in the bar. She didn't care that they were putting on a show for the rest of the pub, this was special. Too soon it was closing time and they had to leave. She really didn't want the night to end and neither did Shay.

'Crystals?' Shay asked and Abby quickly agreed. They walked down Grafton Street and into the club for a late drink. Abby was really impressed when Shay walked straight up to the doorman who ushered them both in; Shay was obviously a regular.

'I do a lot of entertaining here with big clients,' Shay said with a shrug.

They grabbed a seat and Shay ordered more drinks. It was weird, normally Abby would have been really drunk at this stage, but somehow or other the drinks weren't going to her head at all.

Sitting down beside her, Shay looked at Abby for a moment and then, turning serious all of a sudden, said, 'Can I ask you something?'

'Of course,' Abby answered.

'Have you ever gone speed dating?' Shay said with a small grin.

'Maybe. Have you?' Abby answered, non-committal.

'Yeah, once. But it was a disaster. There was a girl there who I really liked. Looked a bit like you, but she never ticked my box! Can you imagine my dinted pride?' he asked.

Abby looked at Shay suspiciously. Was he saying she'd not ticked his box? She had, she was sure of it. 'That's strange. Because when I went speed dating there was a guy who looked just like you there and I ticked his box. He ticked mine too and we were a match. But he never contacted me!' Abby replied.

'I knew it was you!' Shay said with a laugh, before adding more seriously, 'I never got your details though Abby, honestly. You weren't down as a match for me. I was really disappointed as I thought we really connected that night!'

'Me too. I couldn't believe it when you didn't call. Especially when you came over to say hello afterwards,' Abby said shyly.

'Hang on a minute though,' Shay said accusingly. 'You had my details! Why didn't you call me?'

Abby laughed and said, 'Oh I'm just an old-fashioned girl I suppose!'

'God, look at all the time we've wasted!' Shay said with a laugh. Then checked himself, 'Sorry if I'm being too presumptuous. But I really like you Abby. I'd like to see you again.'

Abby couldn't believe her ears. She was so happy she felt like she could burst. 'I'd love to see you too, Shay.'

Chapter Twenty Six

Abby woke up on Saturday morning with a big smile on her face. It took her a moment or two to work out why she was feeling so happy, and then an image of Shay's face came into her mind. She took a look at the alarm clock and jumped up quickly. Shit I'm going to be late, she thought. It was 7.30 already and she needed to get showered and dressed and into the city for 9.00. She knew she should have been dying with a hangover as she didn't get in until 3.30 am, but she felt great. The shower helped wake her up and she quickly dried herself off, grabbing some clothes to wear. Snatching up her handbag and kitbag with all her charcoals etc., she realised she was going to miss the 8.15 Dart. The buzzer rang to her apartment. Who the hell could this be, Abby wondered.

'Yes,' she said into the speaker.

'Darling, it's Gerry. Thought you might like a lift into town!'

'You're a lifesaver, Gerry. I love you! On my way.' Abby ran down the stairs and out the door of her apartment, throwing herself into Gerry's arms. 'I am so late! How did you guess?' Abby said breathlessly.

'Well, when you didn't call me to be rescued last night, I figured the date must have gone well. I thought I'd do my bit for charity today and give you a lift to work and get the gossip at the same time! So come on darling, spill!'

Abby thought for a moment. She wanted to give Gerry an accurate picture of how the date went and the only way to do that was to put it in movie analysis for him. 'Remember the first date that Julia Roberts had with Richard Gere in *Pretty Woman*?' Abby said.

'When he took her to the opera? When Julia is wearing that simply divine black lace dress? Did he take you to the opera?' Gerry said with a squeal, nearly banging into the car in front.

'Watch the road, Gerry. No, of course he didn't take me to the opera, but it was that kind of perfect first date! He told me I looked stunning straightaway.'

'I love him already!' Gerry declared.

'Then he asked me all about my painting. And he had sensible questions too. He seemed to get that it was a career for me, not a silly part-time hobby.' That had meant a lot to Abby.

'What's the catch, there has to be a catch!' Gerry said with a laugh.

'I know, but I don't know what it is! When I told him I'd sold a painting on Thursday, he went up and bought a bottle of champagne for me to celebrate!' Abby knew that would impress Gerry.

'Did you take him home right there and then and shag him senseless?' Gerry asked with a laugh.

'No, I was a good girl. I was tempted, but I've decided I want to take this one a bit more slowly.'

Gerry nodded his approval. Abby had a habit of sleeping with guys on the first date, and then they never called afterwards. He had been telling her for years to hold back for at least three dates!

'But we did kiss! Jaysus, Gerry it was the best kiss I've ever had,' Abby said dreamily.

'Oh my God, you've fallen for him,' Gerry said shocked. 'Abby Nolan, you've fallen for this guy already!'

'I know. I can't help it. I just love everything about him,' Abby confessed.

'Oh darling, I'm thrilled for you. You deserve it,' Gerry said with a big smile. It was just amazing to see Abby looking so happy. Having parked the car in Stephen's Green car park, Gerry helped Abby set up her artwork for display. Then when everything was organised they walked to the Kylemore to order breakfast. Gerry with his usual muesli and fresh fruit, Abby with her usual full Irish breakfast. Between mouthfuls of sausage and bacon, Abby told Gerry about every moment of their date. She was so excited.

'What a week for Abby!' Gerry declared. 'She sells a masterpiece and gets a man!'

'Doesn't get much better than this, does it Gerry!' Then all of a sudden her face fell. 'What if he doesn't call me? What if that's it?' Abby said full of self-doubt all over again.

'Don't be silly, darling,' Gerry said softly. He knew how vulnerable Abby was. 'He'll call and very soon, you mark my words. He sounds like he's as smitten as you are. Guys don't go buying champagne for girls willy-nilly you know.'

Abby giggled, saying, 'Willy-nilly!'

'So juvenile!' Gerry replied with a laugh himself. Grabbing a couple of bottles of water, they walked back to Abby's stand. Gerry decided to hang around for a couple of hours to keep her company. It was always quiet until about 11, and then things usually got busy. Having thoroughly dissected Abby's night out at least ten times over, Gerry decided he wanted a charcoal painting done of himself. Sitting down to pose, Abby started to draw her friend.

'God you're so handsome, Gerry. Tom's a lucky man!' Abby grinned.

'I know. I tell him that every night darling,' Gerry replied with a straight face.

Abby spent about twenty minutes sketching Gerry and was totally absorbed in her work. Then a voice from behind her startled her.

'That's amazing Abby.' It was Shay.

Abby was shy again all of a sudden. 'Hi Shay. How long have you been there?'

'Just a couple of minutes. It was really awesome seeing you work. I'm sorry for disturbing you. Get back to your customer.'

'Oh don't mind me, darling,' Gerry said, jumping up from his seat.

Shay looked a bit worried at being called darling by a complete stranger, and then relaxed as all of a sudden he remembered Gerry: he had met him at that first speed-dating event. 'Hi. I'm Shay. I think we met a couple of months ago.' He walked over and shook Gerry's hand.

'That we did, handsome. I'm Gerry. I'm just keeping the beautiful Abby company for a while.' Gerry noticed that they couldn't stop looking at each other. They'd glance at each other then look away again quickly. It was so sweet.

'Abby darling. Didn't you say you needed a coffee? Why don't you and Shay go get one, I'll stay and mind the stall.'

'That would be great,' Shay said quickly.

Abby gave Gerry a kiss on the cheek and promised him she wouldn't be long.

'I'll call you on the mobile if you get a customer,' Gerry promised.

Abby and Shay walked side by side away from Gerry and he was thrilled when he noticed Shay grab her hand after a moment or two. They walked to a small coffee shop just a moment away from the stall and grabbed a table.

'You must let me buy the coffees at least,' Abby said to Shay. He hadn't let her pay for a thing last night and even insisted on paying for the taxi home.

'If you insist,' Shay agreed.

They both ordered lattes, then sat back to admire each other again.

'I don't think I've felt like this since I was a teenager!' Shay confessed to Abby. 'I couldn't wait to see you again, I hope you don't mind.'

'Not at all, Shay. I feel the same way,' Abby confessed. 'I had a wonderful time last night. It was perfect.'

'I know,' Shay agreed. 'Abby, your art is fantastic. I can't believe that you did all those paintings. They're so cool.'

'Thanks.' His compliments meant more to her than anything else right this minute. She searched his face and realised that he meant what he was saying. He really did like her work.

'That charcoal you did of Gerry was great.'

'It was just a sketch,' Abby said modestly.

'Are you and Gerry great friends? You seem really close,' Shay commented.

'Yes we are. In fact there is quite a big gang of us that are all best friends. I'm really lucky.'

'Tell me about them,' Shay said. He was really interested and wanted to know everything about Abby.

'Well, Gerry you've met. He's gay as I'm sure you've guessed, and his partner is Tom. You met him that same night.'

'Yeah I remember. He was slightly older?' Shay asked, squinting his nose up as he remembered the night a few months previously.

'You're cute when you concentrate,' Abby said smiling. 'Oh crap, did I say that out loud?'

Laughing, Shay nodded in response to her question and she relaxed.

'And yep, that was Tom. Good memory! They've been together for years and have one of the most solid relationships I know. They're great together. They live around the corner from me in Clontarf so I see a lot of them.'

'Gerry seems like fun,' Shay added.

'Yeah, he's as mad as a hatter. I love him terribly!' Their lattes arrived then and Abby paid the waitress. 'Then there is Grace and Liam who have a three year old son, Jack.'

'Is that the blonde or the dark one I met last week?' Shay said, remembering the two girls that were with Abby when they bumped into each other.

'Grace is the blonde one. She's amazing. She's just finished a six month course of chemotherapy and is in remission.'

'God that's tough. Is she okay?' Shay said with what seemed like genuine concern.

'Well, fingers crossed yes, for now anyhow. They're getting married this Christmas and I'm bridesmaid!'

'Big meringue dress?' Shay said with a laugh.

'Nah, Grace is so cool! She's letting us pick our own dresses. She's given us a colour and then after that the style will be our own. Tara is the dark girl you met last week, she's the other bridesmaid and she's married to Sean. That's the gang!'

'Are you all close?' Shay asked.

'Yep, we all meet once a week too for drinks. Usually on a Thursday night. Sometimes we go to Grace's for dinner – she's a great cook – or to Tom and Gerry's. Other than that we usually go to Duffy's in Malahide or the Cock Tavern in Swords.'

'That's great; Paddy and I have been mates since our first day of school. That's over thirty years now! Friends are important.'

'My dad always said that you could tell a lot about somebody by the friends they have,' Abby told Shay.

'How'd you mean?' Shay asked.

'Well, Dad reckons that if somebody doesn't have any friends there's usually a good reason. And you know what, over the years I've found that he's right,' Abby stated.

'Sounds like your dad is pretty insightful,' Shay commented. 'Thank God for Paddy!' He finished with a laugh.

After a few minutes Abby got a text message from Gerry saying to come quickly. Finishing their drinks, Abby and Shay promptly walked back to the stall.

'Here she is, the artist herself, Ms Abby Nolan. You are truly honoured that she is here today, as she often stays locked in her studio working for weeks!' Gerry dramatically informed the couple who were standing with him. He must have done a big build-up of Abby because they practically curtsied when she walked over and shook their hands. Giving Gerry an amused look, Abby asked the couple if she could help them.

'Well, we've just bought a house together,' the lady said with pride.

'Congratulations,' Abby replied.

'And we want to buy a piece of art for our bedroom,' she continued.

'This would be a wonderful investment, darling,' Gerry butted in, pointing to the largest and most expensive piece Abby had displayed.

'What do you have in mind?' Abby asked the couple. 'Is there something here that you like?'

'Well we really like this piece here,' the guy said, pointing to one of Abby's larger pieces. 'But I think it's probably out of my price range.'

'How much do you have to spend?' Abby asked gently.

'About three hundred?' he replied quietly.

The piece he had pointed to was priced similarly to the one she had sold the other day and couldn't let it go for less than a thousand. She explained this to the couple, and then directed them to a smaller piece, that was priced at 400 euro.

'It's lovely,' they both agreed. 'But still out of our range.'

Abby smiled at them and made a quick decision. 'Look, I'm having a good day. I'll let you guys have this piece for three hundred. Just don't tell your friends the price!'

The couple were thrilled and the deal was done. As soon as they had walked out of hearing distance, Abby, Shay and Gerry all started to jump up and down with delight.

'Right you guys, lunch is on me!' she declared. She practically floated to the restaurant with Shay and Gerry. Could things get any better? A new man that had huge potential, her art was finally selling and Grace was really well.

Chapter Twenty Seven

'So what's up?' Tom asked Liam. Gerry was over at Grace's going through some wedding plans. When they had started talking about flower arrangements Liam knew he was in way over his head and had quickly legged it to Tom's.

'Nothing why?' Liam responded.

'Oh, I don't know. Just thought that you looked a bit preoc-cupied. Is it the jar?' Tom asked bluntly.

Liam thought about it for a minute then replied, 'Yes and no.' Seeing Tom's questioning face he continued. 'I think about drinking at least once a week, sometimes once a day. It's always there and I need to respect that.'

'Anything I can do to help?' Tom asked.

'Nah. Nothing at all. Do you know, sometimes I wish I could go back in time, back to when I was in my late twenties and starting to knock them back a lot,' Liam said regretfully.

'What would you say to yourself if you could?' Tom asked. He was genuinely interested.

'Well I'd tell myself to slow down. Appreciate a drink for what it is and know when to walk away. I'd tell myself that if I didn't slow down, I'd have to give up alcohol for the rest of my life one day, and that it can be a real pain in the arse!'

'Do you think you'd listen to yourself?' Tom asked.

'Nah, I'd probably tell myself to fuck off then order another whiskey!' he admitted ruefully. They both started to laugh.

'Seriously though, Liam, I'm amazed you haven't been tempted to have one over the last couple of months. It must have been really tough watching Grace go through everything.'

'That's an understatement, mate. It scared the shit out of me I can tell you. There were days when she was really sick that I just wanted to run to the nearest bar and order a bottle of whiskey. The responsibility of taking care of her was enormous and blotting everything out with alcohol seemed like a good option,' Liam said truthfully.

'What stopped you?' Tom asked him.

'Grace and Jack. I love them both more than I need drink. I don't want to go back to the way I was a couple of years ago. It was shit. I barely lived really, just going through the motions with work, and then drinking myself silly each night. Sometimes I can't believe that I actually managed to write at all and get articles published.'

Tom shook his head in disbelief, 'I don't know how you did it either, Liam. I kept track of you when you disappeared in London. I bought any article that you had published and I have to tell you, they were all good.'

'Thanks Tom. Ma has them all. Every article I've ever written. When I was going through treatment she brought them into me and you know what, I didn't remember writing half of them,' Liam said, shaking his head in disbelief.

'How's the job going now?' Tom asked.

'Great. I seem to be able to get assignments easily enough and the money's good. It's different now though.'

'How so?' Tom asked.

'Well now I think about every job I take. I'm choosy about the kind of work I do. I want to write things that will make Jack proud of me in years to come. I've also started to think about money for the first time ever in my career,' he answered.

'It comes to us all eventually!' Tom said with a wry grin.

'I know. I was living a student's life for too long. But I want to get some money saved, you know, just in case the shit hits the fan again,' Liam looked sad again.

'By that do I take it you mean Grace getting sick again?' Tom said beginning to frown.

'Yeah. She's in remission now, but with AML there's a strong chance the cancer will grow back. Grace's back working again, but only part-time. Unfortunately she lost a lot of jobs in the last six months because she was sick, so it will take time to get back some of her clientele.'

'Things tight?' Tom asked with concern.

'We're getting by. We're not about to lose the apartment or anything crazy, so don't panic.' Liam told Tom. 'But with the wedding and everything we're not saving any money.'

'Welcome to Ireland in 2012.' Tom said wryly. 'I don't know too many young couples who have any savings when they have a mortgage and kids!'

'I know. I'm probably worrying unnecessarily, but if something were to happen to Grace again, I'd like to know I have the money to ensure she has the best possible care. Do you understand?'

Tom could see this was important to Liam. He wanted to help out. 'Look mate, I've some savings. How about a loan?' Tom said.

'Ah Tom, no. Thanks a million and all that, but hopefully we won't need any savings for years to come. As I said earlier, I'm just being overcautious. We've made some good cutbacks on unnecessary luxuries so are saving a few euros from that. And the good thing about my job and Grace's is that because our work's flexible we've been able to cut down Jack's crèche fees. He just goes a few afternoons a week now,' Liam said.

'Makes sense Liam. And sorry if this sounds patronising, but I'm proud of you mate. It makes me happy knowing that Grace and Jack are in such good hands. They're lucky to have you. And always remember, you ever need any money, you only have to ask,' Tom stated.

Liam was chuffed with Tom's words and gave him a quick hug of thanks. It was great being able to talk to Tom and share some of his fears. He knew that his conversations with Tom were never repeated to anyone, even Gerry. 'What about you guys, how's things with Gerry?' Liam asked. It felt like the old days, Tom and him shooting the breeze. It felt good.

'Ridiculous, hilarious, dramatic, romantic, you know what he's like. I've never been happier,' Tom declared with a big smile.

'Do you guys ever fight?' Liam asked Tom.

'God yes, we wouldn't be normal if we didn't. We fight about his visa bill all the time. He thinks if he hides it, then it will go away. We fight about our joint account, because there are always laser transactions for the most ridiculous things. We fight about my waistline! Gerry wants me to cut down on the booze and the cigars and the fat!'

'He has a point there, Tom,' Liam said softly.

'Don't you start, or you're out!' Tom replied, pointing to the door. 'It's bad enough getting it from Gerry every day. The worst thing is I know he's right. So starting from Monday I've promised I'd go on a diet. God help me!'

'God help all of us you mean!' Liam laughed. Tom's diets were legendary and whenever he went on one, his temper got very short!

'I'll ignore that remark Liam. Everyone knows my temperament is as sweet as candy!' Tom got up to refresh their coffees and came back a few minutes later with a piece of paper. 'I'm glad you came over tonight. I've something that I need to show you. I was just waiting for the right time.' He handed the document to Liam. It was a list of people.

'What is it?' Liam asked with a puzzled look.

'Well, remember we thought that Garda Robert Hegarty was a possible lead on Grace's paternity? Well we did a check on his blood type and like a good citizen he's a regular donor. His blood type is O negative and that makes it impossible that he is Grace's father.'

'Damn it,' Liam finished. He had planned on visiting Hegarty and demanding he get tested as a suitable donor if Grace got sick again. But these results put him in the clear.

Tom continued, 'Well, don't ask me where I got this, but I have a list – off the record of course – of all donors from the Wexford area with the correct blood type. That's it, narrowed down to all males aged forty plus. No point looking at any younger ones. And at first glance there are no names there that I recognised.'

Liam looked through the list, nothing jumping out at him either.

'As Grace has decided to let the issue of her father drop, I didn't want to upset her with this without talking to you first. And I want to be clear; if Catherine got pregnant by one of the hotel guests Grace's father could be just about anyone, and living anywhere in the world. He doesn't necessarily have to be on this list. It's just one possible avenue to explore,' Tom said.

'I know that Tom, but you obviously think there's something here that I'm missing if you are bringing it up to me now. Although Grace has reconciled herself to the fact that she'll probably never find her father right now, I haven't. I need to find a donor match just in case.'

'Well, I thought the same too Liam. And yesterday I got a break. I got a call from Mrs Doyle. She was the lady who lived next door to Catherine, remember?'

Liam nodded confirming he did remember.

'Well, when I visited her, I asked her did she know anyone by the name of Michael that Catherine used to hang around with,' Tom told Liam.

'Michael is the name Catherine said was Grace's father,' Liam murmured to himself.

'Yep, that's right. Well at the time I asked her, she had said no, she didn't remember anyone with that name. But then Mrs Doyle rang yesterday and she said that something had been niggling her about the name Michael for months. Then it came to her. She figured it meant nothing, but as she'd promised to ring me, she did just that,' Tom said.

'Come on tell me!' Liam said impatiently.

'Catherine did know a Michael – Fr O'Hara's real name is Michael. But he uses the name Joseph as a priest, as it's his second name.'

'Shit, Tom. That's huge. You don't think…' Liam couldn't finish the sentence.

'I don't know Liam, but it's a possibility. I didn't like the man when I met him. There was something about the way he spoke about Catherine that upset me, and Gerry too,' Tom said quietly.

'So what's the story with this?' Liam said, holding up the paper.

'Well, following my discussion with Mrs Doyle, I took the listing out again. I can't believe I didn't catch it before. Look halfway down the list.'

Liam scanned the names and then saw it, 'Mr O'Hara.'

'It could be a coincidence, the name,' Tom said hurriedly. 'If it had said Fr O'Hara I would have picked it up straightaway. Plus there are no initials, so it may not even be a Michael.'

'So what do we do?' Liam asked.

'Well, I'm going to get on to my contact in the donor agency to try and get some more information on this O'Hara guy. See if it's the same guy or not. If it is, we need to talk.'

'How soon can you do that?' Liam asked.

'Tomorrow morning. I'll give you a call as soon as I know,' Tom replied.

'Not a word to Grace though Tom until we know what we're dealing with,' Liam stated.

'Agreed.'

Chapter Twenty Eight

Tom and Gerry were sitting drinking coffee, waiting for Liam to arrive. Tom had started researching blood donors called 'O'Hara' in Ireland as soon as he got up that morning. The bell rang signalling Liam's arrival.

'Well, what did you find out?' Liam looked anxious.

'Come in and sit down. Coffee's ready,' Tom said, leading the way to their kitchen. 'Right, I checked the registrar this morning and I'm pretty much 99% certain that Fr Michael O'Hara has blood type O positive,' Tom told Liam.

'Which means?' Liam asked.

'It's possible that he's Grace's father,' Tom replied softly.

'Shit, shit, shit,' Liam couldn't find any other words to say.

'I know,' Gerry said. 'Tom and I are a bit shocked too.'

'You guys have met this priest. What's your gut?' Liam asked them.

'He's her father,' Gerry said bluntly. 'Something about him has bugged me ever since we met him but I couldn't figure out what it was. It came to me late last night. His eyes. He has Grace's eyes – they're bright green. The exact same as Grace's.'

'He woke me up to tell me. I can't believe we didn't notice it when we met him. All I can think is that I never for a moment supposed that Grace's father would be a priest. I wasn't looking at him as a possible suspect,' Tom admitted.

'Who the fuck would?' Liam said. 'Jesus guys, this is going to knock the stuffing out of Grace. What should we do?'

'It's just like *The Thorn Birds*,' Gerry said, and then shut up quickly, realising this wasn't the time for his movie speak. 'Sorry, force of habit.'

'The way I see it, we've a couple of options,' Tom said. 'We can go to Catherine and confront her with our suspicions first of all. Give her a chance to put her side of the story in first. Or we can go straight to Wexford and confront Fr O'Hara.'

Liam walked around the kitchen distractedly. He needed to think about this for a moment.

'He might just deny it,' Gerry said. 'We don't have any actual proof. Just circumstantial evidence.'

'That's true,' Tom agreed.

Liam looked up at the two of them. 'The way I see it, we owe it to Catherine to talk to her first. After all, it's her life we're messing in. What do you think?'

'Makes sense to me,' Tom concurred. 'Are you going to tell Grace?'

'I don't know, mate. I promised Grace that I'd never keep a secret from her again when we got back together. But I'm not sure she's strong enough to deal with this,' Liam said, concern written all over his face.

Tom's heart went out to Liam. 'You're not keeping something from her if you just delay telling her the information. As Gerry said, we don't have any actual proof yet. I don't think Grace would have a problem if you kept quiet for a few more days.'

'What do you think, Gerry?' Liam asked.

Gerry was chuffed that Liam asked his opinion. He knew that Liam valued Tom's opinion over anyone else's and it meant a lot to him that he wanted to hear what he had to say too. 'I think you'll only upset Grace by telling her this right now. She's got enough on her mind with the wedding. Let's keep this between ourselves until you speak to Catherine.'

'That means we don't tell Abby, Sean or Tara either though,' Liam said firmly. 'I don't want Grace to think we all had a little secret going on behind her back.'

'When are you going to contact Catherine?' Tom asked Liam. 'Don't envy you, mate.'

'No time like the present. I'll give her a call now. If she's available I'm going to drive to Meath and talk to her immediately. I can't leave this one hanging,' Liam replied.

'Understood. What will you say to her?' Tom asked.

'Just that I'm in the area, thought I'd drop in for a coffee,' Liam replied.

'Do you want company?' Tom asked.

'Would love it to be honest,' Liam said, relief flooding his face.

'You go, Tom,' Gerry told his partner before he asked him what he thought. 'You go for the drive with Liam. In fact you should drive. That way, Liam, you can concentrate on what to say to Catherine when you see her.'

Liam picked up his mobile and hit Catherine's number. She answered quickly and said she'd love to see him if he was in the area. She'd be in the teashop all day. Telling her they'd be there in a couple of hours, the guys jumped into Tom's car and headed off.

The closer to Meath they got the more nervous Liam felt. He wasn't quite sure how to ask Catherine about Fr O'Hara. Catherine was such a lady and it seemed rude to ask her about anything to do with sex. It would be like questioning his Ma about her sex life!

'We're almost here, mate,' Tom said. 'Shall I wait in the car?'

'I don't know, Tom. Maybe. She might feel threatened if both of us are there.'

'Righto. I'll stay here so. Come get me if you need some support,' Tom said, giving Liam a good-natured thump on his arm.

Liam jumped out of the car in front of Catherine's teashop. It was a lovely cottage, whitewashed with a bright red door and window frames. The aroma of freshly baked bread and scones that met you as you walked to the door was powerful and despite his nerves Liam felt his stomach groan in response. Before he had a chance to enter the shop, Catherine was running towards him, a big smile across her pretty face.

'Oh Liam, what a lovely surprise. What brings you to this area?' Catherine greeted him with arms outstretched.

Giving Catherine a warm hug, Liam was slightly surprised that he had grown to care for this woman and really didn't want to hurt her. 'Hi Catherine. Just a story I'm working on, that's all.'

'Come on in. I want you to meet everyone. Girls, this is Liam, my Grace's fiancé,' Catherine said with pride.

There were two women working in the shop with Catherine and Liam was quickly introduced. It was obvious that Catherine spoke about Grace and her family a lot, because the women seemed to know everything about their lives. He was touched.

'Now take a seat Liam. Let's have some tea,' Catherine said as she fussed over him. With that one of the women had brought over a tray of scones, clotted cream and strawberry jam and a large earthenware teapot.

'This looks lovely, Catherine,' Liam said truthfully. She beamed at the compliment. Liam thought about Tom in the car and it made him smile. He would have been in heaven right now!

'Scones are made fresh this morning. Now eat, we can catch up afterwards.'

Liam didn't know how Catherine kept her trim figure, because if he could bake like her he figured he'd be the size of an elephant. Despite his nerves he easily managed to scoff two scones, washed down with the strong sweet tea. When Catherine was satisfied that Liam was completely stuffed she led the way to the back of the shop to her private quarters. Her house was beautiful. The loving care that had been invested into it was obvious. If Liam's eyes didn't mistake him there were several antique pieces in the living room and fresh flowers – white, of course – were in a vase on the sideboard.

'You know it's amazing how alike you and Grace are,' Liam told Catherine. 'I suppose that proves the point that genes are more important than environment!'

'Oh I don't know, Liam. I think they both play an equal part. It tickles me that Grace resembles me so much and I can see so much of myself in her, when I was her age. But there's no denying the influence of Mick and Annie's upbringing.'

'That's true,' Liam nodded in agreement.

'So tell me all the news. How are Grace and Jack?' she asked.

'They're both fine, Catherine. Grace's up to her eyes preparing for the wedding. Gerry has her killed choosing colours and flowers and seating arrangements!'

'Have you chosen a wedding venue yet?' Catherine asked.

Liam realised that this would be a good chance to turn the subject in the direction of Grace's father. 'Well we've narrowed it down to a couple of places. We both want somewhere small and intimate as we're only having about fifty guests. We also want somewhere with its own chapel in the grounds,' Liam said.

'Oh, that sounds beautiful.' Catherine thought this idea was lovely.

'Well, one of the places we're thinking of is in Wexford. Rose Tree Manor,' Liam said.

He watched Catherine's reaction closely. The friendly open smile on her face froze and she looked more guarded all of a sudden. Liam felt lousy. She had no idea what was coming her way.

'Rose Tree Manor. That's a beautiful hotel. I used to work there you know,' Catherine said quietly.

Liam didn't know whether to let on that he knew she'd worked there, so decided to be non-committal for a while. 'Yes, it is beautiful. The chapel in the grounds is amazing too. Tom went to a wedding there years ago and said it was one of the most spectacular events he'd ever been to.'

'I can imagine,' Catherine said flatly.

'Look Catherine, Grace and I know that Rose Tree Manor is close by to Ballymichael. Would it bother you to be so close to home?' Liam asked.

'Ballymichael hasn't been my home for many years now, Liam,' Catherine said sadly. 'But if you and Grace want to get married in Rose Tree Manor, I would never try and stop you. Besides, I still have some friends in the area that I haven't seen in quite some time. I could use the wedding as an opportunity to catch up with them.' Catherine felt a little shaken at this reminder to her past. Ballymichael had so many sad memories for her. She knew that she should let them go, it had been over thirty years, but when she thought about Ballymichael it made her feel like a young woman in her twenties again – frightened and scared.

'I wonder if the Murtaghs are still there,' Catherine wondered out loud.

'Yes they are,' Liam responded. Then seeing Catherine's puzzled look, he explained, 'Tom and Gerry spent a weekend in Rose Tree Manor a couple of months ago. They met the Murtaghs. They mentioned that they knew you.'

'Oh I see,' Catherine started to frown. 'Why haven't you mentioned this to me before?'

Liam didn't have an answer to that. He reckoned the time had come to put all his cards on the table.

Chapter Twenty Nine

'Catherine, I haven't been totally honest with you. I'm not working in the area today; I came specifically to talk to you,' Liam said softly. Seeing the look of hurt cross Catherine's face made him feel like shit. But he was here now and needed to continue. 'Grace was terribly upset when you wouldn't tell her about her father,' Liam paused to let it sink in for a moment or two.

'Why must you keep bringing this up?' Catherine said agitatedly. She had begun to twist the ring on her finger.

'I'm sorry Catherine. We're not trying to hurt you, but please see it from Grace's point of view. She needed to find out more about where she came from. So Tom said that he would help by doing an investigation.'

A look of horror passed over Catherine's face. 'An investigation into my life, my background, I take it,' she said coldly.

Liam simply nodded, feeling lousier by the minute.

'And just what did Tom find out?' Catherine almost spat out.

'Catherine please try to understand why we did this. Grace felt that you were lying to her when you said you didn't know who her father was. It was an intuitive feeling, but she felt then, and still does today, that you were hiding something. And more importantly Catherine, we need to find Grace's father. If he has had any other children there is a strong possibility that they could be a donor match for Grace. If the cancer comes back…' Liam couldn't finish the sentence.

Catherine walked over to Liam and shook him by the shoulders, 'You stupid man. What do you take me for? I've lain awake at night thinking about Grace's cancer and the possibility that it will come back. I've thought about all kinds of ways to find a suitable match. I know that the best chance is with a sibling. For God's sake, if I thought for one moment that her father had any more children I would have told you a long time ago.'

Liam absorbed this information. His eyes never left Catherine's face and he could see fear then resignation wash over her.

'So what do you think you know? What has Tom found out?' Catherine said weakly.

'Grace and I never believed that you were the type of woman to get drunk and have a one-night stand with somebody you didn't know. It just didn't fit,' Liam said, feeling really bad.

'I could have changed. You have no idea what I was like back then,' Catherine challenged.

'We know. That's why Tom went to Rose Tree Manor to try to fill in some blanks. For what it's worth I'm really sorry we did it behind your back. But you wouldn't talk about Grace's father; our backs were against a wall.'

Catherine acknowledged this with a nod of her head.

'Tom spoke with Mr and Mrs Murtagh. He also spoke to Ann Dalton, Mrs Doyle, Garda Hegarty and Fr O'Hara.'

Catherine paled. 'Ann never told me,' she whispered.

'I'm sorry, but Tom did his investigation under subterfuge. He didn't divulge that he knew you and just made general enquiries about No. 3, your house, to get some information.'

'I see. And what did he find out in his "enquiries"?' Catherine asked, sarcasm dripping with every word.

'That you were pretty much the model citizen. Worked hard,

didn't drink, and didn't sleep around. Had only one real boyfriend, Robert Hegarty.'

'He's not Grace's father, if that's what your investigation has turned up. We never even slept together,' Catherine said bluntly.

Liam knew that even without the results he had of the blood tests, Catherine was speaking the truth. 'We know. We did think that maybe he was the father at first because he was the only name that kept coming up with yours romantically. But he has the wrong blood type.'

'Tom is very thorough,' Catherine said.

'Yes he is. Catherine we believe that Fr O'Hara is Grace's father,' Liam said as gently as he could.

Catherine sank into her armchair, putting her face in her hands. 'Does Grace know?' Catherine asked with horror.

Liam noted she hadn't denied it. 'No. Just Tom, Gerry and me. I thought it was only fair to come to you before we confronted Fr O'Hara.'

Catherine started to cry. Quietly, with her head in her hands. Liam did not know what to do.

'Are you okay?' he finally asked.

She looked up with a tear-stained face; she appeared to have aged ten years in the last few moments. 'No I am far from okay, Liam. You have no idea what you've discovered. Yes, Fr O'Hara is Grace's biological father. There, I've confirmed your suspicions. But he won't help Grace. He's an evil man, Liam. He may wear priest's clothing, but he's not a good man,' Catherine said, clearly agitated.

'Does he know that he's Grace's dad?' Liam asked quietly.

'Oh yes, but he won't admit it. Not in a million years. He's too much to lose.'

'Would he agree to a donor test?' Liam asked hopefully. 'Surely for his own daughter?'

'You're not getting it, Liam. He wanted me to have an abortion for God's sake. This from a man of God! He persuaded my father that I was evil and needed to be punished for my sins. My father kicked me out of my home and never spoke to me ever again. He died without talking to me in over twenty years. And Fr O'Hara was partly to blame for his stubbornness. This is the kind of man we're talking about!' Catherine ended on a sob.

'I'm so sorry, Catherine,' Liam said humbly.

Catherine got up and walked over to her drinks cabinet. She poured herself a brandy and sat back down.

'Are you going to tell Grace?' Catherine asked.

'I have to, Catherine. She has a right to know,' Liam replied gently.

'Why, what good will it do her? She's accepted that she'll probably never find out who her father is. Why can't you leave it?' Catherine begged.

'Because that's not my decision to make, Catherine. I think you should tell her. She'll understand. You were young; you fell in love with the wrong guy. It won't be the first time that's happened. She'll understand, I promise you,' Liam said. He stopped abruptly when he heard Catherine laugh. It was a cold mirthless laugh and he felt the hairs on the back of his neck go up.

'You think I had a relationship with that man? You actually believe I was in love with him? Liam, I was helping out at the church because I was thinking about becoming a nun. It was something I'd thought about for a couple of years, ever since I finished with Robert Hegarty. I asked Fr O'Hara for his advice,' Catherine replied coldly.

Liam nodded encouragingly at Catherine. Finally they were getting somewhere. She was opening up. But nothing prepared him for what she said next.

Tears were pouring down her face again as Catherine said, 'He raped me.'

At first Liam thought he'd misheard, she'd spoken so quietly. But she repeated the words again, stronger this time.

'The bastard raped me.'

With that the house of cards came tumbling down. Liam felt like somebody had punched him in the stomach. He couldn't bear to see Catherine in so much pain but didn't know what to do. He felt totally at a loss. He wanted to get in Tom's car and drive to Wexford straightaway and beat the shit out of this so-called priest. He wanted to kill him, God forgive him. Walking over to Catherine, he pulled her into his arms, saying over and over again, 'I'm so sorry. I'm so sorry.'

Finally her tears subsided. 'Now do you understand?' Catherine begged.

'I'm beginning to,' Liam said humbly.

'He destroyed my life, Liam. I trusted him implicitly, and then one day he tore that trust away and violated me in the worst possible way. I was a virgin. He took that from me, and then told me that it was my entire fault. He said I had tempted him, that I was sent by the Devil to tempt him. He told me that if I ever told anyone he'd deny it and paint me as a whore. I believed him.'

'Was there no one you could have spoken to?' Liam asked gently. 'Your cousin Ann? Your friend Mrs Murtagh?'

'You're talking about Ireland in 1980, Liam. Back then the Church was absolute. There were none of these sex scandals that you have today. Not openly talked about anyhow. To accuse a priest of something like that would have been tantamount to suicide. I tried to tell Ann once. But I couldn't find the words.'

'I can't imagine what it must have been like for you. Did it ever happen again?' Liam asked.

'No, I stopped doing the flowers for the church immediately and as you can imagine any thoughts of joining a convent vanished. I felt that God had forsaken me,' Catherine said.

'What happened when you found out you were pregnant?' Liam asked gently.

'I went to see him. He always acted like nothing had happened if I met him in the street. But when I told him I was pregnant his calm facade disappeared. He accused me of being a whore, sleeping with customers at the hotel. He denied being the father. But he knew. He knew that when I told him I'd never had sex with anyone before or after him, that I was speaking the truth,' Catherine replied, anger creeping into her voice with every word.

'Is that when he suggested an abortion?' Liam asked.

'Yes. He said there were places in the U.K. that could help me. He never actually used the word abortion – he was too clever for that – he just delicately suggested that "relieving myself" of the problem would be the best all round.'

'Bastard,' Liam said. He wanted to punch something.

'Yes that he was,' Catherine said sadly. 'The thing that killed me most was my own father's reaction. Telling my parents that I was pregnant was the hardest thing I've ever done, with the exception of giving up Grace. They took it really badly. My father just got up and walked into the living room, closing the door, and didn't reappear for a couple of hours. When he did, he demanded to know who the father was. When I couldn't say, he went mental, breaking up the room, throwing delph and ornaments. My mother and I had to run next door to Mrs Doyle's.'

Liam hadn't thought about what it was like for Catherine to tell her parents. He made a promise to himself that no matter what Jack did in the future, he'd always be on his side.

'Do you know what the irony was? It was Fr O'Hara that my mother called for help to calm Dad down. He came in wearing his cassock with the Bible in his hand. He had the audacity to walk over to me, put his hand on my head and say "May God forgive you", before walking into the living room to talk to Dad.

206

He convinced Dad that the Devil had been at work and that I must be punished for my sins.'

'How could you keep quiet? Surely you felt like telling them the truth?' Liam said.

'You'd think, wouldn't you? I'm not proud of how weak I was Liam. But I was scared. I didn't think anyone would believe me. In fact it may have been worse if they believed me. I think if my Dad had known the truth it may have just killed him.' Catherine walked into the kitchen and put the kettle on. Liam followed her. 'I'm sorry. I'm sure you could use a coffee.' She smiled weakly.

Liam watched her as she began laying a tray. He wasn't sure he even wanted a coffee but was glad of the distraction for a few moments. He needed to straighten his head.

When they were back in the living room, sipping their drinks, he asked, 'What do you want to do now Catherine?'

'About Grace?' Catherine asked.

Liam nodded.

'I don't know, Liam. Do you think that she would want to know that she was born as the result of a rape? Do you think that she could cope with that?' Catherine asked in a small voice.

Liam didn't have an answer for that, so kept quiet.

'That's why I didn't want to meet her before,' Catherine said quietly. 'I was so afraid that when I'd see her, all I'd remember was the horror of the rape. I was terrified that I couldn't love her.'

Liam felt tears sting his eyes as he watched this woman, who he'd grown to love as a mother-in-law, in so much pain.

'I lost so many years because of that, Liam,' Catherine said, silently weeping.

'How do you feel when you see Grace now?' Liam asked.

'Full of love. I thank God every day for bringing her back into my life, giving me a second chance to get to know my child,' Catherine answered passionately.

'Catherine, it's your decision. I'm sorry for not trusting you before. I hope you can forgive us for our deceit, but we did it out of love for Grace,' Liam stated.

'Don't be silly. You've nothing to be sorry for Liam. None of you have. I can understand why Grace needed to know. But I need to think about this for a while. Can you keep it to yourselves for a few days? You were right earlier; if Grace is to find out, it needs to be me who tells her.'

Liam agreed. After a few more minutes he felt it was time to go. He had a feeling that Catherine needed to be alone for a while. She looked punch-drunk and he was so sorry that he had caused her this distress. Kissing him absently on his cheek, she promised she would call in a couple of days.

Chapter Thirty

Tom had never seen such a mixture of anger and sorrow on Liam's face ever before. He jumped in the car thumping the dashboard.

'I need a fucking drink, man,' Liam said with a look that Tom had never seen before.

'I take it things didn't go well so?' Tom asked dryly.

'You have no fucking idea.' Liam looked at his friend and said, 'He fucking raped her, man. He only fucking raped her.'

'Ah Jaysus, no. Fr O'Hara? Tom asked.

'Yes, the one and only. I've never wanted a drink as bad as I do right now, Tom,' Liam said, putting his face in his hands.

Tom started the car. He had been for a scout about earlier on and there was a forest a couple of miles away. Tom figured this would be a good place to go so that Liam could let some steam off. As he drove there, Liam kept cursing and hitting the dashboard, not making much sense. When they arrived at the local beauty spot, Tom was relieved that it was pretty much empty.

'Come on mate. Let's go for a walk. Try and burn off some of that anger of yours,' Tom said.

Liam jumped out of the car and walked furiously on to the forest trail, with Tom panting and puffing behind him. After about ten minutes of this fast pace, Tom finally bent down, exhausted.

'Ah Jaysus, Liam. Hold on there a minute. I'm about to die here.'

Liam turned around and took one look at his best mate's red face, the sweat pouring down it, and started to laugh. 'Oh God I'm sorry Tom. I was just so pent-up.'

'It's all right. But can we take a pew for a few minutes?' Tom lowered himself on to the bench that was at the side of the trail. Liam came back and sat beside him.

'That was awful man. She's in bits back there,' Liam said.

'What happened?' Tom asked.

Liam relayed their conversation to Tom, leaving nothing out.

'The poor woman. No wonder she's never gone back to Ballymichael. Do you think she'll tell Grace?' Tom said.

'Yes I think she will. She just needs a couple of days to adjust to the situation. I'm all over the place about it myself. I can't bear to think how it will affect Grace.'

'If she decides to keep it secret, will you tell Grace?' Tom asked.

'I don't know. I don't fucking know, Tom. What would you do?'

'No idea, Liam. I agree with you that Grace has a right to know. But this could really mess her head up. With everything she's been through already maybe we should just keep it to ourselves,' Tom said.

'How the hell did things get so complicated?' Liam asked his friend sorrowfully.

Tom didn't know and threw his arm loosely around Liam's shoulder. It must have been hell for him in there confronting Catherine. Selfishly, he was glad he hadn't been in the room.

'You're not going to go run to the nearest pub are you?' Tom asked with concern.

Liam grinned wryly, 'Nah. Don't worry. It was tough in there, but you know what, if I can watch Grace go through cancer and do it without a jar, I can pretty much cope with anything. It's a reflex for me; put me in a stressful situation and I'll automatically want a drink. I'm all right now. Still, think I might go to a meeting later tonight.'

Tom was once again stunned by how mature Liam had become.

He was so proud of him. 'Come on mate. Let's get going. But this time promise me no marathons, okay? Let's try a nice gentle stroll, take the time to smell the coffee!' Tom declared.

****

They arrived back to Dublin by late afternoon and Liam collected his car from outside Tom's.

'I'm going to head off, man. I want to go see Grace and give her a hug,' Liam said.

'You go do that mate,' Tom replied.

'Thanks, Tom. I owe you,' Liam said seriously.

'You owe nothing. Now go give Grace a kiss for me,' Tom replied.

Liam drove home quickly, stopping at a florist on the way to pick up a bunch of roses for Grace and a Spider-Man toy for Jack. Walking into the living room he found Grace lying fast asleep on their leather couch, a bridal magazine on her lap. She was beginning to look like her old self and had put on some weight. It suited her. Liam felt his breath catch in his mouth. It surprised him sometimes the depth of his feelings for this woman. Kneeling down beside her, he caressed her cheek. She opened her eyes sleepily, looking a little dazed, and then catching sight of Liam, she threw her arms around his neck, whispering his name softly. He put the flowers on the floor and started to kiss Grace softly, then more urgently as their passion grew. He lifted her sweater over her shoulders and kissed her neck softly. Grace began to undo the buttons on his shirt and they started to make love quickly and passionately on the couch.

'I love you, Grace Devlin,' Liam whispered in her ear, as she moaned softly when he entered her.

'I love you too darling,' Grace whispered back. They climaxed together and lay quietly for a few moments in each other's arms.

Turning to face Liam, Grace said mischievously, 'Can you wake me up like that every afternoon I take a nap?'

'That can be arranged, babe. You'll be sorry you said that!' Liam said with an exaggerated leer.

'Did you have a good day, honey?' Grace asked him as she slowly played with his hair.

'Could have been better, but I'm feeling a whole lot happier now, babe. What about you?' Liam felt his conscience prick him as he averted telling Grace the truth.

'I had a great day thank you. Catherine rang about an hour ago,' Grace replied.

'Oh?' Liam said with a start. 'What did she want?'

'Just to say that she loved me. Wasn't that nice?' Grace said smiling.

'Yes it was, babe. She's a nice woman,' Liam said sincerely.

'Mmm. And I managed to get a new contract too. Mrs Williams has asked me to do her baby's nursery. I did her living room about a year ago,' Grace continued.

'That's great, babe. I knew you'd start getting calls again,' Liam said.

'Abby called around this morning too. Oh Liam she's so happy. She's met this new guy called Shay and they're inseparable. I've never seen her happier.'

'That's cool. I could never understand why Abby wasn't snapped up ages ago. What's this guy like?' Liam said.

'He's the architect guy – remember from the speed dating?' Grace said.

Liam thought for a moment, then said, 'No, doesn't ring a bell.'

'God you men are terrible! Sean was the same. He couldn't remember him either!' Grace said giggling.

'Sure we never met him, why would we remember him?' Liam asked puzzled.

'Well you'll get the chance this weekend. We're all going out on Saturday night. Abby wants everyone to go for dinner. I've asked your Mam and she said she'll have Jack for a sleepover,' Grace told him.

'Fantastic. So we'll have the house to ourselves! Maybe we'll skip dinner and stay at home!' Liam said, grabbing Grace.

'Down boy!' she said half-jokingly. She knew what he meant though. While she was ill she couldn't face having sex, but now that she was in remission she was feeling great and they were trying to take advantage of every spare moment. Problem was a certain three-year-old boy who had a habit of walking into their room during the night for a cuddle! He had almost caught them having sex a few weeks ago and frightened the life out of them. But neither of them was complaining. Things had never been so good between them. Grace worried sometimes that she felt too happy. She worried that things couldn't keep going as well as they were right now. But there wasn't time for those thoughts at the moment.

'Come on lover. It's almost time to collect Jack from Montessori!'

Chapter Thirty One

Sean and Tara were in Siam's, a Thai restaurant in Malahide, waiting for everyone else to arrive. Tonight they were going to meet Shay properly. Tara and Grace had already met him a couple of weeks ago but didn't really get a chance to talk to him. Thankfully Tara was off her Atkins diet; she couldn't stand not eating carbs for the rest of her life, so things were back to normal. She already knew what she was going to order – tempura for starters followed by Thai green curry. Delicious!

Sean watched his wife with a grin on his face. He could tell she was thinking about food. There was always a certain glint in her eye when she did! It was good to see her smiling too. It had been another disappointing month for them both. Last week Tara had got her period once again. The thing that worried him the most was that she had seemed resigned to its presence. Through their work both of them saw babies and expectant mothers all the time. Only today he'd confirmed a pregnancy to a deliriously happy young woman. He couldn't help but wonder what it would feel like to hear the news that he was to become a father. He knew that this was so hard on Tara; he witnessed the crushing devastation the negative pregnancy tests left on his wife every month. They had finally looked for help and had both gone through the gauntlet of tests, only to be told that they had no physical problems as to why they had not conceived. This in itself was extremely good news, but also extremely frustrating as it meant they had no magic solution to solving the mystery why they had not succeeded.

'What you thinking about?' Tara asked her husband. 'You okay, babe?'

'I'm fine. Just wondering if this is the real thing with Abby and Shay?' he quickly lied.

'Don't know, Sean. According to Abby it's going fantastically. It'll be interesting to see how they are together. And don't forget to remind Grace that she's due a check-up with you,' Tara said.

'I know. I did call her on Monday and she promised to make an appointment, which of course she didn't. So I've taken the decision out of her hands and scheduled her in for an appointment on Monday morning. Like it or lump it!' Sean replied.

Tara leaned in and kissed her husband in approval. Even though Grace was feeling fantastic right now, it was important she kept her routine check-ups.

Tom and Gerry were the next to arrive. There were the usual theatrical air kisses between Tara and Gerry, while the boys manfully shook hands.

'Darling, you're looking ravishing tonight. And you don't look too bad either Tara!' Gerry quipped, blowing a kiss at Sean. He loved to rile Sean any chance he could. He knew that over the top 'gayness' made him feel slightly threatened. Although he'd never admit it.

'Leave Sean alone,' Tom told Gerry with a laugh. 'Now let's get the drinks in.' He beckoned the waiter over and ordered a couple of vodka tonics for himself and Gerry. Tara and Sean were already sipping their drinks.

Then Grace and Liam arrived, looking a little bit ruffled.

'You haven't been at it again, have you?' Tara whispered to her friend.

Nodding, Grace replied, 'You're just jealous!'

'Too right I am! Do you two ever stop?' Tara said with a giggle.

'That's enough whispering from you two,' Tom commanded. 'Now listen to me. When Abby asks us later on what we think of Shay, here's what we're all to do.'

Gerry smiled at Tom as he relayed his plan to everyone. He had schemed all the way to the restaurant in the taxi. No sooner had he finished instructing everyone when the couple of the night walked in. Abby looked like the cat who'd got the cream and Shay looked pretty much the same, albeit a little bit worried as well.

'Hi everyone. This is Shay,' Abby announced proudly.

'Shay, you remember Grace and Tara? Well this is Liam – Grace's fiancé – and Sean – Tara's husband.' Shay walked over and shook hands with the guys and bent down to give the girls a peck on the cheek. 'And this is Tom, Gerry you've met.' Shay shook each of their hands too and looked slightly taken aback when Gerry jumped up and kissed him on the cheek!

'Just treat him like one of the girls, mate,' Tom said with a laugh.

'Darling you look gorgeous as usual,' Gerry said as Abby sat down beside him.

'Thank you, Gerry. You look stunning too. So handsome and debonair.' Gerry practically preened himself as she spoke.

Their waiter came and took the drinks orders, leaving the gang to select their choices from the extensive menu. They'd all eaten there before; it was a favourite haunt, so they knew the food would be good. When the orders were given, Tom turned to Shay and asked. 'You're an architect I believe?'

'Yes, that's right,' Shay said a bit shyly. He knew that everyone was watching him closely and he didn't want to let Abby down in any way.

'What type of work do you do? Commercial or residential?' Tom asked.

'Well our firm does pretty much anything, but I tend to work on the residential side mainly. One of a kind houses that are a little bit special.'

'Where money's no object?' Tom enquired.

'Yeah, something like that. It's challenging sometimes to come up with new concepts for my clients, but I love it,' Shay replied.

'Darling, how perfect,' Gerry exclaimed loudly to Abby. 'Just think of the house he'd design for you two if you get married!'

Abby thought she would die of embarrassment and quickly looked to Shay to apologise, but he was just laughing. Thank God, she thought, he's taken it the right way! Soon Grace and Shay were deep in conversation about some of the houses he had designed and Grace had done the interiors on. They had a lot in common. Abby was chuffed to see her friends all take to Shay so easily. He was fitting in just fine. Their starters arrived and as always in Siam's, all conversation stopped for a few moments as all thoughts went to consuming the beautiful food laid out in front of them. When the starters were finished and everyone's glasses of wine were topped up, conversation resumed. Soon talk turned to Grace and Liam's wedding.

'You should see Jack's tuxedo,' Grace told the group. 'Gerry and I bought it today in Debenhams. It is absolutely gorgeous on him. He looks so cute.'

'Did he mind trying them on?' Tara asked.

'Did he what?' Liam joined in. 'He went mad. It was only when I said he could wear his Spider-Man t-shirt underneath, that he agreed to it!'

'Darlings, I was worried for a moment! I thought he was going to insist on walking Grace down the aisle in red tights with webs dangling from his hands!'

Everyone laughed with Gerry at this image.

'Well if so, we could always have had a fancy dress wedding,'

Grace said with a grin, turning to Tom. 'You could have worn your Robin outfit again!'

Tom acknowledged this by simply sticking his tongue out at Grace.

'By the way, you'll all be pleased to know that the venue's booked,' Gerry informed the group. 'They decided upon Rose Tree Manor. December 24th, all set.'

Everyone clapped and whooped with delight, Tom shouting the waiter to bring some champagne.

'Didn't Catherine mind?' Tara asked.

'No, she rang yesterday and said she thought I should definitely have the wedding there. She said it was perfect and that she'd call her friends, the Murtaghs, to make sure we got the best treatment.'

Tom, Gerry and Liam exchanged glances. 'When are you seeing her again, darling?' Gerry asked.

'Well, she said she'd be up in a couple of weeks or so. What did she say to you Liam when she called?' Grace asked her fiancé.

'Just that, babe. She's going to come for a visit soon.' With a slight nod of his head to the guys, Tom realised that Catherine had made her decision and was going to tell Grace.

There were some people in this world that bad things happened to. There was always a drama of some kind in their lives, and Tom sadly realised that Grace was one of those people. He met people like that a lot in his work. Some of the stories of horror he'd come across in the past would make the hair stand on the back of your neck. But Grace was strong. She'd taken every knock in the past and come through it. Losing her parents, Liam's drinking, raising Jack alone for his first years, surviving cancer. She'd learn to live with the horror of Catherine's rape. He knew it.

'Tom, whatever is the matter. You're staring at me very strangely!' Grace said self-consciously.

'Sorry pet. Didn't mean to. Just thinking how lovely you're looking tonight that's all.'

'You're forgiven so!' Grace said with a beautiful smile.

Shay excused himself then to go to the bathroom. As soon as he left, Abby turned to the group and asked them excitedly what they thought of him, as they knew she would. Six faces stared back at her silently. She couldn't believe it. She thought they'd be praising him immediately. They really seemed to like him.

'Gerry, you've met him already. Do you still love him?' she asked smiling.

'Darling, there's something about the way his eyes keep shifting around that worries me,' Gerry replied dramatically.

'Grace, Tara, you liked him right? You both said he was lovely that first night,' Abby turned to the girls.

'His laugh is a bit false don't you think, Tara?' Grace said, to which Tara agreed.

'A man with a false laugh is always a worry,' Tara replied sagely, to which the entire table nodded their assent solemnly as if she had spoken words of wisdom worthy of the Dalai Lama!

'Tom?' Abby turned feeling panicky.

'His eyebrows are really bushy. Very sinister looking,' Tom replied.

'Sean, Liam? Guys come on; I know you all liked him.'

One by one they all shook their heads. Abby looked distraught and couldn't believe what she was hearing. Then looking at their faces again she could see that they were all struggling not to laugh.

'You little shits!' she said crossly. 'You're having me on!'

'That we are darling,' Gerry exclaimed, giving his friend a quick kiss. 'We love him. He's perfect, isn't he everyone?'

With that, the group all started telling Abby how much they liked Shay, going quiet really quickly when he returned to the table.

'Well do I pass?' Shay asked the group. Seeing their faces, he continued with a grin, 'I assume you were all letting Abby know what you thought about me! Will I do or should I pack my bags and go now?'

'They love you!' Abby said with a laugh.

'Thank God for that! I'd hate to get on the wrong side of you lot!' he finished with a laugh.

'We're not that scary are we?' Tom asked him.

'Yes we are!' Liam replied. 'I can remember the first time Grace introduced me to Tara and Abby. That was terrifying! Talk about the Spanish Inquisition!'

'Wimp,' Tara said with a grin.

'Now I've just got to get through Sunday!' Shay said with a mock groan.

'What's happening on Sunday?' Grace asked.

'He's coming to my parents with me for Sunday lunch,' Abby declared. To which the group erupted into whoops of laughter. To their knowledge, Abby had never taken any guy home. She must really be smitten.

'Watch out for her dad, mate,' Tom said to Shay. 'He's been known to meet guys at the door with a shotgun!'

'And you better take a couple of Rennies too; her Ma is a terrible cook!' Liam added.

'What about those brothers of hers?' Sean threw in for good measure.

'You all finished?' Abby asked them with a laugh. 'Don't worry Shay, Dad never shoots the guys the first time he meets them!'

The meal continued with lots of chatter and laughter and the friends all had a great night. As Abby and Shay picked up their coats to go, Grace whispered to her, 'This one's a keeper. I can tell. Give me a call in the morning so we can have a proper gossip!'

Tom shouted to Shay as he was leaving, 'Join us for a jar some Thursday.'

Abby couldn't have been happier, the night had been a complete success.

Chapter Thirty Two

Catherine was spending the weekend with Grace and Liam. She had been avoiding them for weeks now, afraid to finally confess to Grace who her father was. Liam had called her and said he would have to talk to Grace if she didn't talk to her soon. Catherine didn't have any plan formulated. She laughed ruefully to herself when she realised this; she had spent the last four weeks thinking about little else. Every possible scenario played through her mind, what she would say and how Grace would respond. But now that she was driving to Grace's apartment in Swords, the words were all muddled in her brain. She couldn't get them straight in her mind. Half an hour later she was sitting in Grace's living room, listening to Jack tell a story about his best friend in Montessori.

'Ben met Mickey Mouse,' he said excitedly.

'Well it won't be too long and you'll be in Disneyland too pet, and that's where Mickey Mouse lives,' Catherine told him with a fond smile.

'Do you think Mickey Mouse will give me a kiss too, Mommy?' Jack said turning to Grace.

'Of course he will sweetie-pie. But only if you're a good boy!'

They spent a lovely afternoon together chatting away about the forthcoming wedding. Liam came home from a meeting with his editor later that evening.

'Dinner's ready!' he said with a grin when he walked into the sitting room with two bags. He'd stopped for an Indian takeaway on the way home.

'You're not eating very much, Catherine. Are you okay?' Grace asked with concern when she realised Catherine had only been playing with her food.

'Oh I'm grand pet, don't be worrying. Just not that hungry.'

Liam glanced at her quickly and his heart went out to Catherine. He knew what she was thinking about.

After eating, they all watched some TV together and then Grace took Jack upstairs to bed.

'Are you going to tell her tonight?' Liam asked Catherine as soon as Grace had left the room.

'I'm not sure I can,' Catherine replied.

'Of course you can Catherine. You have to,' Liam said firmly.

'That's easy for you to say, Liam. Are you so sure that Grace needs to know? What good will it do?'

'I don't think Grace needs to know Catherine. But she has the right to know. We can't keep it from her. It wouldn't be right,' Liam replied.

'Why not? If Tom hadn't gone snooping around Ballymichael, none of you would know,' Catherine said.

'But he did go "snooping", Catherine. We can't pretend that we didn't have that conversation a month ago. It's not fair expecting me to keep this from Grace,' Liam said once again.

'Keep what from me?' Grace interrupted them both, a curious look on her face. 'What kind of surprise are you two cooking up for me now?' Then taking a look closely at both their faces, Grace realised that whatever they were talking about, it wasn't a good thing. 'What's going on? Liam?' Grace said worriedly.

'Catherine has some news for you, Grace. Come over here babe and sit down beside me,' Liam said, beckoning her over.

'I'm fine where I am,' Grace replied, standing firmly in her spot by the door. 'Catherine, what have you got to tell me?' Grace was beginning to get worried. Catherine and Liam looked so nervous; she began to imagine all sorts of things. 'Oh my God, you're not ill are you Catherine?'

'No pet, I'm not ill. Sit down and I'll tell you,' Catherine replied immediately.

'Thank God. Come on, whatever it is, it can't be that bad,' Grace said with a sigh of relief.

Grace noted the look that passed between Catherine and Liam and felt worried all over again.

'It's about your father, Grace,' Catherine began quietly.

Seeing the puzzled look on Grace's face, Liam clarified, 'Not Mick. Your real father.'

'I thought you didn't know who it is,' Grace accused Catherine.

'I lied to you, Grace. Although I think you already guessed that. I've always known who your father is, but couldn't tell you,' Catherine replied.

Grace couldn't believe her ears. She felt a big smile begin to creep up her face. This was fantastic news. She was going to find out who her father was at last. Walking over to Liam, she sat down beside him saying, 'This is huge. My heart is beating so fast! I can't believe I'm going to find out at last where I came from.'

'Try to calm down, babe. This isn't easy for Catherine,' Liam said, grabbing her hand.

'I'm sorry Catherine. I just got so excited. Please go on,' Grace said with a smile.

'This is very hard for me, Grace. I've been very scared to tell you the truth,' Catherine said in a small voice.

'Why? Look Catherine, nothing you can say to me will shock me. I promise you.'

'I hope you feel the same way when I've told you my story. Liam's told me that Tom looked into my background.'

Grace looked at Liam accusingly. When had he told Catherine this? 'It seems there have been a few secrets going on around here.'

Liam mouthed 'Sorry.'

Catherine continued, 'Liam came to see me about a month ago. He and Tom had discovered something about your father and wanted to check it out with me.'

Grace absorbed this information. She kept quiet although she had plenty of questions running around her mind.

'I asked Liam and Tom to keep quiet about the conversation we had so that I could get myself together. I wanted to tell you myself.' Catherine stood up and walked over to Grace, sitting on the other side of her. 'There was a reason why I didn't want to tell you previously about your father, Grace. It was a difficult and painful memory for me and one I've tried hard to bury for years. This is going to be hard for you to accept Grace and I'm so sorry that you have to hear it,' Catherine said seriously.

Grace had paled as she listened to Catherine speak and she realised that whatever she was going to hear now would change her life completely. Glancing at Liam, he too looked really worried.

'I know Tom told you that I hadn't really had any boyfriends back then and was basically a good girl.'

Grace nodded in response.

'Well that was true. Back then I only ever went out with one guy. Robert Hegarty.'

'Did you love him?' Grace asked her mother.

'No pet. I'm not sure I've ever loved a man to be honest. Robert was a kind man and he was very good to me, but I didn't love him. He's not your father, Grace.' Catherine was concerned that Grace still harboured this possibility.

'I know that,' Grace replied. 'So who is?'

'I was raped Grace.' Catherine watched her daughter's face

closely and saw the shock register with a sharp blow. Grace stood up and started to pace the room.

'Raped?' Grace asked with a small voice. This she hadn't been prepared for. 'My father is a rapist?'

'Yes,' Catherine said softly.

'Did you know him?' Grace asked, horror written all over her face. She felt that now all-too familiar feeling of being completely winded, as if being hit by a truck. Bang! There it was again.

'Yes, I knew him Grace,' Catherine replied.

'Who is he?' Grace asked quietly.

'Are you really sure you want to know? Just think about this for a moment, Grace. Who he is isn't important. Your father was Mick Devlin. That will never change. The man who raped me is nobody. Believe me he isn't worthy of one moment of your thoughts,' Catherine said fervently.

Grace looked at her mother in horror. She couldn't believe what she had just heard. Her mind was racing and she didn't know what to think.

'Are you okay, babe?' Liam asked her.

She looked at him and bit back a sarcastic response. She was annoyed with him but knew that more than likely she was being unfair. She knew that he hadn't done anything wrong and if he'd spoken to Catherine behind her back, he did it with only good intentions. She walked towards the door. 'I'm going for a walk. I need to clear my mind.' Liam made to get up but Grace stopped him, 'No Liam, I don't want any company. Stay with Catherine.' As she got to the door, she paused and turned back into the room towards Catherine, 'I'm not annoyed with you, okay? I just need some time; I'll be back soon.'

Grabbing her coat and bag, Grace walked out the door. Liam knew that it was better to let her go. As it was raining Grace decided to go to her local pub down the road. She hadn't really planned where she would go when she walked out of the apartment, she just knew that she needed to get out for a while. She needed some time alone to try to absorb the information she had just been given. Walking up to the bar, she asked for a brandy and ginger. She spotted a quiet corner and walked over with her drink. For one surreal moment she wondered if she had just dreamt the previous conversation. Had Catherine told her she'd been raped? Fuck. This was a nightmare. Who could have done such a thing? A hotel guest? Somebody from Ballymichael? A family member? God, it could be anyone. A cold shiver ran over her body when she thought about it. Poor Catherine. How awful it must have been for her. She couldn't comprehend it. Catherine had said that maybe she shouldn't know who the bastard was who did this to her. But surely she needed to know who he was. What if she bumped into him and didn't realise who he was? A single tear fell down her cheek. How she wished her Mam and Dad were alive. She'd love to ask them what to do. They'd know what she should do, they always had. She knew she couldn't hide out here forever, so she swallowed her drink and started to walk home.

It had stopped raining and she looked up to the sky. A rainbow was shining brightly. 'Oh Mam and Dad! Is that you beyond the rainbow's end?' she whispered. 'I don't know what to do.' She thought of their faces and felt their love envelop her. And then she thought of Catherine, her mother too, and she realised she loved her and she knew she had to get back quickly to give her a hug. She couldn't imagine what it must have been like for her.

Chapter Thirty Three

'Where do you think she's gone?' Catherine asked for the tenth time in the last half hour. She was pacing the floor of the apartment.

'She'll be back,' Liam assured her. 'It's a lot for her to take in. Give her a chance to absorb the information.' Liam was trying to keep Catherine calm. She was beside herself. He was worried too but was trying to keep that to himself. God alone knew what was going through Grace's mind. It was with great relief that he heard the key turn in the lock. Running to the hall, he pulled Grace into his arms. 'You okay babe?'

'I'm fine, Liam. Sorry for the dramatic exit,' Grace apologised. 'Is Catherine okay?'

Catherine had walked to the door and answered Grace herself, 'I'm grand, pet. Just so very worried about you.'

'Well don't be, Catherine. None of this is your fault. I can understand why you didn't want to tell me before. It must have been very hard for you to tell me. Thank you for being so brave.' She walked over to her and pulled her into her arms for a hug. She actually felt her mother sag with relief. She suddenly felt very frail to her and Grace became aware for the first time that Catherine was almost sixty. 'Liam, make some tea please. I think we could both do with some. Come on in Catherine. Let's sit down.'

Liam was once again amazed by his fiancée. She was taking control and looking after Catherine. She seemed to have digested the information about the rape and dealt with it in the course of the twenty minutes or so she'd been gone.

'Was the man who raped you from Ballymichael?' Grace asked. Catherine nodded.

'Did you know him well?' Grace continued.

'Yes. He was a friend to my family. I trusted him,' Catherine confirmed.

'Did you have any kind of relationship with him?' Grace further probed.

'Other than as a friend, no. He overpowered me. He gave me no choice, Grace.' This, Catherine answered very firmly.

'Catherine please don't ever feel the need to convince me of that. I believe you absolutely. I'm just trying to build a picture up in my mind. Are you okay to talk about this Catherine? We can stop if it's too much,' Grace asked.

'No I'm fine. You have a right to know and maybe it's time I got rid of some ghosts. I've kept this secret to myself for your whole lifetime, Grace. I tried to tell Ann – my cousin – once but it was too hard. So I kept it quiet,' Catherine said sadly.

'What happened when you found out you were pregnant?' Grace asked her gently.

'I told my family, but they didn't handle it very well. My dad threw me out when I wouldn't reveal who the father was.'

Grace felt that she was probably getting an abbreviated version of events from Catherine. She was trying to soften the blow of the story. Grabbing Catherine's hand to show her support, Grace listened as Catherine told the story of how she left Ballymichael and ended up in Dublin, finally giving Grace up for adoption.

Liam came in with a tray with a pot of coffee and tea on it. Pouring drinks for everyone, he sat opposite them.

'Why didn't you tell your dad that you'd been raped? Surely he would have supported you then?' Grace asked with dismay.

'I was scared, Grace. I felt ashamed that I'd been raped, like somehow it was my fault. I felt ashamed that I'd got pregnant and knew it was going to bring shame on my family. I didn't know what to do.'

Although Liam had heard this before he still felt a surge of anger on Catherine's behalf. He could see that Grace was feeling the same anger too.

'You said it was a family friend. A friend of your father's?' Grace asked.

Catherine nodded in response.

'Did he know you were pregnant?' Grace asked her.

'Yes, he did. In fact my father spoke to him about it when I told my parents I was pregnant,' Catherine replied.

'What did he do?' Grace asked, horrified.

Catherine hesitated and wondered how much she should say.

'Please tell me, Catherine,' Grace guessed her thoughts. 'I can take it, honestly.'

'He wanted me to have an abortion. He was scared too. Scared I might tell people what had happened,' Catherine answered, looking at her daughter straight in the eye.

Grace was shocked at this revelation, yet at the same time surprised that she was shocked. What more could she expect from a man who had raped a woman? 'Did you think about having one?' Grace asked quietly. 'I wouldn't blame you at all if you had. I'm not sure I would have had the strength to go ahead with the pregnancy.'

'I didn't, not for a moment, Grace.' This was true Grace realised as she watched her mother's face.

'Thank you for that, Catherine,' Grace replied, brushing aside a tear as it began to fall from her eye.

'For what, pet?' Catherine asked.

'For having me. I can't imagine what it's like to be raped. Then to get pregnant. Nobody could have blamed you if you'd had an abortion.'

'It wasn't an option for me Grace. Plus Ireland was very different back then,' Catherine replied.

'When you wouldn't meet me ten years ago, was that because of the rape?' Grace whispered.

'Partly,' Catherine replied honestly. 'I was scared again. I sound like a wimp don't I? I was afraid that when I met you, I'd be reminded of it. I was also afraid you'd want to know who your father was.'

'You're not a wimp, Catherine. You're one of the bravest women I know.' Grace leaned forward and gave her mother a kiss on the cheek. 'Do I remind you of the rape when you see me now?' She really hoped the answer was no.

'No. I was so nervous when I got your letter the second time. I knew I had to see you because you needed me. But I wasn't sure if I'd lose it when I met you. But I needn't have worried. You were so beautiful in every way and that's what I saw when I met you. I never think of the rape when I see you. Except of course when the subject of your father comes up.' This acknowledgement came with a small smile.

'I'm sorry. No wonder you kept running away when I kept harping on about it!' Grace replied.

They both took a sip of tea. 'Is there any chance that I'll bump into him?' Grace asked with a wobbly voice.

'Very slim, Grace. He still lives in Ballymichael, so unless you go there looking for him, it's very unlikely,' Catherine answered.

'You never have to meet him, babe,' Liam said firmly.

'Who knows about all this?' Grace asked Liam.

'Tom, Gerry and me,' Liam replied. 'We haven't told the others.'

Grace was relieved to hear this. If they had all known, she would have had no choice but to find out the man's identity. 'Well if that's the case, I don't want to know who he is. What good would it do knowing his name. I have no desire to meet him, especially after what he's done to Catherine. My father was Mick Devlin. I don't want or need another father. As far as I'm concerned that's the end of this subject,' Grace said firmly.

Catherine was relieved to hear her daughter say this. It was the right thing. Knowing her father was a rapist and also a priest was too much for anyone to cope with in one day. 'If you ever want to know, I'll tell you, I promise. But I'm glad you feel that way. There's absolutely nothing to gain by learning his name,' Catherine told Grace.

'Liam, will you talk to Tom and Gerry and make sure they keep this information to themselves?' Grace asked.

'Of course, babe. I'm so proud of you. I'm so proud of both of you.' Walking over to them, he gave them both a hug.

Chapter Thirty Four

'One, two, three – go!' Grace, Abby, Tara and Gerry downed their baby Guinness's in a split second.

'Darlings! I swear those drinks are little pieces of heaven!' Gerry screamed, licking his lips.

'I don't think that barman has ever seen a man wearing a tiara and lip gloss downing a baby Guinness with his pinkie finger sticking out before!' Tara said, giving Gerry a dig in his ribs playfully.

The group laughed, then Abby jumped up shouting 'more drinks!' and headed to the bar. They were in Donegal in a small village called Downings on Grace's hen night. She hadn't wanted to have a typical hen night in Temple Bar or, in fact, any big town. Tara had known that instinctively and had come up with this beautiful village on the Donegal coast. It was fabulous and just perfect. They were staying in a gorgeous bed and breakfast, which was within walking distance of the local bar. They'd had a gorgeous steak earlier, but were now ready for serious partying. Gerry had arrived with dress-up gear for each of the girls. They all had tiaras and wands, with Grace having the added accessories of a set of fairy wings. Tara had then spiced things up with a pair of inflatable boobs that looked hilarious mixed with the fairy gear.

'Okay time for a game,' Gerry told the girls, as Abby passed out another round of drinks. 'What I have here is a set of cards and each card has a dare that all self-respecting brides have to do before they can get married,' Gerry said very seriously. 'Now pick a card number Grace and I'll tell you what you need to do!'

'I know I'm going to regret this, but what the hell!' Grace said laughing. 'I'll have card number 4, please Gerry.'

'A good choice Ms Yummy Mummy!' Gerry said with a lascivious wink. 'Stand up on your chair and tell us a dirty joke!'

Abby, Tara and Gerry all started chanting 'Joke, Joke, Joke,' ensuring that the whole bar stopped what they were doing to turn around and look at the group.

'She won't do it' Abby said, laughing.

'Course she will,' Tara said, giggling. 'That one loves the limelight!'

With that Grace jumped up on her seat and picked up her bottle of Budweiser. Holding the bottle as a mike, she turned to the pub and shouted, 'Ladies and Gentlemen, I have a little joke I'd like to tell everyone. This is a story about a man called Paddy. Paddy was a long way from his hometown of Co. Clare. He was working in the Philippines. One night he went to a club for a drink. He walked into the bar and the most beautiful woman he'd ever seen in his life walked up to him. "Would you like to buy me a drink, Mister?" the beautiful woman asked Paddy,' Grace said using a very convincing Philippine woman's voice, much to the amusement of her friends. 'Paddy couldn't believe his luck and as he bought the lady a drink, he thought to himself, Jaysus, they don't make them like this in Clare.' Grace spoke with a strong Clare accent for Paddy's voice. 'Then the woman asked Paddy if he wanted to dance. Leading him to the dance floor, she pulled Paddy in close, running her hands over his body.' Grace demonstrated this, much to the delight of the men in the bar and to the whoops of her friends, then continued, 'Paddy couldn't believe his luck and again thought to himself, Jaysus, they don't make them like that back in Clare! Then the woman whispered in Paddy's ear, "Would you like to come back to my place?" Paddy could barely conceal his excitement, thinking to himself, Jaysus, they don't make them like this in Clare!' Paddy and his new friend were back at her place and she said to Paddy, "Would you like to make love to me?" Paddy nodded yes excitedly, thinking to himself, Jaysus they don't make them like this in Clare!'

Grace was giggling at this stage, she could barely continue with her joke, as quite a few people were joining in with the catchline 'Jaysus they don't make them like this in Clare'. Continuing, Grace told the group, 'So Paddy got undressed and the woman said "Take me from behind!" Paddy nearly had a heart attack, thinking…..' Grace turned to the pub and encouraged them all to say the catchline, which they did! 'Jaysus they don't make them like this in Clare!' Delighted they were joining in, she continued, 'So Paddy entered from behind and ran his hand down the woman's body, until he came to a penis sticking out from the front of her body!'

Gerry squealed, 'Lucky Paddy!' ducking as Grace threw a beer mat at him.

She carried on, 'Paddy couldn't believe what he was feeling – a penis in the front of the woman's body! Then he shouted out "Jaysus they don't make them like this in Clare. In through the back, straight out through the front!"'

The whole pub erupted into a round of applause and cheers and Grace obligingly took a bow!

'Told you!' Tara said to Abby with a laugh.

'Darling, I didn't know you had it in you!' Gerry grinned, blowing a kiss at Grace.

'Oh my God, I need a drink!' Grace replied, but she was secretly delighted with her performance! It felt good to be having fun, no holds barred again, with her friends. 'Okay, need to take the focus off me for a minute!' Grace said, laughing. 'Come on Abby; tell us the latest on Shay!'

'Well, it's going really well,' Abby said with a smile. 'We just have the best time together. It's easy, no hassles, no rows, no misunderstandings. Just great!'

'You want to kiss him, you want to marry him,' Tara started saying in a singsong voice, with the others joining in.

'Maybe,' Abby answered with a laugh.

'Maybe, she says maybe! Darling, you're thinking of getting married?' Gerry squealed, spilling his drink in his excitement. 'I can see it now – Weddings by Gerry!'

'Is it that serious sweetie?' Grace asked Abby earnestly.

'I think so. He brought me to look at a show house at the weekend that he thought would be fantastic for us to live in. It's gorgeous, a three-bed detached house,' Abby gushed.

'Wow, that's huge news, Abby,' Tara said impressively. Grace and Gerry both nodded in agreement.

'Does he know that you don't want to live with anyone until you're married?' Tara continued. Abby had always said this; she reckoned her dad wouldn't be able to deal with her "living in sin", as he delicately put it.

'Yes. He knows all that. We had "the talk" quite early on actually, about what we thought about the whole marriage/living together thing,' Abby told her friends.

'So, if he knows you don't want to live "in sin"' – here Tara raised her eyes to heaven – 'and he's showing you show houses… Oh My God!'

'He's going to propose!' Grace, Gerry and Tara exclaimed together.

'Do you think so?' Abby asked, with what looked like a hanger in her mouth. They all nodded their assent.

'I wonder when he's going to do it,' Grace said dreamily. 'Maybe Christmas. Maybe Santa's got something extra sparkly in his stocking this year!'

'I want to get married,' Gerry said pouting. 'I'd be a beautiful bride.'

'Yes you would, oh gorgeous man!' Grace said laughing. 'Sure what's stopping you now?'

'Nothing. We could have a civil ceremony. Maybe one day,' Gerry answered.

'Would you wear white?' Tara asked with a giggle.

'No darling, I'd wear pink! Right, time for another card,' Gerry said, waving them in Grace's face. 'Choose a number, Ms Devlin.'

'I'll have no. 2 this time please,' Grace said seriously.

'Okay darling, you must walk around this bar and kiss the best looking man in the room – your choice – and also kiss the ugliest man in the bar – which will be our choice!'

'That's evil! Best looking man, that's easy,' Grace said, standing up. 'Come here, Tiger,' she said as she grabbed Gerry by his shoulders for a big kiss on the lips.

'This lady's not for turning!' Gerry said afterwards with a laugh, 'but I'll say one thing for you Grace, Liam's one lucky fella!' To which the girls all roared with laughter.

Tara and Abby then jumped up to go and look for the winner of the ugliest man category, returning with what looked like an extra from *Worzel Gummidge*.

'Grace meet Charlie, Charlie meet Grace.' Taking a deep breath, Grace jumped up and gave Charlie a kiss on his cheek, to which she received another round of applause from the bar.

'Don't marry that other fella, marry me,' Charlie slurred at Grace.

The rest of the night passed by in a blur of vodka tonics, baby Guinness's and even a few rounds of Flaming Sambucas. Singing, 'Going to the chapel and we're going to get married', the gang were the last to leave the bar, with promises of undying love from Charlie.

Chapter Thirty Five

Tara woke up the following morning with what felt like two dozen tiny leprechauns dancing in her brain. Her mouth also felt like it had grown a carpet inside it overnight. Thankfully she had had the foresight to buy a couple of litres of Ballygowan the previous evening; ready for what she knew would be a belter of a hangover. Having downed a couple of pints of water, she felt a little bit better. Taking a look at her mobile, she realised it was early, only 8 a.m. Always the same; when you don't have to get up early, sure as the sun sets in the west, you'll wake up at the crack of dawn, she thought. They had decided to go down for breakfast at 10.30, the last serving. Tara glanced over at Grace's bed, then realised with a jolt that her friend wasn't there. Checking the bathroom and seeing it was empty, Tara noticed a message scribbled on the bathroom mirror in red lippy – 'Gone for a walk. X'

Tara threw some clothes on and headed out the door. It was freezing cold, but dry at least. That's the Irish weather for you in December. Tara figured that Grace would have headed for the beach. She loved the coast and had been talking about going for a walk along the beach since they arrived yesterday afternoon.

It took about ten minutes to get to the beach and Tara wrapped her scarf tightly around her, thanking her foresight to have worn it and her hat. She scanned the beach both left and right, not seeing any sign of Grace in either direction, so decided to leave her decision up to luck. Left winning the contest, she headed in that direction. After walking for what felt like an hour, but was probably only a couple of minutes, she could see the faint outline of someone heading in her direction. Picking up her pace, she was delighted when a couple of minutes later she realised it was her friend.

'Hey you,' Tara said, giving Grace a hug. 'I was worried for a minute; thought aliens had finally come back for you!'

'Ha, ha, such a comedienne!' Grace replied, smiling.

'Oh no my friend, that would be you!' Tara quipped. 'Jaysus, they don't make them like this in Clare!'

'God I'm mortified!' Grace said, laughing. 'What must those locals think of us?'

'I don't think they've ever seen anybody like Gerry before, that's for certain!' Tara answered. 'Did you see their faces when he got up and started singing Gloria Gaynor's *I Will Survive*?'

'Tara, this weekend will go down as one of the funniest times I've ever had in my life!' Grace said. 'Thank you so much.'

'It's a pleasure. So then, what has you up so early?' Tara asked. 'Truth now, Grace. What's up?'

'Don't look so worried. Nothing's up. I just couldn't sleep, so decided a walk would be good. I needed to clear my head; it was feeling a little bit battered this morning!'

'We're getting old Grace; ten years ago we'd have done last night and been ready for action again this morning!' Tara declared.

'Speak for yourself, Cousin,' Grace retorted. 'Fancy a coffee?'

Walking back to the B&B, they went into the breakfast room and grabbed a table. Mrs Dunleavy, the owner, came over to take their order.

'Can we just have coffee to start with please Mrs Dunleavy?' Tara asked with a smile. 'Then maybe we can work our way up to breakfast later on?'

'No bother at all,' she answered. 'I'm sure you'll need a good strong pot of coffee after all your shenanigans last night!'

'Oh no, I'm so sorry, did we wake anyone up?' Grace asked worriedly.

'No, not at all,' Mrs Dunleavy answered with a smile. 'I meant down at the pub. I heard you guys were the life and soul of the party down there.'

Tara and Grace started to giggle as they realised they were the talk of the village.

'We've still got it in us to cause a stir all the same!' Grace said with a grin at her cousin. 'Despite our old age!'

'You're a bit pale, Grace. How you feeling these days?' Tara asked with concern.

'I think even Judith Chalmers would be pale this morning after the amount of alcohol we chucked away last night,' Grace answered with a smile. 'I'm fine honest injuns. Just feeling a bit tired.'

'You all set for your next check-up?' Tara asked.

'Yep, I'm in next week. To be honest Tara, I'm a little scared,' Grace admitted.

'Of course you are, pet. You wouldn't be normal if you didn't feel apprehensive about the results. But you've got to keep positive. I'm sure it will be fine,' Tara said firmly.

'What if it's not, Tara? What if the cancer's back?' Grace whispered.

'Then you get your chemo again and beat the fucker one more time. And I'll be right there beside you, willing you on,' Tara declared firmly.

'Thanks Tara. Anyhow, enough about me. How are things with you and Sean? We haven't seen much of you both in the last couple of weeks.'

'Oh we're grand, Grace. Just lying low for a bit that's all. You know how it is,' Tara said.

But Grace could tell that Tara was hiding something. 'Tara, I've had to keep some secrets in my time, so I think I can safely say when someone's hiding something. What's going on with you, really?'

'No flies on you are there!' Tara said ruefully, pausing to pour a cup of coffee for both of them.

'Righto then, it's no biggy really, but Sean and I have been trying to have a baby.'

Grace jumped up and leaned over to give Tara a big hug, saying 'That's fantastic! A cousin for Jack at last! When are you due?'

'Not so fast Michael Schumacher,' Tara said with a sigh. 'Do you really think I'd have been chucking back Sambucas if I was preggers?'

'Oh right, of course not Tara. Sorry. Just got carried away for a minute. Go on.'

'We've been trying for over a year now.' Seeing Grace's raised eyebrows, Tara guessed what she was thinking, 'I never said anything to you, because you were going through chemotherapy at the time. It didn't seem appropriate.'

'Oh Tara, of course it would have been appropriate. You must never keep anything from me, no matter what's going on in my life. Promise me,' Grace implored.

'Well, there's nothing to tell, Grace. We decided we were ready for a family a year ago; Sean's career is established and mine too. We've a few euros saved, so we can afford for me to take some time off work, maybe work part-time only. We had it all worked out. But nothing's been happening. Despite all our best efforts. So we went to see a specialist a month ago and he ran some tests. Good news, there are no medical reasons as to why we are not conceiving. But get this; he said that it could take some time for me to conceive because of my age,' Tara said ruefully.

'You've got to be joking,' Grace said with shock. 'You're only *thirty two*, there's women having kids who are nearly sixty for God's sake.' She could remember reading something on Facebook about that.

'I know, but according to him, that's old for a first-time mum. It's so unfair. I've spent the last fourteen years using contraception to make sure I don't bring a kid into the world without the right set-up, husband, money, home, and then when we get all our i's dotted and t's crossed, we're told that we left it too bloody late.' She took a gulp of her coffee.

Grace felt so bad for her cousin. She could tell that this was something that she wanted desperately. 'I don't believe for one second that you've left it too late, Tara. What advice did the doctor give you both?'

'God it's like a military operation! We've been working to a schedule, making sure we have sex at the right time, at the right temperature. Sean is wearing boxers, letting it all hang out!' Tara finished with the start of a smile.

'As Gerry would say Tara – share don't scare!' Grace said with a laugh. Then grabbing her friend's hand tightly, she continued, 'It will happen I'm sure it will. If anyone should have kids, it's you and Sean. You are both so good with Jack. You'll be amazing parents.'

'Thanks, Grace. I appreciate that. It's just so disappointing when each month comes and my fucking period arrives like clockwork. Having spent years thanking the heavens when it arrived, it's been a whole different ball game lately! That's why I went to ground the past couple of weeks. I really thought we'd done it this month. I was a couple of days late and had convinced myself that it had happened. But then ten days ago, bingo, there's my fucking period,' Tara said, her voice wobbling with emotion.

'It must be so disappointing for you both. How's Sean doing?' Grace asked with concern.

'He's great, so great that he's doing my head in. He keeps coming up with these stupid platitudes and stories about patients he's met who've tried for kids. I swear if I have to listen to one more story of "there was this lady who was trying to have a baby for six years, had ten miscarriages, then got pregnant and now has twenty kids," I'll do time!'

'Poor cow,' Grace said dryly. 'Twenty kids, ouch.' Then the two girls started to laugh.

'And before you start telling me how lucky I am to have Sean, and how he means well, I know all that Grace. It's just sometimes I wish he'd tell me what he really thinks and show me how disappointed he is too, not try to be super husband all the time,' Tara added. 'I know how upset he is too. I catch him looking at me sometimes so sorrowfully.'

'Well, you've got to try to keep positive and look on the bright side,' Grace said, pouring more coffee. 'At least you're having regular sex!'

'God you have a one-track mind!' Tara replied, giggling.

With that, Gerry and Abby walked into the breakfast room. Gerry wearing big sunglasses, holding Abby's arm for dear life as he manoeuvred his way through the tables like they were landmines.

'Feeling delicate?' Tara asked.

'Darling, I'll be as much use as a chocolate teapot today,' he replied.

Abby as usual who never suffered with hangovers declared she was starving and quickly ordered a fry-up for everyone.

'How can you even think about food? Do you think I could actually eat anything in my condition?' Gerry asked.

'Your breakfast isn't for you silly!' Abby answered. 'It's for me!'

'You just watch it, Abby Nolan,' Tara said, waving a finger in her friend's face. 'When you get to forty, all this food is going to catch up with you! One day you'll wake up and be a size 20, and I for one will be cheering in the wings!!'

Sticking her tongue out at Tara, Abby poured a cup of coffee, spooning three sugars in just to wind her friend up!

Chapter Thirty Six

Grace was sitting in Dr Kennedy's office waiting room, feeling like she was getting ready to be executed. She was terrified. Having been cancer-free for six months, the thought of hearing the results of her latest check-up were unbearable. She was on her own, having chosen not to tell Liam, or indeed any of the others, about this appointment. They thought it was tomorrow. They would have all fussed so much, and with her nerves in shreds already, she didn't think she could have coped with their worries too. It was easier this way.

She noticed that there were fresh flowers on the countertop of the reception area. This was a distinct improvement to her previous visit to see Dr Kennedy; she decided it was a good sign. Then it was time. Dr Kennedy was beckoning her into his office with a big smile. Grace couldn't decide whether the smile was a smile of victory – i.e. her being still in remission – or one of condolence – i.e. ding ding, round 2. Taking a seat (still those uncomfortable seats – damn it, a bad sign), Grace took a deep breath and asked her consultant what the results showed.

'How have you been feeling lately?' Dr Kennedy asked gently.

'Great, fantastic, in fact never better,' Grace babbled quickly.

Dr Kennedy raised his eyebrows slightly. 'You decided to come on your own today, Grace. No Liam or Sean waiting outside?'

'No Dr Kennedy, I'm a big girl. All on my own. Please, can we skip the pleasantries? You are making me nervous. Just tell me, am I okay?'

'I'm terribly sorry, Grace. I'm afraid the AML is back. Quite aggressively in fact.'

Ding ding, round 2 it was. Why wasn't she surprised? Because somehow she knew in the back of her mind that the poison was back in her veins. She could feel it. She had just pretended that all was well.

'Grace, have you any questions for me?' Dr Kennedy said.

'What's the prognosis?' Grace asked firmly. She glanced up at the ceiling and thought that this time she'd better keep her feet firmly on the ground. She'd beaten this once before, she'd do it a second time.

'I'm afraid it's the same as last time. We'll start chemotherapy immediately, another course of six treatments. Then we'll review the situation.'

'Well I'm afraid that it's impossible for me to start chemo immediately,' Grace told the doctor. 'I'm getting married next week. Then I'm going to Florida with my husband and son for two weeks.'

Dr Kennedy ran his hand through his balding head and sighed. This was never an easy task for him, talking to patients about their cancer. But this seemed particularly terrible, a young woman on the brink of marriage. 'Grace, my dear, I strongly advise that you postpone your wedding and we start the chemotherapy immediately. The earlier we start working on this the better. This is serious.'

Grace got up and walked to the window of the consultant's room and looked out at the wet and grey December day. Of course it was raining. Turning back to Dr Kennedy, she said quietly but very strongly, 'I'm sorry Dr Kennedy, I really am. But there is no way I'm going to miss my wedding. I'm getting married on December 24th, I'm going to spend Christmas Day with my family and loved ones, and then I'm flying to Disneyland to introduce Mickey Mouse to my son on St. Stephen's Day. There is absolutely nothing you can say to alter these plans.'

'Okay Grace. I can see you have made your mind up. I'll agree to defer the treatment by two weeks. But I want you to cut your honeymoon in half and return here for treatment the beginning of January. No buts, Grace. I'm sure Liam will agree to a shorter honeymoon when you explain what's going on.'

Grace nodded silently. She got up and shook Dr Kennedy's hand wordlessly. Walking to the door of the consultant's office, she turned back to the doctor and said quietly, 'You've got to help me beat this Dr Kennedy. I've too much living to do yet. You hear me?'

Dr Kennedy smiled, 'I'll see you on the 3rd January, Grace. I'll be in touch.'

Grace got a taxi home in a blur. The busy Dublin traffic that usually drove her to distraction, this time she didn't even notice. She was grateful for the delay on the M50. It gave her time to think. By the time she got home she knew what she was going to do. She wouldn't tell Liam, or in fact any of her friends, about her cancer's reappearance. What was the point in worrying them for two weeks, when they could do nothing? She'd ring the travel agents and change their flights home for a week earlier. She did toy with the idea of only changing her flight, but knew she'd never in a million years get away with leaving Liam behind in the US while she flew home for chemo. Plus in all honesty, she knew she wouldn't have the strength to go through it alone. She'd keep her news to herself and then towards the end of the first week, tell Liam the truth. That way her news wouldn't ruin his wedding day or his honeymoon. Her decision made, she felt better. Time to make some phone calls.

Chapter Thirty Seven

'Darling, wake up, it's your wedding day!' Gerry said, blowing a kiss at Grace as he opened the curtains in her room.

'What time is it? Grace answered sleepily.

'8 a.m. princess. Time to get up. I've ordered breakfast for us all; it will be here any minute,' Gerry replied.

Grace got up and realised she was feeling pretty good. She'd been fighting tiredness and aches in what felt like her whole body for the past week, but this morning, ache-free! Walking over to Gerry, she grabbed his hand and pulled him in close for a hug. 'I love you, Gerry,' Grace whispered in his ear.

'Darling. I love you too,' Gerry said with a smile, kissing her.

'Thank you, Gerry.'

'For what my darling?' Gerry asked.

'For my wedding,' Grace replied.

'But you haven't seen it yet, darling. I just hope that you like it,' Gerry answered.

'Oh but I know it will be perfect. Just perfect. Because you organised it. So thank you. Just in case I forget to tell you later on.'

Gerry gently kissed his friend on her forehead and led Grace to the dining area of the suite they were staying in. 'Sit, I'm going to get breakfast,' he told Grace with a barely stifled sob.

With that, Tara and Abby walked in. 'What's going on with

Franc? Someone mix up his seating arrangement?' Tara said with a laugh. 'He's gone running into the bathroom crying!' Then Tara noticed tears in Grace's eyes too. 'Oh Lord, not you too! It's not even dawn yet and we've started on the Kleenex!'

Abby and Tara both pulled Grace into what was to become one of many group hugs of the day. Gerry came back into the room just as the champagne breakfast arrived.

'This is what I call breakfast!' Tara said as she gulped a glass of Bellini. 'A girl could get used to this!'

Having eaten a good breakfast, Gerry then shooed the girls towards their respective bathrooms for showers. 'Hairdressers will be here at 9.30. No time to waste!'

Knowing it was far easier to agree than argue, they all did as they were told. Grace was having a hairpiece fitted by the hairdresser. Her hair had started to grow back but was still quite short. She didn't feel herself without her flowing locks, so Gerry had organised a hairpiece which matched her strawberry blonde curls perfectly. She was going to wear her hair in a low ponytail tied loosely at the nape of her neck. She had decided against a veil but had tiny white rose-buds that were going to be placed randomly throughout her crown.

The morning passed in what can only be called organised chaos, with Gerry having fits of Franc every hour or so. By one o'clock, Tara and Abby were dressed and looking beautiful. They were both wearing black evening dresses in raw silk. Tara's was a halter-neck design, with Abby's having little shoestring straps. Both had white fur stoles to wear over their shoulders. The hairdresser had swept up both of the girls' hair in chignons. Simple diamond stud earrings and a matching diamond choker finished their look off. These were a gift from Grace and Liam.

'Darlings, I have never seen you both look so lovely. Quite lovely. Now sit, while I put the finishing touches to Grace.'

He walked into Grace's dressing room and literally gasped when he saw her. She turned to face him and Gerry brushed away a tear as he took in the beautiful bride. Grace looked radiant. She was wearing a Vera Wang gown, which in its simplicity seemed to mould itself to Grace's figure. The gown was pure white, with a tight strapless bodice. The skirt of the dress fell in soft drapes around her slim figure with a long train flowing out from behind. The exquisite detail of the design was amazing.

'Will I do?' Grace asked with a catch in her voice.

'Oh, darling. Dump Liam, marry me! It's worked. You turned me! I swear I actually felt something stir down here!' Gerry said, pointing downwards.

Grace burst into laughter. She had needed Gerry to say something to relax her and he had. She knew today was going to be emotional, but she was determined not to spend the whole day crying! Walking into the main suite, Grace gave the girls a twirl. Despite shouts from Gerry of 'no tears girls, no tears', Abby and Tara immediately burst into tears when they saw their friend. Knowing he was fighting a losing battle, Gerry thought what the hell, and thanked God for waterproof mascara! After ten minutes of the girls having their make-up reapplied, it was time to leave. Gerry placed a long white fur cape around Grace's shoulders.

'Darling, you are like a magnificent snow queen. A masterpiece!' Gerry declared. 'Are you ready, darling?'

Nodding quietly, Grace followed Tara and Abby to the door.

****

Liam meanwhile was standing at the top of the little chapel in Rose Tree Manor, feeling slightly sick. He couldn't wait to see his bride. It felt like torture not seeing her the previous night. But Grace had been adamant that they should keep at least one tradition before they got married. Tom and Sean were looking fantastic in their black Louis Copeland tuxedos. All three were wearing thick black silk ties with their suits. Jack was wearing a miniature version of their suits and had left them a few minutes earlier with Gerry to go get his Mommy! Liam glanced around at the little chapel and smiled nervously at his Mam and Uncle Martin sitting just behind him. Looking around them he smiled as he realised that just as he and Grace wanted, all forty or so guests in the chapel were friends of theirs who they dearly loved. There were no strangers whatsoever. The music started. Tom, Sean and Liam stood up and faced Fr Dominic – a family friend of his mother's who had baptised Liam thirty four years earlier. It was all Liam could do not to turn around and watch Grace walk up the aisle, but he knew he was supposed to stay looking ahead.

Then Tom whispered, 'Liam. Look at Grace, she's stunning.'

With that, Liam turned around and smiled at Tara and Abby as they walked to the side of the altar. Then he actually thought he was going to faint when he had the first glimpse of his wife-to-be. She literally took his breath away. He felt Tom grab his arm to steady him. Composing himself, he walked to meet Grace and Jack. He leaned down and shook hands with his son who looked very solemn.

'Here you go, Daddy,' Jack said, grabbing Grace and literally shoving her towards Liam.

With a giggle Grace bent down and kissed her son's cheek, 'Thank you sweetie-pie.'

Tara walked up and took Grace's cape off her shoulders and grabbed Jack's hand. 'Let's sit down, buddy,' Tara told her godson.

Grace then looked up and into Liam's eyes.

'You're beautiful,' he said simply.

'What, this old thing?' Grace said with a wink.

'Still want to get married?' Liam whispered in her ear.

'With my entire heart, babe,' Grace whispered back.

Chapter Thirty Eight

Grace and Liam walked into the banquet hall of Rose Tree Manor to cheers and claps from all their family and friends. The room looked amazing, decorated throughout with both candles and fairy lights. The tables were round and there was a magnificent centre-piece for each one, with extravagant flowers in vibrant colours, red, orange, purple, and green. Crisp linen adorned them, with beautiful ruby red wineglasses. No detail was left out and each guest had a handpicked Christmas gift beautifully gift-wrapped. Grace and Liam were smiling like Cheshire cats, and without saying a word to each other, they both knew that they had never been so happy. They took their seats and the wedding festivities began. They had an amazing six-course banquet and everyone agreed they had never experienced such a beautiful wedding.

Gerry had asked the wedding videographer to walk around to each table and get a quote from all the guests to keep as a video diary. Every comment was full of praise.

'The most beautiful and romantic wedding I've been to.'

'The little chapel was so beautiful with the candlelight lighting up the aisle.'

'The music was so moving. Who was that singer?'

'The food was amazing. I can't eat another thing.'

'Grace looks like a movie star. She's so beautiful.'

'Has Liam got a brother?'

'I wonder how much that wedding organiser, Franc, costs. He's fabulous!'

Before long the meal was over and Tom was standing to start the speeches. 'My Lords, Ladies and Gentlemen, Fr Dominic, friends and family, I hope you all enjoyed that feast.' Tom started to rub his belly as he licked his lips. 'Now before the speeches start, I've got to lay down some ground rules. Liam, my pal here, has stated that nobody, and that means nobody, can make a speech that goes on longer than five minutes.' This was met with cheers and whoops from the guests! 'So, I'll be timing each speech and if anyone goes beyond five minutes then….' Tom bent down and picked up a bell and started to ring it loudly to laughs and cries from everyone. 'And just to make sure you all understand how important this rule is – for every second you go over the five-minute barrier, you have to buy me one drink! Now, representing the Devlins, let's start with a word from the son of the bride, young Jack!'

Grace and Liam looked slightly worried, as they had no idea what Jack might say. Picking Jack up and standing him on his chair, Tom held the mike up to Jack's mouth, showing the bell to Jack who started to grin.

'I'm Jack and I'm nearly four,' Jack told the group. 'That's my Mommy and my Daddy,' he continued, pointing them out to the group. 'Uncle Tom said I should tell a joke. What happened at the cannibal's wedding? They toasted the bride and groom!' he finished to whoops and cheers from the whole room.

Liam stood up and carried Jack from his chair over to Grace and himself, whereby they both kissed and tickled him. He couldn't believe his luck. He'd had chicken nugget and chips and a big bowl of ice cream. What a day! And there was going to be dancing later on. Then Santa was coming tonight. And then they were going to Disneyland in two days to meet Mickey Mouse. Yes!

Tom stood up again and told everyone, 'Well, Jack has set an early record. Thirty seven seconds. Well done my son! Well said. And what a joke. That's set the standard everyone. Now, Liam's Uncle Martin would like to say a few words on behalf of the Ryans.'

'We'd like to welcome Grace to the Ryan family. She's a right bonny lass Liam, you'd better mind her now!' More claps and cheers. 'Your Mammy and I are very proud of you Liam.' Martin sat down with a big grin on his face, feeling delighted with himself.

'A man of few words there! Well said Martin. Good words and a timing of forty eight seconds! Competition is fierce, no doubt about it. Would you all like to hear from the main man himself?' Tom asked, throwing the mike in Liam's hand.

Liam stood up and took a bow, glancing at his watch as he did. He'd better not mess up his own rule! 'Fr Dominic, friends and family, on behalf of my wife and me, thank you all so much for being here today to share our wedding. Thank you to you all for our beautiful gifts. We've been blown away by everyone's generosity. In fact, had I have known what a generous lot you all were, I'd have proposed earlier!' Liam paused to wink at his wife. God, it felt good to call Grace his wife! 'I'd like to thank a few people that have made this day so special for Grace and me. To the staff of Rose Tree Manor for a fabulous venue and their wonderful hospitality, thank you. I'd also like to thank my good friends Tom and Sean who have stood by my side, not only today, but over the past ten years, through good times and bad. We may not be brothers, but I think of you as such.' Sean was grinning from ear to ear and Tom was brushing away a tear. 'I'd also like to propose a toast to the beautiful bridesmaids. You look fantastic. Tennyson once said that "a happy bridesmaid makes a happy bride." And I know that both of you have helped Grace so much over the past couple of weeks in the madness leading up to today. So thank you.' Abby blushed when she heard a wolf whistle coming from Shay's table.

Glancing at his watch, Liam realised he had about three minutes left of his speech. 'I've also got to thank Gerry, or Franc as we've all come to know him. Words can't describe our gratitude, mate. You have given me and Grace the wedding of our dreams. We will never forget it.'

Gerry buried his face in Tom's shoulder, never feeling as proud as he did right then, basking in the applause.

'And now lastly, but not least, my beautiful wife and son. Three years ago I thought I'd lost them. I never stopped loving Grace or Jack, but somehow I got lost along the way. But, with the help of my amazing family, Mammy and Martin in particular, I found my way back. Now I have a son who blows my mind on a daily basis. Jack, in your words, you are way cool and Daddy and Mommy love you.' Jack was grinning madly at this. Taking a deep breath, Liam turned to his wife and continued, 'Grace, you literally took my breath away when you walked into that chapel today. For a moment, it felt like time actually froze and I know that to the day I die I will never forget how you looked right then. I thought you were beautiful the second I met you, but today you have never looked lovelier. I struggle to find words to describe how I feel about you. I would be nothing without you Grace and I'll love you forever. To finish I'm going to borrow a few words from Robert Burns that sum up far more eloquently than I could, what I'd like to express: "Grow old along with me; the best is yet to come."'

Liam sat down, leaning across to accept the kiss Grace was waiting to give him. 'To you Mrs Ryan.'

The entire top table were crying when Liam finished his speech. It was the sincerity in his words that overcame them all, it was so heartfelt.

Having taken a moment to compose himself, Tom rose again with his mike. 'And now, Mrs Ryan herself has decided she'd like to share a few words.'

Grace stood up. She hadn't prepared anything and in fact had told everyone that she wouldn't make a speech, but at this moment she felt it was right to do so. 'Wow. I'm not sure that I can speak following those wonderful words from Liam. This is a bit impromptu, but there are a few things I'd like to share with you all. First of all I echo everything that Liam said earlier, and in order to keep to my timescale Tom, I won't repeat them! But there are a couple of other people that I'd like remembered this evening. I'd like everyone first of all to raise their glasses to my parents – Mick and Annie Devlin, who I know are looking down at this moment with a glass of champagne in hand, feeling very proud of their little Grace. I couldn't have had more amazing parents and I think about them and miss them every day. I wish they were here with us all. But there is someone here I'd also like to acknowledge. She is a very special woman, that I have grown to love and respect with every day I spend with her. Please raise your glasses to my mother, Catherine.'

Catherine had never felt so much pride as she did at that moment. Noel and his wife and three children were sitting at the table with her, as Grace had insisted that they come for the wedding. Noel grabbed his sister's hand and squeezed it, realising that he hadn't seen her look this happy since before she had got pregnant.

'Now as you all know, I've had a bit of bad luck recently with my health, which can cause even the most optimistic of us to reflect on our lives! And you know what, I realised I have it pretty damn good!' This was met with claps and cheers from her friends. 'I have the best friends any girl could ever dream of. I love you guys – Tara, Sean, Abby, Gerry, Tom. I'd never have muddled through my life quite so successfully without all of you. Jack, as Daddy said earlier, you are our world. Always remember that sweetie-pie. Nothing is more important to me and Daddy than you are. And lastly, before that bell rings,' Grace winked at Tom, who'd given up all pretence of timing her, 'my friends, I need to tell you about this man here. My husband. There have been days this year when I thought I couldn't take anymore, but Liam taught me to never give up. He helped me through those miserable days and did so with love and warmth and laughter, never making me feel like I was putting him to any trouble. I know he was scared, but he never showed that to me. He just put his big strong arms around me and held me until I felt better. Liam, I depended on you and you didn't let me down. So everyone, I want you all to know that I am blessed. If this is as good as it gets, I'm happy. I am blessed to have found Catherine, my friends, and most importantly my husband and son. Thank you.'

Liam stood up with Jack in his arms and hugged Grace and the whole room stood up too, raising their glasses, toasting the Ryan family. Finally Tom stood up, taking the mike back from Grace and started his best man speech. 'There's no doubt about it, is there Ladies and Gentleman? Grace obviously loves Liam. Hard to follow all of the speeches, especially those last two. But I'd better try! So, what can you say about a man who came from humble beginnings and is now rising to the very top of his profession? And all of this done purely on intelligence, charm and good looks. Well that's enough about me, after all I'm here to talk about Liam!' Tom was gratified to see he was getting the laughs he anticipated!

'Seriously, I'm very honoured to be a part of this day, standing beside my two best friends, Liam and Grace. I remember the first time that Grace called in to our house, looking very nervous, but also very determined to get the job as our interior designer. Gerry and I both said afterwards, that the second she spoke, we knew that she was not only going to be the designer to decorate our new home, but would also become a great friend of ours. And we were right.' Tom turned to Grace, who blew a kiss at him. 'Very soon we were introduced to her extended family – Liam, Tara, Sean and Abby, and our little family was born. As for the bold Liam, he's a man after my own heart. Speaks from the heart, speaks honestly, enjoys a joke, and if you have a problem, he's a great friend to have in your corner. Your uncle Martin said it earlier Liam, but I'll say it again – you've really got your life together and we all know that at times you've taken the wrong path, but I believe that you needed to go that road in order to come back to where you should be right now – with Grace and Jack. I'm proud of you too, Liam. You're a good man. And now to finish my speech, I'm going to end with some advice for the bride and groom. Never, ever, go to bed mad……. Stay up and fight!!!'

Chapter Thirty Nine

Christmas day went by in a blur of present swapping, too much rich food and more emotional speeches from everyone as the wine flowed into the night. It was a magical place, Rose Tree Manor, and a time that none of them would ever forget. Before they knew it, the alarm was ringing and it was time for Liam, Grace and Jack to head to Dublin airport for their midday flight to Orlando. Jack was literally beside himself with excitement. Grace was beginning to feel tired again, the past couple of days taking their toll. But she was determined not to let this stupid illness ruin her honeymoon.

The journey was long, but thankfully Jack's lack of sleep finally caught up with him and he slept through most of the flight, with Grace and Liam also snoozing. They were staying in the main Disneyland resort, wanting to make sure they had the opportunity to soak up every moment of their time there. They spent the week going to the Magic Kingdom and all of the parks, making sure that they did something every day. Liam had wanted to space their trips to the parks out over two weeks, not knowing about their earlier departure, but Grace insisted she wanted to keep going. It was a magical time for all three of them and one that would never be forgotten. On what was going to be their last day and night, Grace asked Jack which was his favourite park. He of course answered the Magic Kingdom.

'So let's go back again today then,' Grace declared to the boys.

'You sure you don't want to just relax today, honey. You look beat, all this running around,' Liam said worriedly. 'I'm exhausted!'

'Come on wimp! No lying around swimming pools today. Let's go say hello to Mickey one more time!'

'Yeah!' Jack screamed, running to his bedroom to fish out his Mickey Mouse ears.

'And as it's New Year's Eve I've organised a special meal for us tonight. I know we can't go out on our own but I wanted us to have a nice meal together. So once Jack falls asleep, we'll have a room-service banquet in our hotel suite! It's all organised, menu even picked, one that doesn't consist of Maccy D's too!'

'I'm liking that idea,' Liam said with a smile. 'When did you organise all this?'

'Oh before we left, I called the hotel and organised it. You're not the only one who is good at organising surprises!' Grace said to her husband.

They all enjoyed another great day courtesy of Disney, spending most of their time queuing for Thunder Road Mountain, over and over again! The more splashed they got; the more Jack wanted to go again.

'He won't be happy till I'm drenched!' Liam said, wiping his face.

At four o'clock they finally called it a day and walked back to their hotel. Grace and Liam both had showers and got dressed up for their big night in. Tucking Jack into bed at 7 p.m., he fell asleep as soon as his head hit the pillow. Not long afterwards, room service arrived. Having finished their beautiful meal, Grace turned to Liam and said, 'Fancy giving an old married woman a hug?'

'Sure no problem, just don't tell my wife!' Liam quipped in return. They sat holding hands on their balcony bench, full from their meal and feeling very relaxed, Grace with a glass of Pinot Noir, Liam with an orange juice. They watched boats drifting along in the Disney Resort Lake. It was beautiful and very serene. They could hear gangs of revellers in the distance all getting ready to ring the New Year in.

Grace felt a little part of her heart break as she knew it was time to tell Liam about her cancer. 'I've a confession to make Liam.'

'Secrets and lies already. God, woman, we're not even a week married!' Liam said with a laugh. 'Go on then, spill your guts! What did you buy? Another pair of shoes?'

'Afraid not Liam. Three plane tickets. I'm sorry honey, but we're going to have to go home a little earlier than planned. I changed our dates with the travel agent and we go home tomorrow evening,' Grace said quietly, aware that her words were going to hurt Liam so much.

Liam put his face in his hands and sat quietly for a few moments. Looking up eventually, he said quietly, 'It's back, isn't it?'

'Yes,' Grace answered softly.

He pulled her into his arms and held her tightly for a long time. 'When did you find out Grace?'

'Two weeks ago. I lied about my check-up results; please don't be cross with me. The AML is back and I have to start chemotherapy on the 3rd January for another course of six treatments.'

Liam digested this information, before swearing under his breath, 'Jesus Grace, why didn't you tell me? You should have told me.'

'I'm so sorry Liam; I hated lying to you, honestly. But why tell you then? You couldn't do anything and I didn't want our wedding day and honeymoon to be marred by this fucking cancer.'

Liam winced at Grace's words.

'Admit it Liam, if you knew the cancer was back, you wouldn't have enjoyed our wedding. You would have been worrying all the time about me and whether I was feeling okay or not. And I didn't want that as a memory. Our wedding day was perfect and this holiday has been the best time of my life. Please don't be angry with me. I can't take it,' Grace implored. She hated the thought of Liam being angry with her; her intentions were good.

'I'm not angry, Grace,' Liam quickly replied, pulling her into his arms again. 'I understand. I'd have probably done the same thing as you. I just hate the thought of you coping with this all on your own.'

'Well, I wasn't on my own silly. I was with you and Jack. And now you know. Everything.'

'God Grace, this is so fucking unfair. Why now?' Liam shouted. 'Haven't you gone through enough?'

'Liam, it is unfair and believe you me, I want to wail at the world too about the cards I've been dealt, but I refuse to do that. I've beaten this damn cancer once and I'll do it again, with you by my side. Okay?' Grace leaned in and kissed Liam's cheek. 'Remember your speech at the wedding? I've every intention of growing old with you. I know the best is yet to come.'

'Too right the best is yet to come. I've not even started with you yet! Of course you're going to beat this. No bloody way I'm going to lose you a second time!' Liam said defiantly.

'Now, it's almost midnight and I for one don't want to ring the New Year in talking about my cancer, so please, let's just enjoy our last night here and have some fun!' Grace said to Liam.

'Jump up!' Liam said. 'Let's go show these Americans how to party Irish style! Even if it is on our balcony!'

Chapter Forty

Grace was sitting in her hospital room, having the first of her chemotherapy treatments. Closing her eyes, she decided to focus on something lovely, to try and forget about the weird feeling chemo was giving her. She'd almost forgotten how it felt.

'What are you smiling about?' Liam asked with a grin.

'You,' Grace answered. 'I was just thinking about our first dance. That was a lovely moment wasn't it?'

'Yes, babe. It was. Although how I let you get your own way on that first song, I'll never know!' Liam teased.

'Tony Bennett's classic – *The Way You Look Tonight* – it was perfect. You have no taste!' Grace replied in mock annoyance.

'Ah but I have. I married you, didn't I,' Liam declared. 'Now prepare yourself for company. I've called all of the gang to tell them you're back in hospital. I'd say, we can expect visitors in, ooh let's see, Dublin traffic on a Monday afternoon, about half an hour!'

'Liam, I told you not to call anyone. I don't want a fuss. They all think we're still in Florida. Why couldn't we leave it like that?' Grace asked.

'For two very good reasons, babe. One, I'm scared of Tara. She's only just forgiven me for being alive, if I kept the fact that you were in hospital from her, I seriously think I could wake up with a horse's head in my bed one night!' Liam smiled as Grace giggled. 'As well you might giggle Mrs Ryan, but I can see you're not contradicting me! And two, the other reason I told everyone is that we're going to need some babysitting help over the next couple of weeks, while you're in hospital.' This time Dr Kennedy had admitted Grace into hospital and elected that she should have daily chemotherapy sessions, as opposed to weekly.

'Did Jack mind going into Montessori this morning?' Grace asked.

'You are kidding me? He was like a hero returning from war. He walked in with his big bag of sweets for everyone, wearing his Mickey Mouse ears. He was mobbed within seconds. I left him in full flow telling them all about Buzz Lightyear,' Liam replied, laughing.

Grace could picture the scene in her head. Jack would be in his element telling stories to his friends. He was like Liam in that way. He had a way with words. 'Did you ring Catherine?' Grace asked.

'Yes, she was the first person I rang. And she's on her way up. She's just going to organise some cover in her shop, then she's coming to stay for a few days,' Liam said.

'You okay with that?' Grace asked her husband. She knew that having a mother-in-law to stay was not every man's idea of fun. Especially when they were supposed to be on their honeymoon!

'Relieved, she suggested it to be honest, babe. Just because we're not in Florida, you remember that this is still our honeymoon! I want to spend as much time in here with you, and with Catherine at home, then at least I know that Jack's getting fed,' Liam replied, leaning in for a quick kiss.

Liam was not the best cook in the world and Grace had figured that the boys would be living on takeout for the next three weeks. This was definitely a better arrangement.

'How did the others react?' Grace asked.

'Tara screamed abuse at me for not telling her sooner. Sean had to take the phone off her in the end. I explained to him that it was my wife who made the decision to keep us all in the dark, me included,' Liam said, throwing his eyes up to the ceiling.

'Ah she'll calm down. You know Tara. Speak first, think later,' Grace told her husband. And with that, right on cue, in walked Tara.

'Hi cousin,' Grace said with a smile. 'Come on; give it to me, before you explode.'

'You should have told me. I can't believe you didn't tell me,' Tara said with tears flowing.

'Sorry Tara. But it was better this way. I couldn't handle everyone's sympathy and pity. It would have only marred my wedding. And besides I'm fine. Now come over here, stop sulking and give me a hug.'

'How are you feeling?' Tara asked, having done as she was told.

'Oh fantastic. Nothing like this baby to put a spring in your step!' Grace said pointing to the drip.

'Same schedule as before?' Tara enquired.

'No, this time they're keeping me in for three weeks and I'm getting the full lot.'

'How do you feel about that?' Tara asked with concern. She knew that if this was what the doctors had decided, they were taking a more aggressive course of action.

'Happier. It's better to get it over and done with in one go, rather than have to keep coming back. So, bring it on,' Grace answered with a shrug. 'Where's Sean? I'm going to need him to do some translating for me again, about Dr Kennedy's diagnosis.'

'He's got clinic at the moment, Grace. But he's coming here as soon as that finishes. He's going to put a call through to Dr Kennedy too and see if he can get some information. Don't worry he's on it,' Tara said firmly.

'I didn't doubt it for a minute, sweetie,' Grace smiled. Sean was so dependable.

Abby walked in a few minutes later with Shay, and then promptly burst into tears when she saw Grace all hooked up.

'Oh don't cry, Abby,' Grace said, holding onto to her friend's hand. 'I'm fine honestly. You start to cry and you'll have me going.'

'I'm so sorry Grace. I promised myself I wouldn't cry, but this is so unfair. You should be on honeymoon,' Abby said, quickly wiping her tears away.

'I know. But at least I had a week. At first Dr Kennedy wanted me to cancel the wedding and the honeymoon! I felt sorry for myself when I got the results back, but then I realised that wasn't going to change anything. I got through this once before, I can definitely do it again,' Grace said. Looking up, she noticed Shay standing in the corner looking a bit uncomfortable. 'Hi Shay Thanks for coming. I appreciate it.'

'Hi Grace. You're looking good. Did you have a good holiday?' Shay asked.

'Brilliant Shay. I tell you what, why don't you take Liam for a coffee and a sandwich. He hasn't left my side all morning. I want to have a chat with my girls,' Grace suggested.

'I know when we're not wanted,' Liam said with a laugh. 'I am a bit hungry actually. Back soon, babe.'

'What can we do to help?' Tara asked Grace. As always she was the first to sort out the practicalities. 'Where's Jacky boy?'

'In Montessori at the moment. Well, there is something I'd like you to do for me. It's Jack's birthday tomorrow. We had originally booked a birthday surprise for him at Disneyland – a birthday dinner with all the characters. I haven't really got anything prepared. Could you organise a treat for him? He shouldn't miss out,' Grace said.

'Consider it done,' Tara answered. 'We'll organise something Do you need me to get a present from you and Liam?'

'That's done. We bought his present weeks ago. It's at home all wrapped up already,' Grace said.

'Great. Anything else need doing?' Tara continued.

'Nope, not that I can think of. Catherine's coming to stay for a while, so that will sort out babysitting for Jack. Maybe when she goes home, I'll need some help. But for now, it's covered.'

'We'll sort that out with Liam, Grace. Don't worry about a thing,' Abby said. 'How are you feeling? Truthfully.'

'Knackered! I'm absolutely exhausted. I've kind of been on autopilot for the past couple of weeks and lived on adrenalin. But I have to admit, as soon as we got back from Florida, it was as if I ran out of batteries. Everything just caught up with me. My whole body aches. I'm feeling pretty nauseous too. It's funny but you do forget how bad this chemo makes you feel. I don't remember it being this horrible the last time,' Grace said, looking like she was about fourteen.

'When did you tell Liam?' Tara asked.

'New Year's Eve. We went out for dinner and then I told him,' Grace said sadly.

'Must have been a shock for him,' Tara conceded, feeling a bit guilty for shouting at him earlier.

'Just a bit,' Grace answered with a smile. 'But he took it in his stride. Breaking the news to Jack the next morning that we were going home that evening was a different story though! He was hysterical.'

'I can imagine,' Tara said with a laugh. 'Is he alright now?'

'Absolutely. Sure by the time we got home, all he could talk about was seeing all his friends in Montessori. Shit, that reminds me, he needs a cake and sweets for Montessori tomorrow too. Do you mind?' Grace said, feeling bad for putting all this on her friends. Each child always had a birthday party at Montessori, but it was up to the parents to provide the cake and party sweets for everyone.

'I'll call into Superquinn on the way home,' Tara said. 'I know they do Mickey Mouse birthday cakes. I'll drop them all into your apartment, so that Liam has them for tomorrow.'

'Perfect.' Grace was relieved to know that this was under control. She was beginning to feel very sleepy and before she knew it she had drifted off.

Tara and Abby held hands watching their best friend. They were scared.

Chapter Forty One

Tom kissed Grace on the forehead before leaving the hospital room. She'd been asleep for the past half hour. Liam followed him out of the room.

'How are you doing, buddy?' Tom said, giving Liam a big bear hug.

'Not great to be honest. Worried sick about Grace. She looks terrible, doesn't she?' Liam replied.

Tom nodded his response. He'd got a shock when he walked into the hospital room earlier this evening. He'd never seen Grace look so tired and pale. It was such a stark contrast to how well she looked a few weeks earlier at her wedding. 'It's to be expected though, mate. She's probably suffering from jet lag on top of everything else,' Tom added.

'True. We never stopped in Florida, Tom. If I'd only known the cancer was back, I would have insisted that she slow down. But she was like a whirlwind over there. Insisting that we do something different every day. She was trying to fit it all into our first week. Crazy,' Liam said.

'That's Grace for you,' Tom said with a smile. Her courage and strength never failed to amaze him. 'She's one hell of a woman. You're a lucky man.'

Liam nodded in response. He didn't need reminding of that. Every day he couldn't believe his luck that he and Grace were back together and now actually married.

'We're all meeting in the Cock Tavern for a drink. If you fancy calling in on your way home?' Tom asked his friend.

'Thanks, mate. But I need to get home. Catherine is there. She picked up Jack from Montessori and she's desperate for news on Grace. She's also got dinner waiting for me,' Liam replied.

'Alright so. I'll be off. But I'll see you both tomorrow,' Tom said. He walked away with a feeling of dread. Half an hour later he parked his car outside the pub and walked in, spying the gang immediately in their usual corner.

'Darling, I have a drink for you,' Gerry told him, giving him a quick kiss. 'You alright?' Gerry could tell that Tom was upset.

'Grand, love. Don't be worrying,' Tom answered. 'This is a load of bollocks though.'

The others all laughed half-heartedly at Tom's phrasing.

'How did you think she looked?' Tara asked him.

'Terrible. She wasn't that pale the last time, I'm sure of it,' he stated.

The others all nodded in response. Abby turned to Sean and asked, 'Did you get a chance to talk to Dr Kennedy?'

Sean nodded, 'Yep. Her bone marrow function has deteriorated again.'

'Will the chemo sort her out?' Abby asked.

'Hope so. But in all honesty, her best bet is a transplant if she's going to beat it this time,' Sean said ruefully.

'What about advertising?' Gerry suggested. 'You know, asking for people to come in and be tested? You often see people on breakfast TV looking for help this way.'

Nobody answered him. Tom patted Gerry's hand, acknowledging his idea, but he was thinking along another line: Fr O'Hara. He had been thinking about him while driving to the pub. He needed to talk to Liam tomorrow about paying him a visit again. He could be the answer. If Catherine wasn't a match – maybe he was.

'Where's Shay, darling?' Gerry asked Abby; just realising she was on her own.

'He was supposed to join us but rang me about an hour ago to say he was really tired. He's going to have an early night,' she answered. She was a bit disappointed to be honest, as tonight she could have done with his company. She was so worried about Grace and a friendly shoulder to lean on would have been nice. But he was adamant he couldn't go out tonight.

'Everything alright with you guys?' Tara asked.

'Fine Tara, thanks. Just worried about Grace,' Abby answered. 'Can you imagine what it must have been like for her, keeping that from everyone – in particular Liam – for the past three weeks?'

'Darling, I couldn't have done it,' Gerry replied.

'Me neither,' Tara added.

'She's a strong woman is our Grace,' Tom said. 'She was thinking about all of us, not herself, as usual. I just feel so useless. I want to do something to help.'

'Well we've got to organise something for tomorrow. It's Jack's birthday. I promised Grace we'd sort something out. I've bought two cakes. One I've left with Catherine for Montessori tomorrow. The other I've at home. I thought maybe we should bring the party to Grace. I don't want her to miss out,' Tara told the group.

'That's a great idea,' Abby agreed. 'We can all bring our presents for Jack to the hospital and that way Grace can see him opening them all.'

'I'll bring some stuff to decorate Grace's room, make it look festive, darlings,' Gerry added, grateful for an excuse to do something.

'That's settled then,' Tara told the others. 'I'll give Liam a ring later on to make sure he's happy enough with the plan.'

Chapter Forty Two

Grace had finished the second course of her chemotherapy and was trying to recover some energy in time for the party later on. Liam had told her earlier of the plans and she was delighted. She always loved watching Jack open his presents. His excitement was infectious and she needed something to keep her spirits up. Plus, she missed him terribly. She hadn't seen him now for two days and it felt like a year. Then Gerry burst into the room with an armful of balloons and two big bags.

'Hello darling,' Gerry said, bending down for a kiss. 'I can see you've decided to go for the pale and interesting look today.'

'Cheek of you!' Grace answered with a laugh. 'Do I look that bad?'

'No darling. You are, as always, beautiful. But a little bit pale. But never you mind, my darling. Gerry to the rescue!' He bent down and started rummaging through Grace's bedside locker till he found her make-up bag. 'Good girl. Glad to see you didn't forget the essentials when you packed!' Gerry declared.

'Never leave home without it!' Grace told Gerry with a smile. 'Go on; give me a makeover.'

'This will need to be an extreme makeover, darling!' Gerry said as he started applying Mac foundation on Grace's pale skin. 'By the time I've finished with you, Liam will be proposing all over again!'

Grace closed her eyes and allowed Gerry to take over. She trusted him completely and knew that he'd apply just the right amount of make-up to make her look healthy. She didn't want to scare Jack when he came in. Ten minutes later Gerry was finished and Grace was delighted when she looked in the mirror.

'Thanks sweetie. I feel better already!' Grace said, blowing a kiss at Gerry. 'Now what's in those bags?'

'This room is far too bland for a party, darling! I called into Party Zone and we have balloons, streamers, banners, posters, party poppers and party hats for everyone!' Gerry said, clapping his hands excitedly.

'Oh Gerry, that's wonderful. You've thought of everything. Jack's going to love it!'

With that, Gerry started to decorate the room and Grace could feel herself getting more and more excited with every balloon that was added. Then Catherine, Tom, Tara and Sean all arrived. Tara had the birthday cake and they all piled the presents at the end of Grace's bed, ready for Jack's arrival.

'The room looks fabulous, love,' Tom told Gerry.

And it did.

'You're looking pretty foxy today Mrs Ryan,' Sean then said to Grace. 'If only I wasn't married…!'

'In another lifetime…' Grace said with a wink.

'Did you see Dr Kennedy today?' Catherine asked Grace.

'Not yet. He'll probably call in later on this evening. I told him about the party, so he said he might drop by for some cake,' Grace replied.

'That's nice,' Catherine said. She was pleased to see Grace looking better today, but knew that the flush on her cheeks came from her make-up. She could tell that Grace was making an extreme effort to keep things going. Then with a burst, Jack and Liam walked into the room and everyone shouted, 'Happy Birthday!'

'I'm four today!' he told everyone. Then he climbed up on the bed beside Grace, plonking himself on top of her.

'Hi Mommy. You look pretty. Where's my present?' Jack demanded, as Grace did her best to hide her wince. Seeing Liam about to come over and grab Jack, she quickly shook her head at her husband. Every second she could have with Jack she was going to take, even if it caused her the odd wince or two.

Grace turned to her son and started to laugh, 'Compliments will get you everywhere sweetie-pie. These presents are all for you, Jack. Knock yourself out!'

Jack's face lit up with excitement, it seemed to say – all these for me! He couldn't believe his luck as he opened each present. 'Thanks Uncle Tom, Uncle Gerry. Cool!' They had bought him Handy Manny's Tool Box. 'Wow, thanks Aunt Tara and Uncle Sean,' he continued when he'd ripped open their gift. They had chosen a huge Lego set for him. He then moved onto Abby's present, which was a Spider-Man web maker. 'This is what I've always wanted!' Abby was delighted with his response. Liam had given her the tip-off that he'd been eyeing this up in Smyth's superstore. Catherine had bought him clothes, which he looked at quickly, then moved onto the next present!

'What do you say to Nana?' Grace said giving him a little dig.

'Oh, sorry Nana. Thank you. I love them!'

'That's okay, Jack. You're welcome,' Catherine said, making a mental note to buy a toy the next time a present was required!

Then Jack opened his last present from Grace and Liam. 'Mom, this is way cool!' They'd got him a Bob the Builder costume, to add to his already bulging wardrobe. They'd also bought him some Bob toys to add to his haul. 'This is the best birthday EVER!' he declared to the group, cuddling in close to his Mom.

'That's great bud,' Liam told him, ruffling his hair.

'Time to blow out the candles,' Tara told her godson. Sean lit each of the four candles quickly.

'Make a wish, baby,' Grace whispered to Jack.

He closed his eyes really tightly and made his wish. Taking a big deep breath, he blew all the candles out. Then everyone sang Happy Birthday as Jack insisted he blow the candles out a second time.

'What did you wish for Jack?' Tom asked him.

'I can't tell you! I'm not allowed to tell, am I Mommy?' he replied seriously.

'No sweetie-pie. It won't come true if you tell. Good boy.' She gave him a kiss, as he wriggled away.

'Can I put my costume on, Daddy?' he begged.

'Sure you can,' Liam answered him, helping him get changed.

'I'll go get some coffees to go with the cake,' Tom told the group.

Catherine jumped up to go with Tom, offering to help. 'Can I have a word Tom?' Catherine asked him as they walked down the corridor.

'Sure Catherine,' Tom replied. 'What's on your mind?'

'Fr O'Hara,' she answered.

Tom nodded. He suspected it might have been this.

'Grace needs a donor quickly. She can't go on like this, can she? I mean, it's no way to start off married life,' Catherine continued.

'No, Catherine, it isn't. To be honest I've been thinking about paying Fr O'Hara a visit since last night. Do you think he'd agree to be tested?' Tom said.

'I don't know, Tom. I don't think that he'll ever admit to being Grace's father, but maybe if he knew his daughter was ill, just maybe he'd come good,' she replied doubtfully.

'How do you want to handle it?' Tom said.

'I think I should go see him,' Catherine answered quietly.

Tom nodded. He could tell that the mere thought of seeing the man who raped her again was scaring the life out of Catherine. 'What do you want me to do?'

'Will you come with me, Tom? I haven't the strength to face him on my own and Liam needs to stay here with Grace.'

'Of course I will Catherine. I'll do anything to help. When do you want to go?' Tom said.

'Well, I've told Grace that I'm staying here until the weekend but then I have to get back to the shop for a few days. I thought maybe we could go down to Wexford to see him on Saturday. Would that suit you?' Catherine asked him.

'Absolutely. I'll clear my plans for the weekend. Are you going to tell Liam?' he asked.

'Yes. I'll tell him tonight,' she replied.

Chapter Forty Three

'Gerry, I'm telling you, there's something wrong. I'm not imagining it,' Abby said.

'Tell me everything, darling. When was the last time you spoke to Shay?' Gerry asked her.

'The day that Grace started her chemotherapy and I haven't spoken to him since we left the hospital.'

'But darling that's nearly a week ago now! Very strange for sure. Have you called him?' Gerry said with a frown.

'A couple of times, but I keep getting his answerphone,' Abby said tearfully.

'Have you left messages?' Gerry asked further.

'Yep. But he hasn't returned any of my calls. He sent me a text last night, just saying he was busy, but would be in touch soon.'

'Ouch,' Gerry replied. 'What did he say to you when you said goodbye at the hospital last Monday?'

'Love you baby. See you later,' Abby said, tears again filling up her eyes.

'Right, but then he texted you to cancel meeting us all in the Cock Tavern?' Gerry asked.

Abby nodded.

'Did you call him on Tuesday?'

'Yes and then again on Wednesday. Each time I keep getting his stupid answerphone,' Abby said.

'Has this ever happened before?' Gerry said with a frown. It didn't look good to him.

'Never. We speak to each other every day, sometimes twice a day. But it's Friday now and I still haven't heard from him. I'm really getting worried Gerry.'

'This doesn't make sense to me,' Gerry told his friend. 'I mean at Christmas he was all over you like a rash, darling. He used to sometimes make me feel like we were intruding, when we all went out together. I mean a couple of weeks ago he was bringing you to see show houses. This I think is just a classic case of male commitment phobia.'

Abby nodded her head. She thought this was the case herself. A few times over the past month she felt that Shay had withdrawn himself slightly. But then he'd do something so romantic that she'd thought it was all in her imagination. 'So Gerry, what should I do?'

'It's Friday evening. We're going to put our glad rags on and we're going out. Then you're going to stay here with Tom and me for the weekend. When that rascal Shay calls, you won't be at home. I think he's taking you for granted and I think he needs to realise that you're not always at his beck and call,' Gerry stated firmly.

'I don't feel like going out,' Abby said with a sigh.

'And that's precisely why you have to go out my darling. What's the alternative? Sit here feeling miserable? Now go home, get changed and I'll pick you up in an hour. And if Shay calls, don't answer it. Let him feel what it's like to be at the end of an answering machine for a change,' Gerry said, shooing her to the door. Seeing Abby smile at this, he continued, 'That's my girl! Now go put on some lip gloss!'

When Abby had left, Tom arrived, just back from the hospital. They were all taking it in turns visiting, making sure that someone was there all day and all evening. Gerry had been there earlier, as had Abby.

'Hi darling. How was Grace this evening?' Gerry said, jumping up to give Tom a hug.

'Tired and looking it. She didn't say much to be honest with you. So I only stayed for a little while. Any news with you?' Tom asked, relaxing into his partner's arms.

Gerry filled in Tom on his conversation with Abby. 'What do you think, darling?'

'Sounds like he's getting cold feet alright,' Tom answered. 'Poor Abby. She sure does pick them. To be honest, I never had him down as a bastard though.'

'Maybe he's not, Tom,' Gerry said. 'We don't know what's going on with him. He might just need some space for a few days.'

'That may well be the case Gerry, but what I don't like about all of this, is that he decided to go underground just as Abby needs him most. I mean he knows how close Abby is to Grace. He could see how upset she is. His timing is crap is all I'm saying,' Tom replied, shaking his head.

Gerry nodded, he had thought the same, but was determined to try and think the best of Shay. 'Well, we're going to cheer her up tonight. She's been sitting at home every evening this week on her own, pretending everything was okay with Shay to the rest of us.'

'Right. Where we going?' Tom asked.

'I thought we'd go to Trocadero's for dinner,' Gerry said, looking at Tom for his agreement.

'Sounds good, Gerry. But it won't be a late one for me. I'm off early in the morning to Wexford with Catherine.' Tom wasn't looking forward to it. Somehow or other he didn't believe that Fr O'Hara would admit culpability. 'Not a word to Abby tonight about my trip though,' Tom reminded Gerry, who drew a zip over his mouth to show his agreement.

****

An hour later they were sitting in the restaurant, sipping red wine.

'You mark my words,' Tom said to Abby. 'That little iPhone of yours will be beeping away before you go to bed. I'm telling you.'

Abby smiled at his words, grateful for them. 'We've spent every weekend together since that first weekend we met. This is the first Friday night we've not been together. It seems strange.'

'Oh darling. Don't you worry; this will be the last Friday night you spend without him. I bet you Shay's sitting at home right now wondering why you haven't called him again. If you don't hear from him this evening, he'll be on the blower by tomorrow I promise you,' Gerry declared.

Abby hoped so.

Chapter Forty Four

'Do you miss Wexford?' Tom asked Catherine.

'Yes, I do. I still think that it's the most beautiful part of the world. I really enjoyed our few days in Rose Tree Manor for the wedding.'

'The Murtaghs certainly loved seeing you again,' Tom added.

'Yes, it was great seeing them both. It's been well over thirty years, but seeing Molly, well it took me right back,' Catherine smiled. She had expected that going back to Rose Tree Manor would stir up some painful memories. But seeing her beautiful daughter so happy on her wedding day – not to mention her wonderful grandson – nothing could have ruined the day.

'Happy days?' Tom enquired.

'Yes, they were. I loved working in Rose Tree Manor. It was a fun time. Things were so uncomplicated back then,' she finished with a frown. The nearer they got to Wexford, the more her stomach started to turn. She was really worried. She'd wondered if she should maybe call first and make an appointment to see Fr O'Hara. But then, she chickened out every time she'd picked up the phone. In the end, she had called Ann, her cousin, for a chat. She'd casually asked about Fr O'Hara and secretly she'd been hoping that Ann would say he was on holiday. It would get her off the hook. But no, that would be too easy. He was fine, Ann had said.

Tom interrupted Catherine's thoughts, 'Have you had any more thought on how you want to do this?'

'Actually, yes,' Catherine replied. 'I thought that maybe you could go in on your own to talk to him. If you can persuade him without me, to be honest that will suit me perfectly.'

'And if I can't?' Tom asked.

'Then I'll talk to him,' Catherine said with a sigh.

****

They arrived in Ballymichael by midday and drove straight to the vicarage.

'How will I know what's going on?' Catherine asked.

'I tell you what; I've done this a few times before. I'm going to ring your mobile and leave it on while I'm in with Fr O'Hara. That way you can hear our conversation and work out if you want to come in. Does that sound okay?' Tom asked.

'Yes. That's a good idea,' Catherine said.

So Tom knocked on the door, expecting the housekeeper to answer. But when the door opened it was Fr O'Hara himself. He looked shocked when he saw Tom standing there and obviously recognised him.

'No need to remind you who I am, I see,' Tom said as he pushed his way past Fr O'Hara into the hall.

'How dare you come barging in here,' he blustered in response. 'You've no right.'

'Oh, I think you'll find that I've every right, Fr O'Hara. Or should I say Michael?' Tom said, emphasising the 'Michael'.

The priest visibly paled. 'You'd better come in.' He led the way into the living room. 'What do you want?' He sounded nervous.

'Funny that you didn't mention your name was Michael the last time I was here,' Tom stated. 'Must have slipped your mind.'

'It didn't seem relevant that's all,' Fr O'Hara answered. Then he appeared to pull himself together, putting a big smile on his face. 'How can I help you, Mr Whelan?'

'Well, first of all I'd like you to stop lying, Michael,' Tom said coldly.

'I'd prefer it if you'd call me Father. And I don't care for your tone, Mr Whelan.'

'Oh we're all friends here. You can call me Tom and I'll call you Michael. Makes it much easier, don't you think?' Tom sat down in one of the chairs and pointed to the other one.

Taking a seat opposite, Fr O'Hara said, 'You've obviously got something on your mind. Again, how can I help?'

Tom took a deep breath. He figured that there was no point in beating around the bush. 'Let's recoup a number of facts. Fact one, you raped Catherine Dunne. Fact two, you are the father of Catherine Dunne's daughter, Grace Devlin. Fact three, Grace is ill. She has leukaemia and needs a bone marrow transplant. The next fact is yet to be determined,' Tom finished.

Fr O'Hara looked more and more frightened with every word that Tom said. He stood up and turned his back to Tom. Tom knew that he was trying to compose himself. He wondered what his next move would be.

After a moment or two, he turned back towards Tom. 'I'm afraid your facts are incorrect, Mr Whelan. I have no idea who told you those poisonous lies. I can only imagine Catherine's mind turned when she sinned all those years ago. It grieves me to think that she's suffering. That poor delusional soul.'

Then the door opened and Catherine walked in. 'You bastard. How dare you?'

Tom walked over and put his arm around her, whispering, 'Calm down Catherine, it's okay, I'm here.'

She nodded and walked towards Fr O'Hara, 'Do you know that I have spent the past thirty three years literally terrified at the thought of ever having to see you again? For years I had nightmares of that day when you raped me. But do you know something? Looking at you now I'm not scared. I'm just disgusted. You disgust me, Father.' Catherine was shaking as she spat out the word 'Father', but it was true, she was no longer scared. Maybe it was the fact she had Tom in the room with her. But it was probably the first time in over thirty years that she didn't feel afraid.

'What do you want?' Fr O'Hara shouted at her. 'I suppose you're here to cause me trouble, you vindictive little bitch.'

With that Tom grabbed him by his shirt and threw him against the wall. 'Oh I'd watch your tongue if I were you, Michael. I'll be honest; I don't really need much of an excuse to rearrange your face. So go on, say something else, I dare you.'

Fr O'Hara had a feeling that Tom meant every word he said so didn't reply.

Nodding, Tom said, 'You made a wise choice old man. Now listen to what the lady has to say. Sit down and shut up.'

'Thank you, Tom,' Catherine said, and then turning to Fr O'Hara continued, 'We have a daughter. But you know that. She's a wonderful girl and is married with a four year old son. But she's not well. She has cancer.' She paused to let her words sink in.

'I'm sorry to hear that. I'll remember her in my prayers,' he answered her sombrely.

'She doesn't need your prayers,' Tom said sharply.

Catherine continued, 'Grace's best bet for a full recovery is to have a bone marrow transplant. All her family and friends including me, have been tested and we're not a match. You are going to go to Dublin on Monday to have the test to see if you are a match. If you are, you are going to be a donor for her.'

'I can't do that,' Fr O'Hara said. 'What would I tell my congregation? I'd be ruined.'

'For fuck's sake, stop thinking of your own stinking skin and think of your daughter,' Tom yelled at the priest. God, he wanted to deck him badly.

'Tom, sit down,' Catherine told him. Turning back to Fr O'Hara she said, 'Grace doesn't know about you and to be honest I don't want her to. It was bad enough telling her that her father was a rapist. It might just finish her off if she found out the rapist was a priest.'

Fr O'Hara looked like he'd been slapped when she said that.

'So, I want you to be tested and if you are a match, you can be an anonymous donor. I'll talk to Dr Kennedy to make sure he doesn't let Grace know who the donor is,' Catherine said.

'Why are you so sure I'll be a match?' he asked in a small voice.

'I'm not sure. But I'm desperate. I lost thirty two years of my daughter's life because of you. I've only just found her and I cannot lose her a second time,' Catherine finished on a sob.

Tom stood up, 'Right the lady has made her position clear. We've already set up the meeting with Dr Kennedy in Dublin for Monday morning. Here are the details. Don't have me come back here to get you Fr O'Hara. Because next time, I promise you I won't be asking so nicely or so quietly,' Tom finished.

Fr O'Hara paused before finally conceding, 'I'll be there.'

Getting up and walking to the door, Catherine finished by saying to the priest firmly, 'Do this for your daughter, but also do this for yourself. Then maybe there's a small chance you can save your own soul. Because from where I'm standing, there's only one place you are going and that's straight to hell.'

Chapter Forty Five

Abby was a bag of nerves. Shay had finally called her and he was on his way to her apartment for a chat. Judging by the tone of his voice, it wasn't going to be a happy chat either. She was running through all sorts of scenarios in her head as to why he had pulled back so much on their relationship in the past week. Had she done something wrong? But she was really stumped. They seemed to get on so well and were having a fantastic time, right up until last week, when he fell off the face of the planet. She'd been so upset over the weekend, despite being in Tom and Gerry's house. She was worried sick about Grace and felt very selfish that she was also feeling sorry for herself. For once, she thought she had her own special someone to share the worry with. But again she was on her own.

Earlier that morning while eating breakfast with Gerry, he had surmised, 'No word?'

'Nothing. He didn't call once all weekend. But I'm getting worried now Gerry, what if there's something wrong with him?' Abby asked worriedly.

'That did occur to me, darling. It's all very strange. What did you say on your last message?'

'Just that I was worried sick about him. That I'd appreciate a phone call just to let me know that he was okay. I also said to him that I was a big girl and if he didn't want to see me anymore that was fine. He should just tell me,' Abby said.

'Good girl,' Gerry had responded. 'Right, let's give him a couple of hours to reply. Darling, I think this is the first time in my life that I've ever seen you off your food!' he'd added in amazement as she picked at her breakfast. Abby never stopped eating. Things must be bad.

'I haven't eaten anything for days,' Abby said with a sigh. 'I've no appetite.'

Gerry just couldn't work out what was going on. How a guy could be so obviously in love with Abby one minute, and then disappear off the face of the earth the next. It didn't make sense. 'Right. I've an idea,' Gerry said. 'This not knowing is ridiculous. I'm going to call him on my mobile right now. He doesn't have my number, so hopefully he'll answer. We'll know if he's dodging your calls then. And also we can reassure ourselves that he's not lying at the bottom of the stairs with a broken neck.' Seeing the look of terror on Abby's face, he had said, 'Don't worry. I'm sure he's fine. Gerry thought to himself that if Shay weren't lying at the foot of the stairs with a broken neck, he'd soon have one by the time he'd finish wringing it. He dialled the number and within a few rings Shay answered.

'Hi, Shay speaking,' Shay said in a remarkably healthy sounding voice.

'Hi yourself, Shay. It's Gerry here, Abby's friend,' Gerry had replied.

'Oh hi, Gerry. Everything okay?' Shay had asked in a slightly worried voice.

'Everything's just fine now that I know you haven't been abducted by aliens, darling. Abby has been very worried, as you seem to have vanished into thin air,' Gerry said sarcastically.

'Sorry to have caused any worry,' Shay had said. 'I've just been very busy with work.' He did sound sorry.

Gerry had responded, 'I said it would be something like that. I said that there was no way Shay was the kind of guy to just blank his girlfriend for no good reason. I mean if you had decided you no longer wanted to date Abby, you would just say so.'

'Gerry, I'm going to call Abby shortly,' Shay had replied after a long pause.

'Glad to hear it, darling,' Gerry had answered and then hung up.

True to his word, Shay rang shortly afterwards and now Abby was waiting for him to arrive. The doorbell to her apartment buzzed. Checking her reflection one more time, Abby walked to the door to let Shay in. She noticed he didn't lean in for a kiss as was normal for them whenever they met, just nodded at her.

'No Gerry?' he asked, looking around the room.

'No, just me, Shay. Are you okay? I've been worried about you,' Abby said.

Shay ran his hands through his hair and started pacing around the small living room. Eventually he sat down and said to Abby, 'I'm sorry I worried you. I really didn't want to do that.'

Abby breathed a sigh of relief. At least he was sorry to have worried her. For a moment she had thought he was going to pretend that it was normal behaviour to just disappear for no reason.

'But you are right, I have been avoiding you. And I'm sorry about that too. I should have just told you that there was something bothering me,' Shay continued, looking a bit sheepishly at Abby.

'What is it, Shay? You can tell me,' Abby replied softly. She smiled at Shay to encourage him to open up to her.

'It's all going a bit too fast for me,' Shay replied. 'One minute we were having so much fun, enjoying getting to know each other and the next minute it was so…..' he stopped the sentence without finishing it.

'It was so what?' Abby asked.

'It was so intense, Abby,' Shay said. 'It's all this stuff with Grace. It's very hard to deal with.'

Abby actually felt her mouth fall open, 'You're calling Grace's relapse "stuff"?' She was getting angry now.

Shay reddened. 'That came out wrong. I am just so sorry that Grace is ill again. I really like the girl. I like all your friends. But this past few weeks since Grace got ill I've felt like I'm in the way. When you all get together you are a force to be reckoned with. I'm like an outsider.'

'I'm so sorry you feel that way,' Abby said genuinely. 'I know that none of my friends would ever intentionally want to make you feel like an outsider. And I certainly wouldn't.'

'I know that,' Shay said, smiling at her. 'You are just the nicest girl I've ever met.'

'So where does that leave us?' Abby asked quietly. 'Because if you are asking me to choose between you and my friends you will be disappointed.'

'Oh God no, I told you I like your friends, honestly. I just feel like maybe with everything that's going on right now we should just give each other some space, Abby?' Shay answered. 'You have to admit that things have got really serious really quickly. Maybe we should slow things down.'

Abby felt like Shay had slapped her. She was so hurt that he wanted them to take a break. She'd been on 'breaks' before with ex-boyfriends and in her experience, once you mentioned that word, it was game over. She started to get angry. She had given this relationship her everything, her heart, her love. She truly believed that Shay felt the same. But all along he was obviously feeling trapped. She felt really stupid too. Only a month ago she was in Donegal on Grace's hen and they were teasing her about getting engaged.

'What was the past six months about Shay?' Abby asked. 'You told me you loved me.'

'I do love you,' Shay answered. 'But maybe we can just slow things down.'

Abby had heard enough. 'Sure we can slow things down. We can just call it quits now. That slow enough for you?'

'I didn't mean that!' Shay said, looking worried.

'Oh I know what you meant alright. You are just too chicken to say it now. Well I'm not. It's over.'

Shay jumped up and said, 'Abby wait.'

She walked to the front door and turned to Shay and said 'No, I won't wait. I've waited long enough. I want a long-term relationship. I want marriage. I want children. I want love. I really thought that there was a strong possibility all of that would be with you. But what I don't want is a man that can't cope with "intense" moments in life. Nor can I be with a man who obviously has commitment issues. I'm too old and too busy to deal with your bullshit. It's over.' She stormed out of the front door slamming it hard for effect, and was halfway down Castle Avenue before she realised that she'd actually stormed out of her own house, not his! Not to mention the fact that she'd left without a coat or her handbag. Shit, she thought. Well there was no way she was going back now and knocking on the door of her own house. She made her way to Tom and Gerry's, hoping they were in; they had a spare key to her house.

Tom opened the door and took one look at Abby and shouted to Gerry, 'Abby's here, Gerry. You better get out the brandy.' He pulled her into his arms and gave her a huge hug.

Gerry was in the hall in seconds, pulling her to him for a hug too. He said to Tom, 'Make them doubles.'

Pouring three glasses, Tom passed the drinks out. 'You've caught up with Shay so?' Tom said gently. It didn't take a brain surgeon to work out that it didn't go well.

'It's over,' Abby said. She quickly recounted their conversation

'Oh Abby,' Gerry said to his friend. 'I'm so sorry to hear this. He has no idea that he's just let the most amazing person slip through his fingers.'

'I really thought he was going to propose,' Abby told the boys quietly. 'When all along he was just waiting to dump me. How did I get it so wrong?' She started to cry quietly.

'Oh my darling,' Gerry ran to comfort her, tears in his eyes too. He couldn't bear to see her upset. 'He's a monster. And you didn't get it wrong. He fooled us all, didn't he Tom?'

'Absolutely. I thought he was the real deal,' Tom confirmed. 'But he didn't actually dump you though? Unless I'm missing something?'

'No he didn't actually dump me, Tom,' Abby confirmed. 'But it was only a matter of time. He wanted a "break", to slow things down. That's just an excuse to use before you get the Dear John letter!'

'Maybe,' Tom concurred. 'Must be difficult all the same for someone new to come into our little gang.'

Gerry and Abby looked up at him, surprised.

'I couldn't have been more welcoming,' Gerry declared dramatically.

'Yes, true Gerry. We were all welcoming. But think about it. We've all so much history together; sure we finish each other's sentences sometimes. And all the stuff with Grace. We're all crying and devastated by it all. In all honesty, he doesn't know her that well. So it must be very intimidating.'

'I suppose....' Gerry said.

Abby was biting her lip thinking over what Tom had said. 'Do you think I was too hard on him?' she whispered, starting to doubt herself.

'No, of course not,' Tom said quickly. 'He's behaved like a right eejit this past week. But that doesn't change the fact that up to now we all thought he was a lovely guy. Maybe he still is a lovely guy, he just got scared.'

'And I told him it was over!' Abby said, crying again.

'Think we might need another bottle, darling,' Gerry said to Tom as he topped up Abby's glass. Then the doorbell went and they all jumped at the sound. Tom went out to answer it, and standing there looking very worried was the man himself, Shay.

'Tom is Abby here by any chance?' he asked.

'She is, Shay,' Tom replied, not budging.

'Can I see her?' Shay asked.

'Why?' Tom asked him suspiciously. 'What do you want?'

'Well she left without even her house keys,' Shay said, holding them up. 'I was worried she'd be locked out.'

Tom snatched them from his hands. 'I'll go check and see if she wants to see you.' He closed the door in Shay's face. No harm in making him sweat a bit. He had made Abby cry after all. When he went into the living room he started to laugh as he witnessed Gerry quickly trying to wipe away the mascara from under Abby's eyes.

'Give me a minute while I try to sort this out,' Gerry said to Tom dramatically.

'I take it you heard that was Shay?' Tom replied dryly. 'Do you want to see him Abby?'

'Of course she wants to see him!' Gerry whispered in a loud voice. 'There, you'll have to do. A bit pale, but you will go running out of your house with no make-up bag!' he moaned.

'I'll go get him,' Tom said, walking to the door. 'Come on in. She'll see you.'

Gerry quickly whispered to Abby, 'Listen to me, let him do the talking. If he wants you, he'll make sure you know that. Don't put words into his mouth. You need to know that he really wants to be with you.'

Abby nodded solemnly, 'I promise.'

Shay looked very nervous as he walked into the living room. 'Can I speak to you Abby, on our own?'

'Yes,' Tom said at the exact same time as Gerry said 'No.'

Abby almost giggled, but instead turned to Gerry, 'Thank you for everything, but I've got this.'

Before he could complain, Tom grabbed Gerry's arm and steered him to the kitchen.

Abby sat down and said nothing. She looked at Shay and waited for him to speak.

'Abby everything has gone wrong. I've really made a mess of it all,' Shay said sheepishly.

Abby simply acknowledged this with a nod. She mentally zipped her mouth shut, exactly as Gerry had told her to.

'I never wanted to break up with you for good. I just thought we could have a break for a few nights,' he continued. 'I got scared, Abby,' Shay said quietly. He looked at her and thought she would never say something. He was terrified he was losing her. 'Abby, I love you. And it was only when you slammed the door to your apartment that I realised just how much. In that moment I realised that I had literally let you walk out of my life. Abby, please don't let this be the end. Don't let me being a complete gobshite this past week ruin what we've had for the past six months,' he begged.

'You have been very careless with your love for me, Shay,' Abby said to him. 'How do I know that you won't be so careless again?'

'Abby I am certain I will mess up every now and then. But I am also certain that I love you. I want to make this relationship work. I want us to have a future together. I don't want to lose you. Please let me make it up to you.'

Abby almost ran into his arms at this, but there was one more thing bothering her. 'What about all the stuff going on with Grace? It's not going away, Shay. She's sick and I'm going to be there for

291

her. I'm going to get upset at times and I need someone by my side that is not going to bail at the first sign of trouble.'

'I know,' Shay replied. 'I've let you down. It won't happen again. Let me be there for you. And all your friends. I really like them, honestly.'

'We like you too, darling,' a voice shouted from outside the door. This was followed by Tom's voice shouting, 'Get away from there.'

Abby and Shay giggled at Gerry's interruption. It was the perfect tension breaker. Shay walked over to Abby, 'I truly am sorry, Abby.' He looked so sincere.

'I'm sorry too, if I've made you feel left out these past few weeks.' And then he leaned in and kissed her long and hard.

Chapter Forty Six

Catherine and Liam were waiting in Dr Kennedy's office. He was due any minute and they would find out if Grace had found her donor following Fr O'Hara's test.

'I feel sick,' Liam said.

Catherine knew how he felt. She hadn't slept much since her meeting with Fr O'Hara. She'd been terrified he wouldn't turn up for the test, but then when he did, a new fear was keeping her awake. What if he wasn't a suitable donor?

'She's getting worse,' Liam said simply.

Catherine grabbed Liam's hand and squeezed it. She knew that Liam was right.

'She's not sleeping at night. She has terrible dreams,' Liam went on. He'd spent the last couple of nights in the hospital with Grace, as Catherine was back staying with them in Swords. 'Sometimes I can't stand being in that bloody hospital room anymore and I have to get out. But I'm only home for ten minutes and I can't stand not being with Grace. It's just so hard watching her in pain.'

Catherine understood only too well what Liam was saying. Over the past week, Grace seemed to shrink in size. She'd lost so much weight; it looked like you could break her if you hugged her too tightly. She was covered in bruises and Catherine knew that she was in pain a lot of the time.

'Where's Dr Kennedy?' Liam said impatiently. Then with that the receptionist told them the doctor was ready for them. Liam and Catherine walked into his office.

'Please take a seat,' he told them both. 'Right, as you can imagine this is quite unorthodox,' Dr Kennedy started. 'Talking to you both without Grace present.'

'We have our reasons Dr Kennedy,' Catherine said.

He nodded in response. 'Right, well as you know, Fr O'Hara came forward on Friday to check whether or not he is a suitable donor. What we are looking for is a donor who matches Grace' HLA antigens, of which there are six main ones.'

Liam was holding his breath, waiting for the doctor to get to the point.

Sensing their impatience, Dr. Kennedy continued, 'I'm sorry if sound like I'm dragging this out. I just need you to understand the importance of having all six tissue typing groups matched. I'm afraid the news isn't good. Fr O'Hara is not a suitable donor for Grace.'

Both Catherine and Liam sagged at this news. 'I was so sure...' Catherine started.

'What now?' Liam asked. 'What now doctor? What can we do?'

'Well, all is not lost, Liam. I've some good news for you that think may just cheer you both up.'

Liam and Catherine perked up with this and looked at Dr Kennedy puzzled.

'A Mr Noel Dunne, from Perth in Australia, it appears is a perfect match.'

'Noel, oh my God,' Catherine said with a surprise. 'I didn't even know he had himself tested.'

Liam let out a whoop of joy, barely believing his ears. 'Does that mean he's going to be Grace's donor?' Liam asked.

'That it does, Liam.' Dr Kennedy replied. 'He is, I believe currently making plans to travel to Ireland. When he arrives, I'll do some further tests to ensure that he is indeed a match, but I'm confident that he is. Then we'll start preparing Grace's body for the transplant and start harvesting the cells from Mr Dunne's marrow. I'll need to go through all of this with Grace of course.'

Liam jumped up and hugged Dr Kennedy, 'Thank you, thank you.'

'I can't believe it,' Catherine said. 'I've got to ring Noel.'

Dr Kennedy stood up and, pointing to his phone, said, 'Be my guest. Give your brother a call. I think the hospital can stretch just this once!' He was so happy to finally be able to give some hope to Grace's family. He'd grown very fond of her over the past year.

Catherine was shaking as she dialled Noel's number and prayed he'd be at home. Her prayers were answered, because he answered almost immediately.

'Sis, that you?' Noel's booming voice came out.

Catherine tried to answer but couldn't because she had started to cry and couldn't stop.

Liam grabbed the phone, holding it between Catherine and himself, 'Noel, thank you so much. I had no idea you were getting yourself tested.'

'You're welcome Liam. I know I only met you guys recently, but Grace is my niece and I love her. And I love my sister and when she rang to tell me Grace was ill again, I just had to do something.'

'Why didn't you tell me?' Catherine finally managed to get out.

'I was afraid I wouldn't be a match. I didn't want to get your hopes up. I rang Dr Kennedy and he arranged for me to have my tests here in Perth General. I only found out about an hour ago!'

'Words can't say what this means to us,' Catherine said.

'Sure you'd do the same for my lot,' Noel answered. 'I'm leaving tomorrow. I'll see you on Wednesday!'

Making arrangements to pick him up at the airport, Catherine and Liam hung up, hugging each other, laughing and crying at the same time.

'Let's go tell your daughter!' Liam said to Catherine.

Grace was dozing when they walked in, Tom and Gerry sitting by her bed quietly. They were waiting for the news on Fr O'Hara. Seeing the looks on both Liam's and Catherine's faces, they realised the news was good. Liam gently kissed Grace's forehead and she opened her eyes.

'Hey baby,' she smiled at him. 'Sorry. Fell asleep,' she said, turning to Tom and Gerry.

'I've just been to see Dr Kennedy, babe,' Liam told Grace.

She looked up suspiciously at her husband, 'What's wrong, Liam?'

'Nothing, babe. Just the opposite. They've got a donor. They've found a match for you.'

Grace couldn't believe her ears, 'Who?'

Catherine walked up to the bed and grabbed Grace's hand, 'Noel. Your Uncle Noel, Grace. He had himself tested in Australia and he's a perfect match!'

Tom and Gerry let out a gasp of surprise. They assumed the match was Fr O'Hara.

'I can't believe it,' Grace said.

'Believe it, babe,' Liam said. 'He's travelling tomorrow. He'll be here on Wednesday. Dr Kennedy will be in later to go through what's going to happen.'

Grace felt tears streaming down her face. At last, some good news. 'Told you'd I'd beat this,' she said to Liam.

'The best is yet to come,' Liam whispered quietly into her ear.

Chapter Forty Seven

Grace was sitting in her hospital bed surrounded by all her friends and family. They were having a pre-transplant party and everyone was in high spirits. Grace actually felt better; it was amazing what some good news did to improve her spirits. 'I can't believe this,' Grace said for the hundredth time. 'I had hoped and prayed...'

'Darling, "hope is a good thing, maybe the best of things, and no good thing ever dies,"' Gerry said dramatically, standing up to face everyone, his arms outstretched.

Seeing Noel's startled face, Tom said to him. '*Shawshank Redemption*. He's quoting a line from it. Ignore him, we all do.'

'Thank you, Gerry,' Grace said with a laugh. 'Very inspiring.'

Then Liam's mom arrived to take Jack home with her. He was going for a few days' holidays, while the transplant happened. 'I'm praying for you, Grace,' she said to her daughter-in law, kissing her gently on her cheek.

'Mommy, when you coming home?' Jack asked. He looked younger than his four years when he asked this. Although they'd all tried their best to make this easier on him, Liam and Grace could tell that he was anxious. He'd started to wet his bed again, which hadn't happened for at least two years. His Montessori teacher had also called Liam aside the previous day to tell him that she was concerned about Jack. 'He's been very quiet lately,

Liam,' she'd told him. 'And when I asked him what was wrong, he said he was sad.'

'Did he say what was making him sad?' Liam asked her.

'No, I questioned him of course, but he said he didn't know why. Just that he felt sad.'

Liam hadn't told Grace this as she was worried enough about him as it was. Jack had taken to crying whenever it was time for him to go home from the hospital, clinging to Grace. It was breaking both their hearts. Grace had insisted that Liam spend more time at home over the past couple of days. It was too much for Jack to cope with: Grace being in hospital and Liam hardly at home at all. Grace kissed Jack firmly on the lips, 'I'm going to be coming home real soon, I promise. Uncle Noel is going to give me some of his bone marrow and it's going to make me feel better. I promise.'

Jack looked at Uncle Noel. 'Are you?' he asked him.

'Yes I am, Jack. In a couple of days it will all be done. You wait and see, your Mommy will be home in no time.'

Tara was quietly crying. It broke her heart to see Jack missing his Mom so much.

'Can I come in again tomorrow, Daddy?' he asked Liam.

'We'll see, buddy. Mommy has to get ready for her transplant.' Jack started to cry again, throwing himself into Grace's arms.

'Course you can come in tomorrow sweetie-pie,' Grace said, wiping Jack's tears away. 'I couldn't make it through the day without seeing your gorgeous face.' Grace leaned over to her bedside locker and picked up the framed photograph of Liam, Grace and Jack that was taken outside Mickey Mouse's house. In the background of the house was a beautiful bright rainbow. It was her absolute favourite picture. 'You take this sweetie-pie,' Grace said to Jack. 'And whenever you want to see me, you look at this photo and remember the fun we had in Disney. Now dry your tears and go with your Nana.'

Clutching his photograph tightly, Jack gave each of his aunts and uncles a kiss and left.

'Oh my God, Liam. I can't bear it,' Grace said, breaking down.

'I can't bear it either darling,' Gerry said dramatically, tears streaming down his face.

Abby started to giggle at this, which caused Tara and Sean to start giggling, and within minutes everyone was laughing hysterically and crying at the same time.

'Oh Abby, it's good to see you laughing,' Grace told her friend. 'I've been worried about you.'

'I'm fine.' Abby said with a big smile, amazed at Grace's ability to put others before herself even when she was the one everyone needed to look out for. 'I'm seeing Shay later on. We're going for dinner.'

'That's wonderful. I'm so pleased for you.' Grace said, grinning.

Tara jumped up then and walked over to Grace's bed, 'Move over cousin, I've some news for you.'

Grace looked up at Tara enquiringly.

Tara stood up and said with a flair for drama that Gerry would envy, 'I am with child.'

'No!' Grace screamed.

'Yes!' Tara screamed back.

With that the room broke into pandemonium as everyone congratulated Sean and Tara.

'When are you due?' Grace asked her friend.

'Well I'm only barely pregnant, seven weeks,' Tara said, making a face. 'And I know that you're not meant to tell people until you get to twelve weeks, but I thought everyone could do with some good news for a change!'

'That's the best news I've heard in ages,' Grace said to her cousin. 'I'm so happy for you both.'

'So now, that gives you about seven months to get back on your feet,' Sean told Grace. 'Because this baby is going to need a godmother in full working order you know!'

Grace beamed at this news. 'Well if I ever needed an incentive to get better, there it is!'

Tara coughed then said, 'The baby will need a godfather too.' Turning to Liam she continued, 'We thought you'd do.'

Everyone laughed at Liam's expression. He looked like he was going to have a heart attack. 'And I thought you had me down as the spawn of the Devil!' he eventually spluttered out to Tara.

'I have no idea where you got that from,' Tara said haughtily.

'Well I'd be honoured to be godfather to junior,' Liam said walking over to Tara and pulling her in for a big bear hug. 'Always knew you liked me really!'

Chapter Forty Eight

'T-Day had arrived, as Grace had taken to calling it. She'd had a course of radiation to eradicate all traces of her own bone marrow. Following which, she'd been placed in an isolation ward. They had to be totally careful now, as she was wide open to infection. Dr Kennedy had told her that she could expect to call this germ-free room home for at least a month. Only Liam and Catherine – not even Jack, much to Grace's distress – would be allowed in the room, and that was only after they'd put on protective clothing. Everyone else would have to contact Grace via an intercom or on the phone. There was even a hatch whereby all items were delivered into the room to ensure that it stayed germ-free. While this was going on, Noel was on the operating table having one litre of his bone marrow removed. He was going to stay overnight in hospital to recover, but hopefully would be okay to go home tomorrow. Catherine was with him. The doctors had predicted he'd be stiff and sore for a couple of days, but hopefully, nothing worse than that. Grace wasn't sure how she'd ever be able to repay him. It was a debt that was maybe un-payable.

Grace shivered. The room was actually very cold. The nurse had said it was because of the system used to keep the room sterile. Grace was feeling really nauseous and she couldn't work out if it was the radiation – probably – or the waiting for the actual transplant. She hoped Liam got here soon. It was so lonely in the little room. She didn't have long to wait. He walked in a few moments later.

'Not long now, babe,' he said, smiling as he walked in. Grace couldn't help but notice the new lines around her husband's face. Cancer was taking its toll on Liam too, she knew that.

'Come here,' Grace said, patting her bed. 'I've something to ask of you.'

Liam sat on the edge of the bed and smiled at his wife. 'What can I do for you, babe?' he asked tenderly.

'Kiss me passionately. Then tell me you love me. If something goes wrong, I want to go smiling,' Grace said.

Liam leaned in and did just as his wife asked. They sat holding each other until it was time for Grace to leave for the transplant.

A few hours later Liam walked into Noel's room where everyone had gathered to wait for news of Grace's transplant.

'Well, it's done,' Liam told everyone.

'How is she?' Noel asked.

'Worried about you, mate,' Liam told him. 'How you doing? Are you in much pain?'

'Not a bit of it,' Noel said bravely. 'Nothing a few days' rest won't cure.'

'Looking like a florist in here,' Liam said with a laugh.

'Can you believe it?!' Noel answered. He couldn't get over how Grace's family and friends had treated him. They had welcomed him like a returned war hero and he couldn't keep up with the stream of visitors and friends who called in to see him.

'Did you give her our love?' Tara asked Liam.

'Of course,' he replied with a smile. 'She knows you guys are all here willing her on. She said to say she loves you.' It was difficult for them all, not being able to see her. 'Won't be long though and she'll be home again,' Liam said.

Tom walked over and gave him a hug, 'You alright buddy?'

'I'm getting there,' he replied.

'We're all here for you too, you know. Don't forget that,' Tom said.

****

The next three weeks went by intolerably slowly for Grace. It was an endless stream of blood tests, tablets and mind-blowing boredom. She found that she couldn't get up the interest to watch TV or even read a book. She spent all her time wishing Liam and Catherine were with her, but when they did arrive, she didn't have the energy to talk to them. But the good news was she wasn't getting any graft-versus-host problems that Dr Kennedy had warned her about. He had said that some patients find that their body – the host – and the graft – Noel's marrow – don't like each other. In some cases the marrow can start attacking vital parts of the body causing a rash to break out. But thankfully, Grace was spared that. She also managed to avoid getting any infections.

Liam walked in and kissed Grace with a grin on his face. 'Guess what?' Liam asked.

'What?' Grace answered irritably.

'How would you like to give your son a big kiss today?' Liam asked with a big smile. 'That's right, grumpy. I've just spoken to the nurse and you're moving back into your old room today!'

Grace had never felt so happy in all her life. Not being able to touch Jack was unbelievable. He'd come to see her through the window and she'd spoken to him daily on the phone. But he couldn't understand why he couldn't go into her room. It had broken her heart.

'When?!' Grace demanded.

'Any minute! Thought that would put a smile on your face!' Liam said, laughing at his wife's face.

'Go get Jack, Liam. Go get him from Montessori and bring him in right now,' Grace said excitedly.

'Already taken care of. Catherine's picking him up at this minute!' Liam said, well aware how urgently Grace needed to feel her son in her arms.

An hour later, Grace was back in her old room. 'I never thought I'd be so happy to see these old beige walls again!' she said with a smile.

Dr Kennedy arrived then. 'Well, Grace. You're looking very good.' He picked up her chart and smiled. 'Your white cells are 0.7 to 1 and your marrow has started to grow. That's excellent.'

Grace couldn't believe it. This was the first time since all this cancer shit started that Dr. Kennedy had used the word excellent! 'Does that mean I can go home?' Grace asked.

'I'm afraid I'll need you here for a few more weeks, Grace. We need to make sure all your counts rise to an acceptable level. Plus, we need to ensure you don't get any major infections. You're still going to be taking quite a bit of medication, which we have to monitor,' he answered.

'But I'm on the home stretch though,' Grace said with a smile.

'Yes, Grace, I do believe you are,' he answered with a smile of his own. 'But you may continue to feel some nausea over the next few weeks. Keep drinking lots of fluids, that will help. Now, I also need you to start eating again. You're dangerously thin, Grace.'

'I want to eat, honestly. It's just as soon as I do, it comes back again – one way or another,' she finished bluntly.

'One bite at a time, Grace. One bite at a time. It will get easier. But you must keep your strength up,' he advised.

'I promise,' Grace told him earnestly. She was willing to do anything, if it meant that she could get out of hospital quicker. 'Oh Liam. I haven't felt this happy since our honeymoon.'

'Me neither,' Liam replied.

'I'm going to get better,' Grace said with a giggle.

'Never doubted it,' Liam said, giggling too.

'Liar,' Grace said, throwing a pillow at him.

'Well, maybe once or twice. But only for a second,' Liam admitted.

Then the door burst open with Jack screaming at the top of his voice 'Mommy!'

Liam picked him up and he threw him into Grace's arms.

'I missed you, Mommy,' Jack said sorrowfully.

'I missed you too sweetie-pie,' Grace answered him. 'So much.'

'Did Uncle Noel's medicine make you better, Mommy?' he asked earnestly.

'Absolutely. I'm much better now, Jack. I'm getting stronger every day and I'll be home real soon, I promise,' she answered, tears in her eyes.

'Can I see you every day now, Mommy?' Jack asked.

'You better believe it!' Grace said, tickling him until he begged her to stop.

Chapter Forty Nine

Grace continued to get stronger every day, until eventually it was time for her to go home. Liam had packed up her things and she was ready to go. A nurse was standing with a wheelchair to take her out to the car. Grace shook her head though, 'I walked in here on two feet; I'm going to walk out on two feet too.' Holding Jack's hand, she followed Liam out. She had earlier given presents to each of the nurses, without whom she knew she'd have never have got through the past two months. She couldn't believe that it was now almost March. Walking out into the hospital grounds, she actually felt dizzy for a minute. It was a beautiful spring morning and the brightness hit her smack in the eyes.

'You okay, babe?' Liam asked with concern.

Grace assured him she was. She couldn't wait for Liam to be able to start living again. He spent his whole time worrying and caring about her and Jack, and Catherine too. They drove home singing songs. Jack's favourite song was *Maggie May* by Rod Stewart. He just loved it and kept asking his parents to play it over and over again. Happy to oblige, they kept hitting replay and spent forty minutes singing the same song over and over.

'Is Catherine at home?' Grace asked Liam.

'She's gone back to Meath for a few days. She thought we might like to have some time on our own for a while,' Liam answered

Grace smiled. It was typical of Catherine to be so thoughtful. And to be honest, she was glad; it would be nice to have some quiet time without doctors and nurses around, just the three of them.

'Gerry wanted to throw a party for you too,' Liam told Grace. 'He was quite put out when I told him that I'd rather he didn't!'

'I can imagine,' Grace said with a laugh. 'Darling, how could you be so cruel?' she mimicked Gerry's accent perfectly.

'You don't mind do you?' Liam asked with a frown. He hoped he'd made the right choice.

'Liam, I am so relieved. I couldn't face a big party now. I'm too tired to be honest, plus I really want to just relax with you two,' Grace said honestly.

'I wouldn't say you're off the hook though,' Liam told his wife. 'Gerry left muttering about it not being right that we didn't celebrate your homecoming. I'd get ready for a surprise over the next few days!'

Grace felt tears in her eyes as she arrived outside her apartment. It had never looked quite so lovely. Liam fussed as he helped her up the stairs, and Jack was shouting, 'Close your eyes, Mommy!'

'I thought you said no surprises?' Grace said to Liam. But she did as she was told and let Jack lead her into the living room.

'Open, Mommy!'

Following Jack's orders, she opened her eyes and saw a huge banner tied to the curtain rail, saying 'Welcome home Mommy!', obviously Jack's handiwork, with a little bit of help from his Daddy.

'Wow,' she said. 'Where did you buy that fancy sign?'

Jack beamed with pride. 'I made it, Mommy! Daddy, Mommy thought that we bought it!'

'I heard, buddy. I told you it was really good,' Liam said with a grin.

'It's a masterpiece, Jack,' Grace said, bending down to kiss her son. 'I love it.'

'And we have cake!' Jack said. 'Oh no, it's a surprise. I wasn't supposed to say.'

'Oh I hate surprises, Jack,' Grace told him. 'But I love cake! Where is it?'

Liam and Jack went into the kitchen and left Grace with strict instructions that she sit down and relax. They came back in a few minutes later with a laden tray. 'A nice cup of rosy!' Liam told her.

Grace looked at the cake and couldn't believe her eyes. It had the photo of the three of them outside Mickey Mouse's house on the top of it.

'Do you like it, Mommy? I picked the photo!'

'I love it,' Grace said honestly. 'It's just perfect.'

'It has your rainbow, too,' Jack added. 'And Daddy let me pick a DVD for us all to watch.'

'Let me guess – would that be Mickey Mouse by any chance?' Grace asked with a smile.

'Yes!' Jack replied. 'How did you guess? Put it on, Daddy.'

Liam put the DVD on and sat down on the couch with Grace curled up into his chest and Jack curled up into Grace.

'This is perfect,' Grace whispered.

Chapter Fifty

Grace was getting ready; she was going out for dinner tonight. She'd been home for two weeks and was feeling much better. Tonight the gang were all going to dinner at Siam's to celebrate her recovery. Noel was also going home this weekend, so it was a farewell party for him. Both Noel and Catherine were staying at Tom and Gerry's tonight as they had more room for them.

'You look great, babe,' Liam said, walking into their bedroom. 'I think you've put on some weight!'

'I think this is about the only time that a girl wants to hear those words!' Grace said with a laugh. 'Jack okay at your Mam's?'

'Happy we're going out, Grace. Uncle Martin is over as well, so Jack is being totally spoiled. This was the first time I dropped him there in weeks that he didn't start crying when I left. I think he's finally realised that we're both here to stay,' Liam said smiling.

'I know. He's been so clingy with me. But today, when I dropped him at the crèche, he barely said goodbye!' Grace replied.

They got up and left for the restaurant, picking up a wrapped gift as they left. They were the last to arrive. Everyone else was sitting down and when they got there, the others all started clapping and cheering.

'Shut up!' Grace said with an embarrassed laugh. 'Everyone's looking!' She sat down next to Tara. 'How you feeling? Still got morning sickness?'

'No, thankfully that little beauty has gone. Look at the size of me already! Only four months pregnant and I'm huge!' Tara said, but with the biggest smile on her face. She was secretly delighted. She loved wearing clothes that accentuated her bump. She'd never felt so much like a woman, so earthy and maternal all at once. She could barely contain her excitement that inside her right this moment was a tiny little baby, growing every day, getting ready to come into the world.

'You look radiant, Tara,' Liam said.

'Thanks, Liam,' Tara smiled in return.

'My beautiful wife,' Sean said proudly, then placed a hand gently on her little bump. 'You're looking better too Grace,' Sean said.

'I put on two pounds this week,' Grace answered triumphantly. They all raised their glasses to that. The waiter arrived with a bottle of champagne.

'Moet Chandon. Oh la la!' Grace said with a laugh.

'Only the best for you, darling!' Gerry declared.

Everyone took a glass, with the obvious exception of Liam. Tom stood up then to make a toast. 'We're here for two special people. One an old and dear friend, the other a new but equally dear friend. For one of them, we're here to say welcome back and for the other we're here to say a fond farewell. Ladies and gentlemen, please raise your glasses to Grace and Noel.'

'To Grace and Noel,' everyone said.

Grace stood up then. 'My turn! I'd like to say a few words.' The gang clapped and cheered. 'I'm soooooo glad to be back! I feel great and I've never been happier than right now. I couldn't have got through the past couple of months without all of your support and love. Words will never express how grateful Liam and I are for that.' Grace then turned towards Noel and continued, 'Uncle Noel. You gave me an amazing gift. I'll never be able to thank you enough. To me you're my star. So, as a small token of my gratitude, I've got a little something for you.' Grace handed him the parcel.

Noel quickly dabbed his eyes with his napkin, before taking his parcel. He opened it and in it was a frame. He read the words to the group. 'A star has been named in your honour. This unique star will be called Noel Dunne from this day forth. With love always, Grace, Liam and Jack.'

Everyone clapped and Noel jumped up to kiss his niece. 'Well I never, a star named after me. I'm honoured, love. Truly honoured. I'm going to hang this over the mantelpiece at home.' He was chuffed.

The gang spent the night chatting and laughing, talking about the future. Noel invited every one of them to come to Perth to visit him and his family and they all promised to do just that. It was a great night. Finally, at midnight, Grace began to feel tired.

'You okay?' Tara asked, noticing her cousin looking a little pale.

'Just tired. Still not back to full throttle!' Grace replied. 'You look tired too.'

'What are we like? Both nauseous, both tired! There's a pair of us in it!' Tara said with a laugh.

They all decided to call it a night and with kisses and hugs all round they said their goodbyes.

'You're quiet, babe,' Liam said when they got home. 'Tired?'

'I've a slight headache to be honest. Think I'll take a Nurofen,' she answered him. 'Too much excitement!'

'It was a long night,' Liam agreed. 'Straight to bed for you young lady!'

With no argument, Grace climbed into bed and fell asleep almost immediately.

****

The following morning she woke up feeling worse. Her headache had got worse and she felt really warm. Liam decided not to take any chances and rang Sean.

'Let's check that temperature,' Sean said to Grace, sticking his thermometer in her mouth. '103.5.'

'That's high,' Liam said.

'Yep. I'm sorry Grace. We're going to have to get you into hospital straightaway. No arguments.' Sean picked up his phone and called for an ambulance. Two hours later she was back in hospital and her temperature had rocketed to 105. Grace was thrashing about and wasn't really coherent anymore. Liam was standing outside the hospital room with Tara, while Sean tried to find out what was going on.

'This can't be happening, Tara,' Liam said. 'She was fine last night. She was getting better.'

Tara couldn't believe it either. They had all thought that Grace was on the mend. How could she get so bad so quickly? Sean came back and brought the two of them into the relative's room.

'Her temperature is now at 105.1.'

'Fuck,' Tara said.

'That's bad?' Liam asked. 'What's wrong with her?'

'She's obviously got some form of infection. We won't know what until the blood tests come back. But right now, they're concerned about her heart. Her blood pressure has dropped dramatically. They're doing everything they can to stabilise her Liam.'

'Can I go and see her?' Liam said in a voice that sounded like he was a small boy no more than Jack's age.

'In a few minutes I'd say so, Liam. They've a few more tests to do. They'll come and get you,' Sean replied.

Liam dropped to his seat. He couldn't believe it. This was all wrong. 'I'm scared Tara,' he said simply.

'Me too,' she answered, walking over to Liam and taking him in his arms. 'You better ring Catherine, Sean.' He went outside and started making calls. Soon, the waiting room was full with Tom, Gerry, Abby, Shay, Catherine, Noel, Mrs Ryan and Uncle Martin, Tara and Sean. Liam was pacing the hall over and over, waiting to be allowed to see Grace.

'It's been nearly an hour since we got here, Sean,' he said. 'Surely, they've done all their tests now.'

With that, a nurse walked in. 'Liam, you can go in now.'

Liam practically ran to Grace's room and couldn't believe his eyes when he saw her. Dr Kennedy was standing by her bed waiting for him.

'Grace,' Liam sobbed. 'What's wrong?'

'She's unconscious, Liam. We had to sedate her as she was thrashing about so much with the fever. We're giving her meds to bring her temperature down. Grace has a very nasty infection in her blood – she's got sepsis. We've started her on a course of strong antibiotics.'

'Will she be alright?' Liam asked quietly.

'I hope so,' Dr Kennedy answered, patting him on his shoulder. 'She should come out of sedation in an hour or so. Hopefully the temperature should be down by then. I'll be back later.'

Liam sat holding her hand, praying over and over for her to get through this. He didn't even hear Catherine come into the room. She walked over and put her arms around him.

'Dr Kennedy came to see us. He's filled us in,' she told Liam. 'How you doing?'

'Bargaining,' he answered flatly.

'Sorry?' Catherine asked him puzzled.

'I'm bargaining with God. You get Grace better, I'll do anything, sort of thing,' Liam said, his eyes never leaving Grace for a second.

'Oh of course, I've done that myself quite a bit too,' Catherine replied.

They sat quietly for another forty minutes or so, and then Grace began to come out of sedation. She opened her eyes and looked frightened, then calmed down when she saw Liam.

'Don't talk, babe. You've got to conserve your energy. You've got a nasty infection. But you're getting antibiotics to sort it out. You gave us quite a scare, you know. Everyone's here, all outside waiting to say hello,' Liam whispered to her.

Grace smiled faintly. She closed her eyes again. She couldn't seem to be able to keep them open.

An hour later, she opened them again. Liam was still sitting there, but this time Tara and Sean were with him. She smiled. They were back to taking shifts. The nurse came in then and asked them all to wait outside, as she had some more tests to do. Liam joined the others in the relatives' room.

A cup of coffee appeared from somewhere and Gerry had some sandwiches for him. 'You've got to eat darling,' he said very gently.

Liam couldn't taste a thing, but he somehow managed to get half a sandwich down.

Dr Kennedy came back in a moment later. 'Liam, may I have a word in private please.'

'You can talk freely here Dr Kennedy. We're all family,' Liam said.

'I'm sorry, Liam. I'm afraid that Grace isn't responding to our treatment,' Dr Kennedy stated.

'What does that mean?' He looked the doctor squarely in the eye. He was vaguely aware of the others surrounding him. He felt a hand on his shoulder. He heard a strangled sob; he wasn't sure who it came from.

'She's deteriorated quickly, I'm afraid. I think the time has come for you to say your goodbyes. I'm so sorry,' the doctor said very gently.

Liam put his head in his hands and felt himself sink to the ground. Arms reached out to him but he pushed them away. The room was deathly silent. It was as if time froze. After a moment or two, he stood up. 'Does Grace know?' he asked in a strong voice that surprised everyone.

'Yes. She knows,' Dr Kennedy replied.

'How long do we have?' Liam asked.

'I don't think she'll last the night,' Dr Kennedy replied. 'I'm so sorry, Liam. We have done everything but her body is just not strong enough.' He wiped tears from his eyes. He had grown very fond of Grace and Liam over the year.

Liam felt like he'd just been hit by a bolt of lightning. Every fibre and nerve in his body was on edge. The room felt like it was suffocating him. It was still deathly quiet. Nobody was speaking; he supposed they were all, like him, adjusting to the shock. He wanted to run out of the room and out of the hospital. Nobody would blame him. Instead he turned to the others. 'Please. Don't,' he said to his mother as she went to embrace him. 'If you hug me now, I swear I'll fucking collapse. We have to be strong now for Grace's sake. Okay?' Nobody answered him, so he said louder, 'Okay?' They nodded their assent. 'I'm going to see Grace now. Can you give me ten minutes on my own? Then come in. I know she'll want all of you with her. Mam, can you go get Jack?'

'Of course, son,' she answered. 'We're all here for you Liam. Whatever you need.' She walked over to her child. Her heart was breaking for him and for her grandson. She didn't know how they would get through what was facing them. She pulled Liam into her arms and whispered, 'There, there son.' It was something she used to say to him as a baby when she was trying to calm him down to sleep. Liam allowed himself a moment to sink into the familiar embrace of his mother's arms; he allowed himself the luxury of being comforted by her love for just a short time. 'Thank you, Mam,' he whispered back.

Tom walked over to Liam, 'Go say goodbye to Grace, Liam. We'll be in soon. Keep it together just a little bit longer. You can do this.'

Nodding, Liam walked out of the room.

Grace was awake when he got back to the room.

'Bummer,' she said with a small smile.

'An absolute bitch,' he agreed kissing her.

'Jack,' she whispered.

'I know,' he sobbed back. And he did.

'Tell him that I love him,' Grace said softly.

'He knows that, babe. He knows you love him,' Liam reassured her.

'Tell him about the rainbows,' she whispered. 'Tell him that I'll be just beyond the rainbow's end.'

Liam nodded. 'I'll tell him,' Liam promised. 'I'll make sure he's alright, Grace. I won't let you down.'

'I know that, Liam. I know Jack will be fine, because he's got you. No regrets?'

'No babe, no regrets,' he answered her.

'I'm so sorry. I wanted to grow old with you,' she struggled to get the words out.

'Oh babe. I love you so much,' Liam replied, sobbing.

'Always remember what I said at the wedding, Liam. Even right now I feel blessed,' Grace said to him.

He nodded, stroking her hair delicately. Catherine and Noel walked in then. They walked over and kissed her. Noel stood in the corner, unable to compose himself.

Catherine held Grace's hand and said, 'I am so proud of you Grace. I love you so much.'

'I love you too, Mam,' Grace replied with a smile. This was the first time in Catherine's entire life that she'd ever been called Mam. It was too much. She started to cry and Noel walked over

316

her, pulling her into his arms, trying his best to offer some sort
f comfort to his sister.

Tara and Sean came in next. 'Hi cousin. You looking for all the
ttention again?' she said, smiling through her tears.

'You know me. Always the drama queen,' Grace answered. 'Do
1e a favour. Don't call the child Grace if it's a girl. I'd hate to be
1amed after a dead person. Don't put that on her!'

'It could be a boy!' Tara said.

'Oh it's a girl, you mark my words,' Grace said smiling. 'A
eautiful, glorious baby girl.'

Tara tried to smile through her tears. 'I don't think I'll be able
) cope without you,' she told Grace.

'Yes you will. You'll be a great Mommy and you'll be an amazing
)addy, Sean,' she said turning to him.

Sean walked over to Grace and held her hand gently. '*These
'oots are Made for Walking*,' he sang softly.

She smiled remembering the night she had sung that. A lifetime
go. 'Thank you, Sean,' she whispered to him. 'For everything.'

Tom and Gerry walked in together, followed by Abby and Shay.

'Come here, Abby.' Grace held her arms out. 'Be happy, princess.
ll be watching.' She smiled at Shay.

'I love you, Grace,' Abby whispered.

'I know pet and I you,' Grace replied.

Gerry and Tom walked over then.

'Any movie quotes for me now?' Grace asked Gerry gently. He
ouldn't answer just shook his head gently. 'Come here,' she said
) Gerry. 'I've got one for you.' Leaning into his ear, she whispered
) him, '"I'm gonna miss you the most, scarecrow."' It was from
'he Wizard of Oz. It always was her favourite childhood movie.

Gerry strangled back his sobs, determined to be strong for his
eloved Grace. 'I love you darling,' he whispered back, smiling at
is best friend through his tears.

317

'And I you. You two are the best couple I know,' Grace said them both. 'Don't let anyone ever tell you any different. A proper love story.'

Tom leaned in and kissed Grace. 'I'll look after Liam, Grace. Don't you worry about a thing. We'll all take care of them.'

'I'm not worrying about a thing, Tom,' Grace smiled at him. She closed her eyes. She knew she was loved. Wasn't that the greatest blessing of all? She opened her eyes and looked around the room. Catherine, Noel, Tara, Sean, Gerry, Tom and Abby. All watching her with tears flowing down their cheeks, but with utmost love in their eyes.

'Lie with me,' she whispered to Liam. He climbed on the bed and pulled her into his arms.

'Close your eyes and go to sleep babe,' he said quietly. 'Dream of that rainbow's end, my love.'

So she did.

Chapter Fifty One

It was drizzling rain on the morning of the funeral. A damp, grey mist hung over the cold March day. Somehow it seemed apt. It was certainly how a lot of people felt as they made their way to Grace's funeral. The church was packed and there wasn't a single person who didn't feel moved at the sight of Liam, holding Jack's hand tightly, sitting at the top of the church, both with their heads hanging low. Fr Benedict was saying the funeral mass. He couldn't believe that he had to bury the woman he'd only married to Liam a few short months ago. Liam couldn't have got this far without his help. Between him and his mother, they had made all the arrangements.

Sitting beside Jack and Liam was Catherine and Noel and behind were all of their friends. They hadn't left Liam's side since Grace died. He knew they were terrified he'd go for a drink. Liam on the other hand, knew without a doubt, that he wasn't even tempted to have one. He was all Jack had now and he wasn't going to let him down. Not for a bloody drink.

The service went by and then it was time for Liam to make his eulogy. He knew he could have asked Tom or Sean to do this and they would have done an amazing job. But he wanted to do it himself. He wanted to honour Grace and he was determined to do it without any hysterical breaking down. He walked to the front of the altar and took a moment to compose himself, glancing a Grace's coffin. It was surreal to think that his wife, his lover, his best friend was in there.

Looking at his son for a second, he took a deep breath and began his eulogy, his love letter to Grace, 'Hi everyone. I'd like to say a few words on behalf of Jack and myself. Grace, my wife, was an extraordinary person and although her time here has been short, she has lived an extraordinary life. For those of you that were lucky enough to have known her, you'll already know that fact. Grace was one of those rare people on this earth who are both beautiful inside and out. Just being in Grace's company would make you want to be a better person. I know this to be true because she had that effect on me.'

He looked at his friends and saw the recognition in their eyes as he spoke. Taking a deep breath, he continued, 'The happiest day of my life was the day that Grace and I married. I thought I would burst with happiness. How did I manage to gain the love of such an amazing person? I often pinch myself, thinking that I must have dreamed the past twelve months. But then I look at our son Jack and realise it was all true. I look at him and I see so much of Grace in him. He has her sweet nature, her sense of humour, her wit, her creative side, her love. Grace loved you so much Jacky. You were her world. And you are my world, buddy.'

Jack looked up at his Daddy. He couldn't quite understand what was going on. His Mommy was in heaven with his Nana and Granddad, Daddy had told him. Did that mean he'd never see her again? Everyone was crying all the time and they seemed to cry more when they saw him. He was sad too. He wanted his Mommy so much. But somehow or other, he realised that this wasn't going to happen.

Smiling at his son, Liam continued, 'Seeing Grace with Jack was incredible. There was tenderness between them that I was in awe of. I will make sure Jack remembers that feeling for the rest of my life. For me and Jack, for Catherine and for each of Grace's friends, we are all struggling to come to terms with our loss. We want to rant and rave at the injustice of it all. But we have to hold on to our memories of Grace tightly now. I know that I will never forget her and somehow I don't think any of you will either. Grace had an impact on so many of our lives.'

Liam paused, closing his eyes. In that moment, flashes of his life with Grace flew by. He opened his eyes, looking at Jack for strength. 'At our wedding, I told Grace that the best was yet to come,' Liam whispered. He looked down at his family and friends briefly, shaking his head slightly. He wanted to scream at the congregation that he had got it so wrong. How could the best be yet to come without Grace by his side? But then he looked at Jack and knew that he couldn't do that. He had to be strong, for his son's sake. 'This is not the end. Grace is still with us and will always be here. She's right here,' Liam pointed to his heart. 'And when it's my time to go, I know she'll be waiting with open arms to meet me.'

Liam walked down to his seat and scooped his son into his arms. Tom clasped his shoulder reassuringly. He could hear the sobs of everybody as they wept for the injustice of it all. Liam stood up as Tom, Gerry, Sean, Martin and Noel got up to act as pallbearers. He walked to Grace's coffin and touched it lightly, then walked back to his seat and picked Jack up, holding him close. He just needed to get through the burial now. Jack was sobbing, his little body shaking. Maybe it was the wrong choice bringing him here today. He'd spoken to a counsellor at the hospital about it and they recommended that Jack be here. Give him a chance to start the grieving process. He'd discussed it with his friends and in the end nobody could come up with an answer. Jack himself made the decision when he insisted that he be allowed to go.

Twenty minutes later, Grace's coffin was lowered into the ground, beside her beloved Mam and Dad. Each of Grace's loved ones had a single white rose. Tara and Sean walked over together, holding hands. They threw their roses on to the coffin. Gerry and Tom followed, throwing their roses in too, as did Abby. Catherine and Noel then did the same. Lastly Liam walked over with Jack in his arms.

'Time to say goodbye to Mommy, sweetie-pie,' Liam told Jack, using Grace's term of endearment. He threw his rose onto the coffin. 'Give Mommy your rose, buddy,' he coaxed.

Jack was shaking, he was crying so much. He threw his rose in, then sobbed, 'I want my Mommy. I want my Mommy, Daddy.' The sound of his little voice was too much for everyone to bear.

What can you say to a four year old? Liam didn't have an answer. 'I know buddy. I know you do.'

After the burial, the group walked away from the graveside, Jack in Liam's arms.

Suddenly Jack squealed, pointing to the sky, 'Daddy, look!'

Liam looked up and couldn't believe his eyes. Breaking into a smile, Liam kissed his son on his head, 'See Mommy's thinking of you. She's right here with us, just like she said she would be.' The gang of friends looked up to where Jack was pointing excitedly, and there, against the dark, grey sky, was a bright glorious rainbow.

Epilogue

Five months had passed since Grace had died. And once again the gang of friends were gathered in a waiting room; Tom, Gerry, Abby, Shay, Liam and Jack. But this time the waiting room was filled with laughter and the buzz of several conversations as everyone sat waiting for news on the special delivery. Tara had gone into labour earlier that morning. Without having planned it, one by one each of the friends had decided to go to the maternity hospital to await the announcement. Sean had been in and out a few times, with updates for them all, the last time telling them with great excitement that they were finally moving to the delivery suite!

Finally the door burst open and Sean was standing there with a huge smile on his face as tears flowed down his cheeks. 'I'm a Daddy!'

They all jumped up and down, screaming and hugging each other. Jack laughing at his mad aunts and uncles as they got so excited. This was great fun.

'Boy or girl?' Abby screamed at him above the noise.

'It's a girl, a beautiful, glorious baby girl.'

Lightning Source UK Ltd.
Milton Keynes UK
UKHW01f0206110818
327101UK00001B/142/P

9 780007 559565